Praise for *Jewish Noir*

"A little angst, some healthy cynicism, a touch of guilt, a few wisecracks, and some very good stories. What else were you expecting?"
—Michael Moorcock, author of *Mother London* and
the *Colonel Pyat Quartet*

"A hearty *mazel tov* to the ingenious team who created and assembled this vivid and wide-ranging collection."
—Linda Barnes, author of *The Perfect Ghost*

"The words 'Jewish noir' may be redundant, as Kenneth Wishnia points out in his introduction, as brilliant a piece as any in the book. But the authors drill down beneath that surface to uncover a teeming world of hardship and sometime triumph. From a newly translated historical as fresh today as ever to what can only be described as Jewish domestic suspense, gritty tales of childhood to characters appearing on the page for one last dance, this anthology should appeal to readers with an interest in the Jewish tradition and ongoing plight. But perhaps most striking is that *Jewish Noir* will dazzle crime fiction readers of every variety as well."
—Jenny Milchman, *USA Today* bestselling author of *As Night Falls*

"Some seriously good stuff here. This goy loved it."
—Lee Child, #1 *New York Times* bestselling author

"Shining. Evocative. Penetrating."
—Elie Wiesel (on Stephen Jay Schwartz's story "*Yahrzeit* Candle")

"*Jewish Noir* presents a fascinating, kaleidoscopic array of stories of the entirety of the Jewish Experience, sparing no mercy yet with great heart. This anthology demonstrates with great effect that no matter how much man plans, God is always there to laugh."
—Sarah Weinman, editor, *Women Crime Writers:*
Eight Suspense Novels of the 1940s & 50s

JEWISH NOIR

Edited by Kenneth Wishnia

ISBN: 978-1-62963-111-0
Library of Congress Control Number: 2015930893

Cover by John Yates / www.stealworks.com
Interior design by briandesign

10 9 8 7 6 5 4 3 2 1

PM Press
PO Box 23912
Oakland, CA 94623
www.pmpress.org

Printed in the USA by the Employee Owners of Thomson-Shore in Dexter, Michigan.
www.thomsonshore.com

Contents

NIGHT AND FOG

L'DOR V'DOR
(FROM GENERATION TO GENERATION)

SUBURBAN SPRAWL

Introduction

Far dem emes shlogt men.
Tell the truth and you ask for a beating.
—Yiddish proverb

When we first invited the authors to submit a story for this anthology, one of them, Rabbi Adam Fisher, replied with a question: What did we mean by *Jewish Noir*? Anything written by a Jewish author, or did the stories have to deal with specifically Jewish themes?

First of all, how characteristically Jewish to answer a question with a question.

We wanted stories with Jewish themes. What, then, constitutes Jewish *noir*? Practically anything, it turns out. One of the paradigmatic noir themes is that of the person who is at home nowhere, which has been a defining element of the Jewish experience since around 1900 BCE, when God tells Abraham to leave his home city of Ur in southern Mesopotamia, with the admonition, "Know well that your offspring shall be strangers in a land not theirs" (Gen. 15:13).

Even the word *Hebrews* conveys our rootless nomadic origins. When Jonathan son of Saul says, "Come, let us cross over to the Philistine garrison on the other side" (1 Samuel 14:1), the words for *cross over* and *other side* contain the root letters e-b-r, *ebra* and *ever*, respectively. And in the earliest known extrabiblical reference to *Israel*, the Egyptian Merenptah Stele circa 1200 BCE, the word for Israel includes "a glyph that denotes a people without a place" (Golden 122). Thus our ancient tribal names mean to cross over, to wander, to be a stranger, to be rootless.[1]

---

1   Closer to our own era, we are told that the notorious Nazi war criminal Adolf Eichmann "hated Jews because Judaism was 'rootless,' disconnected from the soil and 'universalistic'" (Brent 77).

And things didn't get much better once we got to the rocky high-lands of Canaanite territory. While the farmers in the fertile riverbeds of Egypt and Mesopotamia—both places where the Hebrews had sojourned extensively—could count on regular annual flooding to replenish the soil, producing a culture whose gods were largely benevolent and well disposed toward humanity, agriculture in the arid uplands of Canaan was depend-ent on the whims of distant and capricious storm-gods, who could destroy a harvest by withholding rain or by sending too much rain at the wrong time (Oppenheim 67).

Perhaps for this reason literary scholar Richard B. Sewall writes, "Of all ancient peoples, the Hebrews were most surely possessed of the tragic sense of life" (21). We see this quality in the patriarch Jacob, who is blessed with fathering the twelve tribes of Israel, yet he makes a deathbed declara-tion that his life has been short and problem-filled (Gen. 47:9) because he spent most of his years living as a stranger in foreign lands, according to Rashi's interpretation of the passage.

The God of the Israelites is well aware of that tribe's precarious nomadic existence: after the Exodus, when the children of Israel are wan-dering in the wilderness, God issues a command regarding the Ark of the Covenant: "The poles shall remain in the rings of the ark; they shall not be removed from it" (Exodus 25:15), just in case the Israelites need to pull up stakes and make a quick getaway. One of the more frequent curses that God threatens to impose on the Israelites if they violate the Covenant is that of perpetual homelessness. A typical example:

> The Lord will bring a nation against you from afar . . . A ruthless
> nation, that will show the old no regard and the young no mercy . . .
> The Lord will scatter you among all the peoples from one end of the
> earth to the other . . . Yet even among those nations you shall find
> no peace, nor shall your foot find a place to rest. (Deuteronomy
> 28:49–65)

This curse has been borne out by history. Compare the Israelites' experi-ence to that of other ancient nations—the Persians, for example, who in 1971 celebrated the 2,500th anniversary of the founding of the Achaemenid Empire—2,500 years of continuous occupation and ethnic domination of the same geographic location.

Another key element of noir is fatalism, and not just of the femme fatale variety. To put it in rather simplified form, a majority of the world's Christians are taught that if you follow the right path, everything will turn out well for you in the end. In certain Romantic-style dramas, you can even repent for a life of pure evil at the last possible moment and still be saved. In Judaism, you can follow the right path and still get screwed. *That's* noir.

8

Consider Moses—surely the most important single individual in the Hebrew Bible, who frees the Israelites from bondage in Egypt, leads them across the Sea of Reeds to safety, then to Mount Sinai to receive the Torah, then to the steppes of Moab overlooking the Promised Land. Not only does God tell him, "You may view the land from a distance, but you shall not enter it" (Deut. 32:52), resulting in his burial in an unmarked grave in the land of Moab, but according to the Talmud, when Moses asks to see Rabbi Akiva's reward for teaching the Torah many centuries later in defiance of the Roman prohibition, God shows Moses the results: the Romans punish Rabbi Akiva by stripping off his flesh with iron rakes and then burning him alive. "Such is Your reward?" says Moses. And God answers, "Be silent, this is My will" (Menachot 29b).

If this is the fate of Moses, and the eminent Rabbi Akiva, what of the average Israelite?

Don't ask.

Let's just say that the roots of *Jewish Noir* run deep. And we're especially critical of our own shortcomings. Many of the sayings and attitudes of the Prophets prefigure the reasons why so many modern writers are attracted to the crime fiction genre in the first place—prominent among them the convention of the individual against society, of the working-class hero like the prophet Amos ("a sheepbreeder from Tekoa") fighting for the little guy or gal. This is especially true in the private eye genre, which often includes long passages of social commentary and criticism, and the depiction and condemnation of the endemic corruption that renders the allegedly egalitarian structure of society invalid, for sale to the highest bidder, while the powerless get no justice or, worse, are destroyed by the system.

And society usually doesn't want to hear the message: Elijah has to go into hiding (1 Kings 17:2–5); Micaiah gets smacked in the face and sent to prison (1 Kings 22:24–27); Jeremiah is beaten, jailed, thrown into a cistern, and threatened with death by the entire community (Jer. 37:15–16; 26:7–19); Uriah the prophet is "put to the sword and his body thrown into the burial place of the common people" (Jer. 26:23); and Zechariah is stoned to death (2 Chronicles 24:21 [cf. Orlinsky 134]).

Other books of the Hebrew Bible are similarly dark—Job is forced to confront the reality that God does not appear to reward good and punish evil in this world; Lamentations describes a siege so prolonged and severe that it leads to infanticide and cannibalism; the prophet Micah describes a society built on corruption and blood money, in which no one is to be trusted, not even one's own sons and daughters: "Trust no friend, rely on no intimate; be guarded in speech with her who lies in your bosom. For son spurns father, daughter rises up against mother, daughter-in-law against mother-in-law; a man's own household are his enemies" (Micah 7:5–6).

And then there's Koheleth, the anonymous assembler of wisdom texts, better known as Ecclesiastes, who believes that everything we strive to acquire or accomplish is as ethereal and impermanent as mist. The Hebrew word *hevel* literally means "vapor" (*The Jewish Bible*, 102). Thus he does *not* say "all is vanity" as in the familiar King James translation, but something closer to "All is vapor." Knowledge doesn't lead to enlightenment, it leads to heartache (1:18). Good men die while wicked men endure, so there's no point in being excessively good or wise (7:16). The wise man and the fool both end up dead. So what's the point?

To be fair, at the time Ecclesiastes was written, there was no firmly established belief among the Jews in the promise of an afterlife in heaven, so ultimately the book advises us to eat, drink, and enjoy the love of a good woman, because *this is all we get.*

This theme runs through ancient Near Eastern literature all the way back to the *Epic of Gilgamesh* (which predates the oldest parts of the Bible by at least 1,500 years), in which Gilgamesh, a demigod king who is inconsolable after the death of his closest friend, goes on a futile quest for the secret of eternal life—the key word being *futile*. In other words, he fails.

No happy endings. No life after death.

And we have inherited this fatalistic tradition, in more ways than one. It's not just that the Jews are taught to remember our suffering and enslavement in Egypt every year on Passover, or to commemorate the destruction of the Temple at what should otherwise be one of life's most joyful moments, when a couple's marriage becomes official. Recent studies suggest that our genes have some form of "memory," that the effects of environmental factors such as good or bad harvest seasons, with their resulting feasts or famines, can be detected generations, perhaps even centuries, later in our genes (Carvajal D3). So perhaps Jews are not, as one book recently put it, "born to kvetch" due to some strange and unique confluence of our collective historical traumas and our emotional dispositions. We may actually be carrying genetic traces of our centuries of oppression as well.

When we first proposed this anthology, we had hoped to receive at least a couple of stories depicting these earlier historical periods. But except for Yente Serdatsky's story, which is a special case, all of the stories in this collection are by contemporary authors who have placed their characters in twentieth- and twenty-first-century locales and contexts.

So let's skip ahead, bypassing the Middle Ages, with its forced conversions, bloody expulsions, and accusations that the Jews caused the outbreak of the Black Death in 1348; past the early modern era, when Rabbi

Judah Loew of Prague wrote, in 1598, "This present world belongs to the evil-doers"; and past the nineteenth century, when pogroms and blood libels were so common we *told jokes* about them. One classic example goes like this: a young peasant girl is found dead, and the Jews are terrified that they will be charged with ritual murder, the dreaded blood libel accusation, until the *shammes* runs in and says, "Brothers—brothers! I have wonderful news for you! We've just discovered, God be praised, that the murdered girl was Jewish!" (Ausubel 441). That's some seriously black humor, folks. The underlying causes should be dismissible as relics of the absurd and contradictory attitudes toward the Jews of another era, except that it has recently been reported that anti-Semitic tracts published in Ukraine *still* say that the twelve-year-old victim in the 1913 Mendel Beilis blood libel case really was killed to make matzoh. Really.

Every nation has its violent histories, but how many of them still have to contend with a nonsensical nine-hundred-year-old lie?[2] Two of the authors in this collection, Travis Richardson and Jedidiah Ayres, make references to the resurgent neo-Nazi ideology in twenty-first-century America. In doing so, they are not merely depicting the dark side of American society in classic noir fashion but also the bitter fact that, more than seventy years after the cries of "Never again!" were first heard, such virulent anti-Semitism (and anti–everybody else, too) persists with such resilience, which suggests that we may *never* be free of the disease of violent prejudice. A dark thought, indeed.

Another defining characteristic of noir is this idea that evil is never truly defeated, that the evil doesn't stop at the end of the story. Evil may even be triumphant: Nazi Germany may have lost World War II, but, sad to say, Hitler's goal of destroying the "world of our fathers"—the world of Yiddish-speaking Ashkenazic Jews in Central and Eastern Europe and of Sephardic Jews from the Greek and Balkan states—was largely successful.

Among Moses's final set of instructions to the Israelites is the following:

Remember the days of old,
Consider the years of ages past;
Ask your father, he will inform you,
Your elders, they will tell you. (Deut. 32:7)

Leading a discussion of this passage during Friday evening services, the same Rabbi Adam Fisher who wrote a story for this anthology said that in a post-Holocaust world, "We have no elders. We are orphans in history."

In preparation for a panel discussion on "Jewish noir," another author

---

2   The Torah forbids the consuming of animal blood numerous times (Lev. 3:17, 7:26, 17:10–14; Deut. 12:15–16, 12:23–25) and the Talmud tightened the restrictions even further.

in this collection, Michele Lang, wrote about growing up in just such a post-Holocaust world, a world defined by "anomie, estrangement from trust in societal systems designed to keep the monsters at bay or at least on a leash. As is pointed out every year around the time of Yom Ha-Shoah [Holocaust Remembrance Day], the Nazi regime was completely legal, the Nuremberg laws enforced through an orderly system of judges, administrators and enforcement."

Another panelist and contributor, Alan Gordon, wrestled with related themes from the next generation's perspective, addressing "the American Jewish experience, in terms of stereotypes (both within and without the Jewish communities), assimilation and the failure to assimilate, how the historical ghettoization continued in this country, and how the formation of Israel allowed us to assert a belief in the tough Jew again after the devastation of the Holocaust."

Perhaps this explains something about why three of the authors in this anthology—David Liss, Michele Lang, and Jonathan Santlofer—chose to write about anti-Semitic bullying in small-town or suburban America from the 1950s through the 1970s. There are no pogroms in this postwar America, no organized slaughter of whole villages and their Jewish inhabitants, but these stories suggest that a lot of otherwise fully assimilated Jews are still carrying the memory of these traumatic experiences inside of themselves, and, if these stories are any indication, still harbor thoughts of taking long-awaited revenge on their juvenile tormentors—often with bloody results.

That such emotions should repeatedly come up, with so much passion and vitriol, as if the incidents had just happened yesterday, should provoke some conversations. (And by the way, Harlan Ellison beat them all to the punch more than fifty years ago with his story, "Final Shtick," included here as a vintage reprint.)[3]

Once again, we're not unique in having such a dark history, but what may be unique is the feeling that "it could happen again." For example, while the Irish suffered several centuries of brutal oppression, bordering on attempted genocide, at the hands of the English (followed by decades of bloody infighting), and terrible treatment when they immigrated to the United States, I don't know any Irish-Americans whose grandmothers still keep a bag packed "just in case" they have to flee the next pogrom. (And there's still an Ireland to go back to, if they feel so inclined.)

Yet the celebrated author Dara Horn wrote in a recent issue of *Moment*, "If there is one thing we share with Jews of the past, it is the belief that our

---

3   Full disclosure: I'm enough of a Harlan Ellison fan to recognize that the vision of endless torture described in his introduction to "Final Shtick" comes from his original teleplay for one of the best *Star Trek* episodes ever, "The City on the Edge of Forever," but was not used in the final version of that episode.

generation could easily be the last, and that no one in the future will even know what we have lost" (81). One of the great film noirs of the classic era, *Out of the Past*, has an ending that echoes this motif of being doubly screwed in life *and* in death. Although devoid of overt Jewish content—it stars Robert Mitchum as a former private investigator trying to escape from his past—this underlying dread of being hunted to extinction may help explain why so many American screenwriters and foreign-born directors of film noir were Jewish, and why so many of them were blacklisted for daring to expose the dark underbelly of the American dream.

Unlike the plight of African-American men who still have to deal with their own extremely noir version of the American experience, most of us don't have to worry too much about being mistaken for armed criminals and shot by panicking police officers. But American Jews are still the targets of murderous assaults; absurd conspiracy theories about the Jewish plot to take over global media and finances, along with other hate-filled stereotypes, clearly contributed to the deadly assault in April 2014 by an aging neo-Nazi on a Jewish Community Center in a suburb of Kansas City where, ironically and tragically, all three victims were Christian. And these factors will surely contribute to future attacks as well. In New York City, unquestionably the Jewish-American capital of the United States, you need to pass through metal detectors to get into the Jewish Museum, the Museum of Jewish Heritage, and the Center for Jewish History, while, as of this writing, no metal detectors are needed to get into the Metropolitan Museum of Art, the Museum of Modern Art, or any of the other major city museums.

Welcome to our world.

❧

The recent surge in "noir" anthologies has nothing to do with nostalgia. We live in an age that parallels many of the conditions that gave rise to the first generation of noir writers: economic insecurity, incompetence and corruption at all levels of government, disillusionment with the American dream, while those responsible for it all make their millions and get away with murder.

The stories in this collection run the gamut from noirish literary stories to pulpier crime stories (you'll spot them easily enough), so I'd like to offer a brief guide highlighting some of their key elements. (Note: A story doesn't have to include an actual crime in order to be noir, but it helps.) While film noirs of the 1940s often featured a femme fatale figure who, directly or indirectly, brings about the hero's downfall, by the 1950s the hero (or antihero) was just as likely to be ground up by the gears of a faceless, oppressive system. This type of system can be seen operating in various guises in the first group of stories. R.S. Brenner's "Devil for a Witch" examines the poisonous legacy of America's original sin. B.K. Stevens's "Living Underwater" is a spot-on send-up of our current market-driven approach to education. Travis Richardson's "Quack and Dwight" also gets some great mileage out of another noir staple: obsession. Regarding Steve Wishnia's "The Sacrifice of Isaac," to paraphrase what another editor once wrote: Yes, he's my brother. He's also an award-winning journalist and writer whose tale of money, power, real estate, and race in 1990s Brooklyn is as emotionally wrenching and effective as anything in this collection.

First published in the *Forverts* in Yiddish in 1912, Yente Serdatsky's "*A Simkhe*," which appears here in English translation for the first time, confronts the paradox of assimilation head-on; it suggests that we gained something by it but also lost something. In describing a world long gone, it evokes in the modern reader a sense that we left the stifling Old World ghettos behind, but we also lost the world of our Yiddish-speaking grand-parents as we, their children, assimilated.

Serdatsky's language in "*A Simkhe*" appears to reflect the *Forverts* editor Abe Cahan's policy of writing in "plain" Yiddish for the benefit of that paper's less-skilled readers. The vocabulary is relatively straightfor-ward and many words are repeated. The story, which revolves around the once-radiant and seductive Miss B., reflects Serdatsky's own experience. Like so many radical Jewish women of the period, she came to the United States in search of intellectual freedom but ended up being cruelly isolated due to traditional attitudes and gender roles among her former comrades. (Another classic noir trope: betrayal.) Although the story ends on a rather conventional note, it gives a noirish portrait of faded beauty and promise from the perspective of a woman whom everyone treats as if she were a femme fatale.

It is a great privilege to bring you a new story by Marge Piercy, an author whose work I have taught in my college literature classes. You will find no man-eating femme fatales in "Trajectories," unless you cast the United States itself in the femme fatale role for perpetuating a culture of rootless alienation that leads to the degradation and eventual destruction of the human soul.

My own story, "Lost Pages from the Book of Judith," is set in the fall of 1948, more or less at the precise moment when certain youthful ideals were crumbling under relentless attacks and commencing their long decline into pale shadows of their former glory. The law is definitely not your friend in Wendy Hornsby's "The Legacy," nor is small-town America a welcoming place when you're carrying a suitcase full of secrets from the past (you guessed it: another classic noir motif).

You don't get more noir than the next group of stories. Melissa Yi and

S.J. Rozan both deliver sharply etched, emotionally haunting stories with "Blood Diamonds" and "Flowers of Shanghai," and Michael J. Cooper's "Good Morning, Jerusalem 1948" embodies the noir motif of the earnest cause that may well be doomed from the beginning. As for Moe Prager's provocative and disturbing "Feeding the Crocodile," I just have two words: crocodile tears.

Yet there is no end to the darkness. The next cluster of stories takes on the ultimate noir motif: mortality, the inexorable passing of time, and the ways in which we confront the inevitable. Nancy Richler's "Some You Lose" comes from such a deep heartfelt place that she has since transformed it into the first chapter of her new novel-in-progress. M. Dante's "*Baruch Dayan Emet*" is bone-chilling in its own unique way. And Stephen Jay Schwartz would like you all to know that he wrote "*Yahrzeit* Candle" thirty years ago, just after his father's death, and this is its first publication. It's the story that took him on the path to becoming a writer. The stories by Robert Lopresti, Alan Orloff, and S.A. Solomon are all about taking a leap into the unknown, and finding out just how far you're willing to go to provide for or protect your family, however you might define those terms.

If you need a break from all this relentless noir, there's plenty of dark humor to be found in David Liss's "Jewish Easter" and Rabbi Adam Fisher's "Her Daughter's Bat Mitzvah," a bitter, hilarious, and profanity-filled story in the tradition of Yiddish writer Sholem Aleichem's mono-logues (minus the profanity, that is). Tasha Kaminsky's "Your Judaism" also includes moments of humor, even as it describes a young woman's troubling disaffection and alienation from the modern religious commu-nity. I discussed the stories by Michele Lang and Jonathan Santlofer above.

Now it's time for coffee and dessert, though I should warn you, the coffee is extremely bitter. Most of the authors in the last section of stories go for the adrenaline-fueled gut punch of hardboiled pulp fiction, from the willful self-destruction in Charles Ardai's "Who Shall Live" and Heywood Gould's "Everything Is *Bashert*" to the deadly self-delusion in Alan Gordon's "The Drop." Quite fittingly, Gary Phillips's "Errands" gives the phrase "Jewish noir" a whole new meaning, and in some ways his story is the most authentic expression of the term. One story that specifically references the classic film noir era (as well as the Blacklist, which ensnared so many left-leaning Jews), is Eddie "The Czar of Noir" Muller's "Doc's Oscar," which we are thrilled to include here, even though we had to bump off a few stoolies to get Eddie to play along.[4] Readers with delicate con-stitutions may prefer to skip Jedidiah Ayres's raucous and expletive-filled

---

4   A note to the Yiddishists: We are aware that the phrase used in this story, "*khazerai* wheelchair," is not strictly grammatical, but we believe that the character of Ben King would have said it that way.

"Twisted *Shikse*," but if you're up for a wild ride, this straight-up shot of hundred-proof redneck noir will take you there. Don't say I didn't warn you. Jason Starr's hard-hitting tale, "All Other Nights," is sure to provoke comment. And Dave Zeltserman gives us a cold blast of vintage noir with his twisted crime caper, "Something's Not Right."

One final note: We wanted a multiplicity of voices in this anthology, and while most of the contributing authors are in fact Jewish, we adopted a generous "you don't have to be Jewish to write Jewish noir" policy. (See if you can figure out who's who.)

Kenneth Wishnia
New York

꙳

Thanks to Ramsey Kanaan at PM Press for his ongoing support of this project and for showing the world that the Israelites and the Kanaanites *can* work together peaceably. Thanks to Reed Farrel Coleman, who originally came up with the idea for *Jewish Noir*. Thanks also to Lou Boxer and Deen Kogan of NoirCon for their early support, to the fabulous copy editor extraordinaire Gregory Nipper, and to the rest of the folks at PM Press for doing whatever it is they do when they're not conspiring to overthrow capitalism, globalization, and the imposition of a new world order.

Works Cited

Note: The biblical passages cited in this introduction are from the *JPS Hebrew-English Tanakh*, 2nd ed. Philadelphia: The Jewish Publication Society, 1999. The names of some key noir motifs were taken from David N. Meyer's *A Girl and a Gun* (New York: Avon, 1998).

Ausubel, Nathan. *A Treasury of Jewish Folklore*. New York: Crown, 1948.
Brent, Jonathan. "Eichmann in Argentina." *Moment* 40, no. 1 (January–February 2015): 76–77.
Carvajal, Doreen. "In Andalusia, on the Trail of Inherited Memories." *New York Times*, August 21, 2012, D3.
Golden, Jonathan M. *Ancient Canaan and Israel: An Introduction*. Oxford: Oxford University Press, 2004.
Gordon, Alan. "Re: Jewish Noir Panel." E-mail to the author. October 25, 2014.
Horn, Dara. "The Genial Time Traveler." *Moment* 39, no. 3 (May–June 2014): 80–81.
The Jewish Bible. JPS Guide. Philadelphia: The Jewish Publication Society, 2008.
Lang, Michele. "Re: Jewish Noir Panel." E-mail to the author. October 26, 2014.
Oppenheim, A. Leo. "Assyro-Babylonian Religion." In Vergilius Ferm, ed., *Ancient Religions*. New York: The Philosophical Library, 1950.
Orlinsky, Harry M. *Ancient Israel*. Ithaca, NY: Cornell University Press, 1960.
Sewall, Richard B. "The Book of Job." In Paul S. Sanders, ed., *Twentieth Century Interpretations of the Book of Job*. Englewood Cliffs, NJ: Prentice-Hall, 1968.

BITTER HERBS

Devil for a Witch

R.S. Brenner

**Whither? North is greed and South is blood;
within, the coward, and without, the liar. Whither?**
—W.E.B. Du Bois, "The Litany of Atlanta"

**If you see the teeth of the lion,
do not think that the lion is smiling at you.**
—Al-Mutanabbi, Arab poet, 915–965 C.E.

The funeral for Leon Greenberg was graveside, the service short. As little as possible was said about the deceased. Nothing personal or elegiac. His death blotted out any cause for celebration of his life. If his existence had once been charmed, it was not mentioned. Star chemist, decorated Navy officer, brilliant raconteur, and once holding the enviable title of husband to a beautiful rich woman, no such attributions were uttered. Suicide was a willful negation of life. Out of confusion, sadness, spite, its legatees accepted that the dead man's last act overrode all others.

Across town at the reception, limos dropped the mourners at the Steiners' split-level wonder, a glass and steel extravaganza around the corner from the governor's mansion. It was Atlanta's most prestigious address even if the governor was a murderous bigot.

In the Steiners' living room, *shivah* was under heated discussion. "He's an atheist!" Irene Greenberg shouted.

"*Was*," Phil Steiner said.

"*Was! Was! Was!* I am his wife! I know what he wants!"

"*Wanted*," Phil amended.

"He does not want *shivah*," she insisted. "When my father died, we sat *shivah* because he wanted it. We sat two nights until you went off to a golf tournament."

"He wasn't *my* father."

Irene shook her fist like an impotent human before the throne of God. "He gave you everything!"

"Stop it!" he croaked, holding her wrist and tightening his grip.

"My husband just killed himself! I'm permitted to completely lose my mind!"

"I'm sitting *shivah*," Marilyn Steiner, Irene's sister, said.

"Leon doesn't want it, but now that he's dead, he's helpless. He's in the clutches of Zionists!"

"Helpless!" Phil snorted. "Not with you as defensive end."

"I loved Leon," Marilyn sighed.

"Everyone knows about that," Irene said.

"Shut up!" Phil ordered.

"Your husband wants me to tear my blouse because he knows I bought it on sale at Rich's. I don't wear Vera scarves and Charles Jourdan shoes like my sister. I can't afford to shop in New York." Irene twisted the end of Marilyn's scarf, shortening the loop like a noose. "Would you tear your precious scarf if Phil died?"

"Get a sedative!"

"Phil Steiner is a usurer!" Irene shouted. "Usurer! Usurer!"

Murmurs of sympathy followed as a phalanx of black maids lifted Irene off the ground and carried her to another wing of the house where Valium was forced under her uvula, her mouth clamped shut, and her neck stroked like a dog's. That was only after she broke Sarah Weiner's cane over Phil's arm while Sarah's hands were occupied with lox and deviled eggs. The cane splintered and caught Phil's shirt, ripping it open and scratching his chest. A tiny scratch but Phil agonized as if Irene had bitten his heart out, which she would have if she'd had the strength.

Later, when the pill wore off and she was home in bed, the recollection of the cane, its percussive thwack, Phil's expression, the blood, his torn shirt, and the chaos and confusion that ensued were deeply satisfying. Irene laughed about it for years.

❧

Six months before the suicide, the FBI visited Ace Linens. They brought copies of dozens of checks. Phil Steiner reviewed the list of recipients, the dates, the donation amounts. He was flabbergasted. The checks totaled over $17,000, written to unfamiliar acronyms—CORE, MCHR, SNCC, SCLC, NAACP, and Highlander Center. He studied the signature of Stanley White, comptroller for Ace Linens. It looked genuine.

"I know nothing about this!"

"In other words, they weren't authorized by you?"

"Jesus, no!" he said although he didn't sound convincing. He sounded defensive.

When Stanley White reviewed the checks, he denied any knowledge of signing them. "Fakes," he said. He sounded extremely convincing.

"You know of outside agitators, union organizers, Communists, pinkos, those sorts of people on your payroll?"

"Of course not! Everyone who works here is happy!"

Phil slammed Leon's office door. "I lied to the FBI to save your goddamn ass! In case you forgot, that's a felony! Next time you're feeling goddamn charitable, use your own goddamn profits!"

"We don't have any profits."

"Whoever heard of a pauper giving away thousands of dollars?"

"Stories abound."

"Stories, Leon? Stories mean they didn't happen! You're out of your mind!"

"By my accounting, I took money that belonged to Irene."

"*Your* accounting! I pay overeducated accountants to manage my books. The entire time you worked there, you drew a paycheck and did nothing, Leon. Goddamn good-for-nothing, you listening?"

"Irene hasn't gotten her fair share."

"Irene? I thought you only cared about *shvartses* and commies."

For three years, the FBI had tracked Leon Greenberg's finances, marital difficulties, children's schools, taste in music, love affairs, drinking habits, and contributions to organizations under federal investigation. Agent Whipple unlocked a black attaché case and laid out checks forged by Leon Greenberg with Stanley White's signature.

Leon studied the checks. "I no longer work at Ace Linens."

"We are aware of your employment status," Whipple said grimly. "Nonetheless, we have proof you forged these checks."

"Is that what Phil Steiner told you?"

"We know about your links to Dr. King and Fidel Castro. We know you spent two weeks at a Mississippi Freedom School."

"Are you saying that's illegal?"

Agent Whipple smiled, showing a row of small amber teeth. "You know what's illegal, Mr. Greenberg. You'll soon be facing criminal charges and a long prison sentence."

Leon sat mulling over his Jim Beam. "Like how long?"

"Fraud, forgery, embezzlement are serious crimes."

Leon knew they were serious, serious by intent. He had acted according to conscience.

"In my defense, I can prove the funds were originally embezzled by my brother-in-law, Phil Steiner. Every penny belonged to my wife."

"We call that backpedaling, Mr. Greenberg. Backpedaling is something of an art."

Whipple painted a bleak picture of Leon's future. He had stolen, there was no doubt. He had distributed monies to suspicious causes. Certainly, he didn't believe a jury or judge in Georgia would be swayed by his pinko generosity.

Leon forced himself to stay sober. He considered his choices. *You trade the devil for a witch* was a country saying. Devil, he knew. Witch was unknown.

⚘

Suicide was not farfetched for a man in Leon's predicament. He had contemplated suicide. He'd read the existentialists and accepted suicide as an individual's ultimate act in a world where individuality was valued less and less. Under the multiple threats of the Atomic Age, it functioned as a solace. A last resort. While it carried a stigma of shame, the stigma was one man's act of desperation rather than society's collective condemnation. Avoiding trial and prison meant there would be money for Irene and the kids. Money Leon couldn't otherwise provide.

The FBI would stage the suicide. That would pose no problem. They were adept at theatrics. At their third meeting, Leon handed over suit, shirt, tie, socks, shoes, reading glasses, and wallet with ID. In exchange, he received a bus ticket to Louisville and identification of Dr. Leland Green with a CV that included published articles on the science of white superiority.

"You ready?" Whipple asked.

"How the hell could I be ready?"

"Ready to serve mankind."

"As a white bigot, that's always cause for celebration."

Agent Whipple laughed. "Instead of whimpering with liberal guilt, you can put your ass on the line."

Tears sprang to Leon's eyes. "What if . . ."

"You'll realize you made the right decision," Whipple sympathized.

"It wasn't a decision. You gave me no choice."

At the same hour Leland Green boarded a bus at the Greyhound station, Leon Greenberg's car was locked inside a garage, its tail pipe stuffed with rags, its engine left running. Inside was the corpse of a Caucasian man of medium height with broad shoulders and a barrel chest, wearing Leon's best blue suit, pin-striped shirt, and gray knit tie. The man was the same blood type and shoe size as Leon and shared the same shade of thinning brown hair. Obviously, they weren't identical. Rather than take measures to destroy the body entirely and with it proof positive, the bureau decided to blow off enough of the stranger's face to turn it into pulp.

Leland's bus headed into the starry countryside. He pressed his nose against the window. The nose of a man who no longer existed. Or existed but no longer lived. The memories intact but the man gone. The inverse of amnesia.

In Louisville, he read the hand-printed sign—DR. LELAND GREEN.

"Welcome," Hugh Martino said jovially. "Long ride?"

"An eternity," Leon mused.

Martino showed Leon his Buick with Oregon plates, his new driver's license and passport, a strongbox of cash and traveler's checks, a camera and telephoto lens, a first aid kit, an ice cooler, and a portfolio of articles.

"You think I can pull this off?" Leon asked.

"I don't think anything, that's why they keep me around. Here's your gun and ammo."

"Jesus, I don't know how to shoot. I never fired a shot in the whole goddamn war."

"They don't expect you to know what they know. You're a thinking man, not a redneck. Hell, most of them can't read or write. Try to get in target practice. Squirrels, possums, cans. Go into the woods with your buddies. They know how to shoot. Anyway, woods is where talking gets done. It's trees that keep the secrets."

※

Phil Steiner whistled as he drove. He was an excellent whistler and was often asked at club or synagogue events to whistle a friend's favorite song. "Ebb Tide" was a spectacular tune to whistle. He parked his Lincoln next to the rundown apartment complex on Buford Highway. Constructed quickly after the war, the three-story buildings had not been well maintained. There were cracked windows, missing roof shingles, and greenways intended for playgrounds long overgrown with weeds and scattered trash.

Moshe Berger's apartment was on the second floor in building D. "Phil," he muttered, holding out his hands in European fashion and drawing Phil toward him in an affectionate hug.

"Moe," Phil said with genuine feeling.

Years ago when Moshe and his son first arrived from Europe as refugees, Phil Steiner had been their American sponsor. He'd found them the apartment on Buford Highway. He'd arranged for the synagogue to take up a collection of discarded furniture, kitchenware, and clothing to get them started. He'd given Moe a job driving a truck for Ace Linens.

Moe moved into the kitchenette for coffee and Sara Lee cheesecake, waving Phil to the living room sofa. "You look well," he said.

"Well enough. And your teaching?" Phil nibbled at the cake.

"I'll be teaching until I drop dead," Moe laughed. He was on the history faculty at Spelman College. "You said on the phone?"

Phil had alluded to help. Spiritual help, Moe surmised. Whatever he could do, he would make himself available.

"We had an unexpected death in the family."

"I know about Leon. I used to bump into him on campus. Always brimming with life, wasn't he?"

"A nonbeliever but wonderful," Phil said begrudgingly. He'd not forgiven Leon for his humiliating encounter with the FBI. Phil's fingers clasped and unclasped. "It's difficult for me to speak."

"I know about difficult things," Moe said.

"That's why I came to you. Many times, I thought to come."

"Not to speak makes it worse."

"There's something I have to tell someone. You're the only one in the world."

Moe was taken aback. "I hope I won't disappoint you."

"Leon took his car into a garage and stuffed a rag in the tail pipe." Phil halted and started to weep.

"I'm sorry," Moe said softly, taking Phil's hand. His own wife and daughter had also been suffocated by gas.

"After the police found the garage, the car, the body, they asked me to identify him. Of course, I agreed. I was standing by for the task. His wife couldn't possibly do it. I was the obvious choice."

Countless times, Moshe had wished, dreamed and wished to have a single minute to gaze at the corpses of his wife and daughter. If only for an instant, Moe could have touched their lovely faces serenely composed like the dead often are.

"It was the hardest goddamn thing I ever did," Phil said in a sweat. "When I got to the morgue, they tried to prepare me. They told me I might be shocked. I didn't understand what they meant. It's true I'd only seen corpses in funeral homes, laid out and embalmed. I wasn't in the war. I never saw carnage, only photos and films." With the cuff of his shirt, Phil wiped his eyes. "They pulled Leon out of the freezer and uncovered him. I never told a soul, but I fainted."

There was silence while Phil composed himself.

"He'd blown his face off. Moe, you understand? A man goes to kill himself in a car with carbon monoxide and then shoots himself? What did this last message mean? I couldn't tell his wife he'd mutilated himself beyond recognition. I couldn't tell my wife. She was devoted to Leon. If

I told anyone, it would have turned Leon into a freak. This face, it gives me nightmares. He must have been out of his mind. That's the only way to explain it."

❦

The Natchez Trace is bordered by dense woods, rivers, pastures, and hills. It's a beautiful drive, but Leland Green failed to notice scenery. He was occupied with a temptation to abandon his new identity, steal the car, the cash, the passport and beeline over the border to Mexico. A romantic notion for a man without guilt. Equally occupying him was Leon the hero. Daniel heading into the pit. But he was incapable of ennobling his cause with romance or sainthood. Neither brave nor guiltless, not a Daniel or a Zygielbojm, he was penitent, tired, deflated, and by Jackson city limits, he'd shed any illusions of free will.

He checked into a downtown hotel. His preference was a new motel with a swimming pool, but the agency wanted him to present as bookish, indifferent to modern comforts, content with chintz bedspreads and dust ruffles, Gideon within arm's reach, and paintings of buggies and barns. After dinner in the hotel dining room, he strolled through the thick, stagnant air relieved by the occasional steamy gust from the river. Inside a phone booth, he took a fortifying swallow of Jack and inserted a dime. He gave his home number to the operator, hoping to hear his daughter's voice for a moment.

"What?" his wife hissed. "What? What? What? Can't you leave us alone?"

He'd disturbed her. Maybe, she was sleeping. There was no doubt she was mad. As mad as she'd been at the living Leon, she was likely madder at the dead man. Mad and relieved. His suicide had diminished her grievances. It would now appear *his* grievances overshadowed *hers*.

At the hotel, the clerk handed him a note in poorly printed letters: Meat 11 A.M. by stat U. Hairy B-E-R-G-S-T-A-D-T

"You read it okay, sir?" he asked timidly.

"How long you been working here?"

"Two nights, sir."

"You might consider another profession."

"I want to be a lawyer, sir."

"You got to know how to spell to be a lawyer."

"Nigger lawyers know how to spell?"

Leon closed his eyes. He conjured Daddy King in his pulpit at Ebenezer Baptist. It was there he'd been introduced to *The Beloved Community* and called *brother*. There, he'd perceived what it meant to love an enemy. Only love conquers hate, King said.

"They spell right?" the clerk sneered.

"You better believe they do."

The next morning, he walked to City Hall. He took a seat between the imposing bronze statue of Andrew Jackson and the antebellum building. At the appointed hour, a gentleman with a white standard poodle leisurely approached him. "Dr. Green?" he inquired.

Leon jumped up as Harry Bergstedt pumped his hand. "Meet Puss," Harry said.

Leland Green held out his biscuit-and-gravy fingers for Puss to lick. He found himself trembling.

Let them lead the conversation, Whipple instructed.

Bergstedt's smile brightened. "We've read your work with great admiration."

"Thank you," Leland whispered, unable to catch his breath.

For two years, the writings of "Hailstorm" had appeared in Klan publications and circulated in White Citizen Councils. Agent Whipple never divulged who wrote the articles or how the plot evolved. Leon suggested a local infiltrator was more sensible than an elaborate ruse, but they disagreed. With the country's international reputation at stake, they needed an intelligent outsider. Leon Greenberg put a man on their side who was capable of reasoning through information and responding with measured caution. He had the bonus of a personality that could win the confidence of both crackers and patricians. Violent crackers, the agency could identify. They were status quo. The planners and financiers remained clandestine. The agency wanted to know which bank president owned a white robe.

"I understand this is a research tour?"

"For a new book."

"And the subject, sir?"

"There's only one subject," Lee said, surprised by his resoluteness.

"In Jackson, you'll find many sympathizers. They've sent me out as welcome wagon to invite you to dinner. Meanwhile, what can I do to make you feel at home?"

"I already feel at home," Lee said, his left hand in spasm.

At seven o'clock, he stood stone sober on the doorstep of Harry Bergstedt's Belhaven home, its facade as stately as Harry. Lifting the polished brass knocker, he tapped politely. The door was opened by an arthritic butler who ushered Lee to the parlor where Bergstedt immediately rose and hailed the guest of honor.

"To Dr. Leland Green, pioneer and preservationist."

Lee hesitated. Surely, he wasn't meant to dine with these men in this house. Surely, it was a scene from theater of the absurd. The butler was wrong, and he was wrong, too. His will hung back, but his body swam into the room, shaking hands with seven men and one stunning woman.

"East Texas," Bergstedt said in lieu of a profession for Sally Shaw. "She owns it!"

She turned to Lee, fluffing the mound of tawny hair that fell loosely on her thin shoulders. "Can you tell?"

"Evidently, she owns Paris, too!" Lee riposted, referring to her YSL frock, the black patent heels, the brimless horsehair hat, and an enormous diamond pendant.

Sally Shaw blushed with false modesty.

"What are you drinking, sir?" Harry asked.

Lee wavered, staring at Mrs. Shaw's gleaming russet eyes.

She held up a glass of Campari. "That's what I'm partaking of," she said.

"We might all be writing books if we didn't irrigate our cerebral cortex every night," Peter Smithson said. He was the local GM dealer.

Bergstedt handed over a crystal tumbler of carmine liquid. "Dr. Green has been out West too long."

"I once was a drinking man," Lee said.

Don't offer any personal information, Whipple instructed.

"But?" Sally Shaw grinned.

"It got away with me," he explained what would likely be his only truthful words all evening.

Her penciled eyebrows arched. "*Away* with you?"

They crossed the foyer to the dining room, the walls hung with oil paintings of men in uniform, each dated from a war, the uniforms more distinctive than the faces—1812, 1862, 1898, 1917, 1942, and a recent portrait of a youth in the garb of a Green Beret, Harry Bergstedt's son, Hank, serving in Vietnam.

Harry sat at the head of the oval mahogany table. At each place setting was a white gilded charger, an acid-green porcelain plate, six pieces of festooned silver cutlery, a crystal goblet also gilded, two wine glasses, and individual crystal decanters of cucumber water.

"Dr. Green sir, will you kindly lead us in the blessing?"

Around the table, they linked hands. Lee had rehearsed such things, but he needed to sound unrehearsed. He paused to listen to the paddle fan overhead. Then, he began to paraphrase words of gratitude for the munificent bounty, remembering to ask the blessing in the name of Jesus Christ, Our Lord. An utterance that terminated Leon Greenberg. Again.

Dinner conversation was filled with complaints about business, weather, family, golf. Although Sally asked Leland questions, he resisted. He did well at redirecting. After dinner, Harry ushered them back to the parlor for Napoleon brandy, chicory coffee, cake, and contraband Cuban cigars.

"We like your point of view, sir. We like how you phrase things. That's what a good writer does."

"Thank you, sir," Lee said, forgetting for a few seconds that he was merely a good charlatan.

Never let down your guard, Whipple instructed emphatically.

"Jackson will be my base, but I want to roam around. I may even go as far as Texas."

"You talking my country," Sally said with gusto. "I got plenty of cotton pickers working in *peaceful equilibrium*."

He noted with disappointment that Sally Shaw had read "Hailstorm."

"*Peaceful Equilibrium* and *Compassionate Segregation* are slogans to propel a man to the mansion. Maybe, Harry wants to be gov'nor."

"I think we have a convincing case, sir," Harry's voice crescendoed. "What does counsel think?"

Billy Clarkson brayed, "Counsel thinks he'll have another brandy."

"Our real concern isn't the Negra. Negras, we know how to handle. We been handling Negras for hundreds of years. Feds don't worry me. Excuse me, Missus Shaw, feds don't know their bassackward from a hole in the ground. It's Jews who know the difference. Jews are putting their money on the black. If you're a roulette man, that's worrisome. Jews are funding the entire goddamn nigger insurrection."

Lee visibly shuddered.

"They're not as smart as you think!" Billy Clarkson exclaimed.

"They are! They're the smartest people in the world!"

Lee folded his arms. "I've met stupid Jews," he said, thinking of his college roommate.

"Not possible," Smithson interrupted.

Don't come across as overly opinionated, Whipple instructed.

"There are stupid people everywhere," Lee blurted.

"If you got stupid Jews, maybe you got genius Negroes," Sally Shaw reflected.

Harry winked theatrically. "Try to walk a straight line, a woman throws a curve every time."

※

Leland Green rented a carriage house in the Belhaven district and settled in with a portable Olivetti and a ream of paper. Except for Sunday church, he spent mornings at the library reading crime paperbacks. His favorites by Ian Fleming and Eric Ambler, the more vicious the better. Otherwise, he wrote notes to Whipple or made feeble attempts to outline Hailstorm's new book. In the afternoon, he drove around the countryside, looking for signs of menace. Beside rail fences and at crossroad stores, he stopped to converse. It proved impossible to talk to frightened men. No one wanted a cold drink or a joke. No one except children let him take their picture. The Oregon license plate made him a foreigner.

Sally Shaw offered to escort him in her sporty Mercedes. To help him find "happy whites and happy coloreds," she said.

Colored surprised him. He considered it enlightened, but the car made him squeamish. In Atlanta, no Jews drove German cars except his sister-in-law, Marilyn Steiner. "I accept," he finally said despite the car and outfits that would feed a sharecropper's family for months.

She headed east toward Bienville, swung off the blacktop at Morton, and bounced over a rutted dirt lane into the forest. The deepest ruts filled with chartreuse scum and mosquito larvae. She parked beside a small river underneath a splendid white oak. Lee lifted the metal cooler from Sally's trunk, his eyes scanning her bare tan legs and the sleeveless cotton dress dotted with violets. The dress came with a matching parasol she carried in one hand and in the other a dainty wicker picnic basket.

"This isn't much of a work mission," Lee said, chewing a drumstick and sipping a cold beer.

"My work mission," she lisped through her coruscating teeth.

"I'm not worth a mission, Mrs. Shaw," he laughed. In fact, he laughed freely.

"I thought I'd show you where *your* boys hang out."

"What do *my* boys do?"

"Boy things like drink, shoot at Coke bottles, hunt and fish. Who the hell knows? Chiggers are fierce so I stay over here and swim."

"You don't go for fish and game?"

"As uncouth as I am, I don't like killing. I eat it once it's dead, but I'm not a killer."

A quarter-mile from the river was a crude log construction, a deep fire pit for trash, an outhouse, and an outdoor sink and shower fed by a rain barrel on the roof. Lee peered through a window, surprised by the shabbiness. Sally removed a bobby pin from her hair, twisted the wires, and stuck one end into the padlock.

"Y'all needing he'p?" a soft country voice called from the woods.

A man, ramrod straight and freshly shaven with bloody nicks on his neck, stepped forward. He stood with his hands in the pockets of well-worn overalls, soiled and busted canvas shoes, and on his head a faded shako whose provenance could have been the Napoleonic Age. He was a black Indian with Choctaw blood, his skin flushed red, his eyes different colors, one bright blue, the other muddy brown. He was called Hark although Hark was not his Indian name, Bending Willow, or baptized name, James Willie Johnson. It was a nickname bestowed by the plantation owner where his family used to sharecrop. Hark had lived near Bienville for eighty-six years. He was caretaker of Harry Bergstedt's clubhouse.

He lifted his hat from his hairless head and held it. "Missus Shaw, I saw yo' car over by the river."

Sally relaxed. A colored man made her feel as if she had every right to be there. "This is Dr. Green."

"Thought I'd fish but didn't bring my pole," Lee said.

"They got them plenty poles inside, Missus Shaw. They got them plenty everything you need, sir. I know the best place to dig for worms. Y'all wan' I can open up?"

Hark's gnarled fingers pulled a ring of keys from his pocket, dozens on a string with a rabbit's foot for good luck. He inserted a key in the padlock and another into the discus lock, then opened the door, moving aside to let Sally and the doctor pass into the hot, stuffy room that smelled of stale beer and sour terrycloth. Antlers hung on a wall, baseball bats and golf clubs leaned in a corner. Lee noted the guns, including an Enfield 1917 rifle, the type that killed Medgar Evers. Hark reached for the rods and an aluminum case stamped with the Wheatley mark. "Unless y'all like flies, sir."

"They play golf?" Lee asked Sally.

"All talk in Mississippi divides according to class. Serfs debate the wonders of the combustion engine and gentry discusses golf. You'd think there wasn't another subject in the world except college football. So to speak, Ole Miss Rebels is common ground. Hark will back me up."

"Yes'm, I back Missus Shaw any day."

ꙅ

Leon complained to Whipple he was getting fat. Fat and useless. He was close to hating Leland Green and the vigilance required to mold him into a temperate, chaste Christian man. He certainly hated Whipple. Any discussion of timetable had been vague. Could the agency ask him to stay indefinitely? Yes, he thought they could. They could do whatever they wanted. He worked for them.

Then, there was the evening he felt himself crack.

You'll reach a point when you can't go on, but you'll push through, Whipple said.

"Of course, it happened," Lee shouted, socking his fist against his palm. "I was in the war, were you?"

"Not defending Jews."

Fuming, Lee rose. He walked out the front door and paced across the lawn.

Deep, slow breaths, Whipple instructed. *Once you get control of your breathing, you can think clearly.*

He composed himself and returned to the gathering. "It gives a good cause a bad mark to distort history," he said quietly.

Harry Bergstedt concurred. He supported Leland Green. He liked sound reasoning. "Dr. Green and I are on the same page about that. We can't depend on primitive emotions and ignorant falsehoods. That's over, gentlemen."

Randy McIntire didn't agree. He thought emotions and falsehoods were highly dependable. They'd served the cause very well. What didn't serve were pretentious theories.

In early November, Lee was invited to the country for hunting, drinking, and cards. As the weekend approached, he grew frightened. He might be asked to commit a crime. Whipple told him he was under no obligation to perform a violent act. If his loyalty to Harry's gang was tested, he wasn't sure how to refuse. He wondered if he should bring his gun. If cajoled into skinny dipping, his circumcised pecker might become a topic of speculation. A joke or worse. Randy McIntire had planted the seed that Dr. Green was an apologist for Jews. Whatever was required, he was afraid he would fail.

On Friday night, they drove to Bienville beside the spectral towers of dead kudzu. There were no oncoming cars, no roadside lights, no moon or stars, only black sky and mammoth clouds. At the cabin's back entrance, Peter parked his Fleetwood Eldorado on a patch of flattened weeds beside two pickups. Five men stood nearby, smoking in the chilly dark under the pines, cigarettes glowing like fireflies.

"Come on in, boys," Harry waved.

Lee felt his stomach lurch. He lifted the case of scotch from the trunk, trying to read the license plates on the trucks, heart pounding like a jackhammer, deafening as he bent down and scribbled the numbers on his calf.

Harry lit the kerosene lanterns. Billy made a fire to drive out the cold and damp. The visitors took seats at the square, sturdy table. They looked average, Lee thought. Average Mississippi bigots—farmer, merchant, plumber, bartender, and sheriff's deputy. Mugs and a bottle of Cutty Sark were passed around. One of the strangers had a bushel of boiled peanuts. Harry and his boys were garrulous, almost giddy in contrast to the visitors' silence. None of them spoke. They were busy enjoying the luxury of scotch.

"Who's he?" Pawley asked. He was older than Harry, white-haired with wolf eyes and a nose like a baked yam.

"Dr. Green, y'all call him 'Lee.'"

"Somebody needing a doctor?" Bee Jay asked. Bee Jay was Pawley's fifty-year-old nephew, bald with chubby gray cheeks, a drift in his left eye, and a nickel wart on his chin.

"Only if we have to shoot y'all!" Billy said.

"Not funny when we doing yo' dirty work," Pawley groused.

"Doctor of religion," Harry said, stirring his drink with his finger. "You can get to be a doctor of anything."

"None of us got all night," Pawley said. He liked the money but didn't care for the company. Harry Bergstedt and his men were arrogant. They acted as if they owned the world.

Peter Smithson unzipped his overnight bag, removed a map, and unfolded it on the table. Sloppy circles were drawn around Greenwood, Port Gibson, Vicksburg, Meridian, and the capital.

"Hear, hear! Meeting convened!"

Pawley ran his finger across the state, north to south. "Jackson?"

"Sure, why not?"

"You boys like the sound of that?"

"I don't go for Jackson," Bee Jay whispered.

"Can't hear you," Pawley snarled.

"Jackson got Yankees. No secrets in Jackson."

"What about Port Gibson?"

"Gemi-luth Chessed or however hell y'all say it, it's a Jew house. I seen 'em."

"Fishin' good over there," Bee Jay said, worrying his wart, his hands skittish.

"Jew house got a dome on top just like goddamn commies in Russia."

"Town too goddamn small. Somebody notice us, for sure."

"I agree with Bee Jay," Bergstedt said. "I veto Jackson."

"You aiming to burn or bomb?"

"Fire's easier," Pawley said.

"Bomb makes an instant statement," Peter said. "With fire, you gotta wait through an investigation. By time investigators finish with their rigama-role, it's old news. Nobody cares. Something else done stole the limelight."

"I prefer bombs as long as the building is empty," Harry said.

"Harry's got a soft heart," Billy giggled.

"I don't happen to believe in random killing."

"Since when?"

Pawley took a swig from the bottle. "Since them Yankee niggers come down here with them white niggers, everything gone to hell. Nothing been the same."

"Murder isn't productive," Harry said. "Unless you can't help it."

"Murder means we're serious. It means they have to contend with a militia of self-defenders."

"What's doc say?" Pawley asked.

Lee's eyes were closed, his head sweaty, his bowels in turmoil.

❧

The next afternoon, Lee drove with Harry to Forest, the county seat. They drove in Harry's new marlin blue two-door Eldorado as big as a Chris-Craft. The exact date had not been set, but the rabbi's house in Meridian and the synagogue in Greenville would be bombed on the same day. Code name, MARY PHAGAN. Although Lee now had concrete information for Whipple, he didn't feel proud. He felt poisoned.

"You like those guys?"

Lee grunted.

"Pawley is something of a pyromaniac. I guess fire is an extra kick for him. That's why I insist on bombs. I don't want him sticking around to watch anything burn."

When the Temple in Atlanta was bombed, it was speculated the bomb was prompted by the rabbi's alliance with Dr. King. The next day with police surrounding the building, the rabbi invoked the vision of Jonah who tried to escape the difficult task that God demanded. He spoke of the dual sides of living history and the impossibility of escaping what was right and what was wrong. It was the last time Leon Greenberg had been in synagogue.

Harry parked at the curb across from the post office. The sidewalks were crowded with farmers who'd come to town to shop. Black and white. Sometimes a black man stepped into the street. Stepped or was shoved.

Harry went to buy ice while Lee picked up a bucket of ribs and cole-slaw. Harry put the ice in the trunk and climbed into the driver's seat. As he started the car, a child dashed across the street.

"Mr. Greenberg!" he cried, squatting beside the passenger window. "'Member me?"

Leon shaded his face with his hand.

"You gave me my own book," the child said proudly.

Leon glared at the bright, eager eyes nearly level with his own.

"Boy, you're slobbering on my car!" Harry shooed. "Get on with you!"

The man next to the child dragged him upright. "What foolish talk you talking now? Stepping into other people's business, making trouble." He boxed the boy's ears.

"Yeow-ow!" the child squealed. "Mr. Greenberg done come to my school."

❧

When Hark was already dreaming, he heard an owl. From across the river, he heard it. A hoot, a yelp, a cry, a scream of predator or prey.

The next morning was Sunday. He sat in his rocker and read from Genesis, the book of Beginnings. The beginning of paradise, sin, despair, hope, murder—brother against brother. At nine, he started for the club-house, following the path by his fields through the woods and over a plank bridge that crossed the small, meandering river. He was surprised to find the door locked, the yard empty, no cars or trucks, only muddy tracks.

He unlocked the door. The room was upside down. Smashed bottles, toppled chairs, the table and couch flipped on their side, bloodied cushions scattered on the floor. He circled the room, corner to corner, mumbling, "Lordy, Lordy, Lordy." He didn't stop mumbling as he set the furniture right and opened the windows to air out the alcohol and blood. In the outdoor sink, he soaked the stained cushions in vinegar and hydrogen peroxide. He swept aside the shards of glass. The golf clubs he picked up slowly because he was tired. One by one, he put them in the bag. He mopped the rough pine floor. As he worked, he felt worse and worse, remembering the hoot owl.

Tucked inside the screened porch was a generator and a large chest freezer. Mostly used in deer season, Mister Harry occasionally put birds, squirrels, and possums in it. For big weekend parties, they stored white wine and vodka. A padlocked tow chain was wrapped around the sides, the handle, and the coil panel in back. Hark had never known Mister Harry to use a lock on the freezer, but he was sure he had a key. After a dozen mismatches, it opened. The chain was not so simple to unwind. It took all Hark's strength to wrestle with it. When he opened the heavy lid, he saw a man with a pillow over his head. He touched the body. Cool but not stone cold. He removed the pillow. The side Hark could see was drenched in blood. It was impossible to recognize a face, but he reeked of liquor. Hark stepped back to consider. He could leave the man. It wasn't his business. On the other hand, the man would probably die without his help. The death would be on Hark.

He went back inside the cabin. He gathered blankets and piled them on top of the man. He propped the locker open with a golf club. He left the cabin and walked as quickly as he could manage. At home, there was no one. He wrote a message on a piece of rolling paper, stuffed it into a hollow tube, and opened the dovecote. He wrote, "Bring truck & boys." The message was for Estelle May, Hark's daughter, his seventh child and a healer. He fastened the tube to Yosh's leg, lifted his hands, and tossed the bird into the air.

"Hurry!" he cried.

Hark walked out to the blacktop. It was a cool, overcast day. Under his overalls, he wore a flannel shirt and sweater. He wore a skullcap. There were wintery undercurrents in the air. The redbuds and sugar maples had turned red and gold. If Estelle was home, he reckoned it would take an hour to get to him. An hour was optimistic. Optimism was part of Hark's nature. He believed things could get better. Even a nearly dead man in a freezer could get better.

From his overalls, Hark pulled out his pocketknife and a small piece of wood. He was not accustomed to idleness. If there was nothing else to do, he whittled. He didn't whittle with intention. He waited with childish anticipation to see what might emerge. A face, a flower, an angel, a pony. He was considerably skilled, and sometimes others asked him to whittle them a talisman.

When Estelle arrived with the boys, he lifted himself into the cab. She leaned over and kissed her daddy's forehead.

"Clubhouse," he wheezed.

"If you messing in white people's crazy business, that make you crazy, too."

His blue eye glowed. "We can bring him back."

"When they comes around to finish up their business, they gon' ask for you. You be the person they gon' ask. Where the man be? Where the man gon'? You ready?"

"I been ready."

Estelle turned into the dirt lane that led to the back of the clubhouse. From the tracks, Hark could tell no one had come or gone. He pointed to the screened porch. Estelle waddled after him. She peeked under the propped lid, pushing it back so it rested against the shed wall. She put her index finger on the man's neck crusted with blood.

"I got something." Her eyes glowed like Hark's. It was what he had counted on. Estelle May, seventh of seven in a line of three generations of sevens, born to heal.

She motioned to the teens, shrinking against the truck. "He ain't dead so you gotta lift him gentle." She raised the man's head. He moaned softly as each boy took the end of a limb like the four corners of a flag. He was broken, the white man. He'd been beaten everywhere.

Estelle drove slowly. It was bumpy until they reached the blacktop. Hark sat in the back of the truck with two of the boys. He held the man's head in his lap, speaking to him. He prayed over him and sang hymns. The boys held his legs to keep him steady. On the Bienville road, Hark covered him with a sheet. Estelle floored the accelerator until they reached the town limits. She pulled the truck behind her garage. The boys moved the man to the back of her washhouse. She ordered them to light the stoves, boil the kettles, bring basins and towels from the closet.

Estelle cut off his clothes and began to clean him. First with warm, soapy water, followed by a warm rinse. After the blood had been dabbed and wiped away, Hark recognized the man. It was Sally Shaw's friend. Estelle rubbed the man's chest and abdomen with lemon juice. For swelling on his arms and legs, she placed compresses of comfrey, dandelion, horsetail. She girdled his cracked ribs in a mustard plaster. She splinted his ulna with strips of sheets and a garden stake. The leg, she stretched out and splinted with a crutch. The crushed thumbs, she set between popsicle sticks. The eye was nasty, but Estelle didn't flinch. Into his empty eye socket, she squeezed lemon juice and laid a paste of turmeric and ginger over the hole.

When they turned him over, she saw sets of numbers written on the back of his calf. Two letters and four digits. She didn't know what they signified, maybe license plates. She wrote them down. She washed his back, his buttocks, his legs, erasing the numbers. Deep inside his trouser pocket, she found two more. By the ten digits, she thought they must be long distance with an area code outside Mississippi. Everybody in Mississippi was 601. These were 404.

"Maybe, they ain't aiming to come back," Hark said.

"They aiming. They gon' dump him in the river. Or put him out for buzzards. The river's no problem if they dump good. They trained to do that. They already know that's what they gotta do. What you plan to say if them boys swing by?"

"I plan to sleep in the fields."

"You gon' tell them you went there to make breakfast. Corncakes, like Mister Harry ask you. When you done found the mess, you say you done start to clean everything. Somebody come up the drive so you left. You didn't see nobody. You came on home. You don't know nothing."

Hark crossed his index and middle fingers. Whenever he lied, he crossed them like a child. Lying had never agreed with him. But lying was a strategy of survival. That was the fate of his life.

※

A month before Lee's outing to the clubhouse, Sally Shaw left Jackson to visit the Smokey Mountains. She left to get away from Harry after he declared he was willing to marry her. "*Willing*?" she cackled.

Six weeks later when she returned, cold rain and wind had battered the countryside. From the Atlantic to the Mississippi, the land was sodden and bleak, the trees stripped bare, the fields filled with stubble, the shacks weathered to colorless wood, the empty lots piled with rusted machine parts, all of it streaked with red ferrous dirt.

While Sally was away, she didn't contact Leland Green. She resisted, hoping to enhance his expectations. On the outskirts of Jackson, she stopped at a phone booth and dialed his number. There was a buzz, then silence. After several tries, she asked the operator to check. The phone had been disconnected.

Her second call was to Harry. He dropped the receiver with excitement. "Sally Shaw! Where the dickens are you?"

At the hotel, Sally took a slow bath. She rubbed her body with African shea butter and her face with Clarins. She put on her navy Pierre Cardin slacks, a cashmere sailor sweater, a collar of seed pearls, stacked Ferragamo heels, and a waxed cotton Barbour jacket.

At the curb, Harry and Puss waited under an umbrella. Harry had aged impressively. Distended bags under his eyes, unwashed hair, parched sallow cheeks, the smell of smoke on his clothes, signs of sleeplessness and neglect.

"Mrs. Shaw, you are a sight for sore eyes."

"Looks like you been weeping ever since I left."

Harry rubbed his poorly shaved chin. "I do have bad news."

"Dr. Green?"

Harry sank into a chair. Sally Shaw was an uncanny creature.

"Hark died," he whimpered.

"Hark was old."

"Hark has been with me my whole life. He was my best friend."

"It was his time," she consoled.

"He was murdered."

"No!"

"Negras!" Harry muttered vacantly as if he'd had a stroke.

"Is that who killed him?"

"They gone insane. Killing an old man and burning everything."

"And Lee?" she winced.

"Same day Hark got killed, Dr. Green disappeared."

Sally gulped her whiskey and glanced out the window at the rain. "Well, surely?"

"They brought in Hark's daughters and grandsons. They brought in the Johnson boys. I guess Singlet Johnson has most to gain if they acquire his land. River bottom land, nothing more beautiful on Earth."

"And the funeral?"

"I bought the prettiest casket they make, lined with cream satin with genuine pewter handles. We filled the church with gladiolas."

Sally held up her glass for a refill. "Leland Green is quite the mystery. Where you suppose he went?"

"To hell," Harry said positively. "I doubt we'll ever see him again."

❧

Leon lay in a room, curtains drawn, a small table and dim lamp beside the bed. His left arm and right leg in a cast, his thumbs in splints, his ribs wrapped so tightly he could hardly breathe, his head bandaged, every part of him in pain. He wondered if he'd been kept alive only to be beaten again. His tormentors had wanted to know who sent him. They accused him of lying and spying. They said he could save himself if he confessed. Who stood behind him. Jews? Yankee niggers? Commies?

A small moth circled the lamp, occasionally leaving its orbit to glide over Leon's face. It was company, but visitor or visitation he wasn't sure. He reached out for it with his best working hand and felt a convulsion from his shoulder to his groin. He snatched the moth and enclosed it inside his weak fingers. Such commotion its wings made. Such life force. Like him, fighting to live.

"You woken up?"

Leon scrutinized what parts of Irwin's face he could see. African black with pebble-colored eyes. "You save me?"

"We nurse you. Estelle and Uncle Hark save you."

"Estelle?"

"Hark's girl brought you three days ago Sunday."

"They almost killed me."

"They did kill you. They left you dead. Bleed out, suffocate, starve, all different ways you be dead. Or they come back to fetch you and throw you in the river. River filled with bones. You can't make me swim in no river."

"Hurts like hell." Leon patted the bandaged portion of his face. His skin itched beneath the gauze.

"Dr. Patterson came here. He want us to take you to the hospital. Hospital ain't no option. Hospital too dangerous. All of us in danger if you in hospital. Dr. Patterson stop over every night."

"What they done? Concussed me?"

Irwin stepped to the window and pulled the drape aside. "Your people come by," he said.

"What people?"

"Soon as you wake up, they plan to fly you out at Hawkins Field." He reached in his pocket and pulled out a card with a name, a number, and several hundred-dollar bills. John Whipple's card, taxpayers' money.

"We afraid to take it to the bank. We afraid to spend it. Everybody wanna know where we get money like this. They think we stole it."

"My people left it?"

"For medicine, doctor, extra for our trouble. They want us to swear we don't tell nobody. I told them I wasn't raised to swear."

"They ain't my people," Leon said gruffly. "They're swine." He'd been put out as chum worth a few hundred dollars.

Leon blinked at the white walls, the muted TV, the rain battering the window. He wished he could cry. He tried, but tears wouldn't come. Physiological or emotional, he wasn't sure. He leaned back on the hospital bed, awash with relief that the sham of Leland Green was behind him. Another version of himself was dead.

"You're a lucky man," Whipple said.

"To hell with you."

"Once you're better . . ."

Leon yanked Whipple's sleeve. He would have pummeled him, but one sleeve was all he could manage. "I'll never walk right or see straight again. I fared better under the brunt of a world war than your shenanigans."

"Whenever doc says you're ready."

"You'll leave me alone?"

"After you choose a name, we'll get your papers ready."

"I can't think about a new name."

"What about 'Bar-do'?"

"Bardo?"

"Something you muttered. Something we tried to trace. No one by that name in Mississippi, but we found a town in Poland."

"It's a place in your head, Bardo."

"It doesn't sound real."

"Is that an ontological assessment?"

"Whatever you want to call it, that's your right."

"What about Bergstedt's thugs? They still have rights?"

"Peanuts," Whipple said.

"Peanuts kill same as anybody else."

"We can't arrest them until we catch them in the act."

Leon patted his head. "This act doesn't count?"

"We know nothing about it."

"I'd have told those boys anything. 'I love niggers' they made me say it. I was proud to say it."

"You did good, Leon. You've been a big help."

Whipple sipped the lukewarm coffee. It had been two harrowing weeks, but the screws had started to turn. Bergstedt, Smithson, and McIntire had been placed under IRS investigation. Although impossible to get cooperation from local law enforcement, the agency had made inroads in the governor's office. There were enough offenses on Bergstedt's henchmen to harass them into good behavior for a year or so.

"Won't they worry I'll talk?"

"We took care of Leland Green."

"What's that mean?"

"We made sure a body was found in the woods."

"Something you're actually good at."

"It was messed up, gnawed by animals and things."

Leon gagged. "I can testify Pawley and Bee Jay killed me."

"You're dead, remember? Otherwise, we'd be accused of entrapment."

"And Hark's family?"

"We're taking care of them, too."

"Is that called human sacrifice or quality control? What's the new term you use, collateral something?"

Later, Dr. Josephs visited Leon to discuss the new eye. "They do wonders with glass," he said. "It'll be a perfect match."

Tears flowed down Leon's face onto the bed sheet. "I don't want a match," he cried. "I want the brightest blue you have."

The Sacrifice of Isaac

Steven Wishnia

The wineglass crunched. Ari the groom, his beard just beginning to sprout under his earlocks, stomped on it decisively. The white-cloth napkin wrapping it trapped the shards like a condom. Malka the bride beamed radiantly under the *khupah*, a white-satin headscarf covering her newly shorn hair.

The band played a slow tune, "The Bride's Waltz," in three, almost freely enough to be a *doina*, a flowing, rubato improvisation. The minute they got a break, the bass player, Zak Katz, headed for the kitchen area that doubled as a dressing room. He was tired. He needed to sit down. This wedding, on the far south side of Williamsburg, was his fourth gig of the weekend. Fortunately, it wasn't far from home.

He saw a skinny, black-gabardined figure hunched over the steel counter by the wall, heard the distinctive sound of lines being snorted. Just what he could use, a bit of artificial energy.

"Yo, you got any more of that?" he asked when the guy stood up.

"Yeah." It was Zev, one of the groom's party. His father was supposed to be some kind of big wheel. The kid was all business. "How much you need? Grams, fifty; half-grams, thirty; eight-balls, a buck and a quarter." Zak went for the half-gram.

He needed the stimulant. It was a good-paying gig, but they made you work for it, playing for four hours as the men in black danced. Men in round black hats wrapped in double-breasted coats, the younger ones cigarette-thin inside them, the big-bellied older ones stretching them. Some of them were shikkering the liquor pretty hard.

The band was a five-piece, clarinet and violin on top, synthesizer in the middle, bass and drums laying down the bottom. Zak was playing electric bass. Yesterday he'd had to shlep his upright bass and a small amp all the way to the Upper West Side, to a *shul* on Ninety-Ninth Street and West

End Avenue. Secular weddings like that one preferred more traditional klezmer. They wanted the music from the old countries their great-great-grandparents had fled, that their great-grandparents had danced to at an occasion on the Lower East Side or in Brownsville in 1924. The Hasidim's taste was more modern and arguably cheesier. They liked to hear the traditional melodies combined with dance-club rhythms and textures. Zak put a funky bump and slap, some '70s-disco thumb-and-forefinger octave licks, on the keening D minor and the Middle-Eastern-sounding *freygish* scales. But the keyboard player grated on his nerves, introducing songs with space-wind and thus-spake-Zarathustra bombast, playing tinny imitation-horn sounds.

Zak's mood perked up when they did "Yikhes." The word meant ancestry or family heritage, a selling point for matchmakers back in the shtetl, but the tune's original lyrics were a Yiddish yo-mama snap, far too crude for a *frum* wedding—"your mother steals fish in the market . . . and your sister sleeps with a Cossack." He rocked into the C section, driving the band with a burbling, galloping groove, and when they punched out the six G notes that heralded the chorus—ahh! ahh! ah-ah-ah-ah!—the men went wild, dancing with a frenzy that bordered on religious moshing.

Zev Asher was back at work early on Monday morning, in the offices of Asher Yotser Management, his father's property-management company, on the third floor of an old building overlooking Broadway and the Williamsburg Bridge. The rusty exterior and shabby office furniture belied the money that came through it. The company owned all or part of more than three hundred buildings around the city. And it was moving up as a player in the big redevelopment projects, the ones you needed serious political connections to get in on, along with the patience and clout to hold on through years of planning, land-use review procedures, and who-gets-what bargaining. But the rewards were potfuls of public subsidies, of tax abatements, low-interest loans, and property transferred for a dollar, all in the name of the public good, of "revitalizing," "affordable housing," and "creating jobs."

If you stuck your head out the office window and craned your neck to the west, you could see the first big deal they'd made, new buildings on a three-block stretch south of the bridge that had been so abandoned in the '70s that the only occupied structure was the clubhouse of a biker gang called the Chingalings. The deal had been tied up for years while the Hasidim and the Puerto Ricans to the north fought over it, but Shaul Asher, Zev's father, had brokered a compromise with City Councilmember Roberto Colon, "the baron of Bushwick," the unofficial boss of the

Brooklyn Democratic party. His company got to oversee it, Colon lined up the subcontractors, and the housing was split 2–1 in favor of the Hasids, with Colon's nonprofit organization getting dibs on a tract further east.

It had made Shaul Asher a pillar of the community. He'd become a major contributor to the local *shuls*, and earned a reputation and gratitude for delivering apartments within walking distance, big and cheap enough for a four-child family whose breadwinner spent most of his waking hours studying Torah and Talmud. Portly, almost professorial with his rectangular gold glasses and a light-brown beard, he contrasted sharply with his son, who was shorter, thin, and darker, his beard barely reaching his cheeks, surveillance-camera eyes behind smoke-rimmed glasses.

They weren't looking out the window. They had a ten o'clock meeting with Dick Weinstock, a political aide to Mayor Steve Schwartz. The sixty-ish secretary bustled about, preparing salami sandwiches and coffee with nondairy creamer for it. Zev spieled about his favorite topic, that they should expand eastward, into the working-class and ghetto neighborhoods that were just beginning to get artists and wannabes.

"Look at what happened in the East Village," he was saying. "The neighborhood got better block by block, from Avenue A to B to C. And the smart ones who got in on the ground floor made big bucks. They bought buildings for $10,000 and sold them for a million. Remember the guy who said 'we'll give them life-preservers and push them into the East River'? Those people didn't go swimming, they're coming over here now. Anybody with an ounce of *seykhel* in their head can see what's happening."

They should buy up more buildings further out along the L subway line, he urged. They already had two in the Italian neighborhood by the Graham Avenue stop, the third one in Brooklyn, and one on Montrose Avenue, near the fifth.

"It's good business if it works, but you're on your own," his father cautioned him. "You don't want a piece of property where you're stuck with Puerto Ricans on Section 8 and *shvartses* complaining about the heat and hot water for the foreseeable future. It's worth it if you can get them out and bring in a better class of tenant, but it's a lot of *mishegas* and aggravation. You have to create a climate that encourages them to leave, and if they don't want to, we have to pay the process server, the lawyer, maybe somebody to help expedite things a little. You make good money when the better people move in, but listen to me, you have to be prepared to sit for a while on a property that's not earning. We work with the city, it's bigger and safer."

"I'm not stupid," Zev reassured him. "I know we shouldn't get too far out in front of the wave, where our money's all tied up and yields nothing but *tsuris*. But it's like chess, you gotta think two or three moves ahead. If we see where it's going and put our money in the right places, we'll get an incredible ROI in a few years."

"Not a bad idea, but if we get this deal locked down, we've got a license to print money. They back us on the financing, we get tax credits for the lower-rent units, and it's a mitzvah for our community."

Weinstock had arrived while Zev was still spieling. Shaul introduced them. "He's a sharp kid," the aide complimented. "I can see where he got it from. He's got good *yikhes*."

They met around a table with an architect's design that looked like a Hollywood version of the Warsaw ghetto, beige buildings with old-European details, speckled like matzoh, bent-iron balconies doubling as security and space for *sukkahs*, with a shopping center on the west side, facing toward the Brooklyn-Queens Expressway. It was a development planned for the Flushing Avenue corridor.

Of course, there were politics involved. The Democratic primary was four weeks away, and Mayor Schwartz was being challenged by a black candidate, City Councilmember Herman Clarkson. Wiseasses were calling the race "Schwartz vs. the *shvartse*." It was close, and the city's veins had been pounding with aggravated racial tension since the police shooting of Denroy "Echo" Eccles in June. Eccles, a twenty-one-year-old aspiring DJ born in Jamaica, had been stopped by cops while urinating behind a dumpster in Crown Heights. He'd made a "furtive motion" toward his pants and gotten shot eighteen times. The mayor had scored law-and-order points talking about the half-smoked blunt found in the dead man's pocket, but had not endeared himself to the city's black community. They didn't like him that much to begin with, and now they sympathized with Eccles's mother, a licensed practical nurse bleary from night-shift work, grief, and rage.

"It goes without saying we're gonna need your help," Weinstock told them, "but I know you think it's a mitzvah for all of us." In other words, Schwartz was counting on them getting out the bloc votes from Hasidic Williamsburg.

"Don't worry about it. Now what's new on Flushing Avenue? Have you talked to Roberto?"

"I think he'll work with us. He wants to play. It's just a matter of the details. He's gonna want some units for his people, but he's flexible. We give him a piece of this, we do the next one at his end of the neighborhood, we'll be all right."

"The *shvartses* are going to be a problem." The Flushing Corridor plan crossed the border into Bedford-Stuyvesant.

Vance Dawson would have played ball, they thought. The former Bed-Stuy state legislator had once dominated the political machinations of

Black Brooklyn, of Bed-Stuy, Brownsville, Crown Heights, and Flatbush, and he'd worked well with Weinstock and Colon as they all rose in the '80s. He'd had the prescience to get funding for a drug-rehab clinic just before crack exploded onto the streets—and the weakness or stupidity to get caught embezzling $260,000 from it. That and the blurry surveillance video of him in a motel room with an unidentified female companion, a rolled-up Benjamin, and a mirror railed with cocaine made him Purina Tabloid Chow. Dawson got twenty-one to twenty-seven months on federal fraud charges, and Clarkson and his upstarts had seized the opening—a big enough base to challenge the mayor, and indirectly, Colon.

"Yes, they're different," said Weinstock. "They don't do things like us. They're ideologues. They'd rather posture and make a rhetorical point than make an agreement where it's a win-win, where everybody gets a little something, everybody walks away happy."

"When they're not making excuses for murderers," Shaul seethed. "Yankel Rosenbaum, a good man, an innocent man, and they killed him like a dog in that pogrom. They had the chutzpah to say it was an eye for an eye, to compare a tragic accident in which a little boy was killed to a heartless murder."

The Crown Heights riots of 1991 still rankled him. Weinstock brought the conversation back. "We win the election, they won't be such a problem. Officially, Roberto's neutral, because of his leadership position, but between you and me, he won't be against us. He doesn't like Clarkson and his people. That's almost as good as an endorsement, because they need the Hispanics if they're gonna beat us."

Zak Katz lived on Flushing Avenue, the southern border of Williamsburg, on a block with a derelict warehouse, three auto-repair shops, and two vacant lots with weeds growing inside chain-link fences, one a depot for the Hebrew-lettered school buses that got the workers home in time for Shabbes. The three-story maroon-brick building was divided into six small lofts, the gray steel door covered with graffiti. He was on the first floor, with an iron-barred window looking at the street.

He liked the place. It was isolated, but he could practice without getting noise complaints from the neighbors. They were artists and musicians too. And the hipsters on the third floor had no right to complain, they had rent parties on the last Saturday of every month, three-hundred-odd people and three bands. He was doing well, steady work, his weekends full of jazz and klezmer and wedding gigs. He'd been in the right place at the right time to catch the klezmer revival. The joke was that it had started when the Milliner, a jazz and rock club occupying a former hat factory on Allen Street on the Lower East Side, had been trying to figure out what they could book that might possibly draw on Christmas Eve, and had discovered a house-packing alternative to the venerable holiday tradition of Chinese takeout and movies. He was making more money than he had in the late '80s, when he was young and in a rock band that thought they were kings of the world because they had a buzz and an album out.

How long it was going to last he didn't know. Everybody else had moved out except for the hipsters. Mike and Marcia, the sculptor-painter couple on the third floor, had left last month, moving to a small town upstate. The landlord wanted them all out. There were rumors they were going to turn the block into luxury condos. Who would pay Manhattan-style rent out here, he couldn't imagine.

Asher Yotser had offered him $5,000 to move out. That was a sick joke. He was paying $550, and you couldn't find even a studio the size of a little kid's shoebox for that now—never mind a place where you could play music. The former industrial lofts in the area, from the old Gretsch guitar-and-drum factory south of the bridge to the warehouses at the northern tip of Greenpoint, were getting snapped up as a tide of priced-out artists flowed across the river from the Lower East Side, followed by yuppies and the real-estate speculators calculating and betting on where to cash in. Same old story, he thought, you move somewhere because it's cheap and you can afford to live there and do your art, you take a risk living in a neighborhood that's pretty sketchy, and you just being there makes it trendy so they can push you out. You're an unwitting pawn.

"Colon's okay with you getting most of the units," Weinstock told the Ashers on Wednesday afternoon. "As long as he has enough to show his people, he's all right. He'll play on the apartment sizes, the height of the buildings. He cares more about the subcontractors and the management. He's always got a *comare* who needs a job, or one for her nephew. It's gonna be a *shandeh* someday, he won't leave the women on his staff alone. The guy makes Clinton look like a priest."

"What's the timetable?"

"If we can get the buildings delivered vacant by the end of the year, we can break ground in the spring. We can use eminent domain if we have to, but then we could be tied up in court for a couple years, and it doesn't always look good in the public eye."

"No, that's not good. The press is nosing around Keap Street," Shaul told Weinstock. That was the building where a construction worker named Jesus de Atitlan, an illegal immigrant from El Salvador, had been killed when a jerry-rigged scaffold gave way and he plunged three stories into wet concrete. The contractor had chased a *Village Voice* reporter off the block last week.

"Don't worry," Weinstock told him. "The *Voice*, they're such drama queens, they'd sit *shivah* when a battery dies. Nobody reads it outside of Manhattan. Only if it catches on with the rest of the media, then we have to worry. And we're working on something that's gonna be a lot bigger."

"The commercial tenants will go at the end of their leases, but some of the residential ones are still there," Zev pointed out. "They're rent-stabilized."

"Offer them buyouts."

"Of course we did," Shaul said. "Not everyone was willing."

"Maybe we should send them a message," Zev said.

"I don't want to know about it."

❧

Zak said goodbye to his band and the bartender, left a tip, and wheeled his upright toward the L train. This was his Friday night jazz gig, at the 12 Blue, a two-room lounge in the East Village. It was practically charity, a four-piece splitting $100 plus tips for three sets. But he had to keep his jazz chops and network up. The wedding gigs dropped every year in the seven-week layoff after Pesach. He also liked playing with these guys, Malik on alto fronting them, Jason on piano, and Leonardo on drums, an older cat who'd played with Cannonball Adderley in the '60s before sinking into dope and then recovering.

They'd hit a perfect late-night mood on the last set, stretching out on "All Blues," then doing his new tune, "Ceiling Cat's Blues," a slow twelve-bar in E minor with a hypnotic four-note bassline and a flatted-fifth turnaround. Soft and stark, spacious and intimate, weaving a lace of notes with the other musicians.

Zak shlepped the bass down the stairs to change from the L to the G. He got off two stops later, at Flushing Avenue. The three sets, two drinks, and a joint smoked with Jason before the last set were weighing on him. The station felt like an oven, fetid with the stench of baked rat urine. The two flights of stairs to the street loomed like a mountain.

He waited for everybody else to leave the platform, one tired work-ingman and two couples coming home from clubbing. He lifted the *zaftig* doghouse and steeled himself for the ascent. He stopped after three steps. A wave of fatigue smoked with dizziness hit him. He recovered, scanned the area, then discreetly dumped the last of his coke into his hand and snorted it. Refueled, he finished the climb, one step at a time, and wheeled the bass across the street and down the sidewalk, past the plumbing-supply shop with the black-and-white Yiddish sign.

He looked around to watch his back, saw nobody. He leaned the bass against the wall, steadying it with one arm around the neck, and reached into his pocket for his keys. A car passing by shook the block with big-booty bass and gunshot snares, the old-school beat of Notorious B.I.G.'s "Gimme the Loot."

He found the keys, opened the door, and—*shove!* He went reeling onto the floor. The bass fell to the ground, its strings smacking loud on the wood as the bridge cracked. Two thugs were on him. Big muscled fuckers in beefy dark clothes. He scrambled to get up, but stumbled or tripped back to the floor, tried to roll away from the blows. He crashed against the speaker cabinet he used to use for rock gigs, five feet high and ninety pounds. One of them pushed it over on him. Tan Timberland boots pummeled his broken ribs. The last one he felt slammed his head.

The younger thug grabbed the case containing Zak's electric bass. The other one noticed it as they ducked around the corner.

"*Déjalo*, motherfucker!" he snapped.

"C'mon, that shit's worth money, yo. Somethin' for ourselves."

"*Donde está* your fuckin' brain? That shit's traceable, son."

They slipped it next to a parked van, in the space between the curb and the tires, before creeping down the block to their car.

Sunday afternoon was slow at Billyburg Music on Bedford and North Fourth, just two solitary guys browsing. The two clerks talked gear. One played guitar through a '60s-vintage Magnatone amp they'd just gotten in, getting a watery, rippling sound from its vibrato. "This is a nice piece. Lonnie Mack used one. And Robert Ward. He's pretty obscure, you probably never heard of him. He played on Wilson Pickett and the Falcons' 'I Found a Love' in 1963, started putting out records again a few years ago."

The doorbell rang, signifying a customer. They both looked up. A skinny, raggedy-ass black dude, uncomfortably lugging a rectangular bass case. His FUBU-logo T-shirt was clean, but his acid-washed jeans, out of fashion for almost a decade, were grayed with ground-in grime. Dirt dulled the navy blue of his Yankees cap. He might as well have been wearing a neon sign that blinked "crackhead" like it was grabbing eyes for an all-night carwash.

"Yo, how much y'all give me for this?"

He put the case on the counter and opened it. A sunburst-finish Sadowsky, they saw, a high-end version of a Fender Jazz Bass. No way this belongs to him, they both thought. It's a $2,000 custom-made instrument, and he doesn't have a clue what it is.

"You want cash or consignment?"

"Cash."

"How much?"

"I'm selling it for my cousin. He's in jail. He needs $200 for bail money."

"All right. We're gonna need to see your ID. Hold on a minute. Tommy, can you get the forms?"

He nodded to the other clerk. A deeper suspicion was half-forming in their heads. The grapevine said something about a guy killed in a push-in robbery the other night, a bass player, was he the one who came in every once in a while who wanted flatwound strings? Zak or something like that? The papers called the victim "Isaac Katz, a 35-year-old musician."

Tommy got the message. He ducked into the bathroom to call 911.

⁑

The suspect sat handcuffed to a chair, fighting the urge to squirm. Donnie "Nickel Bag" Nicolls, 35, aka Lawrence Nicholson, aka Laquan Norman, aka Nicholas Donaldson. Last known address 33 Nostrand Ave., Apt. 4B, his mother's home in the Marcy Houses projects. More than two dozen priors.

Two mustachioed detectives questioned him. Bernardo Toro, the younger and shorter one, and Vince Esposito, his boss, a bulky man with a shaved head. Nicolls claimed he'd found the bass.

"It was a dope ground score," he said. He came off a little simple, not cocky. Toro worked the not-amused angle.

"You're telling me you found a $2,000 guitar on the street? You expect me to believe that?"

"I swear on my mother's life. I found it."

"Where?"

"Somewhere near Flushing. Around the corner."

"It was just laying there?"

"Yeah."

"Tell me another."

"I'm telling it like it happened. It's the truth. And the truth will set you free."

"You ain't telling me the truth." Toro leaned over and steamed the suspect's face for a few seconds. "Look in my eyes, Donnie. I'm treating you with respect. But you're not respecting me, you expect me to believe this shit. You're starting to piss me off, Donnie." He pulled back a few inches and toned his voice down, just enough to seem like he was relaxing the forced intimacy. "Can I ask you a question?"

"You gonna ax it anyway."

"YOU THINK I'M FUCKIN' STUPID?" Toro exploded, spattering Nicolls's lips with spit. He slammed a blackjack on the table.

Esposito intervened. "Hey, calm down. You want something to drink, a Coke?" Donnie nodded. "Bernardo, take a minute. Get him a Coke." He uncuffed the prisoner's right hand.

"Okay, Donnie. Let me tell you something. You're in big trouble. You were caught trying to sell property belonging to the victim of a homicide. You understand that?" He paused. Donnie stayed stony, or tried to. "But I'm not a bad guy. I'm gonna try to believe your story for a minute. Hey, you're innocent until proven guilty. But really, I have to say it's not looking too good for you. Unless you can tell me something that helps me find whoever else did it."

"I don't know what else I could tell you."

"Let me tell you something. Donnie, you been on the street for a long time. You're a playa, you know how the game works. You help out on the big stuff, the little stuff ain't so important. You help me clear a homicide, I don't give a fuck you were poking around cars with a crack pipe in your pocket looking to rip out somebody's CD player.

"But right now we got you on a 165.45, minimum. Criminal possession of stolen property. An E felony. With your priors, that's a couple years upstate. Automatic. And if somebody else did this and they don't get caught, you're the one that's going down. You're not gonna plead this out. Now we're talking fifteen, twenty-five years. A long time, Donnie. So if I were you, I'd be thinking really hard about what I could do to help myself."

"I'm telling it like it happened. For real."

"Okay, Donnie, you wanna play like that, you'll be in so long, you'll be goin' to your mama's funeral in handcuffs."

※

"I don't know that I don't believe him," Toro said when they took a break. "Look at his priors. Larceny, coupla burglary, bunch of controlled-substance-sevens, possession with intent, dis con, one attempted robbery one, pleaded out to menacing two. Not a lot of rough stuff, and the one looks like a botched mugging."

"Fuck him, he's a mutt," Esposito answered. "How do you know he's lying? His fuckin' lips are moving. We got him with the vic's property, he says he found it, and he says he found it right around the corner from the vic's house. Like he expects us to believe his junkie-ass crap."

"Yeah, he's a mutt, but I don't read him as a thug. Look at him, he's a scrawny fucker, no muscles. He's a lowlife piece of shit, but he's a scavenger, not a predator."

"You got it right he's a piece of shit. I can't read his fuckin' mind. Maybe it was a crime of opportunity. He sees the vic with an instrument, he knows it's worth money, so he takes him off, and shit happens. Fuck him, it's cleared. That's what's important. We got him in place near the T/P/O, and we can take that to the ADA. We got twenty other cases on the board, we don't got all year to dick around with maybes."

❧

The *Voice* story, "Jesus in Concrete: How an Immigrant Died for $5 an Hour," came out the Wednesday before the primary, on page 13. It was overshadowed by the day's *Post* headline, "HERMAN'S LITTLE HITLER." The Clarkson campaign had funneled get-out-the-vote funds to a Brownsville activist named Khadijah Omowale, who as an eleventh-grader named Charlene Duncan at Franklin K. Lane High School during the 1968 teachers' strike had handed out flyers denouncing the "racist Jew pigs denying Black youth our education." Channel 7 interviewed Omowale for the six o'clock news. All the channels led with the clip at eleven, her spieling in an orange kente-cloth headwrap.

"I don't have a problem with Jews per se," she told the massed microphones. "I have a problem with white people."

Also overshadowed was a police-blotter item on page 17 of the *Daily News*, about two men found shot to death in an abandoned car under the Brooklyn-Queens Expressway. The victims were identified as Felipe Bonilla, 24, and Derrik "All That" Allston, 20. The killings were believed to be drug-related.

❧

On primary night, Dick Weinstock sat in Mayor Schwartz's Midtown headquarters biting his nails, drinking coffee, barking into the phone. He had a computer whiz kid tallying the results, entering them into an Excel spreadsheet as the field people called them in. Yeah, the math models helped a lot, he thought, but you still needed an old pro who knew the precincts.

The exit polls looked good, but there'd been record-high turnout in Harlem and Black Brooklyn, and you knew they were going to break 90 percent for Clarkson. Would there be enough turnout in the white neighborhoods, in Co-op City, Bayside, and Forest Hills, in Bensonhurst and Sheepshead Bay, to counter that? How enthusiastic would the Latinos be about a black candidate? If Schwartz could pull 30 percent and turnout wasn't that heavy, they were in good shape there. And how would the liberals on the Upper West Side and in the Village and Park Slope break? This wasn't the '60s anymore, they might not be so PC once they got alone in the voting booth. In New York, he mused, a conservative is a liberal who bought a co-op.

By ten thirty he was relaxing, sitting by the computer with a cold beer.

Williamsburg had delivered well, with heavy turnout in the precincts south of Broadway, putting up an 11,000-vote margin for Schwartz in the Fiftieth Assembly District and 5,500 in the fifty-third. The mayor was holding a twenty-thousand-vote lead, was going to squeak through with around 52 percent of the vote.

Donnie Nicolls lay in a seventh-floor cell in the Atlantic Avenue jail. It was eleven o'clock, after lights out. He couldn't sleep for ruminating. The public defender said the best deal she might be able to get him was manslaughter, four and a half to nine. The ADA has a weak case, she said, all circumstantial, no evidence but the bass and the location, but they were betting that a jury would connect the dots; they weren't moving. She wanted him to plead, said if he went to trial it would be murder two. He'd be risking fifteen to life on the limited chance the jury would believe him. Jesus help me, I know I've done some foul shit in my life, but I swear to God I didn't do this. Bitch won't believe me.

He had one and a half cigarettes, wrapped in the cellophane from a pack, stashed on his bed frame. He smoked the half, held it in like he wished it was rock in his lungs, saved the whole one for the morning. He could hear the tinny sound of a tiny TV, the guards on the gate watching the election news.

Balloons popped and a band played in the Midtown hotel ballroom where Schwartz was celebrating victory. The cameras tracked him as he approached the podium to wild cheers.

The mayor panted a bunch of thank-yous. "And thank you to the people of New York City!" he climaxed. The crowd erupted. He waved his arms for quiet.

Donnie heard one of the guards curse. "Jew motherfucker won."

"In my second term, I promise once again to be the mayor of all New Yorkers, not the special interests," Schwartz orated. The camera panned around the stage and the three dozen people crowding it, the mayor's wife and two kids, his staff, and leading elected officials and supporters, as diverse a mosaic as he could muster. The one black tile was a Haitian prosperity-gospel preacher from Queens called Boukou D'Argent, whose church was in line to build a 121-unit senior-housing development in Cambria Heights. The Hasidic tile was Shaul Asher, and the Latino one was Roberto Colon.

Living Underwater

B.K. Stevens

He had always feared people like her—perky, enthusiastic people, people who smiled a lot and sprinkled their e-mails with emoticons and exclamation points. From the moment Helen Stavros stood up at the September faculty meeting, he knew she was one of those people. When she stepped to the podium, when she flung her arms out wide and spoke, moist-eyed, of her respect for faculty autonomy and her eagerness to learn from others, a wave of dread washed over him. Helen Stavros held a PhD in Institutional Effectiveness and had come to Edson College to serve as associate dean for academic assessment. She had the power to drain his life of all dignity, all reason. And he felt sure she had the will.

Before the first week of classes ended, she made her move. On Wednesday afternoon, he climbed the three flights of stairs to the seminar room where the English department held its meetings. There she was, sitting near the head of the long rectangular table, to the right of nervous little Dr. Simpson. Behind them loomed the Cuthbert Window, a magnificent floor-to-ceiling stained glass collage donated to the college by an alumnus who had learned to love William Blake during his time at Edson. Decades later, after he'd made a fortune in rubber, he'd commissioned an artist to piece together intricate, vibrant images of shepherds and laughing children, of bards and chimney sweepers and a naked child on a cloud. Beneath the glory of that window, Helen Stavros spoke to Dr. Simpson in a rapid whisper, her face warmed by the late afternoon sunlight filtering through a languishing glass rose.

Dr. Simpson looked away from her, spotted him, and waved. "Sam," he said, "have you met Dr. Stavros? Dr. Stavros, this is Dr. Sam Meyer, seventeenth-century English literature."

Helen Stavros looked him over. She was blond and buxom, probably midforties, prettier than most, eyebrows plucked to high, thin arcs. She wore a gray pinstriped suit and a silky red top that plunged deep. "Great to meet you, Sam," she said, seizing his hand. "These are exciting times, aren't they? Ready for a challenge?"

Had he ever before in his life taken such an immediate, intense dislike to another human being? He forced a tight smile. "That depends on the nature of the challenge."

"Oh, the best kind of challenge." Her grip on his hand tightened. "The kind that helps you think in new ways and makes you feel better about going to work every day. How does that sound?"'

"Unlikely." He pulled his hand away, walked to the other end of the table, and sat down next to Jake Nachshon, his mentor since his first day at Edson, the only other Jew in the department. "My God, Jake," he said. "Where do they find these people? And Simpson won't stand up to her."

"He probably can't," Jake said. "But wait and see. Maybe it won't be so bad."

It was bad. Dr. Simpson mumbled a bit, welcoming the one new tenure-track department member and the six new adjuncts, then turned the meeting over to Helen Stavros and sank into his chair, wheezing. She popped to her feet and pressed a button on a remote, and a screen descended from the ceiling, covering the Cuthbert Window.

"Here's the scoop!" she declared, and pressed a key on a laptop.

Nothing happened. She pressed the key again, nothing happened again, and a lank young man in an olive-green T-shirt rushed forward. For the next several minutes, he fiddled with things, she fiddled with things, and they consulted in whispers. Finally, somebody did something right, and the image of a cone topped by a perfectly symmetrical mound of strawberry ice cream appeared on the screen.

"Here's the scoop!" she cried again. "For many years—far *too* many years—higher education in America was all about accounting."

"ACCOUNTING" appeared on the screen—all capitals, in a thick, squat font—surrounded by random gray numbers that came in and out of focus.

"For too many years, we just kept track of the numbers," she said. "We made sure students sat in classrooms for a certain number of hours each week. We made sure they piled up a certain number of credits each semester. When the numbers looked right, we said the students were educated and handed them their diplomas. Had they actually learned anything? We didn't know. We'd never bothered to find a way to keep track of that. The only things we kept track of were the numbers. Hours. Credits. We didn't care about anything else."

"Dr. Stavros," Jake said, "that's hardly a fair or accurate way to describe—"

She whipped her head around to smile at him, a broad, joyless smile taut with warning. "Please. Call me Helen. And this isn't a time to get defensive. It's a time to listen, and to learn. Things are about to get very exciting."

She pressed another key, and "ACCOUNTING" morphed into "ACCOUNTABILITY" and then into "ASSESSMENT!"—hot-pink letters in a jazzy, peppy font, with multicolored sunbursts constantly exploding in all directions.

"But that couldn't go on forever," she said. "Parents wanted more. The federal government demanded more. And we finally realized our students *deserved* more. Reforms were introduced, laws were passed, and now we have the Central Association for College Accreditation to guide us toward ways of making sure our students *really* get an education. We're moving from mere accounting to true accountability, to genuine assessment. But so far, Edson College's efforts at assessment haven't been terribly successful, have they?"

She paused long enough to cast one sorrowful glance around the room, not long enough to let anyone else speak. Two halves of a blood-red heart appeared on opposite sides of the screen and moved toward each other, merging in a shower of fireworks as the word WHOLE-HEARTED pulsed forward.

"We need a whole-hearted commitment to assessment from every one of you," she said. "That's why the college created my position. No more simply going through the motions. It's no wonder Edson was nearly put on warning last spring. I read your eight-year status report—all 456 pages of it—and I won't lie. It was shabby. *Damn* shabby. It was evasive and incomplete and shallow. No wonder you got three solid pages of cautions about things that have to be done better for the final ten-year report. If I'd been on the visiting committee, I would've voted for warning. I might've voted for probation. And you know what *that* would mean."

They knew. The college had been placed on warning after its five-year interim report. Press accounts had turned scorching, enrollment had dipped, alumni donations had sagged, campus morale had soured. Probation would be far worse, and denial of accreditation would be a death sentence—all federal funding cut off, no government loans for students. It would be time for professors to launch desperate searches for new jobs, for the college to start converting dormitories into motels and hiring bankruptcy lawyers.

Dr. Madison, a senior member of the department, sat forward. "But the cautions weren't based on anything *real*," she said. "Nobody criticized the quality of our teaching, and nobody denied our students find good jobs and get into top graduate and professional schools. The only problem was that we hadn't fully documented—"

"If you can't document something," Helen cut in, "how do you know it's real? You can tell yourself that you're doing a good job, but why should anyone believe you? Luckily, *I'm* here now, and I'll show you how to document what you do. I warn you—it'll take hard work."

An image of Rosie the Riveter flexing her biceps appeared on the screen.

"And sometimes, it might get scary," Helen said.

An image of a dark hallway appeared, with ghosts popping out of doorways, saying, "BOO!"

"But in the end," Helen said, and paused. She half-closed her eyes, inhaling long and deep as her shoulders drew back and her bosom heaved upward. Then she exhaled, slowly, and opened her eyes. "In the end," she said softly, "it's going to be beautiful."

Sam glanced at the screen long enough to get a general impression of bunnies frolicking amid daisies, of a waterfall and a rainbow and some sort of bird. He bent forward, staring down at the table, gripping his forehead with both hands. I did fine on the LSATs, he thought. Why didn't I go to law school?

Not that he thought professors shouldn't be held accountable. In theory, he favored vigorous assessment. He worked hard, and he knew some professors barely worked at all. They came to class unprepared, graded quickly and carelessly, made students wait weeks before handing essays back, sneaked out of office hours early. If assessment ever focused on trying to eliminate such offenses, Sam would be all for it. But assessment never aimed that low. It sought, instead, to enforce grandiose, amorphous theories about what education should be, and to quantify results with scientific precision. And since the people who designed assessment programs usually hadn't spent much time actually teaching, their theories tended to be silly, and they had no idea of which sorts of results could be measured objectively and which had to be estimated in a spirit of humility.

Helen gave herself a little shake, as if coming out of a trance. "I wish we could've gotten started last spring," she said. "I like at least two solid years of data heading into a ten-year. But we'll do what we can to salvage this semester, and before spring semester starts, we'll have everything in place. So. The first step, obviously, is that you all have to redo your fall syllabi."

Every professor in the room made a noise—a groan, an exclamation of disbelief, an obscenity. "I spent most of August reworking my syllabi," Dr. Madison said. "I've already given them to my students. That's like handing them a contract. How can I make changes at this point?"

Helen gave her a smile—a kind smile, sympathetic but firm. "You'll simply have to, won't you? Your students will understand. And I have to be honest. The English department's syllabi are probably the weakest in the whole college. Let's start with first-year composition. You all teach sections of that course, right? And the director of composition is Jacob Nachshon?"

Jake half-raised his hand. "For over twenty years. Yes."

"Ouch!" She grimaced, as if embarrassed for him. "Then it's high time to start doing it right. For one thing, from now on, everyone teaching first-year composition will use a common syllabus and the same textbooks."

"You can't do that," a young professor said. "Administrators don't have the right to tell us how to teach our classes. It's an infringement of academic freedom."

"Lots of composition programs use common syllabi and common textbooks. The Central Association prefers that, and the dean's approved it. And I've checked with the college lawyer. If it's my professional opinion that a change is vital to Edson's accreditation efforts, I *can* insist the change be made." She smiled. "So that's what we'll do. Now, all composition classes will have the same student learning outcomes, or SLOs. We'll need at least four, all stated in clear, specific language—for example, 'By the end of the course, students' ability to identify and correct the following grammatical errors will improve by 70 percent.' The syllabus must also list the specific steps you'll take to achieve each SLO—how much class time, how many individual conferences, how many Writing Center visits—and you'll need to keep careful records to show all these steps have in fact been taken."

She went on for nearly another hour. She spoke of the need for multiple assessment tools, of the need to evaluate each student's progress toward each SLO at least four times each semester. No, grades on regular assignments could not count as assessments. She spoke of pretests and posttests, of developing a special template to evaluate essays used as assessment tools. No, neither the pretest nor the posttest could count toward the student's grade in the class, and the templates could not double as rubrics for grading essays. Assessment and grading had to be separate, and professors must keep separate records for each. She spoke of the need to write end-of-semester reports evaluating SLOs and assessment tools. She spoke of the importance of using language precisely and showed a ten-minute video about the difference between "goals" and "objectives." She spoke of turning "can't" into "can," of immersive learning and differentiated learning, of utilizing educational technologies to promote new literacies.

At first, Sam tried to take notes, but after ten minutes he threw down his pen and sat brooding, staring at his legal pad. She's an idiot, he thought. She actually believes this garbage. And she's an idiot with power, an idiot who can force me to fill my syllabi with nonsense, use language I hate, and devise useless assignments to measure things that aren't worth measuring. He pictured himself counting grammatical errors, computing percentages, keeping two sets of records, writing reports assessing his attempts at assessment. It's absurd, he thought, absurd and wrongheaded. And she's loving every minute of it, because she's a bully who thrives on humiliating people.

At least she seemed to be winding down. She beamed at them, eyes sparkling, every pore of her exuding goodwill. "I'll need those revised fall syllabi by Monday," she said, "and your spring syllabi in two weeks. Then I'll come to your October meeting to review them. The good news is that you don't have to worry about whether students actually reach your SLOs. SLOs can always be adjusted—they *should* be adjusted, every semester. If not enough students reach them, lower them; if too many students reach them, raise them. The important thing is to state SLOs in appropriate language and document everything you do to facilitate them. Remember, there's no such thing as failure or success in assessment. It's all about continuous learning."

"More like continuous busywork," Sam muttered.

At least, he'd meant to mutter it. He hadn't meant anyone but Jake to hear it. Apparently, though, he'd said it out loud, because Helen turned to him with a determined little smile.

"What's that, Sam?" she said. "Busywork? You think all this is busywork?"

He lifted his hands. "I'm sorry. That was rude. And I'm sure you mean well. But I can't honestly agree—"

"You aren't comfortable with this new way of thinking yet, are you?" she cut in, and winked at him. "That's okay. Give yourself time. You'll catch on eventually—I promise! Now, I hear you folks always have a holiday party in December, and you serve some pretty potent eggnog. I *love* eggnog! So I'm inviting myself to that party, to celebrate all the progress we'll make this semester. And we *will* make progress. Probably, some of you are worried about whether you can pull all these changes off. In fact, right now, you may be feeling like this."

She pressed a key on her laptop, and an image of Munch's *The Scream* appeared on the screen. She chuckled. No one else did.

"It's natural to have doubts at first," she said, "but you'll get past them. By December, you'll be feeling great!"

The man on the bridge morphed into an image of Santa Claus, a red-cheeked Santa doubled over with merriment, the jolliest Santa Sam had ever seen.

"Now, *here's* someone who makes us all feel great," Helen Stavros said. "And by the time he comes around to visit you in December, you'll be feeling great about your new approach to assessment, too. But remember—between now and then, just like Santa, I'll be watching you! I'll be making a list and checking it twice. So you'd better make sure you're nice, not naughty, or you could end up with a big lump of coal in your stocking! Now I want to come shake hands with each of you and start to get to know you."

Sam felt his chest heaving with panic. I can't stand it, he thought, not another second of it. Before she could reach him, he fled, running down the three flights of stairs, out of the building, down the gravel path dividing humanities buildings from science buildings. He didn't pause until he heard Jake behind him, calling his name. Then he leaned his back against an oak and waited for his friend to catch up, his face burning from the run and from the end-of-summer heat.

Jake came to stand next to him. He raised an eyebrow, shook his head. "Not an especially tactful exit. She noticed. She didn't like it."

"I couldn't take any more," Sam said as they continued down the path, heading for the faculty parking lot. "It was Kafkaesque. It was beyond Kafka. That inane PowerPoint presentation—did she expect us to take that seriously? What's wrong with her?"

"Common rhetorical mistake," Jake said. "Failure to understand one's audience. She's not an academic at heart."

"There's an understatement. She's got a doctorate in a make-believe discipline, she's determined to quantify things that can't be quantified, and she's probably never taught. Twenty years ago, what college would have hired an associate academic dean who'd never taught? And the way she talked to you, the way she sneered at everything you've done for the composition program—how could you stand it?"

Jake lifted a shoulder. "It wasn't fun. But if that's the worst thing that happens to me this week, I'll live."

"We've got to get rid of her," Sam said. "Simpson's a coward, the dean's a fool, but we could go to the president. Or the board of trustees. You've got a former student on the board, right? Could you call her?"

"It wouldn't do any good. Even if she wanted to help us, she couldn't. Neither could the president. This is the future, Sam. It's not just Edson, not just the Central Association. There are a dozen other accreditation agencies just like it, and they can do pretty much whatever they want. The federal government's given them that power. If we resist, they can shut us down. Every college in the country is going through what we're going through."

"So we just give in. Is that what you're saying? We let this ignoramus reshape our classes, we spend endless hours scrambling to generate meaningless data she can plug into her report?"

They'd reached Jake's car. Jake unlocked his door and turned to face Sam. "Let me tell you a joke."

Sam grimaced. "Not in the mood, Jake."

"This is a good one. It's relevant. Top scientists from all over the world got together, they did studies, and they went on TV and announced, 'In three days, there's going to be a huge flood, and every inch of land on the planet will be permanently covered by water.' The Christians said, 'It's all right—you still have three days to accept Jesus Christ as your lord and savior.' And the Jews said, 'It's all right—we still have three days to figure out how to live underwater.'"

Sam rolled his eyes. "Fine. Very funny. But there's no way to live with this."

"What other choice do we have? Pumping out the basement isn't an option—the waters are too deep."

Sam sighed impatiently. "What about building an ark?"

"That worked for forty days and forty nights. This flood will last a lot longer. So. You and Leah are coming over for dinner Saturday, right? Mira and I are looking forward to it."

"So are we," Sam said. "Thanks." Probably, they spent too many Saturdays having dinner with Jake and Mira. Leah liked them, and she never complained, but he could tell she was bored.

Bored or not, she baked an elegant French apple cake for Saturday night. Leah was, among other things, an accomplished baker, an inventive cook, and a cheerful, energetic mother. Their twin boys adored her. They loved Sam too, of course, and always ran out to greet him when he came home from work—he suspected Leah had told them to do that—but she was close to them in a way he could never equal. Sometimes, in the evenings, he felt as if he were visiting Leah's charming family. She was successful professionally, too, already the director of a senior residence center that included both assisted living units and a nursing home. And she was probably smarter than he was. Sam worked hard at trying not to resent any of that.

He also worked at trying not to sound petty around her. While they were eating Mira's overcooked chicken piccata, though, Jake started talking about Helen Stavros, and Sam was doomed.

"She and I met yesterday to discuss the composition program," Jake said, "and I think I sneaked in a couple of small victories. We agreed everyone would use the same grammar handbook—all the major ones are very similar anyway—and that'll be the textbook for the course. I asked if individual professors could also assign 'supplemental readings.' She fussed a while but finally said okay, as long as we don't call them textbooks. So you can still use that prose anthology you like so much—we can all use the ones we prefer."

Sam lifted a shoulder. "It's ridiculous that we can't call them textbooks. I hardly use the handbook. The anthology's the main textbook for my course."

"The point is, you can use it. We also agreed on four SLOs I think we can live with."

"What's an SLO?" Mira asked.

"Sorry," Jake said. "A Student Learning Outcome. It's a kind of goal. For example, one of our SLOs will be that students will write an essay containing at least five unified paragraphs developing a central idea."

"You agreed to that?" Sam put down his fork. "Well, *I* can't. It's setting the bar too low—it sounds like a middle-school standard. It says nothing about the complexity or originality of the ideas developed, or the quality of the writing. Five unified paragraphs developing a central idea! That's how you define a good college essay?"

Jake sighed. "No. That's how I try to get Helen Stavros to back off so we can teach. And it's something we can evaluate quickly. It's only for assessment, Sam, not for grading. Stavros *wants* us to keep those separate. So we take a few minutes to check things off on the assessment template, and then we grade the essay. Conceivably, a student could get 100 percent on the template and an F on the essay. We can use any grading standards we consider appropriate. We just can't put them in the syllabus."

"So we withhold information from our students," Sam said, "and we play word games to trick Stavros. This is one of those 'small victories' you were talking about?"

"Calm down, Sam," Leah said. "That's no way to talk to Jake."

Sam raised a hand in acknowledgment. "Sorry. Jake knows I didn't mean anything by that. And I know he's doing the best he can. But we should be able to state our real standards straightforwardly, and we shouldn't have to waste time filling out meaningless templates that have nothing to do with what students really need to learn."

"I wish you could see how many meaningless forms *I* fill out every day," Leah said. "I have to comply with all sorts of regulations and provide documentation for everything. Sometimes, it gets pretty silly. But it's part of my job, so I do it. Well, now it's part of your job. You'll get used to it."

She'd been like that all week. Whenever he'd tried to explain about Helen Stavros, Leah had shrugged and walked off to check on the boys, or on dinner. He pushed down his irritation, clasped his hands, and tried again. "This is different. Professors are hired because they're experts in their fields, because they're the ones who know what should be taught and how it should be taught. What does Helen Stavros know about literature, or about writing? She misuses language in appalling ways, and she communicates through glitzy, childish PowerPoint presentations, through cartoons and captions. Why should she have the power to shape courses in things she knows nothing about?"

There was that shrug again. "You think all the officials I have to satisfy know what they're talking about? Anyway, Jake's showing you how to handle the situation. You can still teach pretty much the way you want to."

"Yes, only 'pretty much,'" Sam said, feeling his face grow hotter. "And only if I'm willing to lie and mislead, and only by spending hours on useless busywork. Where am I supposed to find the time?"

She started drumming her fingers on the table. "You can cut back on other things. All the time you spend writing pages and pages of comments on students' essays—half the students probably don't read them anyway. And you don't have to reread a book every time you teach it, not if you've already read it a hundred times. That's a *real* waste of time. You'll have to make some compromises, Sam. The rest of us do. Stop thinking you're so special and brilliant that you shouldn't have to do it, too." She turned away from him, twisting in her chair to look at Mira. "How does your daughter like law school?"

They didn't make love that night. Leah barely spoke to him on the drive home, lingered in the bathroom, marched straight to bed, and turned to face the wall. He lay awake a long time in the darkness, brooding. Compromises. Yes, that was the easy answer. Tell a few lies, bend a few principles, skim a few hours from work that made sense and devote it to appeasing bullies. As time went on, there would be more compromises, and things would keep getting worse. And Helen Stavros was the symbol of everything wrong with what he'd be forced to do, the embodiment of the lie.

He got a cheery little e-mail from her a week later, briskly identifying eight major problems and four minor glitches with the revised fall syllabi he'd sent her. She misused "enormity," misused a semicolon, and made two errors in pronoun agreement; he took comfort in printing the e-mail and circling the errors in red. She also reminded him to get busy on his spring syllabi, so she'd have time to evaluate them before the October department meeting. "Don't worry, Sam!" she wrote. "You had a rough time with these, but I KNOW you'll do better with the spring syllabi! You WILL figure this out! I believe in you! ☺"

Bitch, he thought, and stayed late at his office, missing dinner with Leah and the boys, rewriting his syllabi again and again. He'd compromise. He'd use some of the hideous jargon Stavros loved. But he would not sacrifice his integrity. He'd concentrate on making the syllabi so good she couldn't possibly criticize them. At 2:00 A.M., he was satisfied and sent the syllabi off. He drove home, spent an hour pulling old class notes together, decided his Intro to Lit students would have to wait another two days to get their essays back, and crawled into bed beside Leah. She didn't stir in her sleep.

Two weeks later, he climbed the three flights of stairs to the seminar room again and sat waiting for the meeting to begin. He stared at the Cuthbert window, at the image of a person lying, arms outstretched, beneath the low, mottled branches of a poison tree. Blake's poison tree, he thought. That would be so much better, if we could simply think our enemies dead. If all we had to do was to hide our anger, and nurture it, and watch it grow. If we never had to do anything violent, if we could simply wait until our wrath became strong enough, bright enough to draw our enemy into death.

Helen Stavros walked into the room, laughing, talking to Dr. Simpson. She sat at his right hand, smiling and nodding as he rushed through regular department business, gazing at him tolerantly. He sat down, she stood up, and the screen descended from the ceiling. She gave them all a bright, happy look.

"Let's get down to brass tacks!" she cried, and pressed a laptop key.

Nothing happened. The lank young man, today wearing a gray sweatshirt, rushed forward, and eventually an image of dozens of glistening tacks appeared.

"Let's get down to brass tacks!" she cried again. "The good news is, all of you sent me your spring syllabi! Thank you! I'd like to give you all a big hand!"

A grinning, fuzzy-haired cartoon figure with a right hand the size of a border collie appeared on the screen. Helen Stavros giggled. Sam pictured the building collapsing around her, pictured the ceiling beams crushing her skull. He pictured the earth opening to swallow her up.

She tilted her head to the side, turned down the corners of her mouth, made her eyes go wide. She looked glum, pouty, adorable. "But here's the bad news. A few of you have absorbed some fundamental principles of formative, diagnostic assessment, and you've produced syllabi that'll promote multidimensional learning. Yay for you! But the rest of you—well, the rest of you still have a long road ahead. Let's look at some examples, starting with a very good example."

Now, the screen showed the syllabus for Eric Burke's Introduction to Literary Theory course. That figures, Sam thought. Somebody who wrote a dissertation on transgressive modalities in fictive postcolonial constructs probably wouldn't have much trouble adjusting to the way Helen Stavros used language. Helen went through the syllabus quickly, praising the wording of the Student Learning Outcomes and the variety of assessment tools and methods.

"How about you, Eric?" she asked. "How do *you* feel about the changes you've made?"

Eric Burke was sitting back from the table, his right leg draped over his left, his arms crossed over his chest. "Oh, I've drunk the assessment

Kool-Aid," he said. "I love setting things up this way. I've got a clearer sense of where I'm headed, and I can give students more concrete feedback."

She beamed at him. "Good for you! I know how tempting it is to stick to the old, familiar ways. That's the comfortable thing to do, the easy thing. But it's great when professors are willing to work a little harder, to climb out of their ruts for the sake of their students. The transition can be challenging, but the results are worth it."

"No question," Eric said. "*Totally* worth it."

Well, Eric Burke had always been trendy and shallow. But Sam was dismayed to see most of his colleagues listening intently, taking notes, studying the screen without a hint of rebellion on their faces. Some of them, of course, might be prudently hiding their disgust—but if they'd decided to hide it, they probably wouldn't act on it. If Sam took a stand against this garbage, he'd probably have to stand alone.

"There were other promising syllabi," Helen Stavros was saying, "but Eric's was the best of the best." She paused and sighed. "And then, sadly, we have the worst of the worst."

The first page of Sam's Introduction to Literature syllabus appeared on the screen. People looked at it, saw his name in the upper right-hand corner, and chuckled. It was a sympathetic, unsurprised chuckle, as if all his colleagues had expected him to produce the worst of the worst.

Helen tilted her head to the side again, winced a cute little wince, and smiled. "You don't mind, do you, Sam? You seem like a good sport. I figure you can take it."

"It's fine," he said. She's a moron, he thought, a corrupt moron. If she thinks my syllabus is the worst of the worst, that's a compliment.

But he'd always been an A student. He'd always felt driven to excel, to be at the top of the class; he felt embarrassed when he couldn't ace a vision test. Whenever his teachers had used an assignment of his as an example— and they'd done that a lot—they'd used it as a model for others to try to emulate. And now something he'd done was being used as an example of what not to do, and everybody else in the room would feel superior to him.

"Let's make this an interactive learning experience," Helen said. "I could simply stand here and list all the problems with Sam's syllabus, but that wouldn't get *you* involved in the process. You'll learn so much more if *you* tell *me* what the problems are. Sam, if you start to get a sense of where you went wrong, feel free to join right in!"

No, he didn't feel like joining right in, but hands shot up all around the table.

"His Student Learning Outcomes are messed up," Eric Burke said. "For one thing, he uses 'should,' not 'will'—'Students should strive to understand and appreciate various literary genres more fully.' It should be 'students *will*,' right?"

"But I can't see into the future," Sam said. "I can say what *should* happen, but not what *will*. And I know from experience that not all students will reach these goals. How can I make a statement that goes contrary to what experience and common sense tell me?"

"Have a little confidence, Sam," Helen said. "Eric's absolutely right. Always use 'will.' And get rid of 'strive to.' If some students don't achieve an outcome, your assessments will reflect that. But don't get all mealy-mouthed. State your SLOs in bold, clear language."

"And he shouldn't use 'understand' or 'appreciate,' should he?" Dr. Madison asked. "You told me to avoid them."

"Right," Helen said, "because they don't mean anything."

Sam sighed. "Of course they mean something. That's why we teach Introduction to Literature—to help students understand and appreciate literature more fully. That's our central objective in that course."

"Oops," Helen said, wincing prettily. "You mean 'goal,' not 'objective.' You'd better watch that video again. But any goal or SLO that uses 'understand' or 'appreciate' would be too vague to be useful. What does it mean to say a student 'understands' literature? How would you measure something like that?"

"By reading the student's essays," Sam said, "and seeing if they reflect an enhanced understanding of—"

Helen Stavros laughed. "Try getting two professors to agree about *that*! It's too vague, too subjective. Using language like that is a crutch. It allows you to claim you've achieved your outcomes without having to back it up with solid data. Now, you refer to 'various literary genres.' Who can give me a well-stated SLO relating to literary genres?"

One of the younger department members raised her hand. "Students will be able to identify and define five literary genres."

"Excellent!" Helen Stavros fist-pumped twice. "Woo hoo!"

Sam pictured fire descending from heaven, consuming her. "Fine. But that's a tiny part of what we do in Introduction to Literature. That course isn't about memorizing definitions. It's about helping students become more careful, perceptive readers who can recognize the value of—"

"More meaningless words," Helen cut in. "You have to learn to use language more precisely, Sam. Now, what's wrong with Sam's other SLOs?"

"That was brutal," Jake said nearly an hour later, as they walked to the parking lot together. The air felt cooler, fresher now, and leaves had begun to brighten and break free. "I'm sorry you had to go through it."

"That was revenge." Sam drew his foot back, then brought it forward sharply, sending a few bits of gravel skidding down the path. "She was punishing me for running out of the room last month, for not giving in completely on the syllabi. Well, she did a good job. To have to sit there in front of the whole damn department while Helen Stavros tells me *I* need to use language more precisely—God!"

"I know," Jake said. "I'm sorry. Well, at least you're tenured. If you weren't, I'd worry that she'd go after your job. And she seems satisfied with my syllabi, so maybe I can help you with yours. I know you don't want to make more concessions, but—"

"I don't want to," Sam said, "and I won't. There's no point in trying to work with that woman, Jake. I bent as far as I could, and she responded by humiliating me. So tomorrow, I'm making appointments to see the president and the college lawyer. I've looked into the Board of Trustees Committee on Academic Affairs. It's got a couple of academics who might be sympathetic. I'll write to them. Then there's the American Association of University Professors—it's a big defender of academic freedom. I'll see if I can file a grievance with AAUP."

Jake shook his head. "You might as well paint a target on your back. You know I don't like Stavros any more than you do, but defying her is dangerous. We've just seen how she treats people she views as enemies. Worse, it's useless. We can't win by opposing her openly. We'll do better if we focus on damage control. We pretend to swallow her nonsense, we smile, we never disagree with anything she says, and meanwhile we preserve as much as we can."

Sam half-smiled as memories of long-ago religious school history lessons came back. "Sounds like you're talking about Marranos. As I recall, a lot of them ended up getting burned at the stake, once people figured out what they were up to."

Jake lifted his hands. "And a lot of people who refused to hide their Judaism left Spain in leaky ships and died at sea."

"In your metaphors, people who aren't crafty enough always drown."

Jake shrugged. "Whatever. I'm not saying any approach is completely safe, but I think mine has a better chance than yours does. What do you say?"

It was tempting. Taking on the whole college, constantly getting involved in arguments, perhaps having to speak out in public—that would take up so much time, and involve so much conflict. And Jake was probably right. It would probably be useless anyway. But to capitulate after that woman had embarrassed him in public, to let her think she'd won, to let his colleagues think she'd intimidated him or, worse, persuaded him—no. He couldn't stand that.

Over the next two months, he spent many evenings making phone calls, sending e-mails, writing letters. He made appointments and met with people. Many professors said they hated Stavros and her ideas, too, but only a few agreed to support him publicly—and their support didn't count for much anyway, since they were as powerless as he. Even people who agreed with him began finding reasons to avoid him. He sometimes heard people whispering and chuckling after he walked by them. He suspected he was becoming ridiculous.

No administrator or trustee admitted to agreeing with him about anything. Everyone told him the actions he was taking were inappropriate and pointless for one reason or another, and all urged him to look for ways to cooperate. Dr. Simpson called him in to discuss his application for promotion to full professor and hinted it might be easier if he gave up this hopeless campaign against assessment.

Several times, Leah also tried to persuade him to give up. He couldn't help getting heated when he explained why she was wrong, though, so she stopped mentioning the subject and retreated into silence. One day, when he came home from work, he realized that his sons had stopped running out to greet him. In fact, he realized, they'd stopped a week or so ago. He just hadn't noticed.

He heard regularly from Helen Stavros, who sent him friendly little e-mails with suggestions about ways to improve his syllabi. She also sent him inspiring articles to read and urged him to come to her office to discuss their differences. He labored for hours on his responses, drafting them in Word and revising them meticulously before pasting them into e-mail. He refused to make any further changes in his syllabi, or in anything else.

One chilly Sunday afternoon, two weeks before the department's December party, he and Leah took the boys to the zoo. The boys raced ahead of them, running from enclosure to enclosure, calling out to the animals, laughing and jumping. He and Leah reached the Great Cats exhibit and paused at an enclosure where a male Indian tiger paced, massive but agile, his entire body rippling with every step. Sam pointed at it, grinning.

"Maybe I should see if I can rent this guy for an hour or so. *He* could take care of Helen Stavros for me."

She didn't smile. "That's a horrible thing to say. Don't ever say anything like that in front of the boys."

He stared at her. "Of course I wouldn't. You know me better than that."

"Do I?" She turned away from him to gaze into the enclosure. "I *thought* I knew you, but you've become so obsessed with this thing that sometimes I wonder if I ever really knew you at all."

"Don't get melodramatic. Look, I don't expect you to understand. You're not an academic, so how could you? But I'd think you could trust me that it's important. I'm taking a stand for academic freedom. And I'm not giving up."

She looked ahead to where their children were pointing and laughing in front of the cheetah exhibit. "Well, *I* may be giving up, Sam. I've been thinking about it. I've put up with a lot, for a long time. I work hard, but I leave my job at the office. You grade essays and prepare classes every evening, every weekend. I don't like that, but I've accepted it. This semester, it's worse. It's much worse. I don't like having our boys grow up in a house so full of anger and frustration. I don't like having to answer their questions about why Daddy seems so mad all the time, why he doesn't talk to them much anymore, why he doesn't really seem to be listening when they talk to him. Frankly, I don't much like living in that kind of house, either. I've been thinking it might be best if you moved out, at least for a while."

It was a shock, but only for a few seconds. Then it seemed inevitable, and he blamed himself for not seeing it coming. She was right—he *hadn't* been paying attention to her, or to the boys. "But you love me," he said. "Don't you?"

She still wouldn't turn to look at him directly. "I did. I could again—I'm quite sure I could. Right now, I don't know how I feel. You have to focus on loving *me*, Sam, and on loving the boys, and on making things right at home. You have to focus on that more than on other things. If you could do that, I think we might be all right."

"I will," he said. "I promise. Classes will end soon, and then I just have to deal with exams and turn my grades in, and finish revising a reply to the chair of the academic affairs committee, and get past the December party. Then we'll have the semester break, and I can really focus on home. Once I revise my spring syllabi."

She sighed, and gazed at the tiger. "Well," she said. "We'll see."

The day of the December party arrived, and Sam climbed the three flights of stairs to the seminar room again. The food service had supplied big trays of thick, hard sugar cookies in festive shapes, decorated with white frosting and blue sprinkles. There were also cheese trays, vegetable trays, and the famous English department eggnog, though why it was famous Sam didn't know. He couldn't imagine any adult wanting to drink a mixture of egg yolks, milk, heavy cream, and sugar.

He got himself a cup of it, though. Normally, he stuck to bottled water at these parties, but today he needed more. He took a first sip. The consistency almost made him gag, but now he understood why people drank this stuff. He'd known it was spiked, but he'd thought that meant he'd detect a faint trace of bourbon. No. The bourbon overwhelmed every other taste, and he could feel it clear through his body. Someone had been feeling very jolly indeed while mixing up the eggnog this afternoon.

He drained his cup and refilled it, then stood listening as Eric Burke and Jake talked about basketball. Ten more minutes, he thought, and he could leave without seeming unsociable. Helen Stavros had said she'd come but hadn't shown up yet. With luck, he could leave without seeing her at all. He could say he had to pick the boys up from school. It wasn't true, of course. Some sort of carpool brought the boys home from school every day; Leah had set that up long ago. But nobody here knew that. They shouldn't have any trouble believing Sam was the kind of father who sometimes picked his children up from school, a good father.

They didn't yet know how close he was to losing his sons, or at least to losing the right to live with them. This morning, after the carpool took the boys away, Leah had poured Sam a second cup of coffee and said they needed to talk. It wasn't working, she'd said. She needed a break from all the tension and anger, and so did the boys. He needed to move out, and he needed to do it now. For fifteen minutes, he'd tried to reason with her, and she listened politely. Then she'd stood up and handed him several sheets of paper. She'd found some listings for suitable apartments on the internet, she said, and she wanted him to start checking them out today.

He got a third cup of eggnog and turned to gaze at the Cuthbert window. Blake's illustrations had clearly inspired the stained-glass artist, but he hadn't copied them exactly. His figures were more solid and realistic, less dreamlike. The lamb and the tiger, for example, facing each other at the center of the window—the stained-glass lamb was fuller and fluffier than Blake's. Did that make it an even more tempting sacrifice? And the tiger. Sam had always thought Blake's tiger looked like a marginally out-of-shape stuffed animal. This one looked more like the tiger Sam had seen at the zoo two weeks ago, more in line with the poem's allusions to rebels such as Icarus and Prometheus.

Sam glanced at his watch. A quarter of four. He could go. He started for the door, feeling slightly unsteady. Well, it hadn't been smart to drink so much eggnog so quickly, but driving still shouldn't be a problem. Even the few minutes it would take to walk to his car would clear his head.

But Helen Stavros walked in, together with a slim young woman he'd never seen before. Damn, he thought. I can't leave the minute she arrives. It'll look like I'm running away from her. Ten more minutes, then. I just have to leave before she begins whatever asinine presentation she has planned.

She headed straight for him and put a hand on his arm. "Sam!" she said. "Great to see you! Merry Christmas! I'm *so* glad you're here. I can't *wait* to have you see our presentation!"

He hated the weight of her hand on his arm, hated any physical contact with her, even through layers of clothing. "Unfortunately, I have to leave right now. I'm picking my sons up from school."

Her face creased with dismay. "But you *can't* go yet! There's some-thing you *have* to see! Three minutes, okay? Your sons won't mind waiting for three little minutes. Come on, Sharon!"

She bustled up to the front of the room and stood waving her arms while the other woman went to the podium to set up the laptop.

"Everybody!" Helen Stavros cried. "Everybody! I'm not going to take up much of your time. I know this is a day for celebrating, not for talking about assessment, and I can't wait to enjoy some of your eggnog, but there are a couple of things I *have* to tell you! First, I want you to meet my brand-new assistant dean for academic assessment, Sharon Olson. The dean *finally* agreed there's far too much assessment work for one person to handle, so Sharon's joining our team. She has a master's in higher educa-tion administration, and I *know* she'll have *so much* to contribute. Let's give her a big Edson College welcome!"

Sam made himself clap. Assistant dean, he thought. She looks twelve years old, and she's got a degree in another make-believe discipline. Just yesterday, the English department had learned that, despite near-promises made last year, it could not hire someone to replace Dr. Madison when she retired. For the first time since the Depression, the department would not have a medievalist. The college had to cut costs, the president had said, and that, unfortunately, meant eliminating some faculty positions.

But they can always find money to hire another administrator, Sam thought. The size of the administration seems to be increasing faster than the faculty is shrinking. He felt his spine stiffening, his pulse quickening, his blood pulsing hot through his body. He got another cup of eggnog.

"Sharon has *lots* of special gifts," Helen was saying. "One that I *espe-cially* appreciate is that she's a *genius* with technology. So from now on, she'll handle the PowerPoint whenever I do a presentation. And we have a special presentation for you today—short, but very special. We finally have our Edson College Assessment website up! Sharon, show them the home page!"

Sharon pressed a key on the laptop, and this time there were no glitches. The home page leapt onto the screen. The Edson College colors, catchy graphics—and a striking still photo of Sam Meyer, smiling broadly as he and a student looked through a brochure together.

He recognized that picture. It was taken about two years ago, when he was showing a student brochures about summer study-abroad programs. It had nothing to do with assessment.

He heard gasps all around him, exclamations of surprise, a chuckle. And then more chuckles, then a horrible second when the entire room exploded in laughter.

Helen Stavros's face flushed hot red, and her eyes burned. "Ladies and gentlemen," she said, "meet the new face of assessment at Edson College!

And don't think you can get out of this, Sam! Remember that little green form you sign every year when you sign your contract, the one saying the college can use your image for any promotional purposes it deems appropriate? I've got you—one way or another, I knew I'd get you! *You* are my official assessment poster boy!"

The laughter grew louder. Sam looked around desperately. People were doubled over, unable to control themselves, panting, choking. Even Jake was chuckling, hiding his mouth behind his hand. Sam felt the laughter pounding against the walls, billowing on all sides, rising above his head. At the front of the room, Helen Stavros bounced in place, helpless with glee.

The hatred surged upward, nearly blinding him. He threw down his cup and charged her, running to the front of the room, grabbing her by the throat and slamming her body against the wall. He looked deep into her eyes, savoring the terror he saw there, savoring the power he'd finally gained over her. And she couldn't speak—her lips were moving, she was trying to call out, but only a gurgle emerged. He'd silenced her. He tightened his grip on her throat.

But people were pulling on his arms, pushing him away from her, prying his fingers loose. Then someone managed to punch him in the face, and he lost his grip on her. He stumbled backward, away from her, away from all of them.

She half-collapsed against the wall, massaging her throat and taking deep, ragged breaths while people rushed in to support and comfort her. Everyone else in the room stood staring at Sam, afraid to come closer to him, too stunned to speak.

Had he really done that? A lifetime of tightly controlling his actions, all negated in a moment. He staggered back another step, the room swirling in front of him, his eyes unable to focus. Somewhere behind the blur, he had quick, sharp images of Leah looking grim but unsurprised, his boys confused and frightened, disgrace, dismissal, arrest, prison. And already, Helen Stavros was standing up straighter, breathing more evenly. Everyone would sympathize with her. No one would dare oppose her, for fear of being associated with his madness. He hadn't stopped her. He'd strengthened her.

He had to get out of there, but the door was too far away. They'd never let him reach it. He looked at the window, at the image of the tiger, its eyes so knowing, its body so tensed and ready.

Sam threw his head back and roared. Then he ran forward, hurling himself against the window as hard as he could. He heard glass crack, felt cold air rush against his face, felt himself falling. And then the frozen ground.

People ran to the window and stared at the body spread-eagled on the snow.

"Dear God," Dr Simpson said. "What happened?"

Jake looked down at his friend for a moment before turning his face away. "He drowned," he said.

Quack and Dwight

Travis Richardson

I considered not answering when I saw Shirley Chung's name on the caller ID. We'd been friends forever, going back to high-school AP classes. She eventually went to law school while I got a PhD in psychology. Last time I took on a client for her, he was a six-foot plus brute named Aaron. His junkie mother had dumped him with her abusive, drug-dealing brother when he was five. Shirley, the LA County prosecutor in Palmdale, was hoping that the fourteen-year-old would testify against his uncle, considering the multiple bruises he had on his backside from disciplining. The boy, however, had developed a paper-thin temper that craved for any opportunity to explode. I discovered this when he lunged at me and broke my nose.

I answered the phone.

"I've got an emergency situation and need your help ASAP," Shirley said without a hello.

"When and what?" I asked, opening up my calendar.

"We're going to trial in two days and we need help with a child witness."

My week was already full with my regular patients. Moving them would be an aggravating hassle.

"That's too soon, Shirley. You should've called me a month ago."

"We had somebody else, but he dropped out," Shirley said in an apologetic voice.

"Why?" That was crazy to take a contract with the county and then drop out unless there is a family emergency. You'd be blackballed for any sort of expert witness testimony.

"Personal reasons, he says." Shirley's sarcastic tone let me know that she didn't believe him. "Regardless, we need you bad, and I've been authorized to double your hourly rate for an entire week, whether you're needed or not."

That was a lot of money, and I could always reschedule my patients.

"Tell me about this kid. Is he going to try to kill me?"

"He's eight. You can hold your own against that, right?"

"What's the situation?"

"We busted a meth cook and his wife several months ago. They had a trailer next door where they baked the drugs for a prison biker gang. We're coming down hard on the kingpin, a shitstain named Jack Taft. Neither the cook or his wife will testify against Taft, but the boy says he saw him there several times and witnessed Taft giving his father money."

"Is he the only witness?"

"We're working on the mother. She gave testimony and then recanted. Somebody got to her. I've told her she'll never see her boy if she doesn't open up. If we can get her and the son's testimony, we can take the bastard down."

I was intrigued. "So Taft is bad news."

"The worst. He scares people shitless. We usually bust his crew, but never him. Nobody testifies against him. Ever."

"Is the boy in danger?"

"He shouldn't be. Gangs, as lawless as they are, usually don't kill kids. It's taboo. But . . ."

"But what?"

"It's the kingpin, so the rules are more . . . flexible."

A little voice inside of me screamed: *This isn't your problem, Ben. The money isn't worth it.* But another voice, the side of me that stood for law and order and craved to be a cape-wearing-crime-fighting crusader said yes . . . out loud.

❧

I called my part-time assistant telling her to clear out my calendar for the week while Shirley faxed over a contract with my rate doubled. The number looked nice. After I sent a signed copy back, she faxed over several dozen pages about the case. Shirley called before I could start reading.

"I need you to run up to Northridge and see Dwight. The address is in the packet that I'm sending you."

"Who's Dwight?"

"The witness."

Dwight. That was a name I had never run into in person.

"Get a sense of him and what he can do on the stand," Shirley continued. "Then bring him up to my office around noon. Got it?"

Shirley hung up before I could get another word in. She had the diplomacy of a bulldozer and attention span of a gnat. Driving up to the San Fernando Valley was never easy, but the Antelope Valley would be a serious hike. At least I'd be going against traffic since I'd be coming from Santa Monica.

Reading the file, I couldn't help but shout, "Are you freakin' kidding me?" This had to be a practical joke, right? Had Shirley installed hidden cameras to catch my reaction? Dwight Adolf Lange. Nobody names a kid Adolf by accident. And the further I read, I confirmed my suspicions that the boy's parents were a part of a white supremacist sect. At first I pondered God's twisted sense of humor, but then the more I thought about it, I felt like this was meant to happen. I was helping the universe by taking out the leader of this hatemongering organization. This was personal to me. My family lost several relatives to a paintbrush mustachioed jackass and his nation of goose-stepping followers. Anybody evil or stupid enough to salute a Nazi flag will always be an enemy of mine.

Opening up my desk drawer, I searched through notepads, pens, and business cards until I found the small jewelry box in the back. I pulled out the solid gold Star of David medallion and studied it. It still felt as heavy as the day I received it from grandparents on the morning of my Bar Mitzvah. I clasped the chain around my neck. I wanted to see how little Adolf responded to that.

❦

The boy's social worker, Nancy Gonzalez, met me outside of the group home in Northridge where the boy was staying. It was a typical two-story house set in a suburban neighborhood. Typical except for the police officer posted outside the door.

"That isn't normal," I said, nodding at the officer scanning the street from a chair on the porch.

"No," she said brusquely. I had worked with Nancy before. She was sincere, somehow avoiding cynicism that her work often breeds. A wave of resentment radiated off of her. "Children aren't usually called on to testify against known murderers."

"The DA is trying to take that murderer off the streets."

"Do they really need a boy to do it?"

"None of the adults have stepped up."

"So the DA's going to use this kid for their own means and then throw him back to us with even more damage. Not much different from his screwed-up home life."

I didn't know what to say to temper her outrage. She couldn't change my mind since I knew I was doing a greater good.

"This prosecution has cost Dwight," Nancy said, glaring at me. "Two foster home families sent him back after receiving threats. That's why he's at a group home with police protection."

"Surprised anybody wanted him considering his middle name."

Nancy gave a half smirk. "Definitely makes a tougher sell. But Dwight is unique in spite of his biological parents." She touched my medallion. "Is this your way of starting a confrontation?"

"I want to see where the boy stands. If I'm going to work with him through this trial, he needs to know who I am."

Nancy shook her head. "You'll be surprised. Come on."

The officer nodded at me as we went inside the house. Apparently I didn't look like a threatening biker.

Nancy introduced me to the home's administrator, Jamal. Shaking the beefy yet kind man's hand, I couldn't hold back a smile. The boy's family would flip if they found out their son was being cared for by a black caretaker. He led us to a small room with a couch, a few chairs and a bookshelf. Posters with positive words and images of men and women exerting themselves by climbing mountains or running marathons hung on the walls. Nancy went over a few details with Jamal about me taking Dwight out of the home for the next few days. I gave him my best estimate about what our schedule might look like.

"But nothing's certain," I added.

"We're all on edge here with the cops hanging around our door, motor-cycles rumbling past," Jamal said. "Sooner this is over the better. Not just for Dwight, but all of us."

Nancy excused herself, dashing off to another case. Jamal stepped out for a minute and brought a scrawny boy into the room. He had a natural blond mullet ending with a rattail curl. His oversized Harley Davidson T-shirt, faded to gray from years of use, hung loosely off his shoulders. No doubt a hand-me-down. His jean shorts looked filthy. A white-trash Aryan dream. Yet I couldn't detect an ounce of hate in those blue eyes.

"Dwight, this is Dr. Steinberg and he's going take you up to Palmdale for that case."

"What happened to Sam?"

Jamal looked at me, and the boy followed his gaze.

"I'm taking Sam's place," I said, trying to convey confidence and authority. "He had to go out of town."

Disappointment crossed the boy's face as he looked down at his worn sneakers. Let down by an adult again.

"Hey Dwight, after this trial is over, how about you and me go out for some ice cream?" Jamal said, bending down to the boy's eye level. "What do you say?"

Dwight smiled, giving a nod. Jamal patted him on the back and left us alone.

"Take a seat, Dwight," I said, motioning to a sofa across from me. I wanted to know him better before we got on the road. See what I was going to deal with for the next few days.

Sitting, I noticed his feet did not touch the ground. For an eight-year-old, he seemed small.

"Dwight, you can call me Ben." I reached over and shook the boy's reluctant hand. "So how are you doing?" I asked in a soft tone complemented with a smile and open body language.

He shrugged, looking at his feet. I let a moment pass, and just before I was going to ask him about his upcoming testimony, he knit his brows in a perplexed expression.

"How come you aren't wearing a white coat? Don't most doctors do that?"

"I'm not that kind of doctor."

"Do you have that metal thingy to listen to people's hearts?"

"No, I don't."

He paused for a second. "What do you do then if you're a doctor?"

"Normally I listen to what people say and then help them out in ways they need."

"So you're a duck doctor."

"A what?"

"A duck doctor," the boy said, twisting his face. "At least I think that's what Daddy calls them."

"Hmm." I made mental note about the father's influence. The apple falling next to the tree. Wonderful. Although it wasn't too pertinent to the case (the father pled guilty to manufacturing meth and was sentenced to sixteen years for cooking over ten kilograms), I wanted to know more about the bastard's influence. "Tell me about your daddy. Do you miss him?"

The boy shrugged. "A little, I guess."

"You don't always miss him?"

The boy shook his head, looking at his scabbed knees. There was something on his mind. It looked painful.

"Why is that, Dwight? Can you tell me?"

Dwight shrugged, letting out a sigh. "I dunno. Sometimes he was mean. Especially to Mommy. But not always."

"Can you tell me what you mean when you say mean?"

Although the boy looked at a bookshelf full of Dr. Seuss and Shel Silverstein, his stare was a thousand miles deeper. "Sometimes, he'd yell at Mommy and throw things around the trailer. Especially if he'd been drinkin' or testing product with his friends."

Product was the word he'd heard for the crystal meth cooking in the nearby laboratory, according to the report. "Was that all he did, throw things?"

Dwight looked down at his hands, twisting them back and forth.

"Slapped Mommy sometimes. And . . . hit her with his fists and then kicked her when she was on the floor. He usually cursed a lot too."

"Did he ever do anything to you?"

The boy froze, his little shoulders sunk inside of his oversized shirt.

"Dwight, look at me please." The boy turned his sapphire blue eyes my way. "Did your father ever hit you?"

"A little," he said meekly. His pale face whitened further. "But he spanked me more."

"How do you feel about that?"

The boy shrugged.

"Did your daddy say why he did it?"

He scrunched his face for a moment. "Sometimes it was because my room was a mess or I left a toy or something outside. I tried to clean up, but he'd always find something wrong I did. Said he didn't wanna piss off JT."

I hated seeing children growing up with domestic violence, not knowing that life didn't have to be that way. Not knowing that it wasn't their fault.

"You know, Dwight, you should never be beaten by an adult. Even by your daddy."

The boy's face brightened. Shocked, I believed for a second that my words got through to him. That would be a first.

"Quack," the boy said.

"Excuse me?"

"Quack. That's what Daddy says you guys are."

"Oh really?"

"Yeah, like a duck."

"Hmmm," I said, scratching my chin and giving him my best comical, perplexed look. "Do you think I'm a duck? I don't seem to have any wings." I looked at both of my arms.

The boy laughed. "No, of course you're not a duck. It's just a sayin'."

"Oh."

"But it would be cool if you really were."

"Really? Why's that?" I loved children's theories on the world.

Dwight's eyebrows knitted again. "I wouldn't mind being a duck 'cause I'd go swimming every day and if there's any trouble, you know, I'd just flap my wings and fly away."

I leaned back, stunned with a lump in my throat. Damn this kid. He was breaking my heart with this sincere simplicity. I've met hundreds of kids, but there was something special about Dwight. He had some unique quality that struck me hard. Expecting hateful confrontation, I encountered something totally different.

"You okay, Dr. Ben?" the boy asked.

"Sorry, just thinking. Continue what you were saying, Dwight."

"I wasn't saying anything. Just waiting for you."

I pushed my glasses up to the bridge of my nose and smiled. I needed to get back on track and do what the county was paying me to do. "Let's talk about a friend of your family, a guy named Jack Taft, okay?"

"JT," Dwight whispered, his eyes registering a hint of fear. Still, he bravely nodded.

When Jamal led us to the front door an hour later, I noticed Dwight's face became rigid. He glared at the police officer from the open door.

"Wait just a second," the officer said, looking up the street through his mirrored sunglasses. He mumbled something into a microphone on his shoulder. In the distance, we heard the high-pitched whine of a motorcycle engine. The officer motioned us to step back inside with his left hand as his right hovered near his holstered pistol.

Dwight shook his head in disgust. Thirty seconds later the officer, listening through his earpiece, told us it was safe to go to my car. I wondered if I should wear a bulletproof vest for the next few days. After we were strapped in and on the road, I asked Dwight more questions. It was going to take us almost an hour to get the Palmdale DA's office.

"You didn't like that police officer, did you?"

"Pigs are stupid." He practically spat out the words.

I gripped the steering wheel, stunned at the hatred that he had not shown earlier. "Why do you say that?"

"That idiot can't tell the difference between a rice burner and a hog."

"How could you tell? We didn't even see any motorcycles drive by."

"Hogs' engines rumble, rice burners whine," he said with a confident grin.

Had he heard that from somebody or come up with this insight on his own?

"So you know motorcycles really well?"

Dwight shrugged. "I know a little."

"What do you think about the police?"

Dwight shook his head and narrowed his eyes. "Hate 'em."

"Why's that?"

Dwight gave out an exasperated sigh. "'Cause . . . they're not nice."

For a kid who was abused by his father, neglected by his mother, and called "Little Shit" by Jack "JT" Taft, he was placing all of his anger on the one group who freed him from a downward life trajectory.

"Is that because they arrested your daddy and mommy?"

He shrugged, signaling that was all I was going to get. I switched tactics, realizing he hadn't noticed my medallion.

"Anybody else you hate?"

Another shrug from Dwight as he stared out the window.

"What about Jamal? He's black."

"I don't care. He's a good person."

"Nancy? She's Latina."

He turned to me, his eyes furious. "What's your problem? Don't you know it doesn't matter about a person's skin color as long as they are decent?"

Dwight's directness surprised me. I felt like an asshole, being called out for trying to elicit racism from a child. "Where did you hear that from? I know it wasn't your daddy."

"Daddy hates a bunch of people. Mommy does too. But Grandma told me not to judge people until you meet them."

"Tell me about your grandmother."

Dwight stared at the cars we cruised by in the carpool lane. I had read a little about her in the file.

"I understand she passed away last year," I said in soft voice.

Dwight nodded, still looking away.

"I'm sorry."

He nodded.

"My grandmother died three years ago."

Dwight turned. "Sorry."

"Thank you," I said. "Know one of things I miss most? She used to make apple strudel for the holidays and pretty much anytime I'd come over."

"What's strudel?" Dwight asked.

"It's a pastry. Flakey and sweet with sugar, cinnamon, fruit, and jam. I've eaten other strudels, but nobody made them better than my grandmother."

Dwight nodded, his eyes telling me he understood.

"Grandma made really good peanut butter cookies," he volunteered.

"You miss her?"

"Yes." His eyes glistened as he held back tears.

"Anything else you'd like to tell me about her? Sounds like she was a wonderful woman."

"Yeah, she was."

As Dwight talked about his grandmother, he filled in the blanks, helping me understand what made him tick. His father, Gerald, had only recently come back into Dwight's life. He'd started a six-year sentence months after Dwight was born. His delinquent mother, Tracy, had dropped Dwight at her mother's house for weeks at a time. From what I could gather, the grandmother was a warm and nurturing soul. It seemed like her kindness rubbed off on Dwight. Then two years ago, Gerald was released. He took Dwight and Tracy and stuck them in a trailer in the Palmdale desert.

As if that wasn't bad enough, Dwight's grandmother, his only known relative, was killed in a traffic accident. She died coming up from the San Fernando Valley to visit her grandson. I sensed that Dwight felt responsible. The burden was too much for an eight-year-old to carry. The poor kid couldn't catch a break.

❧

Shirley and her colleague, a young guy named Tom, sat across from Dwight at a conference room table. I sat behind them, watching. It was a risky strategy to put a child up on the stand, but after our brief conversations, I believed Dwight had the grit to pull through. He may hate cops, but he was honest. The prosecutors were going to test the boy. If it didn't go well, then I would have to tell a jury reasons why Dwight could not stand as witness while also pushing for his statement from nine months ago to be included. Dwight's identification of Taft from a six-pack of mug shots and his statement that the notorious kingpin had visited the meth lab several times led to Taft's arrest.

Shirley started with questions about Taft being at the house and inside the lab. She provided photographs of the locations for Dwight to look at and confirm. He also reconfirmed he'd seen Taft paying his father and nicknamed Dwight "Little Shit."

Tom followed with a vicious cross-examination.

"Are you certain it was Jack Taft, not another biker friend of your father's?"

"It was JT."

"Is there anybody else you know with the initials JT?"

Dwight thought about it. "No."

"What about Justin Timberlake?"

"Come on, Tom, objection," Shirley said, looking like she wanted to throw a pen at him.

"You know they're going to try to trip him up with those initials."

Shirley scribbled out a note. "You're right, I'll have to define JT better on my end."

They continued like this, Tom confounding Dwight with questions about his certainty of specific events. Dwight looked at me from time to time and I gave him a supportive "man" nod. Letting him know he needed to stay strong.

After Tom was finished, Shirley started over with her questions, trying to preemptively neuter Tom's most potent inquiries. On his cross-examination, Tom came up with a new set of questions to boggle Dwight.

"How can you be sure you saw Mr. Taft give your father money in the middle of the night? Wasn't it dark outside?"

I stopped Shirley before she started a third round.

"We need to get Dwight some food. He didn't have lunch yet."

"The kid is a champ," Shirley whispered to me. "What did you do?"

"Nothing. We just talked." I glanced to make sure Dwight wasn't behind me. "We bonded over our grandmothers."

Shirley and Tom conferred over notes, while somebody in the office made a run for In-N-Out burgers and shakes. Dwight came over and sat next me.

"You're doing a great job, Dwight."

"Thanks."

He stared at point below my eyes.

"What's that?" he asked, touching the Star of David around my neck. "I was going to ask you earlier, but I forgot."

I too forgot about the medallion hanging in front of my open collar. A feeling of panic hit me. I looked over at Shirley and Tom, fine tuning their notes. If I told him I was Jewish, would Dwight flip out on me? Would he feel betrayed and then scuttle the prosecution's star witness? I had planned to tell the neo-Nazi spawn about my background, but I got distracted with his duck theory and all around personality. Sure Dwight believed you shouldn't judge somebody by their skin color, but he had blanket hate for cops. Would he feel the same way about Jews, a community of people with separate beliefs than his own?

"It's nothing . . . just something I wear," I said, stuffing the medallion under my collar. I felt an overwhelming sense of shame and cowardice.

He wanted to ask more questions, but probably sensed my discomfort. The food came in moments later, and we ate non-Kosher deliciousness.

❦

We didn't leave until after 8:00 P.M., when Shirley declared they were "bulletproof." I hadn't paid too much attention as I had spent hours chastising myself instead of watching the testimony. I was determined to tell Dwight who I was when we got into the car.

As we were making my way out the door, Shirley mentioned that the mother, Tracy, might be willing to testify.

Dwight's exhausted demeanor flipped into excitement. "Does that mean I'm going to see her?"

"I'm not sure, Dwight. I'm going over to Chino tomorrow to see if she wants to help us out. I hope so," she said, mussing his hair.

Driving from highway 14 to I-5, we were mostly silent.

"Do you think my mom will testify?"

"I hope so," I said truthfully. It would take pressure off of Dwight, and I could wipe my hands clean of this case. I remembered the promise I made to myself. I had to do it, this case be damned.

"Got a question for you, Dwight."

"Okay."

"What do you think about Jews?" I tried to keep my voice nonchalant, but I'm sure it had some residual emotion in it.

"Why?"

I'm sure the last thing Dwight wanted to do was to answer another series of questions.

"I'm curious."

"You're talking about those people who own all the banks and movies?"

I was breathless. Dwight's racist father had already indoctrinated him in spite of his grandmother's best countermeasures. I felt the urge to pull over and lecture him about stereotypes. But I needed to explore further. Was there hate? "What else do you know about them?"

Dwight leaned back, thinking. "Well, Daddy says they're the people who killed Jesus and control the world. That's why he hates them."

"Do you know any Jews?"

"I don't think so."

"Do you hate Jews?"

"I don't know." Dwight looked perplexed. "I'd need to meet one to make up my mind."

I couldn't help the huge laugh that escaped my lips.

"What's so funny?" Dwight asked, hurt.

"Nothing, I'm sorry," I said wiping tears from my eyes. Though I lost it, I managed to keep the car on the road. "Got a trivia question for you. Did you know that Jesus was a Jew?"

Dwight blinked twice as his mouth opened. His mind was blown. "Are you fooling me, Dr. Ben?"

"Not at all. Mary was his mother, and you can trace her ancestry all the way through Moses."

"Wait, you're saying Moses was a Jew too?"

"He most certainly was."

Dwight rubbed the back of his head, flipping his rattail up and down. He was thinking hard.

"Can I tell you something else, Dwight?"

"If you want."

I lifted the medallion from my collar. "This is the Star of David." I pulled chain over my head and handed it to him. He held it up in his hand, trying to look at it in the passing streetlights. I turned on the overhead light so he could see it better.

"Looks cool. Is it real gold?"

"It is. It's also a symbol of Jewish identity."

Dwight did a double take as his eyes almost bugged out of his head. Then he narrowed them, examining me. "Does that mean . . ."

"It means I'm a Jew."

"But . . . but you don't look like one."

"What does a Jew look like?"

Dwight took a few seconds, trying to recall the racist propaganda he'd encountered. "Aren't you supposed to have a big nose?"

I smirked. "It isn't small."

"What about a big hat and long beard and stuff like that?"

"That's a more strict, orthodox sect of Judaism. Most of us don't do that."

Dwight nodded, but it was obvious he didn't comprehend what I was saying. Regardless, he didn't hate me. He kept looking at the star, trying to comprehend it. I wondered why I cared about an eight-year-old's opinion of me.

❧

Pulling into the Dwight's neighborhood, the road was blocked by police cruisers. Firemen, glowing in the red flashing lights of their fire trucks, sprayed water on the smoldering group home.

"What happened?" Dwight asked.

"I don't know." I pulled out my cell phone, remembering that I had turned it off inside the conference room since there was no reception. Pressing the "on" button, I waited for the software to boot up.

Somebody knocked on Dwight's window. We both screamed like we were in a haunted house. It was Nancy. I rolled down the window.

"What happened?"

"The home got firebombed. I've been trying to call you." She motioned with her eyes for me to get out of the car.

My phone finally engaged. There were seven messages on it. Dwight looked unnerved, twisting the star in his fingers.

"I'll be right back." Dwight's eyes widened. I pointed to his hands. "Hold on to that for good luck."

He hinted a smile. I got out of the car.

"How did it happen?" I asked in a whisper. "Where were the police?"

"They were here, but that gang sent a decoy, popping off shots and getting the officers to pursue him. Another a-hole came through seconds later and threw the firebomb."

"Is everybody okay?"

"They are. Jamal got the kids out in time."

I looked over at my BMW. Dwight clutched the star, his eyes locked on mine.

"What's going to happen to Dwight?"

"I've been working on it, but it's late and he's a high risk. Most families won't take him. He needs a witness protection program or—"

My phone rang, and I answered.

"Shirley, did you hear?"

"Yes. I've talked to Nancy."

Nancy raised her eyebrows at me as if saying there was one more thing.

"I need a huge, crazy favor from you," Shirley continued.

"What's that?" I asked, realizing our friendship had been a one-way street for a long time. But it was that way with most people. A constant pleaser. A man who will make others happy, even at the loss of my own personal identity. I'm not sure if it came from anticipating my mother's mood swings or from fitting in with the public school cool kids or combinations of that and more. I'd spent years of my life analyzing this fault, contenting myself with the argument that I could have much worse flaws like egomania or substance abuse. Shirley's firm, yet cautious voice brought me back to the present.

"I need you to take Dwight home to your place. Just for tonight. I'll get a couple of officers posted there so it'll be safe."

"I can't put Rachel in danger."

"Nobody knows about you yet. Please Ben, Dwight has bonded with you. Over grandmothers, remember?"

Although Shirley's manipulation was obvious, as I looked into Dwight's frightened, trusting eyes, I knew I had to say yes.

⅍

When I called my wife, Rachel, and told her about the situation, she was less than thrilled. Yet she didn't put up as much resistance as I had expected.

"One more thing, Rach. Can you check the freezer and see if we've got any strudel in there?"

"Why?"

"I'll tell you when you meet Dwight."

⅍

I spotted an unmarked police car when I pulled into my driveway. Stepping inside the house, my beautiful wife was waiting for us in the kitchen.

"Dwight, I want you to meet my wife, Rachel."

I saw strudel sitting on the table, but she didn't mention it. Her mouth was open, as she scanned the boy from his blond mullet to his stained T-shirt and scabby knees. Dwight wasn't the boy she had in mind.

He held out his hand to her. "Nice to meet you, Dr. Rachel."

"Oh no, I'm not a doctor. Just a lawyer," she said, coming back to her senses.

Breathless for moment, I feared Jewish lawyer stereotypes escaping Dwight's mouth.

"But don't lawyers have something special about them?" he asked.

Rachel gave a wide-eyed grin. "I have a juris doctor, but—"

"See you're a doctor, just a funny sounding one."

Rachel let out a snort. "I guess you could say so, Dwight. Come have some strudel," she said, pointing at the table.

"Like Dr. Ben's grandma used to make?"

"Well, it's not as good as hers," Rachel said with a little reluctance.

"Nobody's as good as Grandma Steinberg," I said, taking a dish and cutting a piece for Dwight. "But this isn't bad."

"Of course it's not," Rachel said, giving me her "watch it" look.

"This tastes awesome," Dwight said, after taking a bite.

In spite of the mullet, he had won Rachel over.

🦆

After we put Dwight to sleep in the guest bedroom with the smallest T-shirt I could find, Rachel and I talked in bed. I told her more details about the meth lab and white supremacist background.

"I still don't understand how he turned out the way he did," Rachel said. "I didn't detect an ounce of hate."

"He had a special loving and nurturing grandmother who raised him during a crucial development period."

"He knows we're Jewish, right?"

"Yeah. We're the first Jews he's aware of meeting. I think we're making a good impression for the tribe so far. We need to keep it up."

She pulled my face close kissed me hard. Her eyes had a spark I hadn't seen in years. She locked our bedroom door and dropped her pajamas on floor. Even though we had a guest in the room next door, we made quiet, vigorous love.

🦆

Two days later I sat with Dwight outside the courtroom waiting for him to be called. Dwight wore a dark-blue pinstripe suit that Rachel had bought from Macy's along with a new wardrobe. She had taken the previous day off work and went on a shopping spree. She also convinced him to get a haircut. A maternal side had emerged that I hadn't seen since we learned we couldn't have children.

Nervous, Dwight played with the star medallion, flipping it back and forth in his hands. My grandparents had given it to me at my Bar Mitzvah. I thought it was too gaudy at the time, but I cherished it now even if I didn't wear it often.

Toward the end of opening arguments, a sheriff's deputy escorted a scraggly woman in an orange prison jumpsuit across the lobby.

"Mom!" Dwight shouted. He leaped from the bench, running over to her. The escorting deputy tensed, but then relaxed. Dwight's mother, Tracy, bent down and opened her arms as far as her shackles would allow.

"Oh baby darling, I'm here. I'm here."

They hugged. She pulled back her long unkempt hair and wiped tears off of Dwight's face and her own.

"Look at you, honey darling. In a suit. You look so much like a man." She gave him another hug. Her emaciated arms trembled. "Listen here. After I do this . . . thing in there." Her eyes went over to the courtroom door. "They're supposed to cut me some slack. I'll get out in a few months and after I jump through some hoops for them, I'll come and get you, all right? We'll be a family again."

Dwight nodded. Tracy embraced her son again, and I read fear across her face. Like she knew she made a promise she couldn't keep.

※

We waited for an hour. Dwight was anxious, and so was I. He swung his feet back and forth while playing with the medallion.

"You doing okay?" I asked.

He nodded. "You think Mommy's going to be okay in there?"

"I think she can handle herself." I imagined she'd be an emotional wreck when the defense lined up all her prior drug possession charges and questioned her reliability. I patted him on the back. "Don't worry either. You're going to kick butt in there."

He nodded and handed the medallion back. "This is yours."

"Why don't you hold on to it for good luck?"

"Really?"

"You bet."

Dwight stuffed it into his pants pocket with reverence.

※

When Dwight was called to the stand, he kicked butt, pointing out JT, even with his hair cut and beard shaved off. When the defense tried to impeach his testimony, Dwight didn't waver, saying unequivocally that he saw what he saw.

Shirley was delighted, giving me the thumbs up more than once. At the end of Dwight's testimony, the defense asked the judge if they could meet in her chambers. They were looking for a plea bargain.

We celebrated with milkshakes and burgers at Crazy Otto's in Lancaster. Nancy called my phone.

"I hate to do this to you, but can you hang on to Dwight for one more day? I'll have him in a home or a foster family by tomorrow, I swear."

"That depends on what Dwight says."

Dwight looked up from the food he was stuffing in his face, a question on his face.

"Would you want to stay another night with us, Dwight?"

Dwight grinned with a mouthful of fries and nodded.

When I told Rachel, she was delighted and proposed we give him a home-cooked meal, considering he might not get one for a while.

"We ought to make it traditional too," she added. "He'll probably never get a Jewish meal again in his life."

Rachel gave me a shopping list and later that night, all three of us crowded into the kitchen. Rachel put together her family's famous raisin-and-carrot *tsimmes* while Dwight and I peeled and shredded potatoes for latkes. Rachel joked about "making a big *tsimmes* over Dwight," but it went over his head. We were also going to have brisket and matzoh-ball soup. I thought it was cheesy, but Rachel insisted on playing the *Fiddler on the Roof* soundtrack.

"These recipes have been with our families for hundreds of years, Dwight."

"That's cool," he said, shredding the potatoes. "At home, we usually have microwave dinners. Sometimes."

Nancy had told me that *sometimes* meant he didn't get any food at all. The way he scarfed down burgers, it was like he might never get another meal in his life. While I fried the latkes, Dwight asked if he could help out.

"Do you want to set the table?"

"Sure."

Rachel handed him a stack of plates. He took them to the dining room, a place we rarely used. Usually we spent dinner zombied out in front of the TV. Hearing a crash, I turned to see Dwight wide-eyed with broken shards at his feet. His lower lip trembled as his body drew into itself.

I stepped away from the oven. "Dwight, it's . . ."

Dwight shot out of the room. I looked at Rachel. She was perplexed too.

"Dwight," I shouted, running after him. "It's okay."

He ran into the guest bathroom, locking himself inside.

"Dwight," I said in a kind voice, knocking on the door. "It's okay. We're not angry."

"I—I'm sorry," Dwight said through the closed door. "I didn't mean it. They slipped."

"They're just dishes," Rachel said. "I'll buy more tomorrow."

It took several more minutes to coax him out with us swearing not to beat him over some lousy broken dishes. When he finally opened the door, the smoke detector wailed. All three of us jumped at the eardrum-piercing shriek. A latke was burning in the pan. Once the smoke cleared, we sat at the table and had a terrific meal.

❧

"So Dwight goes back into foster care tomorrow?" Rachel asked in bed.

I nodded. "Nancy's supposed to pick him up before nine tomorrow."

Rachel took a deep breath and squeezed my hand. "I don't want him to go." Her eyes were big and imploring.

"I don't think we're ready for fostering yet."

"But if we don't step up, what will happen to him?"

"He'll go to a foster family or a group home."

"And if he breaks another plate with somebody else, what will happen to him? Will he get smacked around?"

"I don't know, Rachel," I said with a lump in my throat. "This is a big decision."

"Remember Bubbe Previn's story? How her Polish neighbors took her in as one of their own while the Nazis carted away the rest of her family . . . my family."

I gave a supportive nod, but her logic was apples versus oranges. "This isn't the Holocaust though."

"No, but it's karma asking me to return the favor. That's why I was okay with Dwight staying the first night." She stroked my face. "Who knows, maybe this is the reason we couldn't have children in the first place."

My mind did backflips. We weren't atheists, but we didn't believe in an active hand of God either. Rachel's eyes had an intense determination rooted behind her unasked request. I've had my share of marital mistakes, but I am no fool.

We woke Dwight. Even though he was sleep-drunk, he came alive when Rachel asked if he would like us to be his foster parents.

"Yes, please," he said with enthusiast nods.

We did a group hug. Tears streaked down Rachel's face while Dwight and I did our best to keep our manly emotions inside. We were starting a family.

⅔

The following eight months after taking custody of Dwight were the biggest upheaval in my life. I had some of the most spectacular life-fulfilling moments. Early on there were bumps as Dwight tested boundaries, subconsciously sabotaging our relationship in order to test the elasticity of love. When we talked to him about stealing money or intentionally not coming home from school one day, he admitted to not knowing why he was acting out. He was just doing it. Slowly we built the bonds of trust.

Both of our parents, at first reluctant to accept a kid with a hateful lineage, were won over by Dwight, accepting him as a grandson. Rachel pushed us to become more active with the local synagogue. Rabbi Levy and the congregation took Dwight in as one of their own. We celebrated Hanukkah with a Christmas tree, and Dwight ended up with nine days of presents.

All the while, Dwight's mother, Tracy, was released, sobered up, joined NA, and took parenting classes. We never followed her progress because nobody thought she could make it through. Then a week before we were going to apply to have Dwight adopted, she moved to reclaim her son with the help of a lawyer. We were about to head out to a baseball game when Nancy called me with the news.

"After all we've been through, Nance, you can't let this happen," I said, keeping my voice down to a violent whisper as I walked into my office. Dwight and his new friend Alec were waiting for me in the living room, decked out in Dodger blue.

"I'm following the rules, Ben," she said flatly over the phone. She was too chickenshit to tell me in person. "I'm sorry."

"But who do the rules benefit? It's supposed to be the child, right? But there is no way that's going to happen if he goes back to her."

"Reunification between child and their biological parent is—"

"Nancy, stop. I know what the rules are and the motivations behind it, but tell me, truly, what are her chances of keeping Dwight?"

She sighed. That was not a good sign. "We're going to monitor her with weekly visits. And she has to pee in a cup every time. One violation and it's over for her. But she really has shown progress and a will to turn her life around—"

I hung up, not wanting to hear any more. I kicked a trashcan and let out a primal shout. While Dwight was ambivalent about his father, I knew he missed his mother. I remembered her strung out look in prison orange. She was no suitable mother.

"What's going on?" Rachel asked, walking into the office. She still had on an apron from making a waffle brunch.

I shut the door. "We need to talk."

Rachel did not take it well. She said something I never thought I would hear her say in a million years.

"I'll kill that bitch if she takes Dwight away from me. I'll do it, Ben."

Her cheeks flushed, and her hands trembled. The savage look in her eyes said that she would rip the mother's heart out of her chest with her bare hands if she walked through the door. She had bonded to Dwight like a sealed envelope. To separate them would cause irreversible damage. Rachel read to him every night as he fell asleep. The attentiveness that she gave Dwight, as he explained the minutiae of his day at school was nothing like I had ever seen from her before. At times I vacillated between parental love and petty jealousy.

"She has a history of drug use and neglect, Rachel." I used my words very judiciously. "We should be able to win in family court, but it's not guaranteed. A sympathetic judge—"

"I'm going to call Sarah Levine," Rachel said, picking up her iPhone and scrolling through the directory. She was the attorney we were going to use for the adoption.

While Rachel talked to her, I came up with an idea. A horrible, awful idea, but it could save our family. Save Dwight from a life of destitution. A life of neglect.

When Rachel got off the phone, her eyes were moist. "Sarah's on it. But she says it could go either way." She bit her lip to hold back a torrent of tears.

"Rachel, I have a plan." Then I told her.

❧

Walking through the steel door, Aaron saw me through the glass at the juvenile delinquent center and stopped for a moment, squinting. Then he recognized me as an angry, surly mask morphed across his face. It was the same face he had when he attacked me ten months earlier. That case for Shirley which only netted me a broken nose.

"What do you want, asshole?" he said after picking up the phone.

"Why do you say that, Aaron?" I couldn't help falling into therapist mode.

"'Cause of you I was put in isolation for three months. 'Cause of you, I ain't ever gonna see daylight until I'm eighteen."

"You attacked me, Aaron. There are consequences to your actions."

He was already on his way to juvie hall, when I had been hired to see if I could pump some information out of him for the county.

"You were talkin' about my mama. That was none of your business to be askin' about her."

"I was just asking if . . ." Aaron's eyes widened, anticipating an insult so he could go berserk. That wouldn't help me at all. "Let me ask you something else. Do you like being in juvie?"

His eyes narrowed. He was ready to play ball. I was going to make a promise I couldn't keep.

❧

I waited at a Denny's in Palmdale. Sitting in a booth facing the parking lot, I had arrived thirty minutes early and watched the cars roll in. I was looking for a 1993 blue Pontiac Bonneville. That's what Shirley told me Tracy drove. That was the only thing I could get out of her about Dwight's mom, besides apologies. I got that information by saying that we wanted to make sure she wasn't driving by to kidnap Dwight.

"She testified, so we made good on our promise to cut her loose on probation," she had said. "Most of the time they get nailed for a violation within their first few weeks out."

That did not make me feel any better. Ten minutes after our appointed time, the filthy junker pulled into the parking lot. I called Rachel.

"She's here."

"Where? Oh, I see her . . . are you sure that's her?"

I squinted out the window. The woman that I had seen in the courthouse had been bone thin with stringy blond hair. If it weren't for the county-issued orange, I imagined she would have worn a Jack Daniels T-shirt with ripped up jeans. This woman looked like her healthy, professional sister. She had her hair cut short and bobbed. She wore a cheap powder-blue dress with modest heels. She could have been a small-time real estate agent in a rural town.

Tracy walked inside, scanning the tables for me. I waved, and she looked at me as a cloud of confusion crossed her face. She hustled across the diner, dodging customers and waitresses. Her eyes looked from me to the empty booth seat.

"Is Dwight here?"

"He's not."

She bit her lip and shook her head. I could tell she saw me as yet another obstacle in a string of disappointing life events.

"You said Dwight would be here, Mr. Steinberg. That's why I came here. I want to see my baby boy. Where is he?"

The lie was the only way I could arrange a meeting with her. She looked like she was ready to leave.

"Take a seat and let's talk about—"

"No, I'm jetting if he's not here. My attorney told me to not to come here without him."

"He's with my wife," I lied. "I wanted to talk to you first and make sure everything is all right before you met with Dwight. If your attorney were here it would be all legal mumbo-jumbo. I have to say, I'm impressed. You seem to have made positive life changes. Please sit."

I waved my hand to the open chair. She hesitated, as an internal debate, no doubt, raged in her head. She had smiled briefly when I mentioned the positive change. I believe that is what got her to sit.

A young waitress came up with an air of unfiltered affability. "Hello, my name is Mindy, would you like something to drink before I take your order?"

"Diet Coke, please," Tracy said in a low, apologetic voice.

"Can we get an order of mozzarella sticks, too?" I asked. The coffee I had been nursing was burning a hole in my stomach.

"Sure thing." Mindy scribbled the order and left.

"I don't have much money—"

"Don't worry, this is on me," I said. "Order whatever you'd like."

Tracy picked up the menu with hungry eyes, not much different from Dwight when I first took him out to eat. This would be a treat for her. She suddenly paused and closed the menu. "No thank you, I've already eaten."

An obvious lie. I wanted to insist, but there was no need to offend her . . . yet.

I saw Rachel get out of our car and start to cross the parking lot. Tension racked my bones.

"So tell me about your progress." I also wanted to know how she could afford a lawyer too, but wasn't sure how to bring it up.

"Gradual. One step at a time. But I'm turning my life around now. And I mean it."

"Are you working anywhere?"

"At a beauty parlor, and I'm getting my GED. I used to have a beautician's license."

"That's great," I glanced out the window again, noticing Rachel approach Tracy's car with unnecessary caution.

Tracy's Diet Coke arrived. "The mozzarella sticks are on their way. Anything else I can get you?" the waitress asked.

"We're good for now," I said.

After the waitress left, Tracy leaned forward. "Tell me how Dwight's doing. He's been okay under your care?"

"Things have been great. We lov . . . care about Dwight a lot."

"Do you have pictures of him?"

"Sure . . ." I said, fumbling for my phone. I swiped through several pictures, skipping snapshots of him wearing a yarmulke at the synagogue or wrapped in a tallit with my parents at Passover. I settled on pictures at Disneyland.

"My boy," she said taking the phone from me. A sob escaped her throat. "He's growing so fast." She scrolled through a few photos when the phone buzzed. I snatched it back, giving a curt sorry.

It was a text message from Rachel. I was hoping it read *mission aborted*. But instead one word glowed on the screen. "Done." My breath caught, the machine we designed was operational.

"Mr. Steinberg . . ." I didn't want to correct her with my PhD title. Her eyes were glassy with tears. "It looks like you've done a wonderful job with Dwight. Thank you. But I want . . ." Her chin trembled for a second. "I need my boy back. He's the reason I'm sober. The reason I'm turning my screwed up life around. I need him if I'm going to survive."

She wiped away tears. Mindy showed up with the mozzarella sticks.

"And here are—" she saw Tracy and went silent. She gave me a sympathetic nod and scurried away.

"How soon are you thinking of taking Dwight back? Do you have a place to live yet?"

"Soon, I hope. I'm in a halfway house now. I had to sell the trailer to get a lawyer, but me and a friend are looking for an apartment."

I saw in Tracy's eyes desperate hope backed by petrified fear. Part of me, an emotional side, wanted to help her. But the other half, the rational, educated side that knew self-delusion and self-destruction were frequent roommates. Nothing good would come from handing Dwight over to Tracy.

"You know that my wife and I were thinking of adopting Dwight before we heard—"

"Thank you again for taking such good care of him. Once I get Dwight settled with me, maybe you two can come visit him." She grabbed her purse, ready to leave.

"Wait, I want to ask you something that been bothering me about Dwight."

Tracy glanced at the door, ready to bolt. "What?" she asked in a tired voice.

"His middle name, Adolf. Why did you name him that?" I held back from calling it the mark of Cain.

She sighed, leaning back against the booth. Her cheeks flushed while she stared at her hands. I noticed that she wasn't wearing a wedding band.

"I was about ready to deliver when Gerald, Dwight's father, got arrested on his second robbery offense. He told me to name the boy Adolf because he knew he was going up to San Quentin and he wanted to get in with Aryans up there for protection." She shook her head. "Selfish bastard from day one."

"But why did you do it? He was in jail anyway."

"He told me I'd better 'cause somebody'd come and check." She looked at me with tears streaking down her cheeks. "Sure enough, a big biker came out to see the birth certificate about two months after Dwight was born."

She clutched her arms and shivered. Although she didn't say anything else, I could tell the biker got more than a look at the birth certificate. I didn't know what to say. I was speechless trying to comprehend what she had told me.

"Good night, Mr. Steinberg, and thank you again for looking after my boy."

I nodded. "Good night."

She rose and walked to the door. I called Rachel.

"Has she left yet?" my wife answered.

"We need to call this off."

"There she is."

"Rachel, wait."

She hung up on me. I threw a twenty next to the untouched sticks and rushed for the door. I saw Rachel's clunker make a right turn out onto the street. I ran to our BMW at the end of the parking lot. Rachel sat in the passenger seat, the blue glow of a cell phone silhouetting her face. When I jerked the door open, I heard her say, "Please hurry." She collapsed the disposable cell phone and glared at me with intense eyes daring me to defy her.

"Everything is in motion."

I sank into the driver's seat feeling like I had inhabited somebody else's body. A dark, sinister man. A conspirator. A life-wrecker. I couldn't believe what we had just done.

❧

We drove down the road in silence. Rachel had her chin jutting out in self-righteousness. I gripped the steering wheel, keeping my eyes focused on the road.

"Over there," she pointed to the blue and red flashing lights more than two blocks away. "I think that's her."

I slowed down to fifteen miles an hour. Tracy's car was pulled over, and she sat on the sidewalk shouting something to an officer who shined a bright ghostly light in her face. A K-9 police cruiser was also there, as an officer led an eager German shepherd into the back of the Pontiac. Rachel squeezed my arm.

"It's happening," she said in a voice mixed with fear and hope, looking through the side-view mirror.

I did a U-turn a block away. Coming back we saw Tracy, cuffed and screaming a fury of words at two officers as they pushed her into the back of a squad car. The K-9 officer held a bag in his gloved hand as the other gripped the dog's leash.

❧

We were on the highway heading home, when Rachel let out a sigh, slinking into her seat. I tried to smile. As we got closer to civilization—Santa Monica, a place far away from meth dealers, filthy air, and tumbleweeds—an ill feeling crept upon me. We did the right thing, I told myself. We rescued Dwight from a fate of poverty and crime. A woman who had messed up her life. A woman who, even with the best intentions to turn her life around would probably not pull it off. And what would happen? Dwight would suffer irreparable damages. Dwight, he was our boy now. I swallowed dryly and repeated to myself, *We did the right thing, we did the right thing*.

In the trunk lay a pile of Goodwill clothes I'd bought trying to blend in with the Palmdale culture, although it had not worked at all. Aaron's Uncle Lewis laughed at me. Lewis had said he would have thought it was a drug bust, but "the cops wouldn't send no candy-ass like you in here. It's too obvious. What's your angle, man?"

I had said I needed it for personal reasons.

"Personal enough you gonna pay out the nose for it, candy-ass."

Three hundred dollars for a little plastic baggie of clear crystal rocks. Three hundred to ruin one life. Three hundred to give a better life to another.

"Hey, Ben," Rachel said, touching my arm.

I glanced over at my wife. By the concerned line on her forehead, she had something heavy on her mind. Was she finally feeling guilt too?

"Yeah?"

"I was thinking, once we get Dwight fully adopted, maybe we can look at fostering a little girl. What do you say?"

THE GOLDEN LAND

A Simkhe
(A Celebration)[*]

Yente Serdatsky

It was near the end of winter, one of those winter days that are the most wonderful days in a big city. No heat wave hangs over your head and there's no dust in the air. There's a fresh blueness and a golden sun. The wide streets, the enormous buildings and the richly decorated stores shine brightly and it seems as if you are seeing them for the first time. How holiday-like it is in the street! The women from the city's best families are all dressed up in fancy outfits—expensive feathers, furs, silk, diamonds—with happy faces and sparkling eyes. On such a day, as you go for a stroll, you forget that there are dark workshops with many disheartened workers, that there is poverty somewhere; you forget so many things. You breathe in the cold, fresh air and your eye drinks in the beauty of God's world.

Others, such as our group of comrades, were not out taking a stroll on such a fine day. It was something we had sort of agreed on. And no wonder, we are very poor here and our clothes are falling apart. Although we earn very little, we share our poor income: one of us supports a sick brother back home, one is making sure that a little sister who has a talent for singing gets an education. One is still paying for a ship's ticket that he sent to a friend. And so we are all poor. In the Old Country we were not ashamed of our poverty. But here, surrounded by such dazzling wealth, you feel as if you're worthless, and unwillingly, the proud head bows.

It was a Sunday. Mary's employers had gone to visit relatives on a farm and were supposed to stay there for a couple of days. The house was left empty. And we made ourselves at home, we who are forever crammed into narrow bedrooms, always longing for what the Russians call *prostor*—space,

---

[*] This story originally appeared in the *Forverts* on May 16–17, 1912, and is reproduced with permission. Translated from the Yiddish by Kenneth Wishnia, with considerable help from Arnold Wishnia.

elbow room. We were happy to take advantage of this opportunity as we gathered in Mary's house.

It was already midday. We assembled in the big, half-empty parlor with the old, wooden rocking chairs. The parlor window looks out the back to the gray walls of the buildings across the way and their sad windows with closed curtains.

❦

The sun doesn't shine into the parlor. But on such a nice day, golden shafts move along the walls across the way, and the room fills with a yellow glow. The yellow light makes us uneasy, it awakens a longing in our hearts to tell the story of the light shining beyond the sad gray walls.

We all sat down, Emotshka and Semyonov and Mary and Maria Davidovna, and B. the poet and short Max and tall Semyon, and clumsy Boruch, and all the rest.

We were all stirred, not from sadness, but from some sort of secret longing for life, for luxury, for radiance, from which we are always so far.

In such a spirit, we didn't even notice as our conversation started to drift toward *pikante* themes, and this time we ended up talking about the lives of old maids. Pale, thirty-year-old Mary gave a nervous cough; but we didn't pay any attention to her, we were all *khakhomim*, such wise men, and each one had something to say about his experience with an old maid. And those of us who didn't have our own stories started to talk about what de Maupassant says and what Chekhov says and what others say, as if the rest of us had never read any such thing.

When it got quiet, Semyonov started to talk:

"I want to tell you, I myself don't know what word to use, an old maid or a woman. Because this is a type that still has no name, either in life or in literature." At that he began to smile bitterly.

Clumsy Boruch also started to smile: he didn't think much about the "new type." Mary stopped coughing, we listened curiously and Semyonov spoke:

❦

Fifteen years ago, when I first came here, I fell in love with her. She was twenty-eight years old then.

At the time there was a small colony of Russian-Jewish intelligentsia here. Most of them had to flee their homes in the Old Country for political reasons. Nowadays somebody comes because they want to live here; in those days they looked like so many "Robinson Crusoes," washed up on an island after a shipwreck, waiting for someone to come rescue them and take them home. Because of that they didn't spread out over the whole city, the way they do now, they all lived in one neighborhood, speaking Russian to each other and keeping all the customs of the Old Country.

She had come eight years earlier. They call her Miss B. She's tall, well built, and graceful in manner. When I first met her, she had black hair and a dark face that was always flushed with that charming color that reminds you of young blood that will never age. She had big eyes with that wonderful expression that great poets and artists are always depicting.

After a while, the "colony" began to feel at home. What can you do? You are so far from home. Some picked up teach-yourself books, some went to work in *shaps* and a few went into business.

Miss B. also worked in a *shap*. It was not hard for her to work; she was strong and nimble, and it was easy for her to make a good living. Her friends advised her that, in addition to work, she should also study a profession, as some of the others in the colony had done. She didn't want to: She said, "I don't see the difference between being a doctor or being a seamstress."

I don't know exactly when her private life with novels began. I mean to say that it was very late, because at that time we were starting to build a movement and Miss B. was busy doing idealistic work. And we knew nothing about "Sanins" at the time.

When she was twenty-five years old she lived with a man for a short time.

Miss B. didn't get married the way her mother did. She didn't take "him" as her lord and provider. They loved each other as comrades, and they both declared themselves to the colony as "chosen." A short time later they declared to the same group that they had incompatible characters, and they separated.

Afterward, the incompatible one "secretly" told a few of his comrades all about his intimate relations with Miss B., and the menfolk were very interested. Love without commitment, and with such a beautiful, intelligent woman no less! A lot of men tried to match themselves with her. There was quite a hunt for her, each one stepping over the other. Grooms left their brides, men neglected their wives, students set aside their schoolbooks, and everyone's thoughts were occupied with her.

Later she became a sort of ruler: At a picnic, at a special event, at a get-together, the whole circle turned around her. And if she happened to be absent one time, we all used to feel disappointed and a bad feeling spread through the whole hall.

And surrounded by so many male admirers, Miss B. did not notice herself how much she was changing: In the past, besides working, she kept herself busy by reading or by doing work for the cause. Now, little by little, she drifted away from reading, she began to pay more attention to her clothing, always dressing with a thin white collar, and her eyes grew bright and shining, and she became more feminine, and the red color in her face blossomed and glowed.

Then Miss B. fell in love with another man, but before she proclaimed him as suitable, she became disappointed in him herself and left him.

I'll spare you the details about how the wives in the colony hated her; but with all the happiness that surrounded her, they too flattered her and didn't show their anger.

Before they introduced her to me they told me everything about her life. I laughed at them. I was a few years younger than her and I was the king of so many fortresses, that is, female hearts. I approached her confidently and with a somewhat shameless pride. But the first time I set eyes on her I felt small and empty; she stood opposite me with her graceful figure, a tall woman with a bright, open face with a wonderful sparkle in her eyes and a calm, assured smile that lit up her whole face. My heart started pounding like a sixteen-year-old boy's. I saw magic in her every movement. Her voice sounded like singing to me, but you certainly know the whole impression that can be made upon you by a person with whom you have completely fallen in love?

I never had any luck in this love, despite the fact that I followed after her like a shadow for months on end: she was the one who chose, and I wasn't charming enough for her.

I don't know how many lovers she chose after that. Although you hear a lot of men shamelessly hinting that "they too . . ." But I know that those are lies. Intelligent Jewish women simply love to flirt.

Later I went away for a while, and when I came back, I found her the same as before. My love for her had already cooled off, and we became good friends. We would go out all the time. We used to walk, talk, enjoy ourselves together, and so fifteen years quickly passed this way.

I saw Miss B. again, not long ago, and once again she made an impression on me, but listen to what happened:

I had just moved back here from a year somewhere else. The first evening I met her in a coffeehouse. Nothing unusual. A forty-three-year-old woman, tall, poised, only her eyes spoiled by eyeglasses and some gray hair. And, just as if someone had hit me on the head, I looked in the mirror: my face had become pale with fright.

I went home. I spent the whole night pacing around in my room. Miss B. had become the mirror of myself.

Mary coughed hoarsely. A couple of us began to take deep drags of cigarette smoke. Semyonov wiped his brow and went on:

Miss B. did not get old all of a sudden, it happened gradually over the years; but when I first met her I was her equal. I approached her carefully, as one approaches a wound, and started to look at her life and how she lived:

She had already been here for twenty-three years, one of the first of the colony. Our whole circle of friends stayed in the same neighborhood. A few tried to settle somewhere else, but they felt sad and came back. Now everyone's comfortable here. Some have offices, others successful businesses. The former workers have become bosses or contractors and are now "well off." Almost all of them have gotten married. The old comrades have paired off, and they've set up houses of their own. They have children, and others already have grandchildren. One, however, Volodya, remained a bachelor, but he has a sister, a widow with four children to whom he is like a father, and they all live in his house.

She remained alone. She herself almost hadn't noticed how that happened, how they had torn themselves from her and shut themselves up in their own nests. Now she works in a *shap* and has a room on the fifth floor with a poor family that lives in the building. She's practically an outcast from our group of friends. The women who once hated her got married to the men who were once in love with her. Now they all hate her, the women because she was once young and beautiful, and the men can't forgive her for having become old.

Almost every evening I see Miss B. in the café. She sits alone at the last table. She looks at a newspaper and sips coffee. Every time the door opens I see the paper in her hand shiver. She doesn't look up, yet she still knows who's coming in. She thinks of almost everyone who comes in as one of her enemies—some more, some less. When the newspaper gives a light shiver I already know that Max has come in. He doesn't even talk to her; but he's a good, kind man. She knows that he doesn't bear any hatred for her. He sits at a table where a couple of friends are already sitting. She buries herself deeper into the paper again, and suddenly the door opens, and the newspaper gives a quick shiver: Samuel has comes in; he was once young, tall and handsome, and he used to follow her every step. Now he's thin and gray. He's sickly and very angry. She feels that he really hates her. She can almost hear his angry look calling her "Old maid!" He sits far away from her and she goes back to reading. And suddenly the newspaper in her hands shakes powerfully. The door opens and in comes Henekh. He is her bitterest enemy. One time, in the good old days, she threw him out of the house. He hasn't ever forgiven her for this. He has a successful business. Sometimes he lends a few *dollar* to a friend and so now he's got many "friends." He is very rude to those whom he doesn't like. He sits at a table and several friends gather around him. The paper in Miss B.'s hand shivers for a long time. I can almost feel her heart beating. A couple of them look at her out of the corners of their eyes. And she knows that Henekh is saying something bad about her.

Between eleven and twelve the café becomes very lively. That's when people come from the theatre, from lectures, from other special events. Everybody's cheerful, people talk and pass the time. The friends' wives don't come to the café; but each one comes with some cousin, or a niece, or a young widow in mourning clothes comes in with a freshly rouged face, or a young woman who is as strong as iron and who isn't afraid of what people will say. It becomes even livelier in there. Eyes sparkle and talk becomes freer.

Miss B. lets the newspaper down on the table. She leans her head on both hands and looks at the guests. She looks directly at them, she knows that no one will even so much as look at her.

I sit apart from everyone. I don't look at her but I can tell that she's looking at me. I am seized by rage, although afterward I laugh at her. "What does she think," I roar inwardly, "that we're equal?" And I answer myself, "Yes." And I become even angrier, but I myself don't even know with whom.

The owner of the café gives her a piercing glance. He's new, he doesn't know her, that when the place opened they used to cater to her, and that when she wasn't there, the place was empty. Now she's just a *nudnitse*, a bother, occupying a table for free. She doesn't spend any money and no one sits near her. He says nothing to her, but she feels his eyes upon her. Several times she starts to rise, and sinks back into the chair again, as if drawn by a magnet; as if she's trying to collect from the chair some piece of her past, of those golden years, long gone.

My heart fills with sympathy for myself and for her. She starts to go. I make a motion showing that I want to stop her and say something to her. Her face brightens with some hidden hope. She makes her way over to me and gives me her hand. We stand there in silence. I'm afraid to look at her. She looks at me as if she were waiting to hear some extraordinarily loving and comforting word from me. I seek that word within me and I don't find it. I become impatient and angry. She starts to get sad again. And I begin breathing again when she walks away from me.

Just as she is about to reach the door, others notice her as if for the first time, several eyes even look right at her, she senses this, and I notice that her eyes are red. She closes the door nervously and, like an evil spirit, whisks herself off to her lonely home.

It's already after midnight when she comes home. She prefers to buy her own key to the door but she always forgets it. The landlord always has to let her in. Once she heard him tell his wife, "Such an old woman, and she shleps around the whole night . . ." Now she thinks that he always says that whenever she shows up, but that he could say something worse. She enters the room, out of breath. Her head is burning and the blood pounds in her face. The room is cold. Half undressed, she lies down on the bed and turns off the gas. She doesn't fall asleep. The ticking of the clock on the night table starts to bother her. She gets impatient and wants to throw it out, only she remembers that she has to wake up in the morning. All this going out is hard on her. More than once, her eyes stare straight ahead, and she sighs, "Already twenty-three years!" For the last fourteen years she has worked in the same place, and has become an important person there. Now a lot of people have left the *biznes*, and other, younger ones are taking the "seat of honor."

She pulls the blanket over her head in order not to hear the ticking of the clock. She starts to get warm, and she throws it off her chest. She lies there quietly. She soon forgets the *tick-tock*. She thinks about something else. She doesn't even know what she's thinking about. Everything is all mixed up into one big chaos. Later she spins a picture out of the chaos. It's a picture of the house where she lives. A poor couple, ugly and common, but still a clean, bright house. A white tablecloth, clean utensils, the enticing smells of supper. She has someone to polish, to cook and to clean up for. A three-year-old girl is dancing around the room. The mother sews little dresses and styles the little girl's braids. The father brings more clothes and kisses. In the evening the children's little voices ring out, and the house is full of laughter and joy.

She begins to feel cold. She covers herself up and thinks, "Why didn't I have a child!" She answers, and almost says out loud, "A child is good when there's a man in the house . . ." She thinks some more, "Why didn't I provide myself with both of these things?" And a proud smile shows itself on her lips: "For whom would it have been as easy as for me?" She stretches out calmly and thinks about her past. Everyone, everyone was chasing after her. She rejected them all. They are all petty and ordinary. They are not worthy of her. So she concludes, and with a proud, calm spirit, she falls asleep.

In the morning, the ringing of the clock makes her nervous. She has *tsuris* in the *shap*, and she goes straight from work to the café and once again sits there until late at night.

Semyonov fell silent and Mary coughed. The yellow glow had long since gone. Silver flecks of light moved along the walls. No one had lit a lamp. Our comrades started to make noises, moving around the floor. A silver strip of light illuminated Emotshka's blond head. Her eyes stared ahead sadly, and she looked like Lilien's portrait of the Queen of the Night. Clumsy Boruch held his head in his hands and thought for a long time.

From the farthest corner, short Max began singing one of Lermontov's songs.

His coarse voice trembled with Lermontov's longing, and that struck all of us. Young people, full of life, also feel such a longing from time to time, but it's like a spring wind that makes things sweeter and pleasanter. But we, broken-down, stay-at-home folks, we feel a longing like a storm in the desert that topples mountains. Our longing is like a physical pain: it starts gnawing and gnawing. Your head feels hot, you have an attack of uneasiness, and you feel that you're dying, you're dying . . .

That's how much Max's voice tore into us. And we remained silent with pain.

And suddenly Boruch's clumsy voice aroused us like a call to arms: "Why, why don't both of you get married? Why are you both living like stones? Why is the world making you sad?"

If this had been another time, one of us would have come up with an argument to counter Boruch, but now, we sat quietly and waited for what Semyonov was going to say. And he answered with a quiet, soft, and loving voice:

"A wound needs to have a plaster, you can't put gall on it . . ."

He had finished. And Mary gave a hoarse cough, began to cry and, starting to sob hysterically, ran into the kitchen. No one went after her; we were already accustomed to that, and we know, at such times, to leave her alone. The atmosphere became even more tense and suddenly Boruch jumped up and went into the kitchen.

An overarching curiosity took hold of us. "What is he doing?" We waited. Mary's sobs became fainter. We heard Boruch's rapid, clumsy voice. One comrade lit the gas, and the glow from the light revealed Boruch and Mary at the entrance to the kitchen. Both of them looked very excited and both of their eyes were shining. Boruch led her to the middle of the room, and as if he were about to give a speech, he said out loud, in his coarse voice:

"I'm not going to leave another 'wound' alone. I want to be the plaster. We want to set up a home and have children. No one should ever waste time."

He had barely finished when thunderous "Bravos" broke out and in the middle of our celebration, Semyonov embraced Emotshka and in his sweet, resonant voice said, "My dear, I want to be the balsam for you!"

And again thunderous "Bravos" broke out, everyone hugged them and kissed one another and in the middle of our celebration the door opened and in came Rosa the *Ollraytnitse*, looking all bright and shiny in a new set of furs. And when Rosa heard what was happening she started dancing around the room and gave Mary her set of furs as a wedding present and she gave Emotshka the diamond ring that her own Mosye had given her as a surprise. And in the middle of all this the door opened and in came tall, straight, mature, but ever-youthful Lazar, whom we call the *Amerikaner patriot*.

And bottles of wine appeared on the table, Champagne, the likes of which we had never seen or tasted, and all kinds of fruits and snacks. And all the gas flames were lit, there was singing and dancing, the poet grabbed "plain" Maria Davidovna in his arms and short Max kissed ugly Helena. And Rosa danced with the "*patriot*" and soon jubilant singing could be heard from all the surrounding windows. I don't know if they shared our joy, or if something happy was going on there as well. And so the celebration continued until we finally realized that it was daytime.

Annotations

Sanins refers to the novel, *Sanine*, by Mikhail Artzybashev (1878–1927), which was published in Russian in 1907 (and in English in 1914). The preface to the Modern Library edition of 1931 refers to critics who looked upon the book as "radicalism spiced with sex."

Lermontov Mikhail Yurevich Lermontov (1814–1841), the Russian Romantic poet and novelist.

Lilien Ephraim Moishe Lilien (1874–1925), Galician-born painter and graphic artist, active in Poland, Austria, Germany, and Palestine. Illustrated a 1903 edition of Morris Rosenfeld's *Songs of the Ghetto*.

Trajectories

Marge Piercy

My uncle Eddy was the eleventh child my grandma Pearl gave birth to, not long before my grandfather was the victim of a hit and run during a snowstorm in Cleveland. When Eddy was seven, Pearl took him to bed with her in their slum apartment—it was January, the heat was not working, and the apartment was cold as a frog's belly. Shortly after midnight, my grandfather's ghost appeared and swore at her, shouting, "Who is this you have taken to our bed?" Eddy always claimed he had seen the ghost too, but we all remember things we never witnessed but heard as stories so often told that we believe we were there.

Late in the Great Depression, Eddy moved in with us. He took the room that had been my brother Harry's until my parents came home early from a party and caught him fucking his girlfriend Shirley on the scratchy old couch. My parents and hers forced them into marriage with the disaster you'd expect, but that's another story. It set a pattern for Harry of marrying, again and again and again, never for long. Where some other guy would maybe give a girl he was seeing a nice birthday box of chocolates, Harry married her.

I slept in my parent's room in our little wooden house near the Detroit Terminal Railroad. Harry and Eddy were only a year apart in age and became best friends. Eddy was of medium height, wiry and strong with curly black hair and green eyes that nobody else in the family shared. All the rest of us had dark brown almost black eyes. Harry was shorter and solidly built, more muscular.

"You're pretty," I'm told I said to Eddy. "You have green eyes like my pussycat." The thoughtless coquettish flattery of a four-year-old who desperately wanted to be liked. Eddy had blue green eyes, changeable as the weather. My cat Whiskers had yellow green eyes. I thought Whiskers the most beautiful creature in the world.

Harry and Eddy bet on the horses together, bent over the racing form arguing records and jockeys, won and lost, mostly the latter, at poker, laid down their money on numbers, whored and generally behaved as if they were both single. I adored my brother because unlike my distant father, he was emotional, warm and funny. Eddy seemed to a four-year-old almost a hero, dashing, spontaneous, handsome. They seldom quarreled with each other but frequently got into arguments and fist fights with other men. Harry would come home with a black eye Mother would fuss over; Eddy usually got the worst of it but he always said, "You should see the other guy. He'll think twice before he calls another working stiff a dirty kike."

I do remember them arguing about the Purple Gang. Harry said, "They were just poor Jews like us. Now they live in big houses, they drive fancy cars and they hang out in nightclubs that would never let us in. They had the guts to go and get what they wanted. So big shots wouldn't hire Jews for decent jobs. So they had to pay the Purple Gang just to get left alone."

"They're vicious fuckers. They were hired to bust unions. They killed anybody. They killed each other. That they ruled this city so long just proves how corrupt the system is."

I imagined men who were the color of grape popsicles.

Both Harry and Eddy'd had Bar Mitzvahs of course, toned down thrown together affairs. Eddy wore a *hamsa* under his shirt that Pearl had given him for protection. Harry would tease him about that. But they were closer than brothers then. When the economy improved, Eddy moved back to Cleveland where Pearl pushed him to marry. She had a bride in mind, you might say, in tow. Eddy told my mother, "I don't want to get married. But Mama's insisting. She cries, she says I'm breaking her heart."

Mother laughed. "Is she praying at the top of her lungs?"

"It's not funny. Last week she wouldn't eat for two days, calling out to *Hashem* to make me do the right thing. Couldn't you talk to her? You know how Harry and Shirley are fighting all the time."

"When Pearl got her mind set on something, dynamite can't move her. You should have stayed here. So what's the girl like? Is she ugly or bowlegged or stupid?"

"She's sweet in her way. Not a bad looker. But I don't love her. I guess she'd make a good wife, but I don't want one!" But he gave in two months later and married what Pearl insisted was his *bashert*. We all went to Cleveland for the wedding, the whole family amounting to maybe fifty of us. Pearl's rabbi married them and the men all danced, even my father, even Harry, although he made fun of it. The bride was very bashful and clung to Pearl. I learned her own mother was dead and Pearl had taken her in. Families did that a lot in the ghetto.

When I was twelve, I took the bus from Detroit to Cleveland to stay for a few weeks with my grandma. Pearl and Eddy lived on the same block of tenements, a neighborhood of poor Jews and Blacks, three story wooden buildings with rickety outside staircases. I got to know Eddy more as a person. He was an anarchist who was bright and read all kinds of literature, mostly political, and owned a jazz collection. He had recently walked out on his first wife and two kids and left everything including his music, but what money he had he spent on records and listening to live jazz. He was proudly and determinedly working class. At that time, he had a job in the steel mills.

"Jazz, that's real music," he told me, "Living music. It has soul. That shit on the radio, it's empty. Full of lies." He played Duke Ellington for me and talked about his genius.

There was not a lot he respected: the government lied, capitalists and bosses lied, the newspapers and news commentators lied. I felt heat from him, a fire that moved me without understanding its source. He was special and I wanted to be an adult like him with passions, excited and knowledgeable about things like a saxophone solo. He accepted my adoration, treating my comments with attention and respect I was not used to from any adult. He took me to the museum, to a ball game, to the fights. Our boxer lost.

I heard stories about him. He had been drafted but refused to salute or say "sir." He was beaten, spent time in stockade, escaped the army by chopping off part of his foot. He would not bend to the government, but he joined the Merchant Marine, was torpedoed at least once. When the war ended, he'd had enough of life at sea. The stories I heard from my grandma or casually told by Eddy himself made him ever more romantic in my eyes. I thought of myself as a rebel like him.

Harry had married Betsy on impulse as he was about to be shipped overseas. She was an East Sider; we were all Westies. He returned from the Marines to divorce her. His marriage to Shirley had ended after three years when she sued him for adultery. She got the few wedding presents and he kept his guitar. He had never actually lived with his second wife, Betsy, so the divorce was simple. He then shook the chemical dust of Detroit from his shoes and moved to California.

He wrote Eddy that the living was good and there were lots of jobs, so Eddy moved to LA, where they shared a bachelor bungalow. Harry worked on the railroad. One of the few things he thought of sending me during those years was a fireman's cap with a union button still attached. Mother wrote him regularly and occasionally he sent a postcard of palm trees or the Brown Derby. Eddy got a job dismantling hot cars in a chop shop. He sent a photo back to Pearl of the two of them standing shoulder to shoulder on a beach in skin-tight bathing suits—Harry in black and Eddy in red—darkened by the sun and grinning widely. Eddy was a few inches taller. Two women in one-piece bathing suits lay on a blanket just behind them in poses imitating pinups, arms crooked behind their heads and busts jutting forward and up like rockets about to launch. Pearl found the photo upsetting and mumbled about *kurvehs* (whores) in Yiddish. "And what was wrong with his wife, that I picked out for him myself? A good Jewish *balabosteh*. Mother of his darling girls."

Even at sixteen I could easily figure out that a good housewife would not appeal to Eddy. If he was ever truly in love, I never knew about it. He had male friends, especially my brother, to whom he was far more loyal than he ever was to any woman. I think he always had something going, but it felt as if all women were interchangeable. Yet he was always good to me. I was in another category. He told me I had a good brain and I should use it. When we spoke, he was always warning me about men, how if I didn't watch my step, they'd use and abandon me. Since one of my central goals in life was to be free and independent, I didn't take his warnings too seriously.

"You don't understand how it is with men. You make yourself cheap. If you can get the milk free, why buy the cow?"

"I am not some fucking cow!"

"If you talk like that, you'll cheapen yourself. You'll sound like a street kid or a whore."

As if he didn't say *fuck* every other sentence. I was furious with him. Like my mother, he couldn't imagine a life for a woman who wasn't a wife or a whore. We didn't speak again (on the phone of course) for two months. All through high school we'd have these late night conversations—not only because of the three hour time difference but because the long distance rates were cheaper then. I had the room that had been Harry's and then Eddy's, so after my parents went to bed, I pulled the phone into my room in case he called.

I remember one postcard Harry sent Mother showing the Hollywood Park racetrack. He had scrawled on the back "This is one great place. Saw Gary Cooper betting twenty dollars on the fourth race. Won a trifecta!" A week later a gift arrived from him, a little round spiny cactus planted in a cart pulled by a gaudily painted burro. I don't remember the ball of spines ever growing but it survived in the kitchen window for as long as I can remember.

In 1959 I followed the family migration to California. At that time, there were cheap lodgings in San Francisco; my neighborhood was a motley mix of musicians, writers, hairdressers, painters, of Japanese and Italians and Blacks and disaffected youth. It smelled of fish, canning tomatoes, and chocolate, and the train came down the middle of the street bringing produce for the canneries to deal with. I rented a studio so called that fronted on the tracks. I had a battered '51 Hudson (my father hated the big three carmakers: Ford was an anti-Semite and supported Hitler; GM had crushed the workers' strikes; I never got straight about Chrysler; but we always had off-brand cars) but I walked to work, tending bar at a local watering hole. I could never get off weekends but I got the other bartender Tim to cover for me Monday through Wednesday nights. I drove down to LA to see my favorite brother and my favorite uncle. And of course to see LA. My images of that city were formed by movies and I expected palm trees and glamour. I had heard about the smog but I figured, growing up in Detroit I'd be used to it, but this gray stuff burned my eyes and my lungs. It didn't feel like air but some other medium. I couldn't even see the mountains I knew were there surrounding us. There were miles and miles of little houses, of stores and small factories and car dealerships and eateries and then more and more miles of the same. There didn't seem to be any end to it, as if it stretched all the way to Mexico.

My brother was a big surprise. On the hottest days he wore a long sleeved shirt to cover his tattoos. He was selling real estate in a development way out in the desert near the Salton Sea, that weird accidental salt lake. He had a little house with an oil well pumping two houses away, the rig dressed up with a chicken head on it. He had divorced another wife I never met and now he had a girlfriend who lived in a lavish house up in the hills with a kidney-shaped swimming pool surrounded by the palm trees I'd expected. She was a widow a few years older than Harry, with two half-grown kids. Obviously there was money. Harry insisted, "This one is different. This is the right woman for me. The fourth time is the charm. I know what I want and she's all of it."

It's true, she was entirely different from his other wives or girlfriends. They had all come from backgrounds like ours and were what he now referred to as "common." He'd somehow acquired a GDS, but he referred to his college days at some vague midwestern school. His time in the brig was abolished and he was proud to have served as a Marine, wearing a button and actively engaged in whatever ex-Marines did when they hung out in their club.

I asked him about Eddy and he looked at me blankly as if he had never heard of him. I kept pressing him, and he finally gave me an address—"If he's still living there. He moves a lot. Can't pay the rent."

"He's not working?"

"Got himself into a hole. Big debts to bookies." Harry shrugged. "He's a loser."

"You used to be best buddies. For years and years."

Harry slicked back his hair over his new balding spot on the crown of his head. "A wise man knows when to cut loose. Eddy would have brought me down to his level. Forget about him. He always said you were smart, so show some smarts. Forget you ever knew him."

Of course I didn't. I found the address, in the Mexican section over a taco joint, but Eddy was long gone. The woman at the cash register in the eatery was cagey at first but finally responded to my high school Spanish. "He got busted for trying to pass bad checks . . . But he never stung us."

"Do you know where he is now?"

"Doing five at Chino."

When I managed to go see him, it was my first time visiting somebody in prison, though by no means my last. The drill was new to me, dumping everything in one of those little receptacles before they buzz you in. The endless wait in a room filled with prisoners visiting with their families. He wasn't a violent or high-risk prisoner, so there was none of that speaking through a glass wall like you see on TV. The children were running around screaming, the wives were clutching their hands in their laps, worrying, leaning on the little gray bolted down metal tables. Noisy, nervous laughter, occasionally a crying fit. I waited for close to an hour.

Eddy was gaunt and grayish coming toward me. He had a bruise on his cheek. His eyes were bright teal in his weathered face. He looked ten years older than Harry.

He was obviously surprised to see me. "You shouldn't have come."

"Why not? You're still my favorite uncle."

"You got no taste." He laughed then and for a moment I saw his old spirit. I noticed two of the fingers on his left hand were crooked, as if they had been broken and never properly set. "So you come all the way out here to see me? How's your mom?"

"Still cleaning houses at her age. I send her a little when I can." I explained I was living in San Francisco, no, had never married and didn't plan to in this life. He didn't seem surprised.

He had never remarried, but he told me he had a kid with a Mexican woman, a four-year-old Pablo, Paul, answered to both names. He corrected himself. Five now. He fished out a photo and showed me. I was half shocked he actually kept the photo on his person, as he'd shown little interest in his ex-wife's two daughters.

"When I get out, I'm gonna make it right for him. He's a good kid."

He didn't like that I was tending bar. "That's no way to meet decent guys."

"It's a good way to make money. I get great tips." I didn't tell him I was going to school part-time to get my degree in psych. I figured I'd heard so many hard luck stories I might as well get paid for counseling lost souls. He said he was coming up for a parole hearing in eighty-five days. He was counting them, of course. I said, "Let me know how it goes. I'll come visit you if you get out."

"Just give me a couple of weeks to get straight and settled."

I felt closer to Eddy than to my brother, I don't know exactly why. After all, I was striving and straining too, taking those courses aimed at hoisting me up into the middle class as Harry was remaking his past to suit the present and future he wanted. He felt fake to me—but hadn't I worked on my accent? Maybe I thought Eddy was more genuine. More of who we all were under the faked education and pretenses. Whatever the reason, I stayed in closer touch with Eddy than with my brother.

I was kind of surprised he managed to finesse the parole board; it wasn't like him. In the past he would have purposely shocked them, questioned their right to pass judgment on him, but obviously, he really wanted to get out of the can. He sent me his address on a postcard of the Hollywood sign. He was back in the Mexican ghetto, said he'd seen Pablo but Luisa had a new man living with them.

I arranged to drive down the next Tuesday, although I warned him he'd have to put me up and I could only stay the one night. It was hot on the drive down, even with all the windows open—the breeze that blew in could have toasted bread. Burned it more likely. Even with sunglasses, the glare gave me a headache, so I wasn't in the best of moods when I crossed LA to his neighborhood, taking the wrong expressway, doubling back and then missing the exit.

With only average difficulty, I found his street and his block—little houses crammed together with a vacant lot where a house had burned down leaving charred earth in the middle of the block. I could see the address he'd given me—a little stucco house, a paved yard in front with a jacked-up Ford and a pickup parked—but there were three police cars out front with their lights flashing. Was he enough of a schlemiel to get busted again already? I had a brief impulse to turn around and go back.

I drove around the corner and parked on the next street. Then cautiously I walked back. A knot of local people had gathered across the street and I joined them. I asked in English and then in my high school Spanish, "*¿Qué pasa?*" "What's up?"

Nobody answered me at first, then an old lady with dyed orange hair sticking out of a bandana asked, "You know him?"

I don't know why I answered "Eddy?"

She nodded and a cold gurgle of apprehension started in my belly. "He's my uncle."

She sighed and nodded again. I started to ask what the police were doing when an ambulance came shrieking around the far corner. "*Veinteocho minutos,*" someone in the crowd said. "*Tarde como siempre. Cochinos.*"

When the medics brought down a stretcher I burst through the yellow tape. "That's my uncle," I said. I saw Eddy's face, pale, distorted, unconscious. I could see blood soaking his chest.

After a brief argument with the medics, I found out where they were taking him. I wanted to climb in the ambulance, but the cops took hold of me for questioning. They held me for an hour asking me all about some burglary of a liquor store and Eddy's associates, shoving their faces into mine, shaking me by the shoulder (it was sore for a couple of days), taking turns threatening me, shouting that I was lying. Finally I was able to persuade them I was down from San Francisco for the day. I put on a dumb and flighty act. After they let me go, a couple of the watchers were friendlier, having seen the cops roughing me up. They told me he had been stabbed and they told me where the hospital was.

I drove there as fast as I could. Eddy was in surgery. I sat in a plastic chair for three hours drinking coffee from a machine. At least they called it coffee. I'd call it ostrich piss. Anyhow, I waited. For what? A doctor finally came out and told me Eddy had passed. I called Harry to tell him. Didn't get hold of him till I was back in San Francisco. He was silent for a bit and then grunted. "I couldn't find out how it happened," I said. "I can't believe he's gone. Just like that."

"Better not to know." Then quietly he hung up, leaving me with nothing but a dial tone. I got a postcard a month later inviting me to his wedding. Eddy's murder was never solved. I wondered if anybody tried.

Lost Pages from
the Book of Judith

Kenneth Wishnia

In the third year of the reign of True-Man son of Ish-Emeth horsemen from the northern lands swept down from the frostbitten heights and swarmed over the plains like a bitter wind until they reached the borders of the broken land. Their leaders were determined to blot out the name of the people who lived by the shores of the great river. And so into the battle she plunged, this holy daughter of Israel.

א

It sounded like buckshot at first.

A volley of small missiles strafed the vessel's metallic hide and hammered at the windows, driven by a punishing wind from the gorge. A girl screamed a few rows behind her, and Judy felt a sudden warm wetness fill her lap as red-faced savages rocked her protective shell from side to side. Bright fall colors swirled around the natives' crazed red eyes as they howled for blood.

"I'm so sorry, dearie," said the elderly spinster dabbing at Judy's thighs with a soiled lace handkerchief to wipe up the half-bottle of warm Coca-Cola she had spilled on Judy's only good coat. Judy raised her arms to keep her white cotton gloves from getting stained. The old woman's face was pocked and pitted like an eighty-year-old slice of stale white bread, and she didn't sound the least bit sorry as she quoted the Gospel on the need to forgive "seventy times seven times."

The eight-hour bus ride had taken Judy through Scranton, then north along the ragged state routes, hitting every rut in the road as the other passengers prattled on about how all the pushy, ill-mannered city boys were fouling the water up here in God's country, till she felt like punching a hole in the roof just to get a breath of fresh air. And now she was being thrust headfirst into a primitive ritual presided over by feverish idolaters in purple-and-gold skullcaps, and all she wanted to do was grab hold of the steering wheel and drive the bus straight back to civilization.

A tribe of bloodthirsty pagans assailed her eardrums, chanting the same crude syllables over and over, then an oblong projectile slammed into the bus and shattered, rattling her nerves. And she wondered if there was some way to appease them, as she had done on the first day of kindergarten a dozen years before, when a taunting refrain had sent her home in tears, determined to change her name from the traditional *Yehudith* to the Americanized *Judith*.

Then she saw their rhythmic incantation spelled out on a purple-gold jersey and the inarticulate wailing coalesced with sudden clarity into the name *Waechtler*, which they pronounced:

"Wax-ler! Wax-ler! Wax-ler!"

"Oh, my stars," said the girl who had screamed before. "We beat the Orangemen!"

The whole bus erupted in cheers, raising the already high spirits of the celebrants battering the sides of the bus and hanging from the trees, purple-and-gold streamers trailing to the wind. As the underclassmen raised this Waechtler kid on their shoulders—the fullback from New Jersey had scored three touchdowns against Syracuse—their ominous Inquisitors' skullcaps transmuted into harmless freshman beanies, and the line of tap dancers in her stomach finally took a bow and exited the stage.

How could they get so worked up over a stupid *game*, she wondered, when an epic battle was looming? Hadn't the union boys advised the war vets returning from Europe and the Pacific to hold on to their guns for the coming conflict between the working class and a growing army of redbaiting reactionaries?

The bus rattled and died, disgorging its human cargo near the summit of College Hill. Judy was dragged along by the crowd, looking for Sammy among the host of revelers, aware of the spreading stain just below her waistline. Thank God her coat was made of dark, absorbent cloth. Her college interview clothes, proper and presentable, but still several notches below the plumage on display on *this* campus. She worked five days a week after classes on the street floor at Gimbels, perched behind the display cases in the glove department, helping gracious ladies try on gloves that cost four times what she would ever dream of paying for gloves even with the employee discount. So she knew the price of high-quality clothes, and played the demure salesgirl while studying radical labor history and forging alliances with the left-wing war vets who had the power to change the world and the courage to do it.

Wild ruddy faces surrounded her, upperclassmen screaming themselves hoarse, rich young toffs leaping and lurching in their crested blazers, tailored shirts coming loose. Some of the women had the men's gold-striped ties lashed around their heads, hair flying loose and socks falling down, swooning with the easy pleasure of not having to care about appearances that belongs only to the very rich and the very poor.

Judy's shoe crunched on broken glass. She bent to make sure the brown shards of a pint bottle of rye hadn't scratched the leather, when someone slapped her on the ass hard enough to throw her off balance. She nearly lacerated her knees on the broken glass, and she almost forgot where she was as she straightened up and spun around, ready to spit fire at the jerk who thought he could manhandle her as if she were a grocery store melon.

A blond-haired prep school grad with pale lips and glazed eyeballs was grinning stupidly at her, his teeth so perfectly white they were practically glowing.

Judy would have had a ready comeback for some groper on Flatbush Avenue or the BMT, but this well-heeled scion of the ruling class knew the terrain around here and she didn't, and he probably had a few hundred friends within hailing distance as well.

"Leave her alone, Chip!" admonished a girl with a frazzled blond perm, giving the boy a playful shove. She put her hands on her hips in a show of pretend jealousy, and the boy pulled her close and planted a sloppy wet kiss in the general area of her mouth.

Judy checked to make sure the wet spot wasn't showing. When she looked up, Sammy was bobbing through the crowd, a towering six-footer in a pea jacket, his dark curly hair tamed into a wavy pompadour with some kind of pomade or cream, struck at just that moment by the brilliant slanting light of the late afternoon sun.

She kept her midsection away from him as he hugged her, but he didn't seem to notice.

"What kept you?" he asked, lips buried in her hair, the stirrings of a six-week-old hunger humming beneath his words like a love song for her ears alone.

She smelled liquor on his breath, but it was a manly smell and she liked it on him. "Been celebrating the big victory?"

"Are you kidding? With these idiots?" he said, keeping his arm around her waist as he guided her through the boisterous crowd. "We've got our own party."

"Can anyone join this party?"

"I'll have to check with the steering committee, but I think I can get you in."

Sammy held her close as the fall colors danced in beautifully choreographed rhythm on the swaying branches overhead. A Romanesque clock tower with a high, pointed roof sparkled majestically in the falling light.

Sammy breathed in the crisp air, drinking in the stippled iridescence of the leafy quadrangle. "Ah—carotene, lycopene, xanthophyll!" he said, enraptured.

Judy smiled at her darling chemistry major's awkward attempt to capture the sublime poetry of this autumnal ballet. She had never seen such a gorgeous campus.

"Too bad you couldn't come up yesterday before all this *mishegas*," he said.

But her mother would never allow her to spend *Erev Shabbes* with her irreligious boyfriend, just like she would insist on a rabbi officiating at their wedding, when the time came.

"Hey frosh, where's your beanie?" A tennis bum in a blue blazer prodded Sammy with the butt of his racket.

"Must have lost it in all the excitement!"

The tennis bum smiled broadly as if he understood completely.

They didn't go in for this kind of nonsense in the city, where the fall semester's biggest rally had been organized in support of the janitors and cafeteria workers who were striking to form a union. She had addressed the rally wearing white gloves, because that was expected of her. She felt overdressed then and she felt overdressed now, but the gloves had helped preserve her dignity when a group of law students tried to disrupt the rally by dumping buckets of ice water on them from a third-floor window.

A flicker of movement caught her eye, and she turned just as a man dangling from a tree burst into flames. The body was hanging from a rope, thick tongues of fire engulfing its tattered clothing in an instant as a mob of students roared with glee, their dark silhouettes outlined by the bright flames.

Oh my God, they're lynching somebody! she thought for an instant before the flames chewed up the ragged orange clothes and chunks of flaming straw fell harmlessly to the ground.

Sammy squeezed her waist protectively as they weaved between the closely packed bodies near the library.

She spied a small mob roaming the quadrangle, intimidating members of the Young People's Socialist League and other dissenters, and scattering their fliers underfoot.

❧

Tell me, their leader demanded, who are these people of the plains, who dare to put obstructions in our path? Where do their loyalties lie?

❧

Judy's pulse was still racing from the shock of seeing the burning effigy as she raised her eyes skyward and beheld the imposing row of Greco-Roman philosophers' names etched beneath the library's topmost cornice. Holding up one end of the frieze, a toga-clad woman representing Knowledge looked out over a rectangular stretch of grass occupied by neat rows of semicylindrical metal structures.

"What are those—spaceships?" she asked, the blood still pounding in her temples.

"Temporary housing for the veterans."

Temporary? The last bombs of the war had been dropped more than three years earlier, on a date that was already being consigned to the history books.

Sammy said, "Yeah, now that the last of the GI Bill bunch are going to graduate, I guess they don't see the point of moving them to permanent housing."

The sun had just slipped below the tree line, and the corrugated metal roofs reflected the stratosphere's diffuse magenta-and-purple glow.

"Some of them are married," Sammy added.

Judy pictured the war veterans and their young brides trying to recover some sense of normalcy after all they'd been through while living in drafty government-issue Quonset huts.

Howls of laughter cut through her dreamy tableau of Spartan domesticity. A group of frat boys with identical crew cuts had commandeered a section of pathway in front of the Phi Alpha Kappa house, chanting *drink drink drink* as a freshman pledge downed four successive shots of cheap bourbon, climbed onto a wobbly chair and recited the opening lines of Lewis Carroll's "Jabberwocky."

He made it up to *the mome raths outgrabe* before his tongue betrayed him and the frat boys grabbed him and dunked him head first into a rain barrel, held him under for a good ten seconds, pulled him up so he could catch his breath, then dunked him again.

They repeated the ordeal once more while a man in a dark wool suit and a short-brimmed hat whom somebody called Dean Whitman stood by watching all this with a local police officer who was probably there to make sure the Ag School boys didn't get too rowdy and drown somebody.

When the frat boys pulled the freshman up for the third time, he doubled over and barfed up a voluminous quantity of liquor and rainwater onto the green while holding his soggy purple-and-gold beanie in place with one hand. Laughs and backslaps erupted as he came up smiling and another fresh-faced pledge got ready to take up the challenge.

"Hey, what'd I tell you about wearing your beanie?" said a lean and muscular frat boy with dirty-blond hair who looked like he was on the sculling crew.

Sammy tried to squeeze by and Judy didn't realize the crew man was addressing him until another refugee from *The Great Gatsby* waved a pennant on a bamboo cane at them and said, "Quite right, old boy. Where's your team spirit?"

The crew man stepped forward, puffing up his chest: "I said, hey, city boy, where's your frigging beanie?"

"Yeah, Vishinsky," said another blue-blooded flag-waver through clenched teeth, his fraternity pin glinting in the fading light as he yanked on Sammy's arm to separate him from Judy and cut off his right flank. "You better decide if you're one of us, or not," he snarled, the harsh words contrasting with his upper-crust Yankee accent.

"It's Vinchevsky," said Sammy. "Andrei Vishinsky is the Deputy Soviet Foreign Minister."

"You mean the sonofabitch who won't lift the Berlin blockade?" said the crew man, anchoring himself in Sammy's path. "Is he your cousin or something?"

"We're not related." Sammy tried to step around them.

"All you people are related."

"Which people? Russians or Jews?" Sammy tried to go the other way. Blocked again.

"Frigging city boys who don't know their place, that's who," said the crew man, shoving Sammy toward the barf-soaked grass.

Judy's heart fluttered like it always did when the *grube yungen* were fighting over territory on Avenue J, before the ethnic divisions were smoothed over, however briefly, by the war effort.

"All right, boys, that's enough," said Dean Whitman, as if he were breaking up a friendly game of marbles. "There's a *lady* present."

The damp-haired freshman sniggered.

"Too bad you can't get your commie friends in the rag trade to hire some muscle to protect you," said the crew man.

Sammy couldn't come up with a snappy comeback to that accusation, since he would have to admit that his beloved ILGWU-AFL had been caught using strong-arm tactics to intimidate the workers in a couple of nonunion shops on West Thirty-Fifth Street in the heart of the Garment District. It looked bad in the press, but what else could they do? The bosses had the mayor, the governor, and both houses of Congress in their pockets, and the workers were losing ground faster than General Lee at Gettysburg.

Sammy faked a move to the right, then cut left and darted through a hole in their defensive line, leaving Judy all alone with the guys smirking at her till she went after him and blended in with the gathering darkness.

❧

The horsemen slaked their thirst and poured out libations to appease the hands of the invisible one. They exulted in the righteousness of their cause, and boasted of their strength in numbers and their superior weaponry.

❧

The sun was down and a cool breeze swept across the indigo skies, chilling the last bit of damp cloth on the front of Judy's coat. She caught up with Sammy as he was crossing the street and looped her arm through his. His stride was swift and strong and it was hard to keep up.

They marched along in silence past a brightly lit drugstore, a bar called the Hollow Furnace full of noisy football fans, and a vacant storefront shrouded in gloom. Her heels clacked loudly on the sidewalk as she searched for a way to soothe Sammy's wounded pride.

This big old melting pot can burn you pretty badly, sometimes, she thought, recalling the years in grammar school when she was required to wear red, white, and blue on assembly day so the principal, a proud member of the pro-Nazi German-American Bund, could harangue the mixed multitude of Micks, Wops, and Yids about the virtues of national unity.

Her voice spilled into the void between them like a bright stream of water arcing into a bottomless gorge, confiding how, when her older sister graduated from high school right before the war, she was told not to bother applying to the phone company because they didn't hire Jews. So it was all right for Jewish men to operate industrial sewing machines and printing presses like her uncles in the ILGWU and the ITU, but it was *not* all right for Jewish women to put on white blouses, pin their hair up and ask, "What number, please?" for the New York Telephone Company.

Of course it was a step up from the life her family had fled in Tsarist Russia, which denied them basic rights as citizens. But there was still a long list of hotels, law firms, medical schools, country clubs, and entire communities across this great land that had yet to open their doors to the children of Israel.

The sky was now a deep violet, and the dusky stretch of sidewalk widened into a vast field of blackness as they drew near the hulking shadow of a darkened movie theater. Her eyes were just growing used to the darkness when the marquee lit up like an air raid beacon.

A pair of pale statues stood frozen beneath the lights, dark hollows under their eyelids and cheekbones where their lips should have been.

Sammy stopped dead in his tracks. In the harsh glare of the marquee, the grim messengers' matching crew cuts were two slabs of unpolished granite.

The theater was showing a mismatched double feature, with *Abbott and Costello Meet Frankenstein* serving as the lowbrow comic lead-in to *Cry of the City* with Victor Mature and Richard Conte and a hot young babe named Shelley Winters who looked like she could have been one of Judy's cousins. Sammy actually looked a little bit like Victor Mature—that big hunk of man—with the same strong forehead and sharp jaw. His nose was just as prominent but a little softer, a little rounder.

"What do you want, Buckley?" Sammy said stiffly.

At least he showed no fear, Judy thought, with a welcome sense of relief.

The first statue spoke: "Simpkin's out looking for you," he said, deep pits forming in the tight mask of his face as his shapeless mouth formed the words.

The *Coming Attractions* showcase announced that next week they'd be showing *Red River* with John Wayne and Montgomery Clift—another sensitive young man who often found himself playing a tough guy because the world demanded it of him.

"Okay," said Sammy. "Thanks."

The statue's unseen lips moved again: "Why don't you just wear the damn thing already before this—"

But Sammy had already plunged into the night, the darkness closing in around him like the frigid waters of the North Atlantic.

❧

Sammy's dorm was a creaky former barracks that was thrown together when the country needed men in uniform as fast as they could make the uniforms. (Judy's uncles had probably done most of the piecework.) Cheap drywall divided the cavernous space into ten double rooms per floor.

The party was still going on when Sammy burst into his room, if you can call three guys with an open bottle of bourbon and some paper cups a party. Their faces were shining in happy anticipation of adding a couple of fresh merrymakers to their ranks, but a cloud passed over their features when Sammy planted himself like a fixed bayonet in the middle of the room and told them what was brewing.

"I knew it would come to this," said Ozzie Baumgarten, Sammy's roommate, a moonfaced fellow graduate of Brooklyn Tech.

Judy introduced herself as Sammy threw his heavy jacket on the narrow cot, scattering a handful of leaflets that had been lying on the thin gray blanket. Sammy pulled back the shade about two inches and peered out the window like Two Gun Crowley checking for coppers.

"There's a bunch of them sneaking through the alley," he announced.

"How many?" Ozzie asked.

"Enough to surround the place and cut off the water supply, if that's part of their strategy."

The room was warm and close. Judy took off her gloves and started unbuttoning her coat, but changed her mind when she saw the caramel-colored stain in the middle of her blouse.

"We've got to face them down," Sammy said, his fading alcoholic haze turning brittle with cold determination.

"We're gonna need more guys," said Zack Rosenzweig, a skinny engineering student who stood a full head shorter than Sammy even though he was wearing basketball sneakers.

"Jeez, you'd think they were preparing for a siege," said Ozzie, peeking out the window.

"Then we're *definitely* gonna need more guys," Zack said, wiping his hands on his faded khakis. "I better go before they get out the battering ram."

The four comrades debated their plan of action, and Zack was dispatched on a mission to round up more troops, leaving the big room feeling awfully empty. Judy sat on Sammy's cot, wondering what the young draftees had felt as they lay there staring at the high ceiling, waiting to receive their orders to ship out across the wind-whipped seas to face Hitler's Panzers or Tojo's Kamikazes.

The fourth conspirator was Al Feinberg, a genial red-haired kid from the Bronx, who had spent most of the day down in Binghamton handing out leaflets to the shoe workers coming off the Saturday morning shift. Only a couple dozen workers had cared enough to stop and listen.

Judy turned over one of the leaflets, which announced an evening of songs and speeches by some big-name Negro artists in a nearby glen to raise money for John Santo's defense fund—the Transport Workers Union's Romanian-born organizer, whom the Immigration Service in Washington had just targeted with deportation proceedings.

※

The great plains trembled beneath their chariots as they raided the mills and threshing floors, demolished the tents of meeting and cut down the idols. They seized the scrolls and made a bonfire that sent such a thick column of smoke into the sky that the sun hid its face for seven days, and they declared that none should be worshipped but the invisible hand that controls all.

※

"Next thing you know, they'll want us all to wear red stars," Sammy said, bitterly.

"Simpkin would be all for it," said Ozzie.

"Who's Simpkin?" Judy asked.

Sammy said, "Just because our parents were working in sweatshops while their parents were playing polo at restricted country clubs—"

"So take it to the Supreme Court," said Al.

"Not *this* Supreme Court," said Ozzie.

"Who's Simpkin?" Judy asked again.

Sammy turned to face her as if she had interrupted a summit meeting at the Yalta Conference.

"The dorm monitor." He turned back to his comrades.

"Maybe we should give up before things get worse," said Al.

"Too late. Things just got worse," said Ozzie, looking out the window.

"You mean, he's in charge of this dorm?"

Sammy turned to her, his face flushed. The atmosphere in the room crackled. Maybe she should have spent the night in a motel.

"What can I do to help?" she said, offering him the full measure of her compassion, the same way she handled difficult customers at Gimbels.

"Maybe this'll come in handy."

The man standing the doorway was a sturdy-looking Negro whose medium-toned skin was a bit lighter, with slightly finer facial features, than Judy was used to seeing in the shadows of the Brighton Line El. He was carrying a heavy iron crowbar, which he set down by the doorframe.

Sammy's face lit up like a charged particle in a magnetic field. Judy felt an odd buzzing in her chest, around her solar plexus, and it wasn't from the spilled soda, unless the secret ingredient in Coke is a trace amount of jealousy.

"What are you staring at?" The man addressed her. His dark blue pants had a sharp military-style crease in them and his black shoes glistened like polished gemstones. "Not all the lefties in this town are Jewish, you know."

"Yeah, one of them's a Negro," said Al.

"Now just a minute, Mr. Feinberg. You know that just ain't so. There happen to be *four* of us."

Sammy couldn't wait to introduce Judy to Roy Marquis, a college senior and a decorated combat veteran, and fill him in on what was happening. Judy stood up to greet him, but Roy kept his eyes level with her chin as he shook her hand lightly.

"Are you living in one of the spaceships?" Judy asked.

Roy raised his eyebrows and gave her a look as if she might have just stepped off a spaceship herself.

"She means the Quonset huts," Sammy said.

"They look just like alien crafts to me."

"Had to get off-campus housing," Roy said flatly.

"Is it hard to find in this town?"

"Harder for some than for others, I guess. Now, Sammy, you just sit tight and I'll go round up some more troops."

Roy charged into the hallway, nearly knocking over the cleaning lady who was coming through with a mop and a pail of soapy water. He apologized—twice—but she still gave him the stink eye as he passed. Maybe he should have apologized *three* times, but it probably wouldn't have made any difference.

Judy stood there waiting for Sammy to put his arm around her and tell her everything was going to be all right, but instead Sammy paced around like a nervous boxer, punching the air with his fists as if he were getting ready to go three rounds with Sugar Ray Robinson.

"There's enough of us to hold them off if we just stick together," he said, pounding out the words as if he could make them come true by sheer emphasis alone.

"You need to get out of here," said Ozzie. "Get some air or something."

"Or hop a bus to Mexico," said Al.

"No. I'm not running."

The iron bar was in Sammy's hands.

"Take it easy, Mr. Clark Kent," Ozzie warned. "You're no Man of Steel."

"He's right, Sammy," Judy said, stepping in close to stay his arm, if need be. "You can win more battles with a sit-down strike than with violence."

"That stuff only works in fables—"

"It worked in Flint, Michigan."

"Besides, these days even Superman has turned his back on his socialist principles," said Al.

"Then why does he still wear a red cape?" said Ozzie, keeping the joke going.

"To keep away the Evil Eye, of course."

"You read too many comic books."

"Yeah, next thing you know I'll be stealing hubcaps and running with street gangs."

"You want me to go get the Dean of Students?" Judy offered.

Sammy snorted in disgust.

"You want me to call the cops? Tell me—where's the nearest pay phone?"

Hearing the *bebop-bop-bam* of footsteps on the stairs, Sammy gripped the iron bar white-knuckle tight and shifted his weight a few inches backward, his right leg coiled tight and ready to launch.

Judy had spent the whole bus ride up imagining what it would be like to lose herself in the raw, unquenchable emotions of their first night together in six weeks. Needless to say, she had something a bit more intimate in mind.

A few syllables of Zack's distinctive Brooklyn dialect were enough to disarm the spring-loaded set-up, and Judy let out a breath she didn't realize she was holding as Zack came back with a couple of gangly Jewish conscripts wearing soot-stained sweaters. Not exactly an army of Maccabean warriors, or even the benchwarmers on Hammerin' Hank Greenberg's ball club, but Sammy set the iron bar down next to the wastebasket by the door and welcomed the newcomers with open arms.

"We snuck in through the coal chute," Zack boasted, as if he'd just slipped across enemy lines and single-handedly blown up a munitions depot.

Judy sank onto Sammy's cot as the six-man squad huddled to discuss the best tactics to use against the opposing lineup. She felt like a spectator in the back row, like in the Russian language class she was taking at Columbia, where she was the only woman in a room full of future military intelligence officers and CIA agents who never turned to look at her when she had something to say.

Her parents had wanted her to go to business school and get a $35-a-week job as a bookkeeper. Working at Gimbels paid for tuition and books, but her mother was annoyed that she wasn't contributing more to the household, like her older sister and her husband, who were moving out of Brooklyn now that the wartime housing shortage was over and staking a claim in Fresh Meadows, Queens, deep in the heart of the white Christian nation.

❧

See how arrogant they are! We will strike them down, the slave with the ruler. They will pay dearly for rebelling against their overlords.

❧

Judy came off the sidelines and took Sammy's hand. Was there no hope of compromise, of brokered agreement, of working with the moderate wing of the opposition? But the opposition had no moderate wing, and the stakes were high: This was about freedom versus tyranny. It was about democracy versus fascism. It was about the kind of world they would leave for their children. Judy's heart swelled with love and admiration as Sammy summoned the spirit of his namesake, the prophet Samuel, railing against inequality and injustice, and so much was going on that they barely noticed the cleaning woman coming through emptying the wastepaper baskets until they heard the steady *tramp tramp tramp* of feet marching up the stairs in unison.

At least the prophet Samuel and his followers could count on the unfailing protection of a jealous God. Such miracles were hard to come by nowadays, but Judy found herself praying for one anyway.

Sammy reached for the iron bar and saw that it was gone as a horde of faces made ugly with hate filled the doorway. The door had remained open the whole time Judy had been there, as if daring the marauders to step inside. Now they stood on the threshold, packed as tight as a bundle of kindling.

And suddenly the spacious room felt very small indeed. The ceiling seemed to have dropped three feet, and the atmosphere hummed with infrasonic frequencies like the inside of a vacuum tube about to get hit with fifty amps of current.

The group of vigilantes seemed surprised that Sammy had raised a posse of his own, as if that was against the rules or something. But the rest of his teammates fell back, leaving Sammy exposed and alone in the middle of the room. The big Ag School bruisers liked that.

This one's left eye twitched.

That one licked his lips.

This one's fingers fumbled with a thread coming out of his shirtsleeve.

Sammy stood there like a dime store wristwatch with its hairspring wound so tight Judy swore she could hear the escape wheel spinning wildly.

Judy opened her mouth to speak: "Listen—"

As if she had thrown a switch, they charged in like a phalanx of Roman soldiers, a pair of beefy guys with standard issue crew cuts leading the pack. The heavier one must have been Simpkin, who went for Sammy's legs, and the others followed, including Buckley and his lookalike, the granite goons who had tried to warn Sammy that this day was coming.

It took eight of them to take him down, four of them just to hold down Sammy's head and shoulders, while Sammy's comrades faded into the wallpaper, their faces frozen in a combination of fear and fascination, like extras on a movie set waiting for the director to tell them what to do.

"What's wrong with you?" Judy scolded them. "Don't just stand there like a bunch of *shleppers*. Do something!"

"At least the girl's got guts," the crew man chuckled, his wavy blond locks dripping sweat on the slippery linoleum.

"You're going to need your jaw wired shut when we're done with you, Vishinsky," said the one with the frat pin and the mainline WASP accent.

"So I can learn to talk like you rich pricks?"

"Cover his mouth, will ya?" one of the Ag School boys growled.

The short beefy guy clamped his hand over Sammy's face.

Judy sprang forward, seized by the instinct to protect her mate, but the flailing fists and legs kept her at bay.

"What kind of ignoramuses are you?" she berated them. "Don't you know you can get expelled for this?"

For a moment she thought Sammy was going to bite the beefy guy's hand, but she held back when she saw that once the big guys had him, they really didn't seem to know what to do with him.

Then the one they called Simpkin pulled a pair of scissors out of his back pocket, grabbed a clump of Sammy's hair, and started to cut off the offending locks.

Judy launched herself into the fray, grabbing Simpkin by the hair while her other hand went for his wrist.

"No, wait—!"

"Don't—!" Zack and one of his friends broke from their trance and rushed in to stop her.

But Simpkin's hair was too short to get a good grip on and he jerked free, so Judy used her nails, elbows and teeth and somehow yanked the scissors out of his hands. She tried to stab him in the neck but the scissors were slick with hair cream and nearly slipped free and Sammy's friends were pulling on her, and Simpkin cursed and backhanded her as hard as he could. The scissors arced toward his neck a second time and Sammy's friends kept getting in the way when a foot or an elbow slammed into her jaw, knocking her backward. She banged her head on the iron bed frame and cringed, curling up for a moment, her lip torn and bleeding.

Simpkin wiped the gunk off the blades and went back to hacking away at clump after clump of Sammy's dark wavy hair, giving him a mangy crew cut of his own.

Judy felt the side of her mouth, and her fingers came away streaked with blood. She probed the inside with her tongue and realized that she had bitten into her cheek.

Zack and his friend with the soot-smeared sweater reached out to help her, but she pulled away from them.

Sammy's other comrades receded so far into the background they could have been figures painted on the walls of an Egyptian tomb, and there were only a few handfuls of hair left standing on Sammy's head when the one with the fraternity pin said,

"Let's leave a fringe."

"Huh?"

The scissors hovered in the air, momentarily unsure of themselves. Then the penny dropped: It would mark him. It would be a sign unto others.

The vigilantes loosened their grips and sat back to admire their work.

The air started flowing back into the room, but the inrushing gust of air reacted with the charged filament and oxidized it, leaving it dangling, charred and dead, and the vacuum tube silently imploded, bits of shattered glass drifting down like snowflakes that crunched underfoot.

It was only when Judy tried to wipe her mouth with her handkerchief that she noticed that her hand was bleeding too. A single slash ran right through her palm from the heart line to the Mount of Venus. She had no idea at what point in the struggle it had happened.

If Hollywood had written this script, she thought, the cavalry would have arrived just in the nick of time. But by the time Roy trooped in with a couple of his buddies, Jimmy Weinstein and Ruby Diamond, they saw that the assault was over.

One of the Ag School boys picked up a flier that had fluttered to the floor. "Boy, they're really scraping the bottom of the barrel. They even brought a nig—"

The frat pin guy cut him off.

Sammy raised his head off the floor.

Weinstein surveyed the scene—eight against one, five shrimpy guys who couldn't lick their weight in feathers, and a girl wrapping a blood-stained handkerchief around her hand.

Diamond stared at Sammy's crudely shorn skull and his eyes blazed with hatred—a deep hatred haunted by a darker impulse that Judy couldn't fathom, at first.

Weinstein kept his voice even. "Okay, you've had your fun. Now what say you Ag School boys get back to your own side of campus?"

"What say you friggin' pinkos go back to the Little Kremlin on College Avenue that you call home," said the crew man.

"Maybe later. It's a free country, you know. We can go wherever we want, when we want to."

"Yeah. For now . . ."

The vigilantes got to their feet and took their time dusting themselves off. They passed around the flier, nodding in some kind of code, until the last guy in line crushed it with his fist and stuffed it into his pocket.

Judy slipped between them, knelt on the scuffed linoleum and cradled Sammy's newly razed scalp in her arms, the blood congealing in the creases around her lips. She could practically feel the hope going out of him like a departing spirit leaving his body.

"And there's plenty more where that came from, Vishinsky," one of the Ag boys explained. "Especially if you try to bring any more of those commie niggers to our campus, like your boyfriend Paul Robeson and that Rustin guy."

"Say, you've been reading the papers," Roy said.

Simpkin offered his own advice: "People like you ought to be lined up against a wall and shot."

"Yeah, that's why we fought the war," Weinstein replied. "So punks like you could threaten us with the firing squad."

Those words went unanswered as the vigilantes walked the gauntlet between the three veterans. They paraded out single file, their laughter echoing throughout the drafty barracks. Judy glared at the rest of Sammy's so-called comrades, who stood around looking at their shoelaces and checking the sky for UFOs.

"Why don't you just lie down in the road and let them run right over you next time?"

"You've got to pick your battles," Al mumbled, to no one in particular.

Roy and Jimmy came forward and helped Sammy to his feet. Diamond held out his big rough hands and lifted Judy off the floor, ignoring the bloody slit in the middle of her right hand, and eased her onto the cot.

Everyone saw the brownish stains on her blouse, but nobody said a word. The veterans' faces were hard to read, as if their thoughts were thousands of miles away in the snowy forests of the Ardennes or the muddy swamps of the South Pacific. The president had issued an executive order integrating the armed forces back in July, but it was only a single step in a *very* long march—and Brooklyn had beaten him to the punch by more than a year, fielding an integrated team back in the spring of '47.

Ozzie looked around and added up the numbers—six comrades plus the girl and the three veterans: "Hey, we got a *minyen!*" he declared.

Judy put her arm around Sammy, and looked up at the three veterans. It seemed like somebody should say something, if only to fill the silence.

"Sorry we got here so late—" said Diamond.

"Where the hell did that iron bar go?" Sammy blurted out.

Ozzie stood there, his big moon face briefly eclipsed by a passing shadow, but he recovered quickly.

Al said, "Yeah, if you'd had it, you'd have given it to them good!"

"Just like Duke Snider hitting a triple!" Ozzie said, sounding so much like a radio broadcaster that Judy half-expected him to pause for station identification and sell them some Burma Shave.

Sammy just sat there smacking his fist into his palm and staring into the emptiness.

The veterans exchanged glances, as if they'd seen this kind of thing before in the faces of battle-weary GI's.

Nobody said anything for a moment.

Then Judy said something so softly they couldn't make it out at first.

They had to listen closely to catch it again: "Jackie Robinson had a better batting average than Duke Snider," she said in a shy, girlish whisper.

Her hand was still oozing blood.

Al stepped in to fill the void. "Yeah, Sammy, you really took one for the team."

Zack hung his head and sighed.

"Robinson hit more triples, too," Judy said quietly.

Sammy finally looked up at her battered face. "Looks like you just broke up a play at home yourself, kiddo."

Ozzie said, "Yeah, wasn't she something?"

The stubble on Sammy's crudely shorn scalp itched and tickled her nose as she kissed the exposed skin above his ear.

"At least we scored a couple hits for Brooklyn, didn't we?" Judy said.

"Sure, baby."

"Well, I'm from the Bronx," said Diamond, like a well-mannered dinner party guest trying to steer the conversation around an awkward subject. "So I guess that makes us crosstown rivals."

"Pittsburgh," Roy said. "But, you know, I heard some of the fans were throwing stuff on the field the day you guys started Jackie Robinson."

"Those must have been the Boston fans," said Judy.

Roy gave a little half-smile. "Well, not much point my sticking around now," he said. "You better get yourselves cleaned up."

"It was nice meeting you," said Judy, holding out her injured hand.

"Uh, yeah. Nice meeting you folks, too," he said, lightly squeezing her fingers.

The clang of an iron bar shattered the moment of peace. All eyes snapped toward the sound, but it was only the cleaning lady making her final rounds of the night.

"Found this while I was cleaning up," she said, dropping the useless weapon on the floor by the wastebasket.

"Huh," Sammy grunted, as if that explained everything.

"Nice to have people you can count on," said Diamond.

"Aah, what did you expect from a bunch of kids?" said Weinstein.

Roy gave Sammy a pat on the back. "He just means some folks aren't exactly ready for combat just yet. Now take care of yourselves, you hear? I gotta go. I'm supposed to be at our own little shindig down by the lake, you know, keeping an eye on things. Maybe I'll see you there later."

"Sure, Roy, sure."

Roy walked out past the cleaning lady, who squinted at him while her mop went *drip drip drip* on the worn linoleum.

"There goes our *minyen*," Ozzie said, snapping his fingers in mock disappointment.

Sammy turned to face his roommate, who might as well have been standing on the other side of the continental divide.

Judy could feel the pulse pounding in Sammy's skull, and she knew what his useless comrades were going to say before they opened their mouths about how they couldn't risk getting suspended for disorderly conduct because that would weaken the movement, and how it was better for one of them to take the hit rather than the whole group because the group was more important than any one member.

Words, words, words.

Sammy's strength was returning, along with something dark and brooding. Judy felt the barely suppressed rage boiling beneath his skin. A rage that would keep on burning inside him for a thousand years, it seemed.

Soon after, Judy went out into the night and followed the glow of the bonfires till she found the row of frat houses, which led her to Dean Whitman, who sneered at the ragged scar on her lip and told her that Sammy shouldn't have provoked the encounter, as he called it, and when Judy mentioned pressing charges she was told, You'll only make things worse, the college will look bad and all the Ag boys would hate your little troublemaker even more than they do already, so she should just forget about it and scoot on home like a good little girl.

But some of the boys had spread the word and soon enough a mob followed Roy to the green stretch of parkland where his people were having their own celebration, and what began as an attack on Roy and his kind quickly spread to include any black face within shouting distance, and pretty soon farmers and housewives were tipping over cars and their young sons were pelting fleeing women and children with rocks. Roy was knocked to the ground and beaten by a sea of white faces sputtering about subversives and undesirables and sending them back to where they came from and he saw the unmistakable flash of a badge on one of their chests as the blood started flowing and the tears ran and the fires raged and the glass was breaking all around him.

א

And the mountains shook to their depths, like water, for the Lord Almighty has thwarted them by a woman's hand. And the children of Israel set up watchtowers on the eastern shores of the great river and lit fires on the heights overlooking the harbor. And from that day till this, she watches and waits, this holy daughter of Israel, she watches and waits over the broken land.

The Legacy

Wendy Hornsby

The 8:32 pulled onto a siding at a packing plant a mile past Marysville to take on two carloads of canned peaches. As the train slowed, Elena pulled her small suitcase off the overhead rack and walked into the passageway between cars, ready to hop off when it was safe enough. Marysville was not a scheduled passenger stop, and there was no depot, but in Sacramento where Elena changed trains, the ticket agent told her that it was none of the railroad's business if a passenger decided to get off anywhere she damn well pleased as long as she didn't screw up the schedule by falling under the wheels.

The air outside was every bit as hot and muggy as it had been inside, but once Elena was clear of the train's exhaust, she felt a gentle evening breeze full of the earthy perfume of San Joaquin Valley farmland, a vast, flat, black expanse broken only by the dim glow of Marysville in the distance. As she picked her way along the tracks, headed back toward town, there was just enough light from the waning gibbous moon to reassure her that no one was following.

The tracks crossed a bridge over a broad, sluggish river and then coursed between a dirt levee and the scruffy backside of town: four blocks of railway and farm worker shacks, the decaying remnants of an old Chinatown, and a few shops, most of them shuttered for the night. The smell of food wafting through the open door of a chop suey house nearly made her faint, she was so hungry. She hadn't eaten since breakfast on the ship before it docked in San Francisco early that morning. Maybe, if service was fast, she could get a bowl of chop suey, though she was already late for her meeting.

Elena took a long look around before she made her way down a steep embankment to the street below, stumbling in the near-dark over rocks and refuse and gopher holes, weighing the risk of being seen by the wrong people against the demands of an empty stomach.

In shadows beside the restaurant, she set down her case to dump gravel from her shoes and get her bearings. When the front door opened, shooting light across the broken sidewalk, out of habit she edged deeper into the dark. Two men wearing farmers' denim coveralls and chambray work shirts came outside carrying beer bottles by the neck. They picked a place to lean against the stucco wall no more than ten feet from her.

"Damn good thing Eisenhower got the nomination," she heard the closer of them say as he pulled a pack of Lucky Strikes from his pocket. "Gonna need a general in the White House if the Russkies decide to invade us like they did Korea."

"That was the Chinese that invaded Korea," the other said, accepting a cigarette. "Not the Soviets."

"Same damn thing. You ask me, a commie's a commie. All o' them need a twelve bore to the brainpan." The first man paused to flame the end of his smoke. "The Reds, you know, they're like polio. They go after the young, suck 'em right in before they know any better."

"I don't know about that," the friend said. "But the guy riding shotgun for Ike this election, this Dick Nixon fella, he's a farm boy from downstate. That can only be good for guys like us."

"Nixon looks too soft to be a farmer. But he's a commie-hating vet, just like you and me, and that gets my vote."

When the first man flicked his match to the gutter, he spotted Elena and took a step toward her.

"Hey, girlie, kinda late for you to be out all alone, ain't it?" He gave her a good looking over, from her plain black oxfords to the dowdy cotton dress she found in a bin at Refugee Relief in Singapore. "You lost, honey?"

"No, I'm fine, thank you."

"You know where you're headed, huh?"

"I do."

"You be careful, hear? It's dark out here."

She picked up her case and walked on. She was a block away when she heard a third voice join the smokers. There was something about the tone of the newcomer's voice that worried her enough to make her quicken her pace. She turned at the corner and when a narrow, unlit alley opened to her right, she ducked in and slipped behind a rank of reeking trash bins to listen. Footsteps approached, a man walking briskly at first, then silence. He retreated a few steps, approached again, and turned into the alley. Elena hunkered down, hugging her case to her chest, and waited. Something—a cat, a rat?—scurried out from between the bins. Her pursuer let out a high-pitched, startled little squeal and hurried away again. When his retreating footsteps had faded to nothing, she risked coming out from her hiding place and continuing on.

The neighborhood began to improve the closer she got to D Street, Marysville's main business corridor. When she passed a tiny, very old wood-frame synagogue, she started counting the doors she passed. At the fourth door, she took another look around to make sure no one was watching before she knocked. The door opened only enough for the man inside to see her.

"You're Elena?"

"I am," she said. "Ted?"

He let her in.

"What took you so long?" The man, Ted, took her case from her and led her down a dark hallway to the windowless stockroom behind a closed jewelry store before he turned on a light. "I heard the train nearly an hour ago."

"Now I'm here."

He was younger than she expected him to be, early thirties, maybe. He needed a haircut, but he was otherwise carefully dressed in slacks and a starched white shirt with the sleeves rolled up. Holding up her case, he asked, "You brought me something good?"

In answer, she took a handkerchief from her pocket and unfolded it across her palm. The single bulb hanging from the fixture above her head set fire to the ruby resting in the middle of her hand. Ted tried to hold a straight face, but she saw the ruby's fire ignite in his eyes. He pulled a jeweler's loupe from his pocket as he lifted the gem.

"Nice," he said, looking up again. "Some small inclusions detract from its value." He took the cover off a gem scale and weighed the stone. "Seven-point-three carats. This is an old-fashioned cut. It will lose some weight when I refacet it for a new setting. So, let's call it seven carats even."

"You'll rarely find a ruby that size with fewer inclusions," she said. "The stone weighs eight-point-four-two carats. If you lose more than a tenth of a point when you refacet it then you're an amateur and I don't want to do business with you."

When she plucked the ruby off the scale and folded it back into the handkerchief, he laughed, chagrined perhaps, certainly surprised. Still holding his loupe, he said, "You know your stuff, honey. Show me what else you have and we'll get down to business."

"We'll start with this one," Elena said. "If I'm happy with the deal, I'll bring more later."

"One stone, that's all you brought?"

"For now."

"But I was told—" He was angry when he picked up her case from the floor, set it on the counter, and snapped it open: a change of underwear, a plain cotton nightdress, a mesh bag of ordinary toiletries, and a book,

East of Eden, with a marker in the center. Using a box cutter, he slit the case lining and pulled it back. His face was crimson when there was nothing to find.

"I don't know you," she said. "I barely know the man who gave me your number. So far, I have no reason to trust you and every reason to walk out the door." Again, Elena unwrapped the ruby and held it on her palm. "We start with this one. Give me a figure. And then, maybe, I'll bring you more."

They haggled over price, briefly. The amount he offered was ridiculous, but it was cash, now, and she wanted to get away from him, so she accepted. Ted opened a drawer under the counter, unlocked a strong box, counted the payment and traded it for the ruby.

"When can I see the rest?" he asked, resecuring the lock box.

"I'll call you." She stuffed the cash into a brown paper bag someone had discarded, and turned to leave. A knock on the back door stopped her. "You're expecting someone?"

He said he wasn't, but he didn't seem surprised. "Wait right here. I'll get rid of them."

Ted went out to the hall, closing the stockroom door behind him. There was a hushed conversation, but it was loud enough for her to hear that whoever was outside had an oddly high-pitched voice for a man and that he and Ted were arguing. She heard, "One stinking stone," and needed to hear no more. On her way out of the stockroom she picked up Ted's box cutter, and abandoning her ruined case and its meager contents, left through the door that led into the darkened jewelry store. As she hurried toward the street entrance, she looked around for something to hurl through the front window so she could get out of the locked shop. But Ted, perhaps covering contingencies should he need to make a fast exit, had left the key in the deadbolt, so she simply let herself out into the night. A few doors down, in front of a juke joint spewing smoke and tinny music from its open windows, a local, obviously someone with a small-towner's trusting heart, had similarly obliged by leaving the keys in his prewar Dodge.

Soon, Marysville was again nothing more than a dim glow of lights in the distance. The old Dodge rattled and shook, and found every bump as she sped east, up into the Sierra. Without breakdown or stop for fuel, Elena reached Lake Tahoe an hour before dawn. She followed the road south along the shore until she found the neon lights of the Bide A Wee Lodge, and pulled into the nearly vacant lot.

A bell over the office door announced her, and brought a sleepy-eyed man in from a back room.

"Elena!" He came around to embrace her. "I was so worried when I didn't hear from you. You said you were coming yesterday."

"I had to make a stop." She kissed his grizzled cheek. "You look well, Uncle Saul."

"And you, you are nothing but bones."

"Then feed me, please."

In back, in the kitchen of his apartment behind the reception lobby, he served her hot tea in a slender glass and set a bowl of cold borscht, bread and cheese, and pickles on the table in front of her. "You eat, and you tell me everything. I have been so worried. Did you have any trouble?"

"Here and there. It was easier getting into Russia than I expected, but there was risk traveling inside; the KGB came around, asking questions. Getting out again, and getting here, that was not so easy." She met his eyes. "Uncle, I killed a man in Singapore."

His face reddened. "Someone came after you?"

She nodded.

"You were hurt?"

"No." The wounds had healed during the long sea voyage home, so why upset him further?

"But how, Elena?"

"He wasn't the first man I had to fight off," she said, resting her hand on the box cutter in her pocket to help fend off the memory of being wakened in the night by the pressure of a gun barrel boring into her temple. "I learned to carry a blade."

He fumed: "I said from the beginning, it was a real bad idea for you to go to that godforsaken place. When I remember what we had to do to get out of there during the Revolution, what could be worth the risk for you to go back?"

"Bubbe made me promise I'd go before she dies."

"Elena, your bubbe, my mother, is old and more than a little crazy."

"Not so crazy, uncle," Elena said. "She wants something better for you, for her. She wants to get sprung from the old folks home Zeyde talked her into before he died. And she wants you to have the wherewithal to walk away from this money pit of a Shangri-La if you want to. If there were resources out there to make good things happen, then why not go get them?"

"It was your life she risked. What do you get?"

"It took nearly losing my life to figure out that I want to live after all; quite a gift she gave me," she said. "Even if I hadn't been successful, that alone would have made the risk worthwhile."

He seemed dubious. "Are you going to tell me that after all these years, you actually found something?"

With her mouth full, she rapped her knuckles against her corseted middle. When she'd swallowed, she said, "I found it exactly where Bubbe said it would be, hidden in a dry well in a forest near Yekaterinburg."

"I'll be damned," he said. "I never believed the stories about Papa's big haul."

She brought out the paper bag with the cash Ted paid for the ruby and emptied it on the table in front of Saul. "Bubbe wants you to have this, to help you believe."

He looked from her to the money, seeming no more convinced than before. "That's American currency. You didn't find that in a well in the Soviet Union."

"I sold something last night," she said. "Bubbe said you should accept this as part of your share of Zeyde's legacy to his family. She told me you could use it any way you want."

Saul gazed out the window at the flashing Vacancy sign beside his nearly empty parking lot. With high hopes, he had used his GI Bill money when he got back from the war to buy the lodge, but hopes don't always become reality. He said, "So, if there really was something worth selling in that well, why didn't my parents take it when we left Russia? My God, what we went through." He looked at the pile of money without touching it. "If only we'd had a fraction of this."

"Bubbe told me that it would have been too dangerous to be found with it if the Bolsheviks had stopped the family. She said that Zeyde thought that when things settled down after the Revolution, he would be able to go back and retrieve his haul, as you called it."

"I always thought it was just a fantasy, a story Papa told in bad times. He would always say, let's just get through this and one day we'll go back and get the hidden fortune and everything will be fine again." He reached into a cupboard and brought out a bottle of brandy, poured a shot into his tea and set the bottle in front of Elena. "He never told us what it was we'd go back to retrieve. Over time, I heard there was a boxcar full of jewels, a ton of rubles—now probably worthless—paid to him by the tsarina, or maybe nothing at all. Take your pick, believe what you wish if it helped you get past the rough spots. In the end it didn't matter, because we never could go back. First came Lenin, then Stalin, and then another world war, the Iron Curtain—"

He canted his head to look at Elena. "What, exactly, did you find in that well?"

"I'll show you." She excused herself and went into a bedroom to take off the corset she wore under her hand-me-down dress. Back in the kitchen, she spread the garment on the table. Though it was stained with age and Elena's own sweat, it was still elegant more than thirty years after her grandfather hid it in a well in Yekaterinburg. The fabric was heavy, canvas maybe, covered in white silk edged with stiff lace, but it was the gems that filled the corset stay channels that gave the corset weight. Along the bottom hem there was a name, Olga, elegantly embroidered in Cyrillic script.

When Saul saw the name it was if a light came on. "There it is. Now I know."

"Who is Olga?" she asked, pouring herself more tea.

"She was the oldest daughter of the tsar. The Bolsheviks shot her in 1918, along with her entire family."

"How did Zeyde come to have her corset?"

He shrugged. "Papa never said, but I can guess. You know that before the Russian Revolution your Zeyde was a famous goldsmith in St. Petersburg, like his father. They made many fabulous pieces of jewelry for the tsar's family and other nobility; we lived very well. But the First World War came, and then troubles for the tsar started, and Papa wasn't getting paid for work he had delivered for the tsarina, and he faced bankruptcy. When he heard rumors that the tsar's family was going to leave Russia, he went to the palace to collect what they owed him. Unfortunately, he went on the day that the Bolsheviks came to arrest the tsar. They didn't only take the tsar, though. The Bolshies arrested the tsar, his family, their servants, and Papa, only because he was there. They all ended up in a big house way out in Yekaterinburg. I know this, because we followed to try to get Papa released. On the night the tsar's family and all of their staff were executed, somehow Papa escaped. He came and got us and we got the hell out of Russia."

"I heard many versions of Zeyde's escape," she said. "But none of them involved a young woman's underwear."

He smiled. "The truth of it is probably less interesting than what you must have imagined," he said. "While Papa was imprisoned, if you could call a mansion a prison, the tsarina had him take the stones out of her jewelry—she took a big trunk full of it with them—so that her maid could sew the jewels into the daughters' clothes. She knew that her husband would be executed, and probably her son. But she was sure that her daughters would not be harmed and she wanted to provide them with something for their future. On the night the soldiers came for the family, Papa was up in the attic, still taking stones out of their settings, some of which he had made himself and never been paid for. He hid up there under a pile of clothes until it was safe, and then he went out over the roof and into the woods."

"Apparently, he took a jewel-filled corset with him."

"And you found it," Saul said with a wistful smile. "Papa is gone, and we'll never know all that happened. And does any of that matter now? You're back, and you're safe, your bubbe has her corset, and it's over."

"Not yet." She poured some brandy into her tea and took a sip. "Uncle Saul, I was very careful, but someone has followed me."

"Do you know who it is?"

"Not this time. The man I killed in Singapore?" She met her uncle's eyes. "He said he was a nephew of the dead tsar and he intended to reclaim his inheritance from me."

"Inheritance, my *tukhes*. Papa took nothing that those bastards didn't owe him. That whole aristo mob, nothing but greedy parasites trying to live off someone else's sweat. Greed, that's what the bastard inherited. May he *peyger* like a dog and rot in hell." Saul turned his head to the side and spit.

When he was calmer, he asked. "How did that guy even know what you had?"

"I was robbed in Vladivostok," she said. "To pay off all the officials I needed to so I could get an exit visa, I took a diamond out of the corset and sold it. The old man I sold it to was very suspicious. He knew it was an old stone and he asked a lot of questions; our family rumors are nothing compared to the rumors in the Soviet Union about lost Romanov treasure. I don't know whom he might have talked to, but I have been followed ever since."

Fatigue washed over her as night gave way to day. To keep her head from dropping to the table, Elena picked up her soup bowl and walked to the sink. "What do we do now?"

Saul took the bowl from her hand. "Now you rest."

The sun was high overhead before Elena wakened. She bathed and put on the clothes her uncle left in the room for her: a chambermaid's starched white shift, an apron, and a headscarf. It had been a long time since the Bide A Wee Lodge had enough paying guests for Saul to afford a chambermaid, but he'd kept the uniforms out of optimism that times would get better. He had no other clothing than his own to offer his niece.

Elena followed the aroma of coffee and toast to the kitchen. After washing her dishes, she went out to help Saul with the two guest cabins that had been occupied overnight. The rooms were clean but threadbare, and she saw that Saul went about his chores with no love for the place. Twice during their conversation, Elena tapped the corset under her shift and reminded him that he had options. They were debating what to do with the old Dodge she had stolen the night before when a black-and-white cruiser with Marysville Police Department on the door turned into the empty lot and parked behind the car. When Saul went out to speak with the policeman, Elena gathered up an armload of soiled linens and followed, to eavesdrop.

"This car belong to one of your guests?" the officer asked Saul.

"Nope," Saul said. "Someone drove it in late last night or early this morning. When I saw it out here this morning I thought one of the guests was sneaking extra people into a room—they do that, you know, try to chisel me out of a buck-fifty. But everyone's checked out and the car's still here. Could be a fisherman, left the car and walked over to the lake. People do that sometimes. I don't mind. Paying guests are more likely to turn in if they see the place isn't empty."

The officer turned to Elena. "You see who drove this car in?"

She shook her head. "It was here already when I got to work this morning."

Saul asked, "There a problem, officer?"

"Yep," he said, pushing his cap back on his head. "We had some trouble last night down in Marysville. About the same time we got a report that this car was stolen, there was a break in at the jewelry store—owner's son got shot. Folks reported seeing the car speeding out of town, headed up this way."

"Was the son badly hurt?" Elena asked, feeling the reassuring heft of Ted's box cutter in her pocket.

"Ted Junior? Yeah, he was hurt bad enough that he's dead."

"My, my," Saul said, shaking his head. "Ever since they opened those casinos over the way in Reno, we've seen a pretty rough element pass through here. Makes my blood boil just to think one of those yahoos chose my place to dump a getaway car. You think they might come back?"

"Hard to say. I'm impounding the car."

"Saul, you've been talking about retiring for a while," Elena said. "Now might be time."

"Might be," he said, smiling as he surveyed his tidy row of empty tourist cabins. "It just might be."

While they waited for someone to come for the car, Saul turned off the vacancy sign and the neon Bide A Wee marquee. He called a friend who sold real estate and told him the place was available, all offers considered. At Elena's urging, he gave no forwarding information but promised to call in regularly. She helped him gather his few mementoes and valuables and stow them in the trunk of his car.

They made two stops on the way out of town, one to drop the Bide A Wee's keys at the friend's sales office, and another for Elena to buy some clothes. With the windows down and a brown bag full of money in the glove box, they were on the road, headed east to collect Bubbe from the old folks home where she was incarcerated—her word—and toward whatever lay ahead.

During the first two hundred miles they watched the rearview mirror, but no one was following.

NIGHT AND FOG

Blood Diamonds

Melissa Yi

1.

Karin kept the laboratory room at a cool 16 degrees centigrade.

She did this for several reasons. The first, although she would never admit it, was vanity. At times her face would blush and shine with sweat, and this tendency was more pronounced in the heat. It wouldn't do for the doctor, or even the patients, to notice this.

The second reason was to contain the smell. She was quite sensitive to scent. One of her first memories was of her parents allowing the dog to dry itself by the fire, despite the terrible stench of wet fur permeating their house. The laboratory air smelled even worse. Fortunately, Karin had grown into a woman in control of her environment. She unlocked the top drawer of her lab bench and withdrew a tiny glass vial. She unscrewed the lid, drew up 0.1 cc's of clove oil with a sterilized dropper, and applied two drops of the light brown oil to her upper lip, one under each nostril. This would further dampen any unpleasant odors. Then she replaced the oil in her drawer, locked it, and placed the dropper in the autoclave.

She was ready.

She glanced at the clock, which showed only 6:33 A.M. The doctor was always on time. Karin approved. Punctuality was a sign of civilization and respect. But the hour would drag on terribly before the doctor was expected in twenty-seven minutes.

She unlocked the filing cabinet below her bench. She refused to turn on the light; she often berated her colleagues, especially Dr. Schreiber, for wasting electricity and hot water, resources that must be conserved for vital research. Yet with only the dim dawn light of a single window barely illuminating the small room, she could not properly make out the files shadowed beneath her desk. She pulled the first folder out and realized it was a copy of her thesis, *Studies on the Physiology of the Butterfly Wing*.

Karin smiled. Her studies at the university seemed so long ago. She had graduated at the age of twenty-four with examinations in botany, zoology, and geology. She had also studied physics and chemistry. One could argue that, eleven years later, she still studied zoology, but in a much more focused fashion. Before Karin's work, the research on eye color was mired in Mendelian genetics, a sort of elementary school equation: two blue-eyed parents equaled one blue-eyed child. Two brown-eyed parents carrying the blue eye allele could yield one blue-eyed child and three brown-eyed children. And so forth.

Karin was one of the first biologists to raise the question of hormonal influence on eye color and to demonstrate its importance in affecting the color of rabbit irises. Still, even as the accolades rolled in, she herself felt dissatisfied. Even if two blue-eyed parents produced blue-eyed children, what about the different shades of blue?

She heard footsteps behind her and turned to see Klaus in the doorway. "Good morning, Dr. Rasmussen," he said.

She greeted him in kind. "Good morning, Dr. Schreiber. Did you sleep well?"

"Better than you, I suspect. Did you sleep at all?" He smiled broadly, revealing his teeth, which seemed too big for his mouth.

Karin was careful not to show her disgust. Klaus was nearly twenty years her senior, but had completed very good work on genetics in his time. She shook her head. "I slept very well," she lied. In fact, even though she had left the lab at eleven o'clock, she had stayed up until three and barely caught two hours of restless sleep. As usual, she'd risen before the sun.

"Did you have time to put on those earrings I gave you?"

Karin made sure her voice remained steady and that her face did not betray her. "I did not find them suitable for the laboratory, Dr. Schreiber."

"So modest. You are a credit to the fair sex, Dr. Rasmussen. The spring of life, indeed!"

Karin's hands quivered, this time in anger. She felt her face flush, despite the coolness of the room. Karl's phrase was a crude pun about the homes where pregnant unmarried women could give up their babies. Although Karin was not past childbearing age, she was no longer in her prime, and it was cruel to remind her of that, even though she had never longed for marriage or children. She had always preferred science. She was extremely lucky to come of age at a time when her skills were needed for the war effort. Her "duty year" as a teacher had turned into a full-time position before she won a research scholarship four years later.

"When are diamonds ever improper? Ah, well. As Friedrich Nietzsche wrote, 'The true man wants two things: danger and play. For that reason he wants woman, as the most dangerous plaything.'"

Karin turned her back to Karl and removed a handkerchief from her lab coat pocket. She blotted her nose and forehead, the areas most likely to shine. Klaus had moved to his own lab bench near the door and was setting up equipment, but continued to ramble about Nietzsche.

Composed now, Karin glanced at the clock. It was 6:54. The doctor should arrive in six minutes. She picked up a glass pipette and held it up in the dim dawn light. It was spotless, as usual. She turned her head to the hallway, hoping to hear footsteps, but all she detected was the everyday noise of soldiers yelling orders and the annoying hum of a mosquito in the distance.

Suddenly, Karl fell silent. Karin lifted her head. If Dr. Schreiber had heard something . . .

Sure enough, a door creaked open downstairs and at least two pairs of well-heeled shoes hammered down the hallway. Karin stood by the bench, arms by her sides, hoping that her face would not betray her excitement this time.

The doctor appeared in the doorway in his immaculate white coat. "Good morning, Drs. Schreiber and Rasmussen."

"Good morning," murmured Karin.

The doctor spread his arms wide, nearly striking the Jewish pathologist who flanked him. The pathologist hurriedly stepped back out of range, clinging to a white box. The doctor barely glanced at him, shooting his gaze at Karin instead. "I have a special present for you today, Dr. Rasmussen."

Karin's heart skipped a beat. She pressed her hands together, willing her face not to sweat.

"You asked me for heterochromic samples of fresh tissue. Yesterday, when I walked the lines, I discovered an entire family with heterochromic eyes. Two parents and two one-year-old twin boys."

"Twin boys," repeated Karin. The doctor's passion for twins could not be underestimated.

"Yes." The doctor's lips split into a smile, revealing the gaps between his two front teeth. "Their cousins are due to arrive today."

Karin's face flushed in joy. This was more than she'd ever dreamed of. "Do you mean—"

The doctor held up one finger. "I would like to study this family myself first, obtain all the members, document their genetics, and so forth."

"Of course," said Karin.

"However, given the circumstances, I no longer required the fraternal twins I already had in service. Thus, I harvested their tissue for you this morning." The doctor nodded at Dr. Schreiber. "They may come to you later today, or tomorrow, Doctor. It depends how long they survive. They are quite tall, five feet eleven and six feet, so you may want to extract their growth hormone."

"Thank you," said Karl, but Karin was no longer listening. The doctor had gestured to the Jewish pathologist, who flipped open the lid of the white box, letting the smell of blood and formaldehyde waft into the air.

Nestled on a bed of ice, four freshly harvested eyeballs stared up at her: two hazel, one green, and one blue. The two hazel corneas were severely ulcerated from previous experiments, but the retinas would probably be untouched. The crown jewels, the heterochromic blue and green irises, with almost pristine white sclerae, seemed almost perfectly alive.

Karin clasped her hands together, barely able to breathe at the sight of the most beautiful gift she'd ever received. "Oh, thank you. Thank you. *Ein herzliches Dankeschön, Doktor Mengele.*"

2.

So I was sitting in the hard chair beside the *farkakteh* hospital bed, wishing that I could knit, but the light wasn't so good for my eyes anymore, and they make you keep the curtains closed now. I guess they worry about all those MRSA bacteria and viruses nowadays, spreading from cubicle to cubicle, but what good is a curtain going to do about it?

It's no good for my back, those hard beds, and those nasty hospital chairs don't have much cover for the *tukhes*, you know what I mean? So I'm sitting, and I'm wishing I could knit, or call my granddaughter on the phone, but you know how they can be funny about phones in the hospitals nowadays, so I'm just sitting. And maybe dozing off, because my stomach hurts so bad, I couldn't sleep last night. That's why I'm here. My stomach.

I can see feet running back and forth from underneath the curtain, attached to legs wearing those funny blue hospital pants. Scrubs, I think they call them. Yes, like that TV show my granddaughter used to like. Oh, she would laugh. Me, I didn't find it so funny, but you know young people nowadays.

Finally, some of the feet stop in front of my curtain. It's a woman in black leather shoes with the toes all scuffed. In my time, you had to shine your shoes, but I guess she's a nurse or a doctor, she doesn't have time. In my day, you took care of things, that's all I'm saying.

Her hand rips my curtain open, and it's a young Oriental girl wearing glasses and a lab coat. Maybe she's a doctor, maybe she's a nurse, maybe she's an axe murderer, I don't know. They don't tell you anything these days, that's what I'm saying. She's wearing a tag, but it's flipped the wrong way. I'm telling you. Scuffed shoes and backward tags. What is this world coming to?

She starts talking, but so fast, I can't understand a word of it. I grab her hand, and she jumps a little. I can tell she's not used to patients touching her, but that's one of the best ways to slow down a motor mouth. My Aunt Bedele taught me that one. When me or my sisters were talking, she'd just grab our hands and tell us to slow down.

Finally, I get this doctor to say her name three times and flip her tag over. She is a doctor, but one of those student ones. A resident, she says. Dr. Hope Sze. Like the letter C.

Well, what difference does it make? I'm old now. Waiting another hour for the real doctor, I can do that. If I die waiting, I die waiting. So I sigh and tell her about my stomach. See how big it is? That's not normal. I look like I'm carrying my son again. Hurts all the time, yes, maybe a little more at night, that's why I came first thing in the morning. I couldn't wait anymore. My family doctor ordered these tests, but he can't see me for another two weeks. My Mordechai couldn't come with me today. He's got his own appointment with his urologist.

This doctor's interested in the tests and scans. Wants to know what kind and when. I want to tell her to look it up on that fancy computer of hers, but it turns out, that's what she wants to do. She pulls out one of those tablets that my great-grandsons like so much, and she starts typing in my hospital number. She double-checks the name and number on my paper wristband, and when she looks up, she sees the other numbers tattooed on the inside of my elbow, and her face falls.

That was a long time ago, I tell her. I was just a little girl at the time.

I'm sorry, she says, and I can see that she means it. She's a good girl, even though she doesn't take care of her shoes.

So I tell her not to worry. And then I look at her name tag again, which is flipped around already, but I remember it. Hope Sze. She's not just any doctor. She's the doctor who solved that strange case of the escape artist who dressed up like Elvis and nearly drowned in a coffin! I should have remembered before, but my memory's not what it used to be. What's she doing at the Jewish Hospital, hmm?

She tells me something about rotating hospitals, and she wants to do emergency medicine, so she wanted to come here because it's busier than St. Joseph's, and they have hospital tablets and electronic records and all sorts of stuff they don't have at St. Joe's.

Well, I knew that! Don't we donate our money so that the Samuel G. Wasserman Jewish Hospital can be better than the other ones?

I guess, working at St. Joseph's, she doesn't see too many survivors. Her eyes are back on my tattoo, so I tell her, go on, touch it. It doesn't hurt.

She wants to and she doesn't want to, but her fingers lightly brush the numbers, and maybe I see tears in her eyes, so I tell her, okay, you don't have to feel bad.

My mother was so beautiful that when the Germans invaded Poland, one of the officers took her as his mistress. You might think he'd want one of the Aryan girls, like Maria Apfel, but no, he chose my mother, and her hair was as black as coal, with pale skin like the moon. The paperboy used to call her Snow White before Hans showed up.

Hans bought my mother real diamond earrings. He kept us out of the camps for a long time, and the earrings protected us a little longer.

Look at me. I survived, didn't I? I married a good man, my Mordechai. He loves me so much, he not only gave me this two-carat ring, he bought me these one-carat earrings. Yes, and my ruby and diamond necklace, too, you noticed.

We did well, me and my Mordechai. But we're generous with our money. Not only to the hospital, but lots of other charities too. *Kinder un gelt iz a sheyneh velt.*

So, nu? You have my test results?

3.

"Hope? Hey, you look horrible," said Tucker, staring me up and down, which was kind of hard to do, since I was hunched in front of the computer in the corner of the residents' room.

"Thanks," I snapped, wrapping my white coat around me. I felt cold, but if anything, the residents' room was usually too hot. As per usual, the place smelled like rotten fish and old fries, and the medical student had left the TV on, blaring MuchMusic.

Tucker dropped his hand on my shoulder. He smelled like lemon cologne today, which was a nice change from the fish, and the slight wiggle in his fingers was a welcome distraction until I belatedly realized that he was also checking out what I'd left displayed on the computer monitor. "Is that what's bothering you? This Jewish couple with a suicide pact?"

I shivered. "I knew them. I was the one who told her she had metastatic cancer. She told me everything was fine, that she and her Mordechai had donated tons of money to the Jewish Hospital so that they'd be the best in the world. She even taught me a little Yiddish. *Zay gezunt.*"

"Be healthy," Tucker translated.

I didn't even raise an eyebrow. Tucker's not Jewish, but languages are his thang. I nodded at him. "But while she was telling me this, she must have had this exit plan all along. I mean, they had pills stockpiled for years, with all the bottles neatly lined up in the car, and they'd sealed up the car windows and doors from the inside. They must have been so scared."

Tucker held open his arms, and I hesitated before I leaned into his embrace. He's such a joker, I'm never sure what to expect, but this time, he rocked me back and forth while Taylor Swift sang "Trouble" in the background. After a few minutes, he murmured into my hair, "I guess this is the wrong time to tell you that I got you a birthday present."

I sat up straighter. "You're right, it's a terrible time."

"So I'll give it to you tomorrow."

"Hang on." My eyes zoomed in on the bulge in his navy jacket. "You can't leave me in suspense like that."

"But isn't that your shtick, detective doctor?"

I tried not to mind that the Yiddish reminded me of Mordechai and Esther Dorn. "I like to solve mysteries, not have them dangled over my head."

Tucker's white teeth flashed in a smile, and I realized that he'd successfully distracted me. He said, "I'll give you a hint. It's not an iPhone."

It really bugged him that Ryan had bought me one, but I couldn't help that. I said, "Good. I already have one."

He pulled a gift-wrapped package out of his pocket. "It's better."

He'd wrapped it in Christmas paper in November. What a nut. Usually, I like to save the wrapping, but for once, I shredded the cheap Santa Clauses spackled on green paper and pulled out a USB stick and postcard picture of a black background, a shot of Earth, and some crude multicolored blocks. On the back of the postcards, he'd scrawled the words, "Diamonds! Happy birthday, Tucker."

"It's a video game," he explained to my blank face. "For a Mac. From 1992. Don't you remember it? I got you a copy on this USB stick."

"Um. Thanks." I was more confused than anything else. He got me an ancient video game for my birthday?

"I thought it was funny because of the Hope Diamond. Get it?"

"Sure," I said, even though I flinched. I'd never thought much about the Hope Diamond before, despite the association with my name. All I knew was that it was cursed.

"And I got you one little thing. *Une petite chose de rien*." He pulled a small, violet velvet jewelry box out of his pocket.

My heart thudded. Tucker knew that I hadn't made a decision between him and Ryan. He couldn't possibly be handing me a ring. He grinned at me, though, and he seemed so carefree, I accepted the case and opened it.

It contained a hairpin studded in diamonds. Even to my uneducated eye, the square pin at the top looked vintage. Maybe even like something from World War II. I know that Mrs. Dorn had said that her mother had received diamond earrings, not a hairpin, but somehow I imagined a little girl holding this hairpin and using it to "protect herself a little longer."

Tucker's brow pleated, and he reached for me one more time. "Don't worry, I picked it up at a pawn shop. It's probably not even real. Are you okay, Hope? You look like you're going to be sick."

The Flowers of Shanghai

S.J. Rozan

Elena stood on the Garden Bridge and regarded the blooms bobbing and slipping between sampans and barges. Pale blossoms, so fresh their velvet petals still curled, floated on the clogged black river. Soon water from a ship's wake would soak them. Iridescent oil splattering off a bargeman's pole would stain them and weigh them down. Or the rain, curdling now out of the cold mist, would pound them under. Elena had watched all of it happen before. None of the river's flowers ever traveled far. Most did not get beyond the harbor; very few escaped Shanghai, she was sure; and certainly none reached the villages in China's interior where mourners had prayerfully sent them.

The body these were meant to accompany had probably sunk to the bottom already.

The first time Elena had seen this soft white hope on the river Johann had been holding her hand, pointing the flowers out. Johann had learned about the burials in their first months in Shanghai, when Elena was still learning about the stench of the river, about the insects and billowing heat of summer, the coal smoke and cold of winter, the rains and never-ending damp of all seasons, about hunger and noise and the crush of people whose words she didn't understand.

Johann said Chinese ghosts could only find rest among their ancestors, in their family villages. People from the interior who died in Shanghai were sent home for burial. The well-to-do placed the coffins on oxcarts for the long trek. The poor couldn't even afford the coffins. They sprinkled their dead with flowers, brought them to the riverbank, and slipped them gently into the water, to make their own way home.

Jews can rest anywhere, while we wait for the Messiah, Johann said. *It's lucky for us, since we have no homes.*

Johann rested now, waiting, in the Israeli Cemetery on Point Road.

A shout broke above the honking and the traffic behind her. Elena turned. The Japanese guard was stabbing at the air with his bayonet, ordering her to move on. She hunched her shoulders and rejoined the crowd trudging across the rusted steel grate of the Garden Bridge.

At home in Prague—Johann had been wrong, they had once had a home—they'd lived in a tiny house and Elena had a tiny garden. She'd grown roses, red ones and pink ones and white ones pale and ghostly as the chrysanthemums in this river. They cascaded over the front fence for all who passed by to see.

In Shanghai the gardens hid behind walls, waved the tops of their trees like teasing fingers above solid brick, poured the scent of unseen flowers into the air in areas where Jews were not permitted to walk.

At the far side of the bridge where it gave onto the Bund, the flow of the crowd narrowed and slowed. Elena peered to see the reason. Outside the guard station, three Chinese women lay flat on the walkway, touching their foreheads to the cold steel in kowtows to the Japanese guards, who berated them in a language the women did not understand for infractions they probably had not committed. The rain was now falling hard. The women's clothes were heavy, sodden. One shivered uncontrollably but none were allowed to rise. When, finally, the shivering one looked up, one of the guards, small and thin and enveloped in his oilcloth raincoat, kicked her in the mouth. Bleeding now, weeping silently, the woman returned to her kowtow. The other two did not move.

Elena walked on. Scenes like these played out across Shanghai every minute of every day. The Chinese and the Japanese shared a mutual, burning hatred as deep as any cold-eyed Aryan's hatred of Jews. The Japanese ruled China now, with a casual brutality toward the Chinese that had ignited Johann's fury. Elena, terrified, had pulled him away from a confrontation with Japanese soldiers more than once, as she had from brownshirts in the streets of Prague. *You'll get killed,* she pleaded with him, here as she had there, *and no one will be saved.*

In Johann's final days, the *Shema* on his lips as he lay devoured by the typhoid fever sweeping through the ghetto, Elena had been struck by this bitter thought: she had prevented him from dying a hero. But she could not prevent him from dying.

Elena trudged on. Last month there was a day in which Ghoya, the Japanese commandant of the Jewish ghetto, felt dyspeptic and abruptly left his office before an hour had ended. The long line of people waiting to see him was angrily told to disperse, as though their coming had caused the Major's illness. Those who had not yet gotten their passes could not leave the ghetto that week for work or school—the only reasons Jews could leave at all. Elena was among them; it was a week of more hunger than usual, more hours spent staring at the wall in the tiny attic room, huddled in the blanket, trying to stay warm. Through a schoolboy fortunate enough to have been at the head of the line, Elena sent a message to the French dressmaker in Foochow Road for whom she worked, informing her what had happened and begging her to retain Elena's position until Elena could return. The following week, when she'd gotten a pass again, Elena sewed as late into the night as the pass allowed. She made up all the work she'd missed, left the shop each night with burning eyes and a pounding head, and also took with her the understanding that were it to happen again Madame Fornier would have no choice but to replace her with a Chinese girl. The Chinese had no understanding of fashion, no sense even of culture, Madame Fornier said. She much preferred employing a European, even a Jew, who valued the art of couture. But her customers must not be kept waiting and the Chinese girls could handle a needle and would do as they were told.

Elena, who could no longer remember what value couture had at all except to keep her, barely, from starving, nodded dumbly and bent to her sewing.

Work and study, those were the only reasons Jews could leave the ghetto, with the exception of funerals. That concession had allowed Elena to bury Johann in sanctified ground, but she had not been permitted back to the cemetery in the six months since. Perhaps that was to the good. In Prague Elena had gone every Shabbos to her parents' graves. Beside a nearby headstone a thin, pale widow could be found, sitting and talking to her late husband. She gave him news of the children and asked his advice. Elena now walked in the world without Johann. Bereft and dazed in this city he had come to love, and she to loathe, in the short years of their life together here, she feared her longing might drive her to do the same: to spend her days near him, and her nights also, were she once permitted to visit the place where he now lay.

Though they had no children of whom to bring him news. Johann had hoped they would, had wanted to start their family in China, to triumphantly return to Prague when the war ended with children born in exile as proof the Jews could not be destroyed. But in the three years of their life in China, as in their single year in the tiny house in Prague before the fires and smashed windows and jackboots forced their desperate flight, Elena had not conceived.

And what advice could she ask Johann for, what could he offer? Advice implied a choice to be made. For Elena, Shanghai offered no choices, just a daily struggle to live, to eat, to stay warm in winter, to breathe in summer. A drowning swimmer doesn't need advice on how furiously to stroke.

Elena clutched her worn wool coat more closely in the spitting rain.

Her pass required her to walk along Nanking Road, and while she usually kept to the far side of the street, today in her weariness she sheltered under the colonnade. She avoided this arched walkway when she could, so as not to pass the former Grand Café, now a German beer hall. The Grand Café had relocated to Hong Kew when all Jews and their businesses had been compelled to, and it was doing well enough. But in this first location she and Johann, desperately poor but still full of hope, had spent what Elena even now recalled as happy Sunday afternoons. The café smelled of coffee and cinnamon; Yiddish was the language of the menus and the signs. They could barely pay the rent on the one room they lived in, but she and Johann nevertheless came nearly every week to the Grand Café for *kaffee mit schlag* and a shared piece of chocolate torte. That night, and the next, there would be no dinner but boiled rice. But Elena would sit with her back to the windows, so she could not see China; and sometimes there was news of home, or of the war, sometimes Herr Baumann played his violin, and always the ardent discussions of Zionism and atheism and art, of God and no God and the death of God, the raised Yiddish voices and the glass pastry case and the hubbub made Elena think for a moment not that she was back in Prague, never that, but that life would again be possible someday.

It would not. Johann was gone. The war continued, the stories whispered out of Europe so horror-drenched that Elena would no longer hear them. She had not read a Yiddish newspaper since Johann's death. She did not visit the new Grand Café, she did not go to *shul*, to the mikvah, she could not go to the cemetery. She went to work, to her room, to work again; she cooked her rice and sometimes a carrot or an onion. She bought boiling water from the boy across the street and made tea. There was no sugar, no milk.

The rain pounded through the night and into the morning. Weak daylight leaked into Elena's room as she struggled to put on her still-damp coat. Without breakfast, because she had nothing left to eat, without tea, because she had no coins for the boiling-water boy, Elena headed once again through the streets of the ghetto. Always, she took the same path to the Garden Bridge although in the ghetto, and only here, a Jew was free to make choices. She would spend the day sewing silk gowns and wool skirts for German and French officers' wives. Today she would be paid, so she would have rice to eat tonight.

On the river the roofs of the sampans ran with water; the polemen's wide straw hats dripped rain onto their thin backs. No blossoms floated today. Jewish schoolchildren, for whom Shanghai was still more than a tangle of reek and damp, of aching for the past and dread of the future, skipped along the walkway with their satchels. In front of Elena a married couple held hands and spoke quietly, heads inclined toward one another. The day would separate them, but they would return to each other in the evening, they would sit together over tea. A trickle of icy water inched down Elena's neck. She didn't reach to tighten her collar.

As the rain drove down harder the paces of people around her quickened. Elena found she could not bring her feet to move faster. She was soaked and cold and she did not feel strong. A commotion at the end of the bridge spread the crowd like pond ripples moving back from a thrown stone. People slipped around the shouting if they could; a wave surged back from it. As much as Elena could not speed her steps, she also found she could not slow them. She continued mechanically trudging and passed through the slackened and the stopped, to find herself at the guard station looking on with a group of her fellows as the thin, oilcloth-coated guard cursed and kicked a bundle on the steel grate. The bundle cried out, and Elena saw it was a Chinese woman, weeping, her arms trying uselessly to protect both her head and her pregnant belly. Three Chinese men struggled to hold a fourth, who shouted her name and pulled against their grip, desperate to reach her. Dully, Elena thought, *That must be her husband. That must be their child, being stomped from her womb.* His friends were right to hold him, though. Attacking the guard would certainly mean death.

Elena had not been able to speed nor slow; now she could not stop. With a howl she flew at the shocked guard, thrust him away, nearly knocked him over. "Run!" she screamed at the girl. "Go!" Of course she spoke in Yiddish and of course the girl did not understand. But as the guard's oilcloth slithered in Elena's grip, the girl staggered to her feet. The crowd parted for her and then came together again with the finality of the Red Sea drowning the soldiers of Egypt. The girl, her husband, his friends all disappeared. Gloved hands and oilcloths and enraged Japanese faces swirled around Elena. A guard behind her seized her coat but she released the buttons and in her thin blouse she ran, not along the walkway but three steps across it, to the railing. A foot in the grille and one on the rail and she was standing high. One teetering moment; then a hand grabbed her ankle and she half-turned. A snarling guard shouted an order. Her free foot kicked out, catching him in eye. He stumbled back, letting her go. She swayed; she desperately tried to maintain her balance so she could turn back, to face the river.

She would do this. It would not be done to her.

Surprised to hear her own voice repeating the *Shema*, Elena stepped off the Garden Bridge. She spread her arms wide to embrace the cold, black water, where today no blossoms floated.

Feeding the Crocodile

Moe Prager

"The piano tuner ran through ascending chords, enjoying the resistance of the heavy ivory keys. His balding head was bent forward, his eyes closed as he listened. The notes rose to the darkened ceiling of the recital hall near Warsaw's Old Market Square, then dissipated like smoke," said Becker, closing his tattered notebook.

"More!" barked Kleinmann. "What happens to the old man's daughter? Does she escape Poland with the documents? Does Pavel, the dirty Bolshevik scum, help her or turn her over to the Gestapo to save his own worthless skin? More!"

"Not tonight, I'm afraid, Herr Lieutenant Kleinmann. I am feeling weak. There was much much work on the ash heap today. Have you ever shoveled wet ashes?"

"You Jews! Always complaining. Always ungrateful. Remember Becker, if not for me, you would be in the heap and not on it."

"I remember. Every day, I remember. I thank the God of Israel for you."

"Good then, write well tonight, Becker. Pray to that God of yours to inspire you, for I will dream again of the piano tuner's daughter and what will become of her."

"But my rations . . . What about—"

"You will have your crusts and soup," Kleinmann said, cutting Becker off midquestion as he always did.

It was as ritualized as the dance of bees, these nightly exchanges between Werner Kleinmann, the SS lieutenant, and Isaac Becker, the Jew. With the exception of Becker's tales, even the words they spoke had become formalized, as if they were the names of words instead of the words themselves. Any implied irony or threat that may have been a part of the ritual when the dance partners took their first awkward steps together had long since been forgotten.

"Thank you, Herr Kleinmann." Becker bowed as he always did, as was expected.

Becker waited for the words. *You're welcome, Isaac.* These words never came. The lieutenant dismissed the prisoner with a curt, backhanded slap of the air as a finger of flame might snap at an impudent moth. It had lately dawned upon Becker that things omitted from a ritual are part of the ritual too, but this revelation did not quench his thirst for praise.

Closing the door behind him and plodding through the mud back to his barracks, Becker cursed Kleinmann in several tongues. In hell, one is educated in many things. He loved Magyar curses best of all. He delighted at the sound and rhythm of the language and the creativity of the curses—usually involving bestiality in concert with more run-of-the-mill profanity—was unparalleled. He had never been to Hungary and had once entertained thoughts of someday visiting. But he had months ago stopped dreaming of riding on a Budapest streetcar just to listen to the people speak. Hell was as close to Budapest as he would ever get.

So caught up was he in his cursing, Becker hadn't noticed the approach of Jacob Weisen. Weisen and Becker were from the same small village on the German side of the Polish border. They had met for the first time when they were five, their hate for one another immediate and mutual. The depth of their loathing was beyond social, beyond merely physical. It was molecular. At home, they had managed, for the most part, to avoid contact. That proved impossible in the camp, their having been assigned to the same barracks. Worse for Becker was Weisen's position as head of the retribution squad.

A death camp is a special kind of prison, but it is a prison nonetheless. In all prisons, there are rules and there are lines and there are lines not to be crossed, ever.

Given the cheapness of life and the ever hungry machinery of death behind the barbed-wire and electrical fences, no one seemed keen on appeals or second chances. This was especially true of the prisoner enforcers. Yes, at its basest level, life inside this place was all about survival: a few more minutes, an extra day, two weeks, perhaps a month. But at what price? How close to the line should one step?

"So, Isaac Becker, you have again been feeding the crocodile," prodded Weisen.

"The crocodile? What nonsense are you talking now, Weisen?"

"Have you never heard it said that the frightened man feeds the crocodile in the hope that he will be eaten last?"

"I am a writer, not a chef. I work on the heap just like you and the rest of the men in our barracks."

"But you eat better than us, don't you?"

This stunned Becker. Kleinmann had assured him that none of the other prisoners would ever know about their arrangement. The change in Becker's expression was not lost on Weisen.

"How typical of you to assume you are the only person in hell to have made a deal with the devil. Do you ever wonder where your rewards come from? For every one of your extra rations, there is a little more smoke, the heap gets a little taller."

Becker felt as if Weisen had just whacked him across the ribs with a plank. He was short of breath, suddenly nauseous, and might've vomited right there in the mud had there been enough food in his system to expel. He had never wanted to think about from where his rations had come. He hadn't wanted to think about it because he knew. He had known from that first day the lieutenant pulled him off the pile.

"You are the storyteller. In such a place as this, your talent is a commodity as precious as gold fillings and hidden diamonds, Becker." The SS man pointed at the crematoria. "If a man's soul is gray when he is stationed here, the smoke will blacken it. If a man's soul is already black . . ."

"And yours, lieutenant, what is its shading?"

"Never mind my soul, storyteller. Your job is to make sure that a little sun shines through the smoke."

And so the deal was struck. Becker would provide the sun and Kleinmann the bread.

"What's the matter? You've gone gray, Becker," Weisen asked, snapping the storyteller back into the moment. "You walk a very thin tightrope between us and the crocodile. His protection extends only so far. One day soon, you will be part of the pile and your rations will go to some other scum who has traded in your soul for an extra day alive in paradise. Sooner or later, Becker, we are all eaten by one crocodile or another."

Becker opened up his mouth to explain, but the words would not come. He knew he could not risk telling another inmate of his plan. Weisen's threats had only reinforced Becker's belief that there were no secrets in Hades.

※

"When he was certain that Christina was well into the tunnel beneath the church, Pavel twisted the hand grenade fuse and pulled Herr Ernst, the Gestapo man, close by his black leather lapels. First, confusion washed across the crystalline azure sea of the Nazi's eyes, then fear like a raging storm roiled the waters. Herr Ernst pounded his fists against the Russian's chest, but to no avail. Pavel simply smiled.

"In that brief second, he was as at peace as any man who had ever lived. He could see his mother's weathered face set against a swaying field of golden wheat, her red and blue babushka snapping in the wind. He smelled the sweet aroma of onions frying in chicken fat and the fragrant steam rising from the boiling buckwheat. When he was certain there was no turning back, Pavel released Ernst's lapels. He pressed his fingers softly to his mouth, remembering the feel of Christina's lips against his. Then nothing.

"When the piano tuner heard the explosion from the nearby church, he smiled and pressed the stolen Luger to his temple. He would not survive long enough to hear the chord his gun hand played as his lifeless body fell to the recital hall stage nor would he see the gun smoke dissipate like so many notes lost to space and time," said Becker, closing the tattered notebook.

It was time for the dance of bees to begin, but it did not. When Becker looked up, he noticed tears streaming down Kleinmann's cheeks. In that moment Becker felt a level of disgust for Kleinmann, his own writing, himself that he never imagined possible. How, in this place where the worst atrocities were perpetrated by one human against another on an hourly basis, could his story make Kleinmann weep? He had witnessed Kleinmann execute prisoners for the mildest perceived slight, for tripping on the heap, even for sport. Becker was not blind to the teenage girls Kleinmann had brought into his office. The crocodile was hungry for more than stories. It was the blankness on the faces of the girls that had motivated Becker to risk what he had risked.

"Bravo, Becker. Bravo!" The lieutenant raved, wiping away tears between claps. "Thank you. Thank you."

At last, Kleinmann uttered the words Becker had longed to hear.

"There will be meat for you tonight, Isaac Becker. Triple rations."

In his head, Becker heard Weisen's voice. *Triple rations. The heap grows taller.*

The SS man smiled. "Or maybe you would like some female companionship instead?"

Now Becker wanted to rip his eyes out of their sockets. "That is most kind, Herr Kleinmann, but the rations will be fine." On the verge of tears himself, Becker stood to go.

"I have not dismissed you, Becker. Here, bring me your book, that magic book of yours."

Becker's body clenched. Fear consuming all the things he had been feeling only a second before. "The magic is in me, Herr Lieutenant Kleinmann, not the book."

"The book, Becker! Now!"

What choice did he have really? He slid the book across the desk to the SS man. The Nazi stroked the book, patted it, picked it up, and caressed it. Then, when he opened the book, Becker had to prop himself against the desk for fear of fainting. The scowl on Kleinmann's face did nothing to improve Becker's equilibrium.

"What is this, Becker? What language is this?" he growled at the storyteller.

Becker sighed silently, thankful for the lieutenant's lack of language skills. He got some string back in his legs. "Hungarian, sir, Magyar."

"Hungarian! The Magyars were once Aryans, but are now interbred pigs. Why don't you write in German or Yiddish? Is this some kind of trick, Jew?"

"I don't dispute you about the Hungarians, Herr Lieutenant Kleinmann, but their language sings to me. Learning Magyar has occupied my mind here and it helps me with my writing. Even you, sir, have said that one's mind must be occupied in such a place as this."

The scowl evaporated. "Yes, I have said this. Whatever helps you with your magic. I suppose the language in which you write is irrelevant, so long as when you read to me . . ." Kleinmann again began to get emotional. "You are dismissed. Go to the rear of Building Five. Your rations will be waiting." Becker stood his ground. "What is it now? I said you can go."

"But my book, Herr—"

"You have no possessions, Becker, only the illusion of possession. That illusion is solely dependent upon me. Savor your meat. Take the night off from your writing. Tomorrow, I will keep you off the ash heap and I will have a new notebook for you and pens, the best pens."

Becker dared not show his panic. He bowed, turned, hurried through the door, and, for the first time in his life, sought out the company of Jacob Weisen.

❧

"Do you know what they will do to you, Becker? For this, it won't be the gas," Weisen warned. "It would be better if they shot you on the spot."

"No. You must see it happens as we discussed it."

Weisen shook his head. "All this for a book. If I had known you were such a fool, I wouldn't have despised you quite so much."

"Then it is a fool's errand and I will pay for the folly, not you."

"Very well."

Becker grabbed Weisen's forearm. "You will give the book to the Gypsy and he will get it out of the camp."

"You have my word."

❧

Jacob Weisen had explained how it was possible to get back to Kleinmann's office without drawing unwanted attention. This part of the camp was dark and not well patrolled. No need, really. On the rare occasions when the prisoners got loose, they did not run to the ash heap. Now Isaac Becker, the storyteller, lay face down in the mud, waiting. For nearly an hour he had listened to Kleinmann forcing himself on one of the blank-faced girls. *Bitch!* he would call her, slapping her as he grunted. Then there was silence. A few minutes later, two guards showed up at his office door.

"She looks like she could use delousing," one of the guards joked.

"Yes, a shower would do her well," said the other.

"No, not this one, not tonight. I am in high spirits tonight. Clean her up and send her to the enlisted men's brothel," Kleinmann said as if he were a genie granting the girl her secret desire.

Shortly after the guards left, the lieutenant headed to his quarters. He had company.

"Becker, what are you doing here? Are you mad? You know this isn't permitted. You could be shot and there isn't a thing I could do about it. Come, walk in the shadows with me." He looped his arm through Becker's and pulled him into the dark.

"My book please, Herr Lieutenant Kleinmann."

"What did you say, Becker? Did you again call it your book? You Jews are a stubborn race. I—"

Pushing his quarry against the side of an empty hut, Becker covered Kleinmann's mouth with his muddied hand. He plunged a sharpened wedge of glass into the SS man's liver and when it was in very deep, Becker snapped the glass off so there was no hope of pulling out the makeshift blade. Just like in his story, there was confusion in the blue eyes of the victim, then fear. Death came soon enough and more mercifully than it would come for Isaac Becker. The storyteller took back his precious book and retraced the path Weisen had laid out for him.

※

It took Becker three days to die on the cross. They had tortured him first and then let him heal enough to make the crucifixion worth their trouble. The cross had been centrally placed so that a large percentage of the prisoners would be forced to pass by the dying man while going to and from their barracks. Those prisoners who lacked a ringside seat had been marched over to watch the long spikes driven into the storyteller's body.

"You got the book out?" Weisen asked the Gypsy, both staring out at the cross.

"This morning in a bag under the ashes for the local farmers. They use it for fertilizer, you know, the ashes? One of the farmers is a Polish Resistance man."

"Where is the book going?"

"An address in Budapest somewhere, I think."

Weisen turned to the Gypsy. "Did you look in the book?"

"I can't read. Did you?"

"No. Becker gave it to your man before the guards came for him. I wonder what was in it."

"Nothing worth that, I can tell you," the Gypsy said, pointing to the crows pecking at the storyteller's body.

"It was to him."

The Gypsy laughed. "No it wasn't. The first time they jolted him with electricity or burned him with a cigarette, I can tell you, he stopped thinking it was worth it."

"Then it was a good thing there was no turning back. Still, I wonder what was in that book."

"Enough! Wondering won't feed us or keep us alive in this place," the Gypsy said. "I'm hungry."

So both men turned their backs on Becker and went behind the barracks to divide up the extra rations Weisen had been received for turning in his old nemesis.

Somewhere a crocodile closed his eyes and fell deeply asleep.

Good Morning, Jerusalem 1948

Michael J. Cooper

I never sleep well under mortar fire. Last night was no exception. The flares hadn't helped either, night shining like day. But once the brandy clubbed me, I finally got some sleep—until the brandy wore off and the mortars woke me up.

Lying on my cot, I open an eye and see that the light splashed on the whitewashed wall of my improvised office and bedroom is no flare. Dawn has broken, and with it, increased fire. In addition to the thud of three-inch mortars, I hear the clatter of Sten guns—ours and theirs—in and around the Old City of Jerusalem. I give up trying to sleep and sit on the edge of my cot.

My temporary quarters is one of twenty-eight small shotgun units within Yemin Moshe, a single-story housing block on the western slope of the Hinnon Valley. We face the walled city, about a quarter-mile away. The place was built by a rich British-Italian Jew, Moshe Montefiore, about a hundred years ago to serve the poor Jews of Jerusalem. It still does, but not now—not with the fighting over the past year. They moved further into West Jerusalem, and we moved in. We're the Palmach, the elite strike force of the Jewish militia, the Hagannah, and Yemin Moshe, with thick limestone walls and its proximity to the Old City, serves us well.

I wince at the daylight, my head throbbing from the brandy. Trying to get some sleep last night, I'd taken a flashlight to forage in the kitchen. There had to be at least one bottle of wine—if only for ritual purposes. All I'd managed to find was a dusty half-bottle of something called "medicinal brandy." I finished it off while I enjoyed my last British cigarette—a Player's Navy Cut. The brandy helped me get some shut-eye, but now I'm paying the price.

I get up and head to the narrow afterthought of a bathroom. Finished with the toilet, I lean over the basin and splash cold water on my face. I towel off and check my beard in the cracked mirror. I shaved last week and there's not enough stubble to bother with.

My khaki trousers lie rumpled on the floor by my cot. I pull them on and walk across the room in bare feet, careful to avoid the jagged pieces of masonry scattered over the floor near the sandbagged window. I keep a pair of heavy green binoculars on a peg by the window, and using one lens I peek through a narrow gap between the sandbags, scanning the crenelated battlements along the top of the wall. I don't see any snipers. But what I do see makes me feel sick—a column of thick black smoke rising in the sky over the Jewish Quarter just beyond the wall.

That can't be good.

There are three quick knocks on my door and a voice calls out, "Good night."

There are plenty of infiltrators who cross from East to West Jerusalem, and by hearing "good night" instead of "good morning," I know it's one of our guys on the other side of the door. The opposite, of course, is used at night. It's simple and saves the effort of trying to remember changing code words that people tend to forget.

A khaki shirt is draped over the back of my desk chair. It looks clean. Clean enough, anyway. I put it on and go to the door, turn the key and peek out. There's a young soldier standing in the doorway—tanned handsome face with moist, dark eyes shaped like almonds and wavy black hair peeking out from beneath his floppy woolen cap. He extends an envelope.

"*Ha'mifaked Rabin*," he addresses me in Hebrew—Commander Rabin, "a dispatch from the Jewish Quarter."

He's new and hasn't yet learned that we're all on a first-name basis.

"Yitzhak," I tell him. "That's my name. Use it. What's yours?"

He seems taken aback. His broad shoulders sag. After a moment he replies, "Isser." He tries to smile, but the effort isn't very successful.

I take the envelope and ask, "How old are you?"

"Twenty."

"I'm twenty-six. Can you give me a few cigarettes?"

"Yes, sir . . . I mean, Yitzhak." He pulls a pack from his back pocket and hands it to me.

It's a local brand, Atid, and the cigarettes are a bit flattened; Isser has been sitting on them. I shake out a few, slipping them into my shirt pocket. I give him back the rest of the pack. "Thanks much."

"You're welcome." He hesitates, "Will there be anything else?"

"Yes. Pass word that I'll give a briefing in the dining hall in thirty minutes." I push the door closed.

I light an Atid, sit down at my small wooden desk and tear open the envelope. I unfold the buff-colored paper and read the cable:

TO: Yitzhak Rabin, Commander, Har'el Brigade, Palmach
FROM: Moshe Russnak, Acting Commander, Haganah—Jewish Quarter,
Old City of Jerusalem.
Sunday, 16 May, 1948—siege of Jewish Quarter continues.
We desperately require reinforcements and resupply. Over half our combat-
ants are dead or too badly wounded to fight.
Current fighters—110, civilian population—1,700.
Weapons:
Rifles—17
Sten guns—42
Machine guns—2
2-inch Mortars—1
Ammunition:
300 bullets for each rifle
500 bullets for each machine gun
0 mortar shells
Other:
374 hand grenades
126 assault grenades
200 Kg. explosives
We recently note that the irregular Arab militia is much more organized and
professional. They've succeeded in cutting off all supply routes from Western
Jerusalem. Our situation becomes more perilous by the hour. We need resup-
ply and reinforcements soon. We're running out of food, water and medicine.

"You're also running out of time," I say aloud and toss the paper on my desk. I lean back in the chair and look across my room at the sand-bagged window. If it weren't blocked up I'd be looking across the Hinnon Valley at the Dormition Abbey on Mount Zion and at the walls of the Old City just beyond. Only a few hundred yards away, it may as well be a few hundred *miles* away.

"What the hell are we waiting for?" I ask for the hundredth time. I have four divisions poised for an attack on Zion Gate. We could break through to the Jewish Quarter, resupply and get out in an hour. But every time I beg central command in Tel Aviv for the go-ahead, they tell me to wait. Wait for what? I hate waiting.

Looking back at the dispatch, I scan Russnak's careful accounting of fighters, weapons and munitions. "Pathetic."

I drag slowly on the cigarette and tap off the ash on the edge of my desk—the small red lettering on the white cigarette paper catches my eye—Atid, Hebrew for *future*. Leave it to optimistic Jews to name a cigarette the future. I look back at the dispatch and shake my head, so much for the future of the Jewish Quarter.

There's something about Russnak's note that bothers me. Sure, it's depressing as hell, but there's just something wrong about it, something that doesn't add up. As I inhale a lungful of smoke it hits me—this sentence:

> *We recently note that the irregular Arab militia is much more organized and professional.*

Over the years, the thing I've come to know about the irregular Arab militia is that they're just that—*irregular*—disorganized and undisciplined, more interested in looting a home than holding a position. Suddenly they're "organized" and "professional"?

It had to be something else. The Arab Legion is organized and professional, but it's still in Trans-Jordan and far from Jerusalem. I know that for a fact. The Legion hasn't joined the conflict. Not yet.

So, what the hell am I missing? I light another cigarette from the stub, unable to shake the feeling. I take a slow drag and decide not to think about it.

I wonder when I'll see Leah again. She's doing clerical work at the Palmach operations center in West Jerusalem and we haven't spent more than a few hours together since my brigade was moved to this forward position three weeks ago. She came by to visit last week toward evening, but she couldn't spend the night. We had a good time for a few hours anyway. And we had the talk about getting married, that is, if we both live through this.

A pair of gray woolen socks loll out of my ankle-high light brown leather boots on the floor by the desk. Squinting against the smoke, I pull on the socks. As I'm lacing up the boots, there's another knock at the door and I'm hoping it's Leah. But then I hear a male voice call out the code greeting, "Good night."

Isser again.

I glance at my watch as I open the door. "It's not time for the briefing yet."

"Another dispatch, Yitzhak." He hands me an envelope.

"From the Old City?"

"No. From Natanel Lorch at the Tannous building. He says it's urgent."

Standing at the door, I tear open the envelope. Unfolding the dispatch, I see that Isser takes a step to leave. "Don't go yet. Wait till I see what this is about."

TO: Yitzhak Rabin, Commander, Har'el Brigade, Palmach
FROM: Natanel Lorch, Haganah, Jerusalem.
Sunday, 16 May, 1948
Just after dawn this morning, a middle-aged woman attempted to breach the
roadblock near New Gate. When her vehicle was disabled, she ignored orders
to halt and somehow eluded Arab snipers along the Old City wall as well
as fire from Haganah fighters behind the barricades. She managed to find
shelter in a stone shack near our position. When the shack was destroyed by
a bangalore torpedo, she was buried under the rubble. Despite sporadic fire
from the Old City, we managed to dig her out. She was bruised and cut but
not seriously hurt. She claims to be a resident of West Jerusalem employed at
the Palestine Archeology Museum in East Jerusalem, but she has no identity
papers. She is, however, in possession of certain diagrams and maps of the
Old City you must see as soon as possible.

"I'll need a Jeep," I say as I stare at the words *certain diagrams and maps.*
"What about the briefing?"

"It can wait." I snap on my belt and stick my Webley service revolver
into the holster. "Let's go."

Isser seems surprised. "You want me to come with you?"

I nod. "If there's no driver, you're it."

Sheltered by the stone buildings of Yemin Moshe and some large
stands of oleander, we make our way up to the windmill on the ridge.
Montefiore built the windmill so that members of the colony might become
self-sustaining by making flour and baking bread. Only there was never
enough wind to turn the millstone, and they never made any bread. Not
one loaf. The windmill serves us well, however, providing shelter for our
Jeeps and giving us an observation point to keep an eye on the Old City
across the valley.

A driver sits in one of two Jeeps parked by the windmill. He's reading
a newspaper. I say goodbye to Isser, who heads back to Yemin Moshe, and
I hop into the Jeep.

"I need to be at the Tannous building ten minutes ago," I tell the
driver.

Pulling away from the windmill, I notice that there's a good deal of
broken stone masonry littering the blacktop. I look back and see that the
top of the windmill is gone.

As the Jeep gathers speed on St. Julian's Way, I turn to the driver and
shout over the roar of the motor and the rushing wind. "What happened
to the windmill?"

"The British blew it up last night!" the driver shouts in reply.

"Why did they do that?"

"They thought we were using it as an observation point."

"We were!" I flash him a smile. "But we'll get by without it."

"We're calling it 'Operation Don Quixote,'" he says laughing.

With everything that's going on, I have to think for a while before I get the joke. By that time we're coming up behind the Tannous building by Barclays Bank and taking fire from the top of the wall by New Gate. The driver swerves into the shelter of the Tannous building and I climb out.

"How long will you be, Yitzhak?" he asks.

"I don't know. Do you have any cigarettes?"

"Sure." The driver snaps open the glove box and hands me a tin of Player's. "Brand new—never opened."

"I can't accept these." I try to give them back.

"Please." He holds up a hand.

I reach for my wallet. "Well, at least let me pay you—"

"Don't be ridiculous, Yitzhak. I have plenty—liberated from the home of an English officer who shipped out last week. Enjoy them in good health. Consider them a gift from our departing British masters."

I slip the cigarette tin into a trouser pocket and nod toward a doorway. "Move in closer to the building. It's safer."

Once through the door, I start down a stairwell littered with pieces of plaster and chunks of broken masonry, the dusty air heavy with the smell of cordite and urine. Reaching the basement, I stop and fish the last flattened Israeli cigarette from my shirt pocket. I light it and head down the hallway toward the closed doors of our improvised interrogation center.

I stop at the first door and knock three times. "Good night," I call out.

There's no response. I try the door handle and it opens to a small room, bare but for a table and chair. I pull the door closed and go down the hall to the second door. I try again. This time a key turns in the lock, and the door opens. Natanel Lorch steps out into the hallway. He's about my age, but with his glasses and thinning hair, he looks more like a middle-aged grocery clerk than a twenty-five-year-old Palmach operations officer.

"I'm glad you're here," he whispers. "I don't know what to make of this woman." He nods toward the closed door.

"You said she was carrying some diagrams . . ."

"Yeah." He slips a green canvas bag off his shoulder and hands it to me. Inside, there's a small leather-bound notebook secured by a rubber band.

"What information do you have on her?"

"Not much." He fishes a piece of paper out of his shirt pocket and reads, "Says her name is Tirzah von Wertheimer, thirty-six years old, a resident of the German Colony, where she lives with her father who's supposedly the curator of the Palestine Archeology Museum."

"She's a German national?" I ask.

"No. She claims she was born here, says her mother was a Yemenite Jewess who died from smallpox when she was a kid."

Holding the notebook in my hand, I hang the canvas bag on my shoulder and take a step toward the door. "Anything else?"

"No." Lorch fidgets with his notes, keeping his eyes down. "Yeah. She's beautiful, Yitzhak, a real looker."

"She's also more than ten years older than you, Natanel."

Lorch fixes me with his eyes from behind his glasses. "This woman is dangerous—"

"All women are dangerous. Let's not keep this one waiting."

I push past him, open the door and step into the room.

Lorch is right—Tirzah is beautiful. And it's not easy for a woman to look this good when her lustrous brown hair is matted with dirt, there's a field bandage on her forehead over her left eye and blood splattered on her white shirt. Though there is the allure of smooth olive skin, serene brown eyes, and her hands bound behind her back.

Turning to Lorch, I tell him to release her arms. He takes a knife from his belt and cuts the rope.

"Thanks," she says in Hebrew as she rubs her wrists and looks up at me with those eyes. "*Efshar l'daber im katzin bachir?*" she asks, her voice low and rich, with a touch of disdain and irritation. "Is there a senior officer I might speak with?"

"I'm as senior as they come," I reply.

"Really? What are you? Twenty?"

"Actually, twenty-six, and you're stuck with me. I'm the commander of Har'el Brigade . . ."

I can see she's not impressed. I hold up the notebook. "Where did you get this?"

"It belongs to my father, Gunter von Wertheimer." She stands up and extends a hand, strong with long fingers.

Lorch flinches and draws his sidearm, pointing it at the woman.

"Please sit down, Miss. You're making my friend nervous." I see that she's wearing a pair of light brown dungarees, a leather belt cinched tight at her slender waist.

She sits down but I can tell she's not too happy. "That notebook belongs to my father. I want that notebook, and I want to get out of here."

"Soon enough, Miss von Wertheimer. First, I need to look at this," I hold up the notebook, "then we talk." As I turn to leave I say to Lorch, "I'll be back in a few minutes. Will you be okay?"

He nods, though his eyes shift uncomfortably. He keeps the gun pointed at the woman.

I stand at the door and look down at her. "Be good now."

She rolls her eyes and shrugs, her brown hair brushing her shoulders.

I head down the hallway to the second room, open the door and step inside. There's a battered brass lamp and a large black telephone on the table. I bend forward and click on the light.

Lifting the canvas bag off my shoulder, I put it on the desk, take the Player's cigarette tin from my trouser pocket, strip off the clear wrapper, and open it. God, it smells good. I light a cigarette, sit down and slip the notebook out of the bag. The worn brown leather cover is embossed with the faded initials, GVW, on the lower edge. I peel off the rubber band and open the notebook.

I glance through pages crowded with careful English cursive along with loose pages. Unfolding these, I spread them out under the lamplight— detailed hand-drawn maps and meticulously labeled diagrams. In about ten seconds I realize that I'm looking at hidden passageways, subterranean chambers and underground aquifers within the Temple Mount. My heart begins to pound in my ears as I glance through pages of cramped notes, page after page.

Minutes pass. I'm not sure how many. I stop reading when a long cigarette ash falls onto the table by the phone.

This notebook—I've never seen anything like it. I don't fully understand its significance, but I know someone who might.

I reach for the phone and lift the heavy receiver. I'm in luck—the phones are working and the operator picks up.

"I need to speak with Brigadier General Yigal Yadin in Tel Aviv."

She puts me on hold.

Yadin is chief of Haganah operations. He's also an aspiring archaeologist. I hold the receiver between my head and left shoulder, freeing my hands to sort through the loose pages.

After a minute the operator is back. "General Yadin will speak with you now." She patches me through.

He gets right to the point. "If this is about getting permission to enter the Old City, the answer is still no. Ben-Gurion is certain that once we enter the Jewish Quarter, the Legion will attack, and that's something we can't—"

"Hold on, Yigal," I cut him off. "This has nothing to do with that."

"It doesn't?"

"No, but it does have everything to do with the Old City."

"I knew it, Yitzhak. You're too clever for your own good—"

"Hold on a minute! I've intercepted some fairly extensive information about tunnels and aquifers within Mount Moriah."

"Okay," he says after a short pause, "I'm listening."

"I have in my hands a notebook full of precise descriptions with detailed maps and diagrams—underground passages, hidden chambers, extensive waterways."

"Where did you get it?"

"A woman I have in custody right now. She practically got herself killed crossing from East to West Jerusalem. She claims this is the work of her father, the curator of the Palestine Archeology—"

"Tirzah von Wertheimer!" Yadin exclaims.

"You know her?"

"Not well, but yes. Like my dad, her father is a biblical archeologist and Tirzah has followed in his footsteps. They're both academically solid." Yadin pauses. "I need to see that notebook, Yitzhak. I want you to courier it to me as soon as possible."

"She says she wants it back."

"I don't care—tell her I'll keep it safe. Tell her I'll return it as soon as I can . . ."

"Will you?"

"Maybe." I can hear Yadin begin to lose his temper. "Look, the battle for Jerusalem may hinge on that information. It's strategically important, vital. Have Lorch send the notebook now with the morning convoy."

"Will do—"

"Good. And if you find out anything else from her, let me know. I'll look forward to seeing that notebook later today."

Yadin hangs up before I can ask again about resupplying and rearming the Jewish Quarter. But I guess he already answered that question. I hate being a *nudge*, but I know that the Quarter won't last much longer without some help—maybe a day or two tops. But maybe Ben-Gurion will change his mind when he sees this stuff.

I rearrange and refold the loose papers and put them back among the pages of the notebook. After securing it with the elastic band, I put it into the green canvas bag and stand up. I click off the light, take one last drag on the cigarette, and leave the room. Time to talk to Miss Tirzah von Wertheimer.

I knock on the door of the interrogation room and say, "Good night."

The door opens and I see Lorch, gun in hand, guarding the woman.

"Natanel, I need to speak with you."

He hesitates. "But—"

"I need you to do something for me."

He backs out of the door and pulls it closed.

"Here." I take the notebook out of the canvas bag and hand it to him. "Put this in a sealed envelope for top secret delivery to Brigadier General Yigal Yadin in Tel Aviv. It has to go out now, with the morning convoy."

He nods and moves quickly down the hall. It's pretty clear he's also anxious to get away from our prisoner.

I push the door open and step in. The woman is pacing.

"Listen, I have to get out of here—" she freezes, her eyes wide. "Where's my notebook?"

"Right here," I tap the green canvas bag as I close and lock the door.

"Give it back to me!" she shouts and steps forward.

"Calm down!" I pull out my Webley pistol and motion toward the chair. "Sit down! We need to talk."

"You'll give it back to me, right?" she crosses her arms, frowning as she plants herself down in the chair by the table.

"Right—just as long as you answer a few questions." Still holding my sidearm, I slide out the chair across from her and sit down. "Want a cigarette?" I try to look sympathetic as I hold up the Player's tin with my free hand.

"I prefer a cigar." She glares at me, then laughs in a gently mocking way. "Sure." She reaches out her hand and takes one. "Do I get a light?"

Still aiming the pistol in her general direction, I toss her a box of matches. She catches it in her hand and lights the cigarette.

"Afraid of a girl?" she asks as she inhales, her eyes narrowing drowsily.

"Just want to make sure we understand each other . . ."

"Oh, I understand you very well, Yitzhak. In fact, I know all about you . . ." She exhales slowly, her eyes shining through the smoke.

"Really," I laugh. "You know all about me? Prove it."

"Ask me something—anything."

"Okay . . . where was I born?"

"Here in Jerusalem, Shaare Tzedek Hospital."

"When?"

"March 1, 1922." She leans back in the chair. "Too easy. Ask me something else, something almost no one knows."

For a minute, I can't speak. My mouth feels dry. It's strange she would know that stuff about me. On the other hand, information like that is public—anyone could find that out. "Okay," I say when I get my voice back. "What do I plan to do after the war?"

"I really don't want to say."

"Because you don't know—"

"No. Because it's kind of boring. You plan to study irrigation engineering in America, at UC Berkeley—"

"Okay," I shout as I push back from the table and stand up, pointing the pistol at her head. "Who *are* you?"

She leans back, crosses her arms, her right hand raised, gracefully cradling her cigarette. "You know who I am—Tirzah von Wertheimer."

"How do you know all that stuff about me?"

"Because we've been watching you."

"*We*? Who is *we*?" Now I'm really shouting.

She draws on the cigarette, as calm as I'm hysterical. "Sit down, Yitzhak," she says quietly, "We need to talk."

"Who is *we*?" I ask again.

"If I promise to tell you, will you calm down?" she asks smoothly.

I nod.

"So," she points at my chair. "Sit down."

I can't believe she's giving me orders. I sit down.

"And put the pistol away."

"And if I don't?" I ask without lowering my aim.

"Then you don't trust me and we have nothing more to say to each other."

I don't know how to respond, so I don't say or do anything. I just sit there trying to figure out how to regain control of this interrogation. Thankfully, she breaks the silence.

"Look, Yitzhak," she leans forward and fixes me with her eyes. "One thing I will tell you is that we not only know who you are, but we like what we see. We believe that you might become the kind of leader who actually solves problems . . ."

"As opposed to . . . what?"

"As opposed to the kind of leader who creates problems—there's always plenty of those."

I'm not sure if she's just flattering me, but I feel no sense of guile from her. I actually find myself believing her, and despite my initial reserve, I find myself beginning to trust her.

She takes a puff and leans back. "So, please—put the pistol away so we can speak as friends."

"Okay, but don't try anything." I slip the Webley into the holster and snap it shut. I reach for a cigarette as I try to calm down. "May I have my matches back?"

"Sure." She tosses the box to me.

I break a matchstick and fumble with another but finally manage to light the cigarette. I can't believe how my hands are shaking. I try to calm down as I exhale. Squinting at her through the smoke I ask again, "So, who is *we*?"

"Before I divulge that information, you must promise never to speak of this to anyone. Do you understand? What I say to you cannot leave this room."

That's a tough one. I raise my shoulders. "How can I make such a promise? What if that information puts the lives of my soldiers at risk? What if it might undermine the success of an operation?"

"Fair enough. I can promise you that our identity won't put any of your soldiers or operations at risk." She leans back in the chair. "It will only put *us* at risk—which is why you've got to promise not to tell anyone."

"Okay, you have my word."

"Good. What do you know about Melchizedek?"

"What has *that* to do with anything?"

"Humor me—what do you know?"

I remember a few things from Bible classes in school, which feels strangely appropriate since I feel I'm being quizzed by a teacher. "He was a king here thousands of years ago, before the city was called Jerusalem—the king of Salem, the king of righteousness. He welcomed Abraham when he first arrived in Jerusalem. But why are you asking me that?"

"Because *we* are the children of Melchizedek."

"And that means . . . what?"

"We are members of a fellowship going back thousands of years—men and women of every race and religion. We're the guardians of the Temple Mount, the guardians of Jerusalem."

I can see she's serious, that she actually believes what she's saying. I hadn't pegged her for a nut, but apparently, I was wrong. "That's it? That's the big secret?"

"Yes, and remember, you promised to tell no one."

"Don't worry, your secret is safe with me," I try not to sound too sarcastic. She may be a nut, but as I look at her through the cigarette haze, I wonder how she knew that stuff about me. Maybe she's psychic. Maybe she's psychotic. Maybe both.

I decide to steer the conversation back to reality. "I have one more question for you, Tirzah." I raise my index finger. "One question—why were you in such a hurry to cross from East to West Jerusalem. You almost got yourself killed."

"The notebook," she answers immediately, nodding at the green canvas bag hanging on my shoulder. "I have to keep it safe."

"Safe? What do you mean safe? Safe from what?—whom?" I feel a stab of guilt knowing that I lied to her—that the notebook is on its way to the command center in Tel Aviv.

Tirzah inhales deeply, the cigarette tip glowing red as she looks off into space. Watching her, I wonder how delusional she actually is. I wonder if there's room for a psychiatric admission at Hadassah Hospital on Mount Scopus. She raises her shoulders, "I don't know if I should tell you . . ."

"Is this part of the big secret I swore not to speak of?"

"No." She shakes her head. "And you'll find out eventually, anyway."

"Okay. So, tell me now."

"Do you remember when Germany's Afrikacorps was defeated in Tunisia?" she asks.

"Of course, but so what? That's ancient history."

"That was 1943—just six years ago . . ."

"And it has nothing to do with our situation here in Jerusalem."

"No, Yitzhak. It has *everything* to do with your situation here in Jerusalem."

"What the *hell* are you talking about?" I have no idea of where's she's going with this. I can't wait to hear.

"What if I told you that some of the Waffen SS troops, with their arms and munitions, left Tunis before it fell to the Allies?"

I shrugged. "I'd probably believe you."

"What if I told you that SS officers escaped from the rubble of Berlin in '45 as the Americans and Russians were closing in? What if I told you that Nazi war criminals escaped from detention centers after the war?"

"Okay. All that might have happened, in fact, it probably did. But what's your point? What does that have to do with our situation?"

Then she drops the bombshell. "Because they came *here*."

I've just taken a puff of my Player's and I start laughing, then coughing. "That's the craziest thing I've ever heard," I manage to blurt out. "This is exactly the *last* place Nazi war criminals would come to!"

"You asked for the truth," she says calmly. "This is it."

I lean back and shake my head. "I've been told you're a good archeologist. Maybe you should stick to ancient history."

"But—it gets worse, Yitzhak. Have you ever heard of General Heinrich Mueller, head of the Gestapo?"

"Who hasn't? Everyone knows he escaped from Berlin and defected to Soviet Russia. He's working with the KGB—"

"Not anymore. Mueller is here. In Palestine. In Jerusalem. Don't your intelligence people know anything about this?"

"Of course not!" I shout at her. "Because there's nothing to know. What your saying is absurd, impossible!"

"That's what I thought. But that's the way it is, Yitzhak. Heinrich Mueller is here with several dozen troops." She sighs and leans back in the chair. "I'm telling you the truth. If you don't believe it, that's your problem."

I figure I'll try to reason with her. "So, Heinrich Mueller and his dozens of troops—where *are* they? Why don't I know about then? Why doesn't anyone ever see them? Are they invisible?"

She nods. "In a matter of speaking, yes. And you're right about part of the reason—no one sees them because no one could possibly believe they're here." She takes a final puff on her cigarette then tosses it to the concrete floor and crushes it out. "The other reason is that they blend in. They've infiltrated both sides—"

That gets my attention. "What do you mean, they've infiltrated *both sides?*"

"Some are disguised as Arab irregulars—under the command of a former SS officer, Robert Brandenberg . . ."

She stops talking. I guess because she thinks she hit a nerve, which she did. In an instant, all my certainty is gone. I feel dizzy, cold and clammy.

"Are you okay?" she asks. I can't tell if she's concerned or amused. Maybe both. "You look awfully pale. Was it something I said?"

I nod silently, thinking back to the dispatch from the Jewish Quarter— that sentence: *We recently note that the irregular Arab militia is much more organized and professional.* Suddenly it all makes sense. I feel nauseated and I hold my head in my hands. We already knew about the Mufti's con- nection with the Third Reich along with a few other operatives and Nazi sympathizers, but realizing the extent of their penetration shakes me to the core. And that's only half the problem. I look up at her. "And you said they've infiltrated *both* sides—*our* side?"

She leans forward, her arms on the table, one hand cupping the other. She begins to speak, calmly and without hesitation, her voice barely above a whisper. "In 1940, Hitler gave a series of speeches inviting any coalition that might isolate and defeat England. Certain elements of the Jewish set- tlement in British Mandatory Palestine jumped at the chance of defeating England and seizing all of Palestine."

I had heard rumors about this and ask, "Are we talking about the Revisionist Zionists, the Irgun?"

"Not the main body of the Irgun. Like the Haganah, they declared a ceasefire in the struggle against England while the British were fighting the common enemy, the Nazis. But a faction saw Great Britain as the *real* enemy and broke away. They continued to attack the British with beatings, targeted assassinations and random bombings. They used the same tactics to terrorize Arabs and any Jews who didn't agree with them. Do you know what I'm speaking about?" she asks and wraps her hands around mine. Her touch is comforting and captivating—I keep my eyes down. I know she's looking at me and I don't want to get lost in her eyes.

Staring at the tabletop I nod. "Of course I know about that faction. You're referring to Lehi—the Fighters for the Freedom of Israel. They've been a thorn in our flesh for years. I know all about them."

"Here's the part you don't know." She gives my hand a gentle squeeze, lets go and sits back. "Early in '41, they submitted a formal proposal to Hitler via a German diplomatic mission in Beirut."

"To fight against the English in Palestine?"

"That and more. They offered to join the war on the side of Nazi Germany, to help defeat England with the promise of receiving control of all mandatory Palestine after the war, to form a totalitarian state bound to Germany by treaty to maintain and strengthen the New Order in the Near East."

"Okay, suppose you're right. But that was then—the situation now is different. The British are on their way out and there's a UN plan to partition Palestine between Arabs and Jews—"

"Which nobody accepts," she says, cutting me off. "The Arabs don't accept it, the Irgun and Lehi certainly don't accept it, and Ben Gurion really doesn't accept it either, though he pretends to for the sake of expedience and appearances."

"And let's not forget another minor detail, Tirzah—Germany lost the war, the Nazis are finished!"

"Oh, Yitzhak," she smiles sadly and draws a deep breath. "They're hardly finished. They had a contingency plan all along."

"What are you talking about?" I ask, irritated that the world I thought I knew continues to crumble.

"The Third Reich disappeared from the world stage and spread out in another form, a dormant state—like spores influencing and infecting anyone they touch. Their goals haven't changed, only their tactics. You asked me why I risked my life to cross from East to West Jerusalem." She points with her chin at the empty canvas bag hanging by my side. "The reason is that notebook. Heinrich Mueller wants that information and he'll do anything to get it. I have to keep the notebook out of his hands."

With a twinge of guilt, I clear my throat and tap the bag. "I saw that it contains details about passageways, aquifers, and chambers within the Temple Mount. What does Mueller care about an archeological survey?"

She laughs at the question in that gently mocking way of hers. "Do you really have to ask?" She takes a comb from the breast pocket of her shirt, sits up straight, and begins combing her hair.

I raise my shoulders. "Does Mueller think it'll give him some strategic advantage in the siege of the Jewish Quarter? I suppose it might—"

"That's only a very small part of the picture, Yitzhak."

"So, what's the big picture?"

She seems to hesitate as she returns the comb to her pocket. When she begins speaking, it's clear that she's choosing her words carefully. "In academic circles, it's well known that my father and I have a longstanding interest in the Temple Mount. We've used Robinson's and Wilson's research and added some of our own." She leans forward and points to the canvas bag. "All that information is in there, and with it Mueller knows he'll be able to move his troops around Jerusalem unseen. It will give him a huge tactical advantage."

"So what if they conquer the Jewish Quarter? They've nearly managed to do that already." I take another cigarette from the tin and offer her one.

She leans forward, touching my hand as I light her cigarette. Leaning back in her chair, she exhales. "It goes way beyond the Jewish Quarter, Yitzhak. Mueller is an agent provocateur. He's very good at it. That's what he did early in his career in Germany and that's what he's doing now. He knows how to use fear and nationalism to create mistrust and hatred, and he has agents on both sides doing just that. He wants to keep the pot boiling, to make sure you and the Arabs are at each other's throats for years to come. And with the British out of the picture, he has the unstable power vacuum he needs . . ."

"A power vacuum to be filled by the thousand-year Reich?"

"*B'di'ook*!" she says with a little smile. "Exactly!"

"Really, Tirzah, that war is over—"

"Not as far as Mueller's concerned. And with the British gone, and with the benefit of the information from that notebook, he'll establish a power base here."

I shake my head. "But he's got so few operatives. How does he believe he'll ever get away with it?"

"Because he'll have leverage, Yitzhak. He'll have a hostage."

"A hostage? Who?"

"Not who. What. The Temple Mount will be his hostage and Jerusalem will be his capital. That's the plan."

I feel sick again. She's right. The Allies could firebomb Dresden and Tokyo, but they can't touch Jerusalem, and they certainly can't touch the Temple Mount.

Tirzah stands up, tosses the cigarette onto the bare concrete floor and crushes it out. "So, if you'll be so kind as to give me my notebook, I'll be going."

"No," I say simply.

"What do you mean, no?" I can tell she's getting mad, and I can't blame her. "But . . . but you promised me!"

"Your notebook is on its way to Tel Aviv, Tirzah."

"What?" Her fists are tight by her side. "I trusted you!" She screams and lunges at me, flailing with her hands, hitting me in the head and chest. I pin her arms back and push her against the wall by the door. I'm not too rough with her because I know she's right. I'm also beginning to like her.

"Let me explain," I say over and over. Finally she stops struggling, but I don't let go of her arms.

"Look, I'm sorry, but I had no choice."

"So where is it now?" She's still shouting.

"I sent it by secure convoy to our command center in Tel Aviv—to be delivered directly to Yigal Yadin for review and safekeeping. He says he knows you, and that you can trust him to keep his word. He promises to keep it safe and give it back to you when he's done."

I feel her body sag and I step away. She wanders back to her chair and sits down heavily.

I remain standing by the table, trying to catch my breath as I look down at her. She's staring past me at the bare wall, and I can tell she's turning the facts over in her mind. I take the opportunity to study her face, so lovely, solemn and brooding, the angular face of a queen.

After about a minute she shrugs. "You're probably right—Yadin can be trusted to keep it safe. He's not one of them." She stands up and heads to the door.

"Where are you going?" I ask.

"Tel Aviv."

"I'll get you a ride."

"No. I'll be fine, Yitzhak, but thanks for the offer."

"I insist, but why Tel Aviv?"

"Yadin will need my assistance. I can help him understand some of the details . . ." She pauses, then adds, "I'll also warn him about Mueller and his troops. He needs to know."

"Why?"

"Because, like you, he's in danger."

"Really? I'm in danger?" I plant a finger on my chest. "We're all in danger!" I point in the direction of the Old City. "In case you haven't noticed, we're at war—"

"No, Yitzhak. That's the enemy you know. That's the enemy you expect, in one form or another, with or without former SS among the Arab irregulars." She looks at me and I see depths of sadness in her serene brown eyes. She leans close and whispers, "You need to watch your back."

I unlock and open the door. She leads the way down the dusty hallway, threading her way among pieces of plaster and broken masonry. Once outside, I see it's early evening, and the Jeep and driver are still there.

"Take her to central command in Tel Aviv," I say and nod good-bye.

She waves as the Jeep pulls away and heads west on Jaffa Road.

I watch the Jeep disappear in the dusk, feeling a hollow weight on my chest, an emptiness.

I draw a deep breath and head back into the Tannous building. I go into the second room, click on the light and ring up Yadin on the telephone. I let him know about my conversation with Tirzah and tell him she's on her way, and that she wants to help. He says it sounds like a good idea. After I disconnect, I still feel terrible.

I figure that since there's no go-ahead to attack the Old City, I might as well see Leah. I ring her up at her West Jerusalem office. She says she'll try to come by and see me after work. I begin to feel a little better.

By the time I get back to my quarters at Yemin Moshe it's already dark.

I leave the light off and go to the window. I move aside one of the sandbags and look across at the walled city. Flames rise from the Jewish Quarter. A single dying flare is banking over the Mount of Olives. When it goes out I look up—the sky is full of stars. And for a change, it's very quiet—I don't hear a single shot.

I do hear footsteps outside my door and three quick knocks. I'm hoping to hear Leah's voice. Instead, a male voice calls softly, "*Boker tov.*" Good morning. It's Isser. I tell him to wait a minute.

I remain standing at the window, looking across the Hinnon Valley at Jerusalem.

Good morning?

No. It isn't good and it isn't morning.

Night has taken hold of Jerusalem—dark and unrelenting night.

L'DOR V'DOR
(FROM GENERATION TO GENERATION)

Some You Lose

Nancy Richler

On the morning after his father's death Morris Elkin woke early and slipped from his mother's house to meet a woman for coffee. The woman was neither friend nor family, and as he drove the quiet streets of the pre-rush hour city he wondered why he was doing it.

He hadn't recognized her name when it showed up in his inbox, one of several e-mails with the subject heading *condolences*. "I'm sorry for your loss," he read, an impersonal message that required no response, but he was in no mood to turn his back on a kind sentiment. "Thank you," he responded, and a moment later she wrote back. "You're welcome."

He glanced at the clock—2:00 A.M. The house was silent, the street outside frozen in the stillness of a winter night. He knew it was not possible that he was the only person in the world still awake, but until a moment ago it had felt like he might be. "Remind me who you are," he wrote, hoping she wasn't someone he had slept with.

"Sonya," came the immediate reply, which annoyed him, felt like a game.

"Do I know you?" he asked.

"Not yet," she wrote back.

Great, he thought. A weirdo who reads the obits every day and then sends off e-mails to whichever mourners she can track down. There were people like that, he knew, people so isolated that their loneliness festered, turning them into stalkers of connection of any kind.

"I can meet you at Café Nico," she wrote next. "Rue Sauvé just east of Lajeunesse."

Right, he thought. It was time to cut this off now.

"I get off work at 6:00 A.M., can meet you at 6:30."

His father's funeral was still a day away but he was planning to speak— was expected to speak—and had not yet pulled together what he wanted to say. He had to shower, sleep, prepare a worthy eulogy. He got up and stretched, hoping the first line of the eulogy would come to him as first lines often did when he turned away from the screen.

"My father . . ." He paced the room. "Was not supposed to die. It was not his time. We were not meant to be here today."

That wasn't quite the beginning he'd been hoping for, but he couldn't forget the doctors' early assurances: *a complication*, they had said, *but nothing we can't treat*; the cheeriness of the nurses: *Why the worried faces? He'll be right as rain in no time.*

"Right as rain," Morris repeated now, an expression as stupid as it was meaningless, that his entire family had clung to nonetheless until the very final days of his father's life.

He heard the ping of an incoming e-mail, willed himself to ignore it.

"My father was . . ." he started again. "Full of surprises."

Terrific, Morris thought. Where could he go from there? *He saved his biggest surprise for last? Fooled us big time? Good one, Dad. The last joke's on you?*

He looked at the new e-mail. "I'm not what you think."

"Then what and who are you?" he wrote back, annoyed with himself the moment he sent it for playing along like a rat being trained to take a bait.

Her answer came within seconds. "Job 13:4"

He stared at it for a minute, impressed, despite himself. It wasn't often that he felt so handily outmaneuvered. And it had been many years since anyone in his life had been able to induce him to voluntarily look at a Bible.

There was a copy of the Bible in his parent's den, but that's where his sister was sleeping, and he wasn't about to wake her by turning on the light or rummaging through the bookshelves. He stood in the doorway to the den, hesitant to enter. The street lamp cast its own light through the window, and he could see the dark shapes of the books on the bookshelves, the dark mound on the couch that was his sister.

"What do you want?" Molly asked in the clear and alert voice of an insomniac.

"I thought you were sleeping."

"So that's why you came in here?"

Morris smiled. He and Molly had been close as children and had never fallen out of the habit of liking each other. "I was looking for something."

"So turn on the light," she said. "I'm not sleeping. In case you hadn't noticed."

"It's okay. It can wait till morning."

At that Molly sat up. "I can't sleep either."

He should have just googled the bloody verse, Morris thought. As fond as he was of Molly, he was not up for a heart to heart talk with her right now, the dissection that he knew she was about to embark on of every decision and wrong turn that had led to their father's unexpected death. Right, he thought, better to play cat and mouse with an anonymous correspondent online than talk to my sister on the night after our father's death.

"It just feels so unreal," Molly said. "I mean, he went in there with a broken leg, for God's sake. People do not die of broken legs. Have you ever, in your entire life, ever *once*, heard of anyone who died of—"

"He died of a blood clot, Molly. It happens."

"What, once in every twenty million cases?"

"Five percent of people who develop a pulmonary embolism die of it."

Molly looked at him. "Don't believe everything you read on the internet." Then, "Do you think he knew?"

"That he wouldn't make it?" He had to have known in those final couple of days, Morris thought, even though he pretended otherwise, continued to speak of his impending recovery for as long as he still had the breath to lie. "He couldn't have felt that hopeful when Simona started reciting the psalms."

"She did *what*?" Simona was their sister-in-law, the wife of their brother Daniel.

"It was very weird," Morris said. "Even for Simona."

"People do weird things when someone's dying," Molly said, and gave him such a long, considered look that he was suddenly sure she knew about the correspondence he'd been carrying on in the next room. "Look at me," she said. "Speaking of weird."

"What about you?"

"Putting off coming in for so long."

"It wasn't so long."

"Three days. Three critical days."

"You had no way of knowing how serious it was."

"Danny and Simona knew. "

Morris couldn't argue with that. As soon as Daniel heard the treatments weren't working he and Simona had flown over all the way from Israel, while Molly hadn't managed to arrive from Vancouver until after Albert's death.

"It's no small thing," she said. "To miss your father's death."

"No," he had to agree. "It isn't."

"I'll never forgive myself."

"That'll help," he said, which did draw a small, somewhat wan smile.

"What were you looking for when you came in here?"

"The Bible."

Molly nodded as if it were a completely ordinary thing for her brother, an atheist since grade school, to come into the den in the middle of the night, looking for the Bible. "For the eulogy?"

"I can't seem to get started," he said, an evasion that wasn't a flat-out lie. He looked over at the bookshelves and saw one of his father's copies of the *Tanakh*. He pulled it out and opened it to make sure that this was the one with an English translation alongside the Hebrew. "Try to get some sleep," he said. "We have the rest of our lives to beat ourselves up over our failures of omission and commission."

Beginning with this one, he thought, as he rushed back to his room, when he knew full well his sister could have used a bit more of his company. He opened the book to Job and found the verse the woman had referred to.

As for you, you whitewash with lies; worthless physicians are you all.

⅍

Why was he doing this, Morris wondered several hours later as he drove up the slope of the mountain that rose in the center of the city and gave it its name. He had managed to fall asleep, but had woken at five, knowing, even before he opened his eyes, that he was going to make that appointment. He knew it was a sick thing to be doing but he tried to convince himself that it wasn't. Who wouldn't be curious, he asked himself. The enigmatic exchange, the bizarre quote from the Bible, the possibility, alluded to in the quote, that this woman might know something that would cast light on his father's inexplicable death? Was she one of the physicians who had attended him? Maybe an intern who had seen something untoward but didn't want to risk her career to raise the problem with her superiors?

He skirted the western flank of Mont Royal along Côte-des-Neiges, then turned into the heart of the mountain along a narrower road that climbed steadily. To his right, below him, were the lights of Montreal. To his left, the city's dead sloped away in darkness. More than half the mountain was reserved for the dead, the cemeteries divided by religion—though no longer by language—as their occupants had been divided in life. The Jewish cemetery occupied a gentle slope of the northeastern fringe, just a short drive from where Morris sat now. Soon his own father would be lowered into the hole there that would be clawed out of the frozen earth to receive him.

Morris glanced at the clock in his car. He had an hour to kill before meeting this Sonya. Assuming she showed up. Assuming she was even a she, that she had any relation whatsoever to the name under which she sent out her cryptic e-mails. He pulled into the lookout, a parking space where he had spent many hours as a teenager, necking with various girlfriends on warm summer nights, though never with Julie, the one girl he had really wanted back then. In those days the cops would come by every so often to move people along. He expected the same would happen now, but it was five thirty on a winter morning and the temperature outside his car was so cold that the exhaust stood upright in a frozen column before dissipating. No one was parking or patrolling tonight.

He looked out at the lights of the city below. Halfway between the mountain and the river he could see the tower of the law firm where twenty years earlier he had been expected to rise like cream and hadn't. Beyond that, closer to the river, was the site of the former scrapyard where his father had started his own working life.

"My father was . . . a fortunate man." Right. So fortunate that he died of a freakish mishap, twenty years before his time. "My father was . . . simple in his desires." Makes him sound like a moron. "My father was . . ." He closed his eyes now. Maybe he should take a break and come at it from a different angle.

He didn't know what type of place Café Nico was, but he imagined a warmly lit diner with windows misted from the condensation of heated air clashing with cold, mugs of steaming coffee on vinyl-top tables, the banter of waitresses with their customers . . . Definitely a more appealing scene than sitting alone in his car in the minus-thirty-degree darkness hitting his head against the wall of his father's eulogy.

He drove down the eastern slope of the mountain, through the neighborhood where his father had grown up. It was a trendy area now, but still comfortably shabby, with its three-story walk-ups unchanged, if less crowded inside, from the days when large immigrant families filled them. He drove north from there, past the furthest edges of creeping trendiness, under the elevated highway that had been built in the early sixties on the eve of the city's glory days. The highway had recently started shedding concrete chunks of itself onto the roadway below—the underside now seemed to be held together by a wrapping of metal mesh. Morris stepped more heavily on the gas to get out from under it and emerged in a neighborhood of low rise apartments, rows of them, squatting against the frozen morning that was just beginning to dawn. Was this the neighborhood where his correspondent lived, he wondered. He looked at the lit windows that checkered the dark facades of the brick buildings and imagined a woman in one of those rooms standing before a mirror, arranging her hair, applying lipstick, readying herself for the meeting she had arranged.

There was no waitress at Café Nico, bantering or otherwise, just an old man sitting on one of the stools at the counter, hunched over the morning paper. Nico himself, Morris suspected. He looked up when Morris walked in and motioned to the empty restaurant, indicating that Morris might take any table he wanted. Morris chose the table by the radiator, ordered coffee, and settled in for the wait. It had taken him longer than he expected to get over here; it was now close to six thirty.

"Combien de sucres?" the man asked when he brought Morris his coffee. He looked even older now than at first glance.

"None, thanks."

When a packet of sugar was plunked unceremoniously beside his coffee Morris wondered if he'd offended the man by speaking in English. He wouldn't have pegged this guy for a language purist—or a francophone, for that matter—but you never knew.

"Il fait froid à ne pas mettre un chien dehors," Morris said.

The man stared at him blankly. "Just a minute," he said. "Haven't got my ear horns in yet." He disappeared into the kitchen, then returned with his hearing aid inserted. "What kind of eggs you say you wanted?"

Morris smiled. "Are you Nico?"

"Who wants to know?" He waited for Morris to repeat the order he hadn't made.

"Over easy," Morris said.

Nico shuffled off to fill the order; Morris pulled out a pen and paper to write the eulogy.

When I was thirteen I made the mistake of referring to my father as a junk dealer.

Too negative.

I was six the first time my father brought me to his smelter.

Better. Noise and heat, the magic of transformation . . .

My father believed in the magic of transformation.

A bit hokey, but he wasn't looking for the Nobel Prize here.

And he believed kindness, faith, and love were the forgers of human transformation.

Good, if not quite accurate, but was *forger* the right word? He'd come back to that later, moved ahead now with specific illustrations of his father's kindness, his faith, his love for his wife and family. Keep going, he told himself, no one is looking for nuance. Or truth, for that matter. His words began to flow, filling one side of the page, then the other. He glanced at his watch; a half hour had passed and Sonya hadn't shown. Neither had his eggs. He motioned to Nico.

"Cook's late."

"How much for the coffee?"

Nico waved away the notion of a charge for the coffee. Morris thought about insisting, then decided to simply leave a few dollars on the table. He put on his coat, his gloves, his hat, and began to make his way to the door.

"I'm sorry for your loss," Nico said.

Morris looked at him.

A burly man came through the door, letting in a blast of frigid air. "Sorry I'm late, Pops. The fucking bus . . . pardon my French," he said, with a nod to Morris. "I thought I'd fucking freeze to death waiting for it." He began to peel off layers of outer clothing as he made his way to the kitchen. "It's not a morning out there, it's a fucking nuclear winter is what it is."

"You want your eggs now?" Nico asked Morris.

"I want to know how you know—"

"Don't be mad. She's a good girl."

"I'm not mad," Morris said, forcing a calmness into his voice that he didn't feel. "I would just like to know—"

"She says your father was a good man. Always polite, always with a smile, a nice word."

"She knew him then?"

"She cleaned his room."

Morris cast through his memory trying to summon an image of the cleaning staff at the hospital, but he hadn't paid attention to them, except to lift his feet when he felt a mop coming his way.

"And how do you know her?"

"She's a regular. Comes in after her shift."

Except today, Morris thought. "Do you have any idea why she would have contacted me?"

Nico looked away as he shook his head, giving Morris the impression he was lying.

"I think she saw something," Morris said. "A mistake the doctors made. Something she shouldn't have seen that she thought I should know about."

"A job like hers . . ."

What, Morris wondered. She sees a lot she shouldn't see? But Nico wasn't inclined to finish his thought.

"She sent me a quote," Morris said. "*As for you, you whitewash with lies; worthless physicians are you all.*"

Nico nodded. "You didn't like the doctors?"

"I didn't like or dislike them. That's not the point."

What *was* the point, he wondered. He had been lured all the way across the city hours after his father's death, on one of the coldest mornings of the year, by . . . what, exactly? The possibility that someone out there—a complete stranger, a disembodied voice—might have something to tell him about his father's death or life?

"The quote, it's from the Bible?" Nico asked.

"What difference?"

"The last one was from the Bible too."

"The last one?"

"And the one before that, it was from Shakespeare. *Hamlet*, I think. Or maybe *King Lear* . . . *Ingratitude, thou marble-hearted fiend—*"

Morris looked at him. "She does this . . . often, then?"

Nico gave the question more thought than a simple yes or no answer would have seemed to Morris to have merited. "You should eat the eggs," he said. "You'll feel better."

"I really can't stay." Was deranged to have come in the first place, Morris thought.

Nico shrugged. As if to say, *suit yourself*. As if to suggest it was Morris who was being unreasonable.

"Order up," the cook called from the kitchen.

Baruch Dayan Emet
(Blessed Is the True Judge)

M. Dante

The call came in while I was at a luxury apartment in Atlanta. I was there as a call girl. A comfortable and lucrative two-week opportunity I had wanted to visit for more than five years. It took patient, hard work, always with a smile, plus a spoon of sugar to get the referral, but I was in! And then on the second day the call came. My father was dead.

His body shipped from Las Vegas to Boston. I was expected to meet the casket at the funeral home back in the area where I was born. I called the anonymous woman who ran the black book apartment, letting her know I had to go. Her voice was soft and kind in that Southern sort of etiquette. She confirmed if I left early, I'd not be able to return for future work. Tears flooded my senses, though I kept my composure. It was one of those moments in life for which there is no coaching, no practice, no preparation like you have with your best friend before a date or practice rounds before speaking in public. Stay and miss my dad's burial. Leave and potentially never have another job of this price point again. I shook my head and sighed in frustration.

At the funeral home, there were roses. Dozens of them. A decadent extravagance ordered from Las Vegas. My dad was Jewish. The funeral home was Jewish. Jews get pebbles. Not roses. The funeral director kind enough to display them without comment other than a polite nod, and quiet sentiment of acceptance. The roses were from my dad's "life companion," a man twenty years his junior, with whom he had lived for a decade. "Love, Sinclair" on each and every card.

In the casket, beneath the roses, lay my dad. Instead of the ritual *taharah*, he had to be embalmed to fly back across country. The first and only person in Lebanon-Tiffereth to be embalmed. Jews are supposed to simply be buried within a few days. Ashes to ashes. Dust to dust. Except for my dad. Eternally preserved with glamorous perfection. His hair blond instead of light silver. His suit stylish. He had stopped wearing suits when he moved from Boston to the Southwest twenty years prior. Trading the business attire in for jeans and brightly colored button-down shirts all the colors of the sunset. There he was, though, embalmed, wearing an elegant yet traditional dark suit and masculine tie, lying beneath the multiple bouquets of love. I have a photograph of me standing beside the casket. Sinclair, unable to be there with us, requested we ask permission to photograph the final process. The funeral director sighed, his expression pleasantly placid from practice, his eyes expressing displeasure as he acquiesced to our request. So there is an actual album of photographs. One of them, me, in my ill-fitting Ann Taylor dress jacket, and a brim hat, standing over my golden-haired, embalmed dad, with roses on his casket. My expression bizarrely perplexed with sadness and the surreal quality of the situation. This is my dad's death. No goodbye. Silent. Spontaneous. Strange.

In the business office, the funeral director sat on the opposite side of the desk from my dad's sister, her husband and me. Dad had no burial insurance. No prepay on the process. The plot, purchased by older family, all since gone, was paid in full, though the cost of the funeral itself was due without delay. I looked at the invoice, thinking I should have stayed in Atlanta. My aunt gently accepting the bill as I started to pull out my credit card, saying she would cover the cost of burial for her big brother. Her husband nodding his head in agreement. Embarrassment sat equal to appreciation.

The Conservative cemetery appeared bleak. At least to me. Utilitarian is a polite way to describe it. No ornaments or decorations. A stark place of almost unsettling silence. Situated off the side of a now busy highway, it is difficult to see the wrought-iron gate unless you know it is there. The turnoff from the main road dangerous even. Off in the distance, down the way, was a mall. Retail therapy being one of my dad's few vices, it seemed appropriate, despite the grounds lacking lush ambiance.

There were less than a dozen people present. Some *levayah*. Though in all fairness my dad had moved away a long time ago. Leaving behind his life with his family. Coming out of the closet as a homosexual. Able to go from whispers of eccentricity to living his truth every day. Besides two employees from a family company closed twenty-five years earlier, I was surprised to see his first man friend present. Not his "life companion," who at that moment would prove to be lying in a stupor of Oxycontin sported after pawning all the gold jewelry Dad left behind, but his first public romance. Ed. I pondered for a moment the humor in how, when my parents first divorced, they both had affairs with men named Ed. Instead of laughter in my ears, the quiet consoled me in a way that only during a death can it do. The silence soothing. Carrying a collage of fragmented memories. I remembered back to when I was ten or eleven, how my mother's boyfriend sat me down in the kitchen of our new apartment while my mother was out, telling me gruffly that my father was a faggot, and that my mother was with him now because he was a man, including being man enough to tell me, which no one else was. Years later he was arrested as a pedophile. I was grateful for my hat keeping the haze and clouded sunlight out of my eyes. I didn't have to see how empty it was there. I didn't like the idea of my dad being lonely for all eternity. After a turbulent life, I wanted him to be at peace. I wondered if the glowing moon rock I buried with my grandpa was doing its job of lighting the eternal night with light of safekeeping. Like a piece of sea glass collected when young, by day it represented the ocean we were raised near, and at night, the moon in the sky. Amid the Hebrew of the service the breeze, and an image of Lilith hiding behind a tree distracted me. Lilith living in one of the trees on the periphery of the grounds. An owl and seven ravens. Emptiness. Wide open emptiness.

Panic played with my senses, but then I realized he would be with the family that most loved and accepted him. No *dybbuk* could break through the veil of love here. The women who all doted over him, raising him while the men were away during the war. The great-grandparents and grandparents he remembered as active people, as opposed to fading photographs and nursing home odors. His mother who died at the same age as him, really, just shy of sixty. All the love buried deep down in the dirt. Ashes to ashes. Dust to dust. A part of me felt there with them. My *bubbe* and *zeyde*, the great-grandparents. My grandma and grandpa. My Nana. The aunts and uncles. All those who traveled the oceans here from far, far away. Ashes to ashes. All those embalming chemicals in with the dust left from the last exhale of life. Someone captured the moment. In the album I have of Dad's funeral, there is a photograph of me standing awkwardly attempting to keep my heels from sinking any further into the soil. My posture curved in a strange sort of serpentine bend. Brushing my hair back off my shoulders. Looking into the space where he would lie, neat and tidy, surrounded by family, eternally cleansed, coiffed and well dressed. A perfect state of narcissism for the eternal rest. This suddenly seemed so fitting. Except, of course, for the roses. The Hebrew service over, the funeral director came and pinned a torn piece of ribbon on my jacket. *Keriah.* Another photograph capturing the moment. My suit jacket and wide-brim hat felt too large for my frame. I wanted to rip off all my clothes. Shred them. Pin the torn ribbon directly into my skin. Instead I stood stoic. Ripped ribbon scratching me in the wind.

I had left him a message. "Good luck tomorrow. Don't forget, Dad, a good attitude is half of the ability to heal!" I said about his appointment to have his heart checked the next day. "I love you." But he was already dead. During the preliminary blood tests, his heart literally exploded right there in the hospital. The casket made its descent while I was lost in thought. Time doesn't always move in a straight line. I was given a fistful of dirt to throw down onto the casket. *Kevurah*. Mix it with tears and it may become a Golem. My dad called home early by a heart tired and slightly broken. He was ready to rest in the bosom of idyllic yesterdays, remembered in ritual visits by the shells and small stones from the shore left on each of the family headstones.

At his sister's house, situated by the ocean near where I was born, everyone was politely pleasant, though it was awkward. What were you doing in Georgia, each person asked? The polite questions burning each time over. I felt dirty. No chemical process could clean the stain I felt spreading through my spirit. The torn piece of ribbon scratching at my throat. An aging whore, daughter of a queer. Again I saw Lilith out of the corner of my eye. Saw her fly by in the wind. A seagull in the distance wailing into the breeze. The echo distracting. Diverting attention. I wondered if seagulls are ever distracted by the glare of the sun on sea glass, or by the moon reflecting off the waves of the ocean constantly in motion.

Yahrzeit Candle

Stephen Jay Schwartz

For my mother, Jean, who never ceases to give me strength.

The flame was blue and yellow and it stained his eyes with its light. Joshua blinked, brushing aside a trail of smoke that sought to engulf him. Please, he thought, no more memories. Let me just sit with you. He stared into the light. Its shape brought a series of confusing images to his mind. He saw a yellow teardrop standing straight while a smaller blue flame lay nestled within its transparent stomach. The flame looked like a torn string of taffy to Joshua. It stood alone in its space like the little blotch of hair that was combed across his father's bald forehead.

Joshua leaned on his tired arms. His heart jumped, colliding with his ribs. Let me *rest*, it seemed to say. He stretched his arms skyward, mimicking the flame. A long deep breath calmed his heart.

"Nothing to worry about," his father would say. "It's just a flutter. What you really need is a little sleep."

Joshua wished he were able to sleep. I could, he thought. I could get up from this chair and leave and give my forty-year-old body a rest. He looked at the candle and knew this was not possible. There would be time to rest and there would be time to sleep, but this time would never return. Joshua prayed to God it would never return.

Joshua continued to breathe normally, letting his body relax. On a final breath he inhaled a cloud of gray candle-smoke. He coughed and covered his face with his sleeve. He felt the stinging in his eyes and knew it was too late.

❦

"Sure is a big candle, Daddy."

It was the biggest candle he'd ever seen. "Did you make your wish?"

he said, excited. Joshua's father stood silent, having used all of his wishes. Reflections from the candle flame danced upon his face. Joshua frowned at the man and turned back to face the candle. It made him feel uncomfortable, a candle left to burn and burn. He'd already seen eight sets of candles in his lifetime and had succeeded in extinguishing them easily after the wishing ceremony. If only daddy would let me blow it out, he thought. A sure stream of air would do it—

His father's hand was a gentle pressure on his shoulder. "No." A soft word hardly spoken. Joshua crouched like an angry gnome. Who needs this stupid candle, he thought. It just sits here like a big, dumb firecracker without the guts to explode.

Joshua left his father and headed to his room. Soccer practice would be starting in an hour and he still needed to get dressed and feed his snake. Bull perked up immediately when Joshua entered. The boy dragged off the heavy bricks that seldom kept his snake in its cage. He reached in and caressed its soft back. The snake had been his Hannukah present the year before. He remembered helping his daddy sneak it into the house behind his mommy's back. The boy had been hinting for three months before the holiday, and his wish had come true. He remembered how his daddy stood up to keep the snake when his mommy threatened to leave. For that, Joshua awarded his father the honor of naming his new pet. After a moment of deep contemplation his father came up with the name Bull. "You know, for *Bull*snake." The man was a good doctor and a practical man, but creative he was not. Bull—a practical name for a bullsnake.

Joshua lifted the hollow Folgers coffee can. With both hands he shook the can in rapid circular motions, listening for the steady *k-thump*, *k-thump* of mouse bouncing off aluminum walls. He removed the lid and let the dazed rodent fall onto the snake's rocky tablecloth. Bull was on top of it instantly, strong muscles wrapping tightly around a fading body.

Joshua still squirmed at the sight of a dying mouse. It bothered him that the little ball of fur could be so vibrant one minute and so still the next. Bull's muscles relaxed and the mouse, thinned and flattened by the pressure, slid like a tear from his grip. The bulging eyes of the rodent were hard, round pebbles that looked as though they might pop.

The eyes reminded him of the first time he fed his bullsnake. It had been hard for Josh to part with that first mouse. He had grown close to it, naming it Sammy. He couldn't bring himself to sacrifice the little creature. Concerned, his father pulled him aside.

"Some die," he said, "so that others may live."

"But I want them both to live."

His father's voice grew into a shaky whisper. "Don't you see, Josh, you're not paying attention to your snake. And because you're not feeding him and you're not spending any time with him, he's dying."

He had trouble speaking to his son of such things. Joshua remembered him leaving the room, leaving him alone with a decision to make. His father's behavior scared him. He wanted to know what it meant to be dying. He wanted to understand the secret his father seemed to know.

Joshua let the mouse fall from his hand into the snake's cage. Bull killed it quickly, leaving a limp carcass with bulging eyes. Joshua's first sight of death made him feel sick, yet he knew it had to be done. After all, Joshua wanted his bullsnake to live.

Presently, Josh replaced the bricks and left the snake to feed alone. He crossed over to the dresser where his soccer shorts were kept pressed and ready for Monday-night practices. He sifted anxiously through a mound of underwear and socks before discovering that his shorts weren't there. He performed a clumsy summersault across his bed and landed beside the dirty clothes hamper, which sat at the far end of the snake's seven-foot cage. Joshua dug through the hamper and surfaced with the dirty shorts in his hand.

"Mommy!" He sprinted the long hallway waving his tricolor shorts like a revolutionary flag. He hurdled their nervous Pekingese and landed at his mother's feet.

"My shorts, Mommy! You didn't do the laundry!"

"Hush, Joshua." She filled two glasses with the dark red wine he'd seen them drinking at Passover.

"But—"

"Calm down, please. There's no soccer practice tonight. I want you to go to your room and do your homework."

"But Seth and Danny—"

"They can do without you this week. Now do your schoolwork and leave Mommy and Daddy alone for a while."

Joshua scrunched up his face and delivered the evil eye. She shook her head dismissively and left the kitchen, a glass of wine in each hand. Joshua stomped off. He picked up the scraggly Pekingese by a clump of fur behind its ears. It yelped in protest before he managed to quiet it under his thick sweatshirt.

His mother's words bellowed from the dining room—"You be good to that dog, Joshua, or you'll lose *all* your pets!" Josh hurried back to his room and slammed the door. The dog leapt onto the bed and hid, shivering, under Joshua's pillow.

Joshua paced the carpet wondering what he'd done to be sent to his room. The only thing he could think was the math test he failed two weeks earlier. Although a few days before that he had accidentally shot the neighbor's cat with Danny's new BB gun. He doubted he was in trouble for that because the neighbors were still out of town and he knew the house-sitter hadn't seen a thing. Josh figured it must have been the math test. With that he settled down and focused on his schoolwork.

Wednesday Joshua returned from school filled with energy. He was hoping his daddy would be home from work so they could kick around the soccer ball. It was a senseless wish, in a way. Joshua's father was almost never home from work and even when he was it was only to pick up something he'd forgotten. Joshua shelved his wish when he saw that all the lights were off in the house.

His feet moved through the house like fingers reading braille, avoiding the subtle obstacles that hid in the dark. The hallway that led to his room was overrun with flickering light. Josh backed away from the collage of shadows, realizing at once that the candle was still burning. His heart skipped a beat as fear filled his body. *How can that be?* he thought. Even Passover candles melted before the night was over. *Why is it still burning?*

"Joshua?"

He turned around quickly and felt the sweat fly from his chin. His father stood in silhouette against the candle.

"You're breathing too loudly. Does your chest hurt?"

"No," Josh lied. His heart was fine for sports, yet fear tended to startle it.

"Come here," his father commanded.

Joshua reluctantly followed his father's order. Lately his dad had been a bore, sitting in front of the candle night and day, skipping dinner, putting Visine drops in his eyes. He'd hardly said a word since bringing the candle home.

The man's hands found soothing pressure points along Joshua's shoulders, arms and chest. Joshua didn't mind the heart condition. All the doctors agreed that it was a minor problem, and Josh could even think of an advantage or two. It kept him from having to go to PE when he felt like sitting out, and it gave his father a reason to hold him close. Joshua liked being held by his father. It made him feel important. He knew, of course, that he could never be as important as his father. Everybody was always saying how kind and understanding his father was and how he was the best doctor in town. His father loved working at the office and spent almost all of his time there. He never missed a day of work, not for anything.

Joshua glared at the candle. Daddy never missed a day until you came along, he thought. If Daddy's going to miss a day he should do something important. He should take me horseback riding or fishing or something, instead of spending all this time with you. Joshua gave the flame the evil eye.

"You appear to be healthy," came the doctor's prognosis. "Are you doing the sit-ups—"

"Can we play Frisbee?"

The father turned slowly from the boy and faced the candle.

"Not today, Josh." His voice a solemn whisper.

Joshua felt a dull shock pass through his body. Tears came to his eyes as he followed his father's gaze.

"I don't like the candle, Daddy. Why is it here?" His lower lip had a chipmunk's quiver. He wiped a drippy nose across his arm. The man brought out a handkerchief to wipe Joshua's face, then lifted the boy to his knee.

"I want you to look at the candle, Josh."

Joshua leaned into his father's chest and did as he was told. The light was too bright in his eyes and he turned away. His father gently pushed his head back to face the candle.

Little Joshua Feder stared into the flame and realized that he hadn't seen his Frisbee in years. He had meant to ask his father if he wanted to play soccer, but somehow Frisbee got stuck in his mind.

"Look into the flame, Josh, and don't be afraid to let the smoke get in your eyes."

Joshua saw the little trail of smoke that drifted up from the flame. It had the shape of a frizzled ribbon on a birthday present.

The flame was an opaque lemon gumdrop. Its center was almost white and seemed flat, two-dimensional, like a thin piece of wax paper tearing through an ebony canvas. It stood prominently and demanded his attention. Joshua couldn't shake the feeling that the flame was watching him as much as he was watching it. Its stare was the stronger one and Joshua was the first to try to break it. But it wouldn't let him. He felt dizzy. The blood was rushing fast and he heard his pulse echo in his temples. His eyes grew tired as smoke drew scribbles around his pupils.

His memory brought visions of his grandfather. They were in a house that was vaguely familiar. There were ghost shapes all around. People that Josh should have known. They talked and laughed and some of them reached out to pinch his cheeks. Baby cheeks. Then they'd fall back into the crowd. Laughing, talking. They jiggled rapidly with their laughter. No . . . it wasn't the people that jiggled . . . it was Joshua. He was riding a small pony or . . . a knee. His pudgy fingers reached into the polyester slacks that hid the knee. Joshua laughed and gurgled and drooled saliva across his flabby cheek. He followed the knee with his eyes, laughing at everything connected to it. An old leather belt, big plastic buttons on a plaid shirt, hairs beginning to gray on a stodgy neck . . . then his grandfather's face. All smiles. The face was kind and sang words to Joshua in baby-talk. His eyes were deep and large; a baby could crawl through those eyes. Josh saw a flickering light deep inside them. Except for the light the eyes were dark and deep and little Joshua crawled into them. He crawled until the others were far behind and there was darkness all around. As he continued toward the light his arms and legs grew. His torso enlarged and his face began to change. He soon found that he was walking and then he was running. Joshua ran with incredible speed until he fell. He pulled himself up and saw that the flickering light in his grandfather's eyes was a candle and a flame. Joshua's body heaved and his eyes began to tear. He turned quickly and smothered his face in his father's chest.

"I'm sorry, honey. I'm sorry." His father's words were barely spoken.

⚘

Friday night had come and Joshua rushed around the neighborhood dragging his helpless Pekingese on a leash. This was the last of his daily chores and he wanted to get home before *Night Gallery* began. He rounded the final corner and the dog ricocheted off the wooden fence and into the backyard. Joshua wore his contempt for the domestic cat and dog like a young Bar Mitzvah wears the prayer shawl on Yom Kippur, with pride.

When he entered the living room, Joshua found that his father had dozed off in the cushioned chair that sat in front of the candle. The man's eyes were puffy like a drowned frog's. The muscles in his back and neck were compacted knobs that barely held his head.

The boy sneaked past his father and turned on the old television set. The TV let out a low hum that would continue until it was entirely awake. Joshua thought about his favorite program. He seldom understood the meaning of the show, but the occasional scene of death and horror intrigued him. *Night Gallery*—Joshua's weekly rendezvous with terror.

The television's hum sharpened into a screech as the sound and picture came together as one. His father jumped at the noise, out of his chair before his eyelids could part.

"Showtime, Daddy!"

The eyelids peeled like separating Velcro, his body flinching at the television's glow.

"No . . . no," his father mumbled. "Not tonight, Josh."

Joshua held back frustration. It took most of his energy to turn off the TV. Past experience discouraged him from watching the show alone because *Night Gallery* gave him nightmares if Daddy wasn't at his side. The boy pulled up a chair and joined his father watching the *Night Flame*.

The candle seemed to notice his presence immediately. It directed its attention toward him and sent a trail of smoke into his eyes. Joshua let the smoke surround him, wanting to share the courage that his father had and to prove to himself that he could stand up to the candle. His vision soon became clouded. The image of the swaying flame blurred into the systematic motion of a rocking chair. Dusty light hid the features of its occupant, but his skinny legs could be seen wrapped in polyester slacks. A cold shiver inched along Joshua's spine and remained even after the vision disappeared.

Josh left his seat and cuddled up in his father's lap. The man was awake but groggy.

"Daddy . . . what's in the candle?"

The doctor's hand made gentle strokes through the boy's hair. His father's unkempt facial hair and casual dress was inviting and comfortable to Joshua. It was hard to see him as a doctor.

The father pulled his son close to his chest and began crying. "It's your granddad, Josh. It's Zeyde."

ж

Saturday morning Joshua awoke in midthought. His sleep had been a fight between semiconsciousness and foggy dreams. He thought about the candle. The candle and the man who huddled before it. It's not right, he thought. That candle should stop making him cry.

And what was it that Daddy was saying about Zeyde? Did Zeyde give us the candle? Why would he want to hurt Daddy?

The thoughts distracted Josh all day. For the first time in his soccer career he was benched during a playoff game. "Open your eyes, Mr. Feder! Watch the ball, speed, speed!" Joshua watched the ball from the bench but his mind was back home with the candle and his father.

He avoided the living room when he returned from the game. He donned a pair of blue jeans and placed his spotless soccer shorts in the dresser drawer. There were things that Joshua needed to think about. He sat lightly on his bed and tried to put his thoughts into words.

First of all, there was the candle. The candle was strange. He'd never seen a candle that could last as long as this one. There was something very wrong about the candle. Then there was the way his father was acting. He hadn't been to work even one day and Joshua could guess from the way he smelled that he hadn't showered for at least a week. He often blurted out senseless words, tying them together with Zeyde's name. The whole week had been a different world for Joshua and he wished he could go back to soccer practice or Hebrew school or anything to get away from the seclusion of his home.

Something had to be done. He knew he was capable of fixing the most challenging of problems, as illustrated in his well-planned disposal of the Millers' cat. Joshua had intended only to graze the cat with the BB gun, and he grieved when he discovered that he had punctured its throat.

The first thing he did was sprinkle dirt over the cat while reciting what he could remember of the Kaddish. But then he heard the house-sitter's delicate song, "Fluffy! Fluuuuffy!" and realized he had to act quickly. He stuffed the hardening animal into his blue jeans and limped quickly past the house-sitter, pretending to have been injured in the war. The house-sitter gave him an awkward look but continued calling for the cat. He walked another few blocks to the riverbed where he dug the cat's grave. It was terrible to have been responsible for such a tragedy, but it would have been much worse if he had been caught.

Joshua knew he could change the way things were at home. All he needed was a plan. Like he had with the cat. He remembered how the cat's big orange and white tail tickled his ankle under his pants. He could even feel it now, alone in his room. He looked down and saw that his bullsnake had escaped again and was wrapping itself around his feet. He picked it up and held its flexible body in the air.

"Bull, you dummy!"

The snake greeted him with a waving tongue and sparkling eyes. Joshua rested the six-foot snake on his shoulders and caressed its smooth belly. "Tonight," he whispered, "Daddy's going to sleep."

At ten o'clock on Saturday night Joshua rolled out of bed. He wore his fuzzy purple pajamas with the plastic feet. They were his favorite for nighttime deeds because the footsies hid the sound of his footsteps. He crept along the hallway cautiously. Candlelight made the shadows a giant spider web that tried to hold him back. It felt like he was walking through the shallow end of a swimming pool.

As he cleared the end of the hallway he could see his father's sleeping figure beside the candle. He slipped gracefully past the man and drew up close to the flame. No sooner had he peeked over the table edge than the candlelight scattered fearfully into its shadow. The flame stood alone, nervous, seeming to know the boy's mission. Joshua addressed the quivering teardrop.

"You're something very strange. You shouldn't have come here." The flame stood still. "I'm sorry, but I have to do this."

Joshua licked his thumb and forefinger and reached out to the glowing wick. The flame belched smoke and Joshua withdrew his hand to protect his eyes. The smoke blurred his vision . . .

He was looking over a deck of cards on the back porch of his old home in Indiana.

"Three of a kind beats two pair," his grandfather announced with an honest grin.

"You told me you didn't have any eights!" Josh yelled.

The old man laughed. "It's poker, not Go Fish."

Joshua picked caramel from his teeth with a Jack of Diamonds.

"It's five-card draw," the man continued, but he could sense his companion was bored. His spotted white hand jostled the boy's hair.

"Come on," he said. "Grab your Frisbee and we'll go to the park."

The memory faded and Joshua screamed. He pounded his fist on the living room table. "Zeyde!" he yelled. He felt his father's hands around his chest, holding him tight. Joshua cried hard, pounding his forearms into his father's side. The doctor's hands, his father's hands, massaged the boy's back, neck and head. Everywhere his hands touched the pain went away. His father kneeled and kissed his son's wet cheek. His tears fell and mingled with the tears of his son. Saturday night at ten o'clock they huddled as one, father and son, while the candle watched from above.

Joshua awoke with the early morning sun and found himself on his sleeping father's lap. The man hunched forward, taking deep breaths, as if his lungs were filtering oxygen through candle smoke. He appeared peaceful, save for the dark semicircles inverted beneath his eyes. The sandman had sealed them tight, Josh thought.

Josh tiptoed up to what was left of the candle—a thin sheet of liquid wax with a blue pencil-dot flame. A trail of smoke rose steadily like a stroke of dark ink from its belly. Joshua saw the flame shrink into itself, coughing one last puff of smoke before disappearing for good. The never-ending trail detached from the wick and rose from a waxed, lifeless body.

Joshua stepped away from the table. Some of the candle smoke drifted toward his father and vanished into his nostrils. A moment later his father woke with a startling, dusty sneeze. His bloodshot eyes revealed a sad, dim light. He chewed the inside of his lip unconsciously, slowly orienting himself. His gaze passed through Joshua and onto the candle, which was already forming into a pool of hardening wax.

For the first time in seven days Joshua saw his father relax. The blood in his eyes drained away, restoring color to his cheeks. He stood with uncertain balance, gently rubbing the tender spot above his temples.

He glanced at the candle and walked away.

Joshua ran to his side and took his hand. He led the weary man to his bed and helped him undress. The clothes were stiff and smelled of sweat. Joshua tucked his father under the covers and kissed his forehead. The man was already asleep.

❧

The vision of his sleeping father returned to a blur and then back to a simple memory. Joshua Feder rubbed his tender eyes. His spine was a steel cable, muscles leeched to every bone. His head throbbed and his heart raced.

He sensed the delicate footsteps of his father behind him. Daddy will make the pain go away, he thought. Joshua felt the gentle touch on his elbow. He turned quickly, his arms reaching out.

But stood there, clasping nothing but memories.

A small voice rang from the child at his feet.

"Are we going to play soccer or what?"

Joshua sat down and lifted his son to his lap. He pulled the boy close to his heart and held him tight. "Not now, David. In a few days."

He turned around in his chair and faced the *yahrzeit* candle.

"Look here. I've got something to show you."

Little David Feder stared into the flame and realized he hadn't seen his soccer ball in years.

Nakhshon

Robert Lopresti

"You ain't doing much business," said Kostin as he strode out of Adam's office, into the main part of the store. He blinked at the light shining through the front windows.

"Tuesdays are always slow," Adam said. He was following Kostin, trying to move deliberately, which was difficult because the bigger man, Molotov—could that possibly be his real name?—was treading on his heels.

"Women don't need pretty things on Tuesdays?" Kostin laughed. He had a slight accent and his voice rose a bit at the end of every sentence, as if everything he said was a question.

He was shorter than Adam, but weighed more, all of it muscle. Even so, the other one, Molotov, could have probably bench-pressed him.

"Things pick up at the end of the week." Adam moved toward the sales counter but didn't step behind it.

"Glad to hear it. Very glad." His voice had a mocking cheerfulness as if he spoke not just in questions but in jokes.

Perhaps in riddles.

"We want all of our customers to succeed. Isn't that right, Molotov?"

The big man laughed and said something in Russian.

Customers, Adam thought. *Is that what we are?*

Kostin picked up a scarf from a show table. He held it by one end and dragged it slowly through the fingers of his other hand.

"Don't want to tell you how to run your business, my friend, but you maybe should dream up some new ideas. Fresh products? Maybe some different marketing techniques?"

"They cost money," said Adam. "I've had a lot of expenses lately."

Molotov laughed, a deep-throated rumble. *So he does understand English.*

Kostin had casually tied the scarf in a knot and was now pulling at both ends. "Maybe you should try—what do the kids call it?—social networks! That's how to make money these days. Go viral?"

"I'll give it some thought." He wanted to open the front door and invite them out, but that would just encourage them to stay.

Kostin dropped the ruined scarf. It fluttered to the floor. He reached toward a display of lacquered hairpins.

Adam put his own hands in his pockets, to keep them still.

The door opened. Not a customer, but Daniel.

Adam felt dizzy. He leaned back against the counter.

"Hi, Pop!" The boy looked at the two strangers with curiosity.

"Daniel, you're early."

"Training day for teachers. I *told* you about it."

"Oh, yes." And this being spring, Rivka's busy season—an accountant at tax time—their son would come to the store after class.

Kostin was smiling. "Well, hello! What grade are you in?"

"Seventh." Daniel was sliding off his bulky backpack.

"Kids your age, I bet you like movies, right?"

"I guess. Sure."

"You ever go to that video store on the corner?"

Daniel looked as if he had been asked about buggy whips. "No. I stream them off the web."

Kostin laughed. He turned to Adam. "You see? That's why our friend Shalom was having business problems. Nobody needs a video store anymore."

"Mr. Shalom had an accident yesterday," said Daniel. "I saw the ambulance."

"What a shame," said Kostin. "Let's hope he's feeling more like himself very soon, yes?"

Adam pushed himself away from the counter. "Daniel, go in the back and start your homework."

Eyes rolled. "Yes, Pop."

Molotov stepped aside to let him pass and watched him until he disappeared down the hall.

"Nice little boy," said Kostin. "You and your beautiful wife must be really proud."

"Are we done here?"

"Are we?" Kostin considered. "I think so."

He picked up a hairpin, tossed it from hand to hand. "Seeing a child like that, so innocent, it reminds me of how we all need to work together, you know?" He smiled. "To make sure they all have a future?"

When the Russians left, Adam wanted to put up the CLOSED sign, but he didn't dare miss a customer.

Customers. Ten years ago he was in charge of large accounts for a major importer of accessories, and his customers were department store chains.

Then the recession hit and instead of being moved up as he expected, the bosses had moved him out.

He and Rivka had taken their savings and opened a store, figuring this was a business he understood. And for a while, things had gone all right.

For a while.

Now he suspected the shop bore the stink of desperation, that mysterious aura that made potential shoppers decide to move on.

He walked past his office to the back room—table, fridge, microwave—and found Daniel sorting through a pile of textbooks. How much homework did they give kids these days? He had never had that much.

Of course, he had gone to public school and Daniel went to a private Hebrew academy.

Adam's parents had been secular Jews who never set foot in a *shul* unless someone they knew was getting married or buried.

Rivka—born Robin—came from the same background, but while pregnant she had unexpectedly found religion.

"I don't know if I believe in God," she had told him. "But I know I'm Jewish and our son will be, too. And that has to mean more than just lighting Hanukkah candles."

Daniel looked up from his schoolbooks. "Can I have some Oreos?"

"You'll spoil your appetite. There's fruit in the fridge."

A dramatic sigh. He struggled to his feet, a martyred man, and opened the refrigerator.

Adam put the water on. "How was school?"

"English is stupid." Daniel bit into an apple. "I hate poetry."

"Okay, what *do* you like?"

"Math. Hebrew."

Adam picked up a tea bag, turning away from his son. Were they going to be able to afford private school next year?

Daniel sat down, but he wasn't ready to resume his homework. "And we heard this really cool story in Jewish studies. We're studying Midrash. You know what that is?"

"Vaguely."

The boy sat up straight, ready to recite. "Midrash are stories the rabbis created to explain weird things in the Bible, like misspellings, or parts that don't seem to make sense."

Adam had to smile. He could hear the inflections of Ms. Ornstein, who taught the Jewish studies class. "Got it."

"So there's this guy, Nakhshon, who gets mentioned a couple of times in the Torah. He was one of the Israelites fleeing Egypt."

"Okay."

"And here's the weird part. The text calls him a *nasi*."

Adam frowned. "A Nazi?"

More eye-rolling. "No, Pop. Pay attention. *Nasi*. It's a Hebrew word meaning prince, or official. In Israel today they use it for, you know, like we'd say secretary of state."

"Go on."

Daniel waved his hands. "So, that's the question. Why did this guy, just another refugee fleeing slavery, get called a prince?"

"Did the rabbis come up with an explanation?"

"Yeah, with a Midrash." He put down his half-eaten apple on what looked like a science quiz. Adam rescued it with a paper towel. "Thanks. The story goes like this: when Moses ordered the Red Sea to open, nothing happened. He told the Israelites to go down into the water but they were too scared, 'cause it looked like the sea wasn't going anywhere."

Daniel pointed dramatically behind him. "Meanwhile the Egyptian chariots are getting closer and closer! Everybody's crowded on the beach, no place to go, knowing the pharaoh will have them all back in chains, or worse, if the army catches up with them."

Adam was so interested he burned his tongue on the tea. "So?"

"So finally this guy Nakhshon said, 'I'd rather die free than live as a slave.' He ran straight down into the water. When it closed over his head—bang!" Daniel slapped the table with a skinny hand. "*That's* when the Red Sea parted."

"Quite a story. What does Ms. Ornstein say it means?"

"Oh, she never tells us that. She says everyone has to decide for themselves." He scratched his head. "Some kids said it means you have to have faith in God. But Michelle says it means the Lord takes care of those who take care of themselves."

He grinned. "You know what book of the Bible *that* line's from?"

"No, I don't."

"Ben Franklin." Daniel laughed. "You sure I can't have a cookie?"

"Positive." Adam put the teacup down in the sink. "We'll go home at five o'clock. Make sure you throw out the apple core."

He walked out front to make sure no customers had managed to sneak in without ringing the bell. No such luck.

Back in his office Adam sat and stared at his phone for a while. Then he picked it up and pushed buttons. He noticed that his hand was trembling.

"Nine one one." The voice was terse. "What's the nature of your emergency?"

"I think I need to speak to a police officer. A detective."

"Is this about an ongoing crime?"

"Ongoing?" Adam frowned. "Sort of. Not at the moment."

Now the voice was irritated. "Sir, this number is for emergencies only. Where are you located?"

"Brooklyn." He gave the address.

"Sixty-Fourth Precinct. Here's the phone number."

"Thanks." Adam wrote down the phone number and killed the call. Then he sat looking at the piece of paper, tapping his fingers. It would have been so much easier if the dispatcher had just transferred the call.

Now he had to decide all over again.

Oh, screw it.

He picked up the phone and pushed the buttons. It took a minute of talking to get through to detectives.

"Sixty-Fourth squad. Royce speaking."

"This is Adam Levy. I want to report a crime."

"Go ahead, sir."

"Look." He ran a hand through his hair. "I don't know what to call it. On TV they call it a protection racket. You know what that is?"

A pause. "I do. What do *you* think it means?"

"A bunch of thugs demand that you give them money or bad things will happen to your business." He swallowed. "Or to your family."

"Yes, sir." The cop's voice got louder. "That's a protection racket. Did that happen to you?"

"It's happening to everyone in my neighborhood. One man on my block got beaten up yesterday, and now they're demanding bigger payments, because they say we know they're serious."

"Okay. Mr. Levy, was it? We'll be there in about an hour."

"No, you won't. You'll come to my apartment tonight after my son goes to sleep."

"Sure. Give me a time and an address."

"And no uniforms."

"No, sir."

"No police cars."

"Absolutely."

When the call was over Adam dropped the phone on his desk. He tried to suck in a deep breath.

Okay, God. It's your turn.

One of Them

Alan Orloff

"Hy Perlstein might be a fat, lying prick, Pop," I said. "But you're not going to kill him."

My father cleared his throat, a thick, phlegmy *glechh* that seemed out of place in his serene, book-filled den. So did talk of murder. "You want me to turn the other cheek, Daniel? That's the excuse *goyim* use for chickening out."

"You don't have to turn the other cheek. But you can't kill Hy."

He tilted his head at me, like he'd been doing for the past twenty-five years whenever I said something he didn't quite agree with. "I can, and I will. And it's Uncle Hy to you."

Hyman Perlstein was not my real uncle, but he'd been Pop's best friend since before I was born. When I was a kid, his family celebrated most of the Jewish holidays with us, and Hy proudly took his seat at the table, right next to a couple of actual uncles. He and Pop had a falling out a few years ago, and when Mom told me about the dust-up, I hadn't wanted to hear the details, figuring it as simply two stubborn old men arguing over something stupid.

"He's not my uncle, but that's beside the point. What did he do to get you so riled up?"

My father wagged a finger at me. He'd aged about fifteen years since I moved away two years ago. "That *ganef* stole our life savings."

I'd never liked Hy much, a feeling that began when he gave me a sweaty handshake as he slipped me a check at my Bar Mitzvah. He'd smelled of cheap aftershave and mothballs.

"Seriously? How'd he do that?" I asked. Mom said Pop's mind was going, and the deterioration had been accelerating. Listening to all his wild stories and paranoia, she figured only about 50 percent of what Pop said these days was true. The trick was determining which half to believe.

"He's been handling our investments for years. Three quarters of the *shul*'s, too. Things seemed to be going fine, then Morty Abel wanted to cash out. Came to find it was all a scam. One of those schemes. You know, with the wop name."

"Ponzi?"

Pop nodded. "Yeah. Ponzi. So then we all wanted to cash out. One thing led to another. Poof! No money."

"Hy admitted that?"

"Of course not. Said to be patient, he's got some kind of mammoth deal in the works and needs all the money as collateral. Horseshit."

"Why don't you report the theft?"

He waved his hand in the air. "Me and the police don't get along too well."

"So what did the others do? Anybody call the authorities?"

"What do you think they did?" Pop sat up straighter, and something flickered in his eyes. "They called me to take care of it. To make things right. Like always."

"Oh, Christ. I thought you left all that behind. I've been trying to." A few years ago, when Pop's health started to decline, they sold the dry cleaners they'd owned for five decades. It had also doubled as a different kind of laundry operation—a money-laundering one. To round things out, they dabbled in running numbers, protection rackets, and similar law-skirting avocations. But if you asked Pop, it was all in the name of altruism. Using his money and his stature, my father took pride in being able to help those in the local Jewish community who needed a hand. He'd watched *The Godfather* too many times.

"If I can support my people, I will. You know me."

"Yeah, I know you." If it wasn't my father involved, I'd have thought it pretty funny that a bunch of bilked Jews were relying on a seventy-nine-year-old geezer with a failing memory and two bad hips to *make things right*.

"What? You think I can't handle it? That I'm too old? I've been making things right since you were a little *pisher*, and I haven't lost a step." He glared at me, then opened his mouth to say something else, but froze. A momentary flash of confusion crossed his face, but he recovered quickly. "Maybe I've lost half a step, but no more."

"Uh-huh." Not only did he have trouble walking, he couldn't drive anymore.

"What are you doing here, anyway?" he asked.

I'd told him when I arrived last night, and then this morning, but I repeated the lie again now. "It's been a while, and I wanted to see how you and Mom were doing. Firsthand, not on the phone."

"Here's how I'm doing—I'm pissed." His nostrils flared.

"I can see that."

Mom had actually called and begged me to come home and talk Pop out of his foolishness. As if anyone could reason with him. She also wanted me to spend some time with him while he could still remember who I was. "Pop, listen to me. You can't just kill Hy. If you don't want to go to the police, get one of your friends to. Let the wheels of justice grind Hy into pulp."

Pop's jaw dropped. "I thought I raised you right, son. There's no way in hell I'm turning Uncle Hy in."

"You'd rather kill him?"

Pop stared at me. "If word of his financial crimes got out, it would give us a bad name."

"Us?" I asked, although I knew the answer. I'd endured his warped logic and attempted brainwashing—with regard to religion—all my life. *The World According to Irv Brickman.*

"Us. Jews. The world thinks we're money-grubbers as it is. Shylocks. Nope, I won't turn on him. He may be a thieving sonofabitch, but he's one of us, after all. I'm going to get my money back, then, *pfft.*" He pretended to choke someone's neck, presumably Hy's. "He's a dead man."

Better to be a murderer than a rat?

❧

I got the feeling Pop wanted to take a nap—the drooping eyelids and nodding head tipped me off—so I left him alone in the study, gently closing the door behind me. I hadn't taken three steps down the hall when I found Mom scrubbing a nonexistent stain on the wall with an old rag.

"Well?" she said.

"Eavesdropping?"

"Absolutely. Someone has to watch over him. I'm afraid he's becoming a danger, to himself and to others."

"Don't you think you're being a little melodramatic?"

"You haven't been living here for the past five years. You don't know the half of it. All those chemicals from the shop, eating away at his brain for all these years." Her eyes misted. Mom performed on a lot of community theater stages in her younger days, even won a few awards, so I never fully trusted what I saw. Pop was stubborn; Mom was shifty. I always wondered who the brains of their operation was.

"I have a feeling that when he wakes up, he'll have forgotten all his threats," I said.

Mom shook her head. "I wish. He's been talking this *mishegas* for weeks."

"Let's have a seat." I took her elbow and guided her into the living room, and we sat on a pair of chairs from the '80s, my tiny mother almost getting swallowed up in the over-upholstered cushions. "Did you really lose your life savings?"

Mom balled up her rag and worked it in her lap. "Much of it, yes. Your father isn't wrong about what happened."

"Then you definitely need to report it. Get everyone else and go to the cops together."

She smiled. "Daniel. You're sweet, but you know we can't do that. Besides, Uncle Hy isn't a dummy. He's probably figured out a way to make it all seem legit. And if we did sue him or turn him in or what have you, we'll all be long gone before the truth comes out. He's got an army of lawyers. He really is a repugnant man. I'll never understand what Irv saw in him."

Probably his own reflection. "So what are you going to do?"

"Well, we were thinking about moving to Florida, but now? Maybe I can pick up some part-time work sewing and hemming."

The idea of my mother working in some kind of self-imposed sweat-shop didn't sit well with me. They'd been talking about retiring to Boca ever since I could remember.

"Or maybe I can clean people's homes."

I should pack my bags; Mom was trying to send me on an around-the-world guilt trip.

"Or I could call people up while they're eating dinner, pushing vinyl siding or those gutter thingies." She shrugged. "Wouldn't that be something, your mother, a telemarketer?"

"I'm sure you'd be very good at pestering people on the phone." I sighed. "How 'bout I go talk to Hy? Get this thing straightened out."

Mom's eyebrows lifted. "Yeah? You think you can reason with him? Get him to return our money?" She nodded, once, twice. "I bet you can. He always liked you."

❦

I drove out to Hy's mansion, up a long winding driveway, not a neighbor's estate in sight. He opened the door himself, and when he shook my hand, I yanked it away before he could pull me close for a hug. He invited me in, and we settled on opposite ends of a floral-print couch in his living room.

In addition to the couch, a gleaming black grand piano, an ornate sideboard, two tables, and several throne-sized chairs conspired to make the large room seem like a closet. The place looked almost exactly like it had when I'd been there seven years ago to pay a *shivah* call after his wife Isabella died. The only difference: Now there was much less food set out.

"To what do I owe the pleasure, Danny?" His porcine eyes almost vanished in the flabby folds of his fat face.

"Visiting Mom and Pop. Thought I'd stop in and say hi to my Uncle Hy."

That brought a smile. When my brother Ethan and I were young, we'd march around during Passover seders chanting, "Hi, Uncle Hy. Hi, Uncle Hy." Little kids having fun, and adults humoring us.

"Well, I'm glad you did. I don't see as much of your father as I used to, you know." He peered at me as if he was waiting for an apology. Or explanation. Or something.

"Oh? Well, I'm sure you're a busy man."

He reclined and draped his arm across the back of the couch, putting his ample gut front and center. "Yessiree. Got a lot on my plate."

"Investments is it now?"

His unctuous smile dimmed. "That's right."

"Business good?"

"Up and down." The smile had been chased off by the slightest of scowls.

"Heard you were handling Pop's money. His retirement fund."

"Among many, many others." He nodded, somber. "A lot of people put their trust in me, and I work hard to do the very best I can for them. I'd die if anything happened to their nest eggs."

Yeah, if Pop got his way. "Pop always said you were a hard worker. But here's the thing. He says that he came to you and wanted to cash out so he and Mom can move to Florida. And you told him the money wasn't liquid right now. Now Pop thinks you're ripping him off."

"Well, that's not the case at all, you see—"

"That's what I thought. I told him Hy would never do that. Not to him. Not to one of his oldest friends in the world. Hy's too much of a mensch."

"That's exactly right." Hy paused. "What did he say to that?"

"He wants his money back."

Hy fiddled with a button on his sleeve. "Yes, well, as I explained, he'll get his money. But . . . there are some pending transactions in play that preclude any immediate liquidation or transfer of funds with regard to—"

I held up my hand. "He wants his money back, Hy. And soon."

"It's not that easy, Danny. If I give Irv his money back now, it'll leave a lot of others in the lurch. He needs to be patient. Something's in the works that's going to pay off huge. Couple months, tops."

"He can't wait. His mind . . ." I let it hang in the air for a moment. "He wants to move. To Boca. While he can still enjoy it. So he'll need his money back. This week."

Hy held out his hands, pudgy palms up. "I'm afraid that's impossible."

I rose and stepped close, looming over him, rolling my shoulders to make my six-four frame even more imposing. "Make it possible."

"Or what?" A thin sheen of perspiration covered Hy's forehead.

"Or I'll come back, and I won't be in the mood to do any talking. In case you forgot, Pop taught me pretty well. And I picked up a few tricks of my own while I was away."

❧

When I turned eight, Mom and Pop put me to work at the dry cleaners, weekends and summers. At first I had the menial jobs: collecting hangers, taking out the trash, sweeping up. Putting the plastic tags with the numbers in order. After I perfected those chores and aged a few years, my responsibilities increased.

When I turned seventeen, Pop started teaching me the other side of the family business, the part that took place in the stuffy, windowless back office. I was a fast learner, spurred on by the opportunity to make some money. And I made my money by collecting Pop's money.

I'd been Pop's right hand man for years until I got busted for cracking open Hammie O'Rourke's skull during a collection that went south. Spent twenty-six months inside for aggravated assault, and when I got out, I left town, plenty aggravated, mostly at myself. For getting caught, for being involved in that life in the first place. I vowed never to spend another second behind bars.

So I moved away from the toxic environment called "home."

Working for Pop had been more lucrative, and—I'm ashamed to admit—a steadier source of employment than I'd been able to find since. I'd been scratching around in a few towns downstate, tending bar, working light construction, delivering packages while dressed in brown clothes. Nothing earthshattering. Of course, I hadn't shattered anyone's kneecaps, either.

But I'd hardly call my life comfortable.

Now my resolve to stay straight wavered. Threatening Hy had come so easily. More concerning, I'd felt a surge of adrenaline. And anger. The money that Hy stole from my parents? That was to be my money someday.

I hated getting ripped off. Maybe even more than Pop did.

❧

The curtains fluttered at the window when I came up the front walk, and a few seconds later, Mom opened the door, mouth already in motion. "Well? Did you talk to him? What did he say?"

"Can you give me a second to grab a soda?"

Two minutes later, after I'd gulped half a Coke, Mom continued her inquisition at the kitchen table. "Is he going to give us our money back?"

On the ride over, I'd been debating how to answer that question, and

I'd gone back and forth without really coming to a conclusion. I turned the soda can in my hands, waiting for a last-minute epiphany, but nothing materialized. "Yeah, I think so. Got a few tiny details to work out, but I think you and Pop will get your money back. It's only right."

Mom practically dove across the table and hugged me around my neck, without even waiting for me to get up.

"Did he say when?" she asked, mouth close to my ear.

"Not exactly. But pretty soon, I think. I need to follow up on a couple things."

She broke off the embrace, and some of the shine drained from her face. "Good. Well, it can't be soon enough. Now, go get ready. Your brother will be here for dinner soon."

⅔

After three helpings of brisket and what seemed like half of the potato kugel, I pushed away from the dinner table and joined my brother Ethan on the back deck, out of Mom's eavesdropping range. Ethan was six years older than me, and he hadn't gotten sucked into the family business— neither aspect of it. Went off to college instead. Smart move.

He popped open a beer and toasted me. "Nice to see you, Bro. You need to visit more often."

I nodded at his drink. "How come you waited until now for that?"

"Why do you think? Even though I've got two kids and a hefty mortgage, Mom still nags me about drinking. One beer, for chrissake!"

To Mom, we'd always be kids, no matter how many offspring or how large a mortgage.

"Glad you came back. Tough to say no to Mom, I guess."

I eyed him. "She told you?"

"About Pop? She didn't have to. I've got eyes. I visit here twice a week and see him at *shul*. I'm glad you came back while he can still remember who you are."

Sounded like Mom didn't divulge their financial problem to Ethan. Which made sense. What could he do about it? He was a high school history teacher.

"Is Pop really that bad?" I asked.

"Comes and goes. Today seems like a pretty good day."

Pop had been fairly with-it at dinner. Just a few confused moments and a handful of repeated questions. "Tough to see him like that."

"Yes, it is. I know you probably won't believe me, but he seems better when he's at *shul*."

"Some kind of divine intervention? Reward for attending services?"

"Don't knock it until you try it," he said.

"Point taken." I'd stopped believing in God the day after my Bar Mitzvah. I considered myself a Jew, but only in the cultural sense. Mom was okay with that; Pop was still peeved.

A moment passed. "You still keep up with Gregg?" I asked. He was Hy's son, a year older than Ethan. I hadn't heard much about him, but I figured he hadn't wandered far from his Dad. Schmuck begat schmuck.

"I bump into him from time to time. He seems fine. Busy."

"What's he do?"

"He works with Uncle Hy. Financial stuff. Why?" He took a swig of his beer and stared at me over the can.

"Pop mention anything about that to you?"

"About what?"

"Hy handling Pop's investing."

"Nope. Why? There a problem?"

I shook my head. "No problem. Can you give me Gregg's number? I need to talk to him about something."

"Sure," Ethan said. "You want him to handle your portfolio?"

"That's one way of putting it."

꙳

Gregg Perlstein was slim, well dressed, and well coifed, the antithesis of his father, at least in appearance. So different that a casual observer might doubt the science of genetics. On the inside, though, he was a Perlstein through and through. We sat at a table by the window at Starbucks, and Gregg interrupted our conversation to check his phone every ten seconds. Mr. Goddamn Important.

"So tell me again what you want, Danny boy."

I *wanted* to smack his head against the table until something broke—head or table, I didn't care—but I gritted my teeth. "As I was saying, my father would like to withdraw his money so he and Mom can retire in the sun. I don't know if you're aware of it, but Pop's going downhill, healthwise."

"Aren't we all, Danny? Getting old bites, huh?" Another glance at his phone. "Beats the alternative, though." He chuckled.

Not always. "About the money."

"Right, right. You already spoke to my dad, and he explained the situation. We've presented a lucrative investment package to an overseas concern, and we need to be patient until it pays off. But when it does, boy-o-boy, it'll be great. Your father will be very glad he waited. He'll be able to retire in high style."

"I think he'd rather retire in normal style, now, so he can enjoy his few remaining years. Or months."

Gregg reached for his phone, and I grabbed his wrist just as he picked it up.

"If you could just give me your undivided attention, I'd appreciate it," I said.

He glared at me. I let go of his wrist, and he set the phone down. "You can have my attention, but you can't have your father's money. Not yet, anyway. You have to believe me when I say there's nothing we can do."

"You wouldn't want Pop suing you. It'd be bad for business."

Gregg laughed, and it reminded me of a donkey braying. "Fat chance. He'd never turn on one of his own and risk shame falling upon the Jews. Let's face it, our fathers have a different way of thinking about things. Old World, you might say. But I told you, everything is on the up-and-up."

Anytime I heard that phrase, I knew things weren't.

He eyed me. "Does your father know you're talking to me? Or to my father?"

I hesitated a beat, and Gregg had his answer.

"Yeah, I didn't think so. Your father isn't the type to send his son to do his business. Now, are we done here?" Without waiting for my answer, he picked up his phone again and started working his thumbs.

I left him to his device.

⅍

When I got back to my parents' house, Mom's car was gone—I remembered her saying something about a beauty parlor appointment—but I found my father in his study, hunched over a table, fiddling with something.

"Hey, Pop," I called from the doorway.

He covered up whatever he was working on and said in a sharp voice, "Your mom with you?"

"No."

"Okay, then. Come on in."

As I came closer, I found out why Pop was acting weird. Spread out on the table was his gun, a rag, and a box of ammo.

"What's going on?" I asked, voice level.

"Cleaning my piece."

"I can see that. Why?"

"Never know when you might need it."

"Cut the crap, Pop. We've been through this. You can't kill Hy."

Pop picked up his gun and ran the rag up and down the barrel.

"Pop," I said, speaking as if I were talking to a child, a dense child. "Why don't you give me the gun? I'll take good care of it. Make sure nothing bad happens, okay?"

He kept working the rag, faster. Not making eye contact.

"Pop?"

"You can't have my gun, Danny. They're not toys. Guns are dangerous."

Exactly. I held out my hand. "I'll put it away in a safe place."

"You can't have it. No way." He stopped cleaning the gun, looked at me, and the pilot light seemed to have gone out. "You still drive that Ford?" he asked.

"The Mustang?"

"Yes. Nice car."

I sold that car ten years ago. "Sure, Pop. It's running better than ever."

"Good. Don't ever buy a Mercedes, okay? We fought the war against the Germans, you know."

Yeah, several wars ago. The mind is a funny thing, but a failing mind is just sad. "I won't buy a Mercedes. But didn't you own a Lexus? Japan attacked Pearl Harbor, remember?"

"Sure. But the Japs didn't have ovens."

🦎

That night, after dinner and after watching some crap on TV, I went upstairs to turn in. While I was visiting, Mom insisted I sleep in my old bedroom, but in the years since, it looked less and less like a bedroom and more like a storage room. Two-thirds of it was filled with plastic storage boxes with such colorful labels as "Old Utility Bills," "School Report Cards," and "Car Maintenance Records."

I flopped down on my old single bed, telling myself I could survive sleeping on a thirty-year-old mattress for a few days. I'd slept in much worse places.

Lying there brought back a few memories, good and bad. I remembered when I was about sixteen and Mom caught me with my hands down Miriam Kellner's pants. Remembering the look on her face—actually, both their faces—never failed to boost my spirits.

A knock on the door interrupted my reminiscing. "Daniel? You still awake?"

Had she been reading my mind? "Yeah. Come in."

Mom opened the door and stepped in. Took a seat at the foot of the bed. "Comfy?"

"Sure." At least the sheets were clean.

"It's nice having you here. Real nice. I miss our conversations."

"It's nice visiting." I didn't remember those conversations but let it slide.

She settled back and told me about Cousin Sarah's wedding. About the neighbor's new cat. About some hen fight in her Mah Jongg group. I listened, waiting for her to arrive at the real reason she came in to talk.

"You know, if there's nothing tying you down, maybe you could move back here." She paused. "Not here in the house, of course, but nearby. Your father and I would like it, and I'm sure Ethan and his family would, too."

"I don't have a girlfriend, Mom, if that's what you're asking."

She donned an expression of shock, and I recalled the time she played Tevye's wife in a local production of *Fiddler*. "Well, will you at least *consider* moving back?"

"I thought you were moving to Florida."

She clammed up, and after an awkward silence, said, "Hy's not going to give us back our money, is he?"

"Sure he is, Mom." I hadn't told her about striking out with Gregg, too.

"Why don't I believe you?"

"I don't know. You should." I'd become a pretty good liar over the years but snowing Mom was always difficult.

"I've known Hy a long time. He's . . ." She shook her head. "Thanks for trying, anyway."

"It's not over yet. I'm going to see him again."

She sighed. "Your father's still planning to do something rash. I can feel it in my old bones."

"I've been trying to reason with him, persuade him to let others fight his battle. But it's not easy getting through." I pictured him cleaning his gun.

"I know, dear. I know." She patted my foot through the covers. "You need to be firm, and repeat yourself. Several times."

"I think I was pretty clear."

"I'm sure you were, dear, but don't give up on him, okay?"

"Okay."

She started to get up, but settled. "One more thing. And it's important. Please don't help him carry out his plans. To go after Hy himself. To make things *right*."

I didn't say anything, but I imagined breaking a few of Hy's fingers until he caved.

Mom raised her voice. "Listen to me. I don't want you taking any chances. If you get caught, no telling what might happen this time. I couldn't live with that." She grabbed my foot and gave it a squeeze. "Promise me, Daniel."

Nice to know my mother didn't want me returning to prison. "Don't worry, I don't plan to do anything more than talk to Uncle Hy. Tomorrow afternoon, in fact."

"Promise you won't do anything but talk?"

"Good night, Mom."

She fixed me with the evil eye, clucked once, then shuffled out. I rolled over as the sagging mattress squealed its disapproval.

❧

The next morning, Mom was already dressed and bustling around the kitchen when I came down to get something to eat. After I devoured a bagel and cream cheese, she slapped a grocery list down on the table.

"Would you mind going to the store to get a few things?"

"Sure." I scanned the list. When did twenty-five things become "a few"?

"Thanks, dear. Your father and I love you. Very much."

At the store, I grabbed a cart and started going up and down the aisles, gathering all the stuff Mom wanted. I wasn't much of a shopper, and I had to backtrack quite a bit as I searched for everything on her list. Green peppers, potatoes, sour cream, herring, egg noodles. When I found the seafood department, I discovered they were out of salmon. Knowing how particular Mom was about her food, I wasn't about to buy a substitute without checking in. I called home. No answer.

I got a few more items on the list, then tried calling Mom again.

Still no answer.

Something didn't add up.

Why would Mom, so finicky about the food she cooked, send me, who barely knows the difference between a rutabaga and an onion, to the store? Thinking back, she seemed especially on edge this morning, as if something were about to happen. Did she guess about my impending confrontation with Hy? Or was something else in play here? And what was with the line about her and Pop loving me *very much*?

Had Pop talked her into taking him to see Hy? Before I had my chance that afternoon?

I abandoned my full cart in the frozen food section and raced to my car. When I got home, Mom's car was gone. I burst through the front door. "Mom? Pop?"

Nobody came running. I dashed through the kitchen, ducked into the family room, stuck my head into the living room. No sign of Mom or Pop. She *had* taken him to see Hy.

Next stop, the den, to Pop's not-so-secret hiding place, where he kept his gun. I pulled out two thick volumes on the bookshelf, hoping that the old Nike shoebox wouldn't be empty.

It was. No gun.

I called Mom's cell. No answer, but she rarely had it turned on. She was only slightly more technologically savvy than Pop, who didn't even own a cell phone. As much as I hated to, I called Hy to warn him.

He didn't answer either. Where the hell was everybody?

Mom and Pop had a head start, but if I hurried . . .

A thought occurred to me. After I'd asked Pop for his gun, maybe he hid it somewhere else to keep me from taking it. I figured I could spare thirty seconds to check his back-up hiding spot—behind his shoeshine kit at the bottom of his closet. That's where he used to hide stuff he'd taken away from me as a kid, and I'm sure he'd forgotten that I knew all about it.

I ran up the stairs and down the hall into the master bedroom.

Before I made it to the closet, I found Pop. Lying in bed.

I watched for a moment, waiting to see his chest rise. Finally, after what seemed like twenty seconds, it did, but barely. His skin seemed a bit gray. "Pop," I said, shaking him gently. "Pop."

Nothing.

I shook harder. "Pop! Wake up!"

Didn't even stir. His breath was faint, wispy.

"Pop!" I slapped his face, softly at first, then hard enough to cause pain.

His eyes fluttered and his lips worked, but nothing intelligible came out.

If I didn't know better, I'd say he was drugged. I rushed to the bathroom. An assortment of medicine bottles littered the vanity. I knew they both took a variety of medications, but an empty vial marked Xanax caught my attention. Had Mom drugged Pop, so she could take on Hy herself? After I didn't promise not to harm him, maybe she'd read between the lines. Had she set off to do the dirty work so I didn't end up back inside?

She never passed up an opportunity to play the martyr.

I pulled my phone out and called 911, gave the dispatcher the address, and reported a possible overdose. Then I called Ethan, filled him in, and barked at him to get his ass over here. I hung up before he could ask any questions, and I ignored his call back as I bolted for my room to retrieve something from my own hiding place. What my parole officer didn't know wouldn't hurt him.

Weapon in hand, I flew down the stairs, out the door, and into my car.

Zipping through traffic, I made it to Hy's house in no time, wound my way up his long driveway, and parked right behind Mom's Chrysler. I hopped out and ran onto the porch. Banged on the door, yelled, tried the knob. Locked.

I scrambled to the nearest window and tried to get a glimpse inside, but couldn't see anything from my angle.

I was about to head around back, when I heard a shot. From inside. No more time to waste. I worked a paver loose from a row of garden edging and smashed in the window.

I drew my weapon and climbed through the opening into the dark room. Waited a few seconds for my eyes to adjust. When they did, I found myself standing next to a china cabinet in Hy's dining room. My first instinct was to run toward the interior of the house, but I'd been in enough situations like this to know better. I crept to the open doorway. Peeked around the corner. Across the foyer, Mom sprawled on the family room floor, head near the legs of the piano.

Screw caution.

I dashed over to where she lay. "Mom! You okay?"

She clutched her hip with one hand and Pop's gun with the other. "I got him, Daniel! I hit him."

"Hy? Where is he?"

"We were talking, and when he heard you banging on the door, he started to get up. I pulled the gun out of my purse and shot him. In the arm, I think. Then he threw a vase at me, and I fell. Oh my God, I can't believe . . ." She trailed off, but the flush of excitement didn't leave her face.

"Take a deep breath, Mom. Tell me where he went." I had my gun up, in case he tried to ambush us.

"I think he ran upstairs." She winced and rubbed her side. "Musta broken my hip or something."

Hy was probably getting his own weapon or calling for reinforcements. Or both. I wasn't worried that he'd be calling the cops. I rose.

"Don't, Daniel. Don't go after him."

"Stay here. And relax, I'll be careful."

I listened for any sound from above as I approached the stairs. Slowly, I climbed them, stepping on the outsides of each tread to minimize creaking. When I reached the top, I half-expected Hy to make his move, but all was still.

The door at the end of the hall was closed. A few drops of blood on the carpet led toward it.

I tiptoed down the hall. Listened at the door. All I heard was heavy breathing, but I wasn't sure if it was mine or Hy's.

I tried the doorknob. Unlocked. Did he want me to enter so he could blow my brains out? I knelt off to one side, turned the knob, and pushed the door open.

A shot rang out. "Shit!" Hy said, when he realized he was firing at air. "I know you're there, Danny. Why don't we talk this over?"

"You give back Pop's money and we'll talk. Otherwise, I'm done talking, and we can wait until you bleed out, for all I care." I made sure to stay out of Hy's line of sight.

"I called the cops."

"No you didn't. You're like Pop," I said, from around the corner. "You'd never turn one of us in."

"You think you're so smart, don't you?" From Hy's voice, I could tell he was on the right side of the room. "I called Gregg. He's on his way."

"Then we'd better settle this quick, huh?" I dove through the open door, rolled on my shoulder to the left, sprang up into a crouch, and fired two shots into Hy's fat gut before he knew what hit him.

Goodbye, Uncle Hy.

His phone was near his body. I picked it up and hit the last number he called. Gregg answered. I hung up, ran downstairs and carried Mom out to her car, then drove it around the side of Hy's mansion, out of sight. Told her to stay put—over her objections. Then I darted back inside and got into position.

My first order of business would be to persuade Gregg to give me all the necessary bank account information so I could get Pop's money back. I wasn't too worried; I can be a very persuasive guy.

But then what? I'd killed a man.

Beside those involved, the only other people who had any knowledge of the real situation—and my motive—were those from *shul*. And they wouldn't turn me in; I was one of them. With the slightest nudge from Pop, they'd close ranks and give me a rock-solid alibi. Hell, they might even gin up some story about an unhappy client who'd been threatening Hy for weeks and had broken in, gone berserk.

One person stood in my way.

Along with his father, Gregg hijacked my parents' life savings, and in the process, wasted some of Pop's precious remaining time. Ripped me off, too.

If he went to the cops and fingered me, I'd be heading back to prison, this time for life. And if he didn't, if he believed in a sacred bond among the Jews—like our fathers did—and refused to turn me in, he'd be honor-bound to take matters into his own hands, coming after me to avenge Hy's murder.

Either way . . .

I wiped an imaginary smudge off the barrel of my gun and gripped it a little tighter, waiting for Gregg to arrive.

As Pop would say, it was time to make things right.

Silver Alert

S.A. Solomon

It was the kind of thing the family would have howled over in the old days, in better days: a Silver Alert issued for a Silver. They'll never find him even if he wants to be found, your sister Ruthie would've cackled: if the Germans and the U.S. Army couldn't track him down, good luck to the NYPD.

But there it was:

NYPD has issued a Silver Alert for the disappearance of Arthur Silver, an 89-year-old white male with dementia, from Sheepshead Bay in Brooklyn. Mr. Silver is described as being 5'10" tall and 200 pounds with hazel eyes and white hair. He was last seen today, 11/26, at 5:00 P.M., on Emmons Avenue, wearing a tan windbreaker and blue pants. A photo of the missing is available. If you see Mr. Silver, please call 911.

First of all—naturally—nobody could agree on which photograph to give the authorities. Jean, your wife, wanted to give them a picture from a Chamber of Commerce banquet circa 1970 because "it looks like Artie, people will know him." She fretted that you'd freeze to death: it was November and still you wore that windbreaker, like a uniform. You could never explain to her that you didn't get cold. You had become impervious to weather during the war: it was an inconvenience, that was all.

Ruthie was dead by then, but she would've chosen the photo of you graduating from army officer training school in 1944, the one she pulled out to show her cronies at the home every time they met for canasta in the activities room. Alzheimer's ran in the family, and Ruthie couldn't always remember who you were—sometimes she thought you were her dead husband and sometimes her dead son (a junkie, that one, who'd never served anyone or anything but himself, so you knew her brains were scrambled)—but still, she was very proud of you.

Your daughter Ellie, a corporate lawyer, insisted on a contemporary photo from a family dinner at the Italian seafood place on Emmons Avenue, all of you standing by the dock, backlit by a Brooklyn sunset. A paunch spilled over your belt even with your windbreaker zipped up tight, and a wisp of cottony hair fluttered like a flag in the August breeze. You hated that photo, or any photo taken of you after 1965.

Ellie won, like she always did. She had inherited the Silver family balls.

They didn't ask your son Larry for his opinion because nobody knew where he was. After receiving a suspended sentence for some kind of financial fraud that none of you quite understood, he had dropped out of sight. One cousin, a black sheep herself, who claimed to be friends with him on Facebook, said that Larry was living in Florida, having adopted a Sanskrit name and reinventing himself as a yoga teacher.

Of course, Florida, they all said. Anything was possible there, the more improbable the better.

(You knew he was really hoping that you'd look for him. As far as you were concerned, his so-called transformation was simply a cry for an invitation back into the Silver fold. But you wanted nothing to do with him. He'd had his chance to work for you, an opportunity to take over the family business, but he was too good for a trade that had housed and fed and put him and his sister through college.)

If you'd been there (but of course you weren't, you were missing, or so they thought, that's why they put out a Silver Alert), you would've taken issue with the description of dementia. They thought you had lost your marbles, but you knew exactly what you were about. You had to take care of business, or, more precisely, the man who was threatening your livelihood. You had to wrap up loose ends.

You were an expert in procurement, a skill you had learned in the Quartermaster Corps during the war and perfected on your return. An army buddy had vouched for you, giving you your start in the jealously guarded business of brokering no-bid contracts to supply goods and services to the city of New York. You connected people you thought would work well together, who were discreet and in the market for a business opportunity. What they did with that opportunity was up to them. You didn't know and didn't want to know.

You were compensated for your matchmaking skills.

You kept yourself insulated from their extracurricular activities. You had your own company, Silver & Sons, into which you plowed your "finder's fees," but you yourself had never contracted with a city agency. Your name was on no documents.

For thirty years you kept a storefront on Emmons Avenue in a small building that you owned. Your firm supplied promotional items for businesses—pens, letter openers, calendars, matchbooks, key chains, magnets—gifts to give a company's customers so they'd remember and refer the business. You leased the second floor to your son-in-law Richard, an accountant. After you "retired," you closed up the shop but kept your office so you had a place to go. Otherwise your wife would drive you crazy with her ceaseless nagging to eat better and exercise and go out with couples you had no interest in socializing with.

You weren't unsympathetic: you knew she was lonely since the children had left the nest, and she couldn't help but dwell on your third child, a son who died young when a speeding car rounded the corner and met his bicycle on your residential street. Compounding the tragedy, the joyriding teenage driver from Manhattan Beach was also killed when he panicked and fled and his borrowed car plunged over the embankment on Shore Boulevard, so there was no one to rail against for your boy's unfair fate. You and Jean both tried to adjust, but your ways of dealing with the loss were very different. Hers was to bond with the parents of the other boy. But that wasn't your way. You preferred to be alone with your memories, which were much more vivid and alive than the present.

You used the top floors of your building to store samples and the detritus of a lifetime that Jean had banished from the house. Your daughter Ellie insisted that the storage floors and empty storefront were wasted space, not to mention a fire hazard. Plus, she thought her CPA husband would attract clients with bigger bank balances in downtown Brooklyn, where she worked. She talked you into selling the building, a good thing, since you more than quadrupled your money. You got out before real estate values plummeted in the Great Recession, before Hurricane Sandy added insult to injury by flooding the place. Ellie had good instincts for a girl, you had to give her that.

You had always run a one-man shop: the fewer people who knew your business, the better. But after Larry's conviction made it impracticable for him to succeed you, you decided that you needed help. It was too difficult to wear all the hats at your firm and keep the wheels turning with city contractors. You couldn't move as quickly as you used to and it didn't inspire confidence when you showed up late to appointments, out of breath and out of sorts after rummaging through unpacked inventory back at the office.

It was then that you employed the man who would become a threat to you. The irony was that you had rescued him from certain deportation. You met in typical Brooklyn fashion: a car accident on Flatbush Avenue. It was a fender-bender, and you both agreed not to involve the police. You didn't want your insurance premiums to go up and the man, whose name was Reginald Dennis, didn't want to attract the attention of the authorities. He was an immigrant, a West Indian, from Flatbush by way of Guyana. Your Eastern European father had made a similar journey to Flatbush, by way of Odessa.

Brooklyn took in all comers and asked no questions, requesting only that you made good and moved up to make room for the new arrivals.

You and Reggie exchanged phone numbers and got to talking. He had entered the country on a tourist visa and stayed on, illegally, after he met Pamela, the love of his life, at a church supper. Although they couldn't risk calling attention to his immigration status with a marriage license, they were husband and wife all the same. He was a devoted father to their son and daughter and would be their sole support, picking up odd jobs in the cash economy, after Pamela died from a heart attack. (It was a bitter and unexpected blow, since Pam, a nurse, took good care of the family and herself. Her doctor called it the silent killer.)

That day, over cake and coffee at a diner, you offered to hire him instead of paying for repairs on his beat-up Honda. He accepted the offer. Technically Reggie was a shop assistant, a factotum, but his real job was as your go-between. He conveyed information and accepted envelopes in situations where it was not prudent for you to be present. Reggie was a quick study and kept his mouth shut. You made sure he was well paid and then some: gifts for the children, money for their education.

You spent countless hours in the car together (with Reggie at the wheel, since you had long ago lost patience on the road), driving to and from appointments, waiting for clients, collecting payments. You traded life stories, shared confidences. You trusted each other, or so you thought.

His son was, like your own, a no-goodnik, a kid who wore saggy pants and kept bad company. You had given him a summer job, but the boy was unreliable, showing up late or not at all and failing to follow instructions. Reggie was apologetic, even agreed with you when you had to let the boy go. He'd had run-ins with the police and had a juvenile record, no surprise there. Okay, so the kid had eventually turned his life around, unlike Larry, graduating from law school and getting a job as a public defender. Still, you would've appreciated a little gratitude for offering him a leg up.

That's what happened when you tried to help people outside the tribe: when things went well, you never got the credit. But when the chips were down, you were blamed.

If the war had taught you anything, it was that you looked after your own.

Like the old Sinatra song, the Silvers had always done things their way, and that's what got you in trouble overseas.

When the U.S. declared war on Germany and Japan, you were still in high school. You signed up, against your mother's wishes, as soon as you graduated from Erasmus Hall High in 1944. You had grown up behind the counter of your father's dry goods store, so the Quartermaster Corps, which fed and provisioned the troops, was a natural fit. Once your mother got over your decision to enlist in the army instead of going to college, she couldn't have been prouder of her son, the officer.

You saw combat on the final push into Germany with the Forty-Second Infantry Division. The Seventh Army captured Munich, the cradle of the Nazis, on April 30, 1945. On the way, troops of the Forty-Second and Forty-Fifth Divisions liberated Dachau, one of the first concentration camps and the model for the others.

Your father, in his letters to you, would always sign off, "Nobody's in the hospital. Everything's okay."

And you, too, would write back that everything was okay. The army was taking care of you; the war was over; you were stationed in Munich with plenty to eat. But everything wasn't okay. How could it be, after seeing what you had seen?

"Nobody's in the hospital." Your father said it even after he himself was in the hospital, because he didn't know where he was or that his mind was gone, or that his wife, your mother, was dead, a lingering and painful death from cancer.

You entered the camp after most of the Germans had gone, after they'd dug trenches and burned bodies to the bone, then tried to grind down by hand what wouldn't burn. It didn't work: they could never erase all that death.

You saw walking skeletons who wept and shook your hand, or just stared from eyes made hollow by the things they knew, by what they'd endured. Nobody should ever have that knowledge.

You didn't flinch at the papery touch of their flesh, like desiccated insect shells.

You acted like everything was okay. Wasn't that the point of liberation?

Looking for enemy holdouts, your squad swept through the complex of buildings that had housed an SS concentration camp guard training school. You weren't supposed to kill prisoners of war, although some of your men were trigger-happy—and who could blame them, confronted with enemies capable of such atrocities? You crashed through doors, overturning desks. In the office of the camp head of command, you pocketed a letter opener with a swastika and the seal of the imperial eagle. Others took more macabre souvenirs.

Your unit was responsible for feeding the DPs. Displaced persons were all those found outside of their national boundaries at the time of liberation. They included the camp inmates: political prisoners, clergy, Jews, Jehovah's witnesses, Gypsies (Roma, they called themselves), homosexuals, and everyone else rounded up by the Nazis as undesirables or enemies of the state. They became slave laborers, worked to death or killed when they became too weak to work, or made the subjects of medical experiments.

Some of the American occupiers looked at the DPs as pitiable ingrates who complained about camp conditions even after being liberated. They were ragged and filthy, louse-ridden disease carriers who had allowed themselves to be not just captured, but subjugated. Most men wanted to believe that they would never end up on that side of the equation, that they were better, stronger, braver: that they would resist or escape or die trying.

And most of them would do nothing of the kind. It was easier just to be contemptuous of the DPs.

The Nazis—the ones who didn't get shot—were at least given the dignity of a trial, the spectacle of world justice brought to bear against them. But what did these DPs have? Their lives, to be sure, but hadn't they already been tried by their ordeal and found wanting? How could anything—liberation, a chance at a future—undo the annihilation of self they had had to endure? Meanwhile, they waited in the camps to be repatriated to their home countries or for the Allies to find them a new home. And they used the skills they had acquired during the war to survive after it.

The Americans provided subsistence rations but could never fill the bottomless hunger borne by these detainees, who had survived on six hundred calories a day and expended triple that in slave labor, consuming their own flesh. That hunger was met by a thriving black market in the warren of streets off Marienplatz Square: cheese, canned meats, butter, Spam, chocolate, coffee, sugar, liquor, and cigarettes. These items quickly became more currency than commodity and your mission encompassed recovering the thousands of dollars' worth of supplies stolen daily from the Quartermaster depot.

In this mission you had help from the DPs, who functioned as informers in exchange for extra rations, drifting in and out of the camps, bartering with criminal gangs that included Nazis using the black market to fund their underground activities. It was a lethal mix of ferocious survivors and savage war criminals. Neither faction had anything to lose: they were consumed by the burning brand they carried in their hearts, either for revenge or for resurgence.

You had established a working relationship with one such DP, a clever fellow who had survived the camp through his bartering skills, trading favors for the SS guards in exchange for food and blankets and other luxuries for the prisoners. You didn't ask what favors had been traded—desperate times called for desperate measures. This DP, who spoke a little English, was a diminutive man with an obsequious way about him, dangerous if crossed. The Americans called him Al Capone for the scar on his face. He said he had been a soldier in Russia, descended from Romany Cossacks. When told that his grandfathers had slaughtered yours, he just laughed. Jews and Roma, we have a lot in common, he said. We should work together.

Still, you couldn't trust him. He wouldn't say why he was still waiting to be relocated or for whom he was working: the Germans, the Russians, the highest bidder. What was certain was that he wouldn't hesitate to betray anyone for a better deal—even a liberator. So it didn't surprise you when the day came that he wanted more than his usual percentage for directing you to a Marienplatz stash. You refused and things quickly got nasty: he pulled a knife and you drew your service weapon. But you were at close range and he slashed at your gun hand, disarming you. You went for the only thing within reach, the SS letter opener that had been sitting in your field bag since the day of liberation. It was pointed, it was handy, and it was effective.

You would've preferred not to report the incident. It was self-defense, of course, but the DPs were a sensitive topic and the killing of a survivor wouldn't sit well with the Occupation authorities. It might even result in your being disciplined: busted down in rank or worse. But you had lost a lot of blood from your knife wound and had passed out. You didn't make it back to the base until the next day, and were considered AWOL while the MPs searched for you. You had to make a full report.

Your worries were unfounded. As it turned out, you weren't court-martialed. You got a medal instead. Like his namesake, Al Capone was a professional operator, heading up a criminal gang that had cornered the market for contraband, partly through eliminating the competition by informing on rivals for the Americans. You were cited for his capture and unavoidable death.

There were things you hadn't told anyone, even your family, because they weren't the redemption stories people wanted to hear after the war. You didn't talk about it when you came back. None of your generation did. You went over there, did what had to be done and if you were lucky, came home. You started a business and a family and supported them. More than supported: you thrived.

You often thought of what Al Capone had said about his people and yours—wandering tribes, rejected by all nations, persecuted, despised—before he pulled his knife.

"We have everything in common but our blood."

You were Jewish, but that didn't mean you had to believe in God.

That was the other useful thing the war had done. It had relieved you of the obligation of pretending that there was a supreme being. A person had to be mad themselves to believe that there was a righteous god reigning over such horrors.

Still, you joined a synagogue, observed the High Holidays, made sure your children took religious instruction. You donated to Jewish causes and supported the state of Israel.

It was important not to let the bastards win.

๚

It was inevitable that Reggie would one day phone and say he wanted out of the business. He had his green card now, he said, and his children were established in their lives. His daughter was an obstetrics nurse and his son was about to go into private practice with a big law firm. You were both old men, he pointed out, or old enough: retired, past your prime. It was time for the young guns to take over, in a manner of speaking, of course.

You didn't buy it. Somebody had gotten to him. You knew his history, as he knew yours. You both understood that you were playing for keeps. He had accepted your money all these years with the knowledge that it was payola and off the books. And now he thought he could dictate terms? It was over when Artie Silver said it was over, not before.

You told him not to say anything more; that you would speak in person. He picked you up in his new Honda and drove to your usual meeting spot off the Shore Parkway. Nothing would disturb you by the bay, just the cry of seagulls and the tidal sounds of distant traffic.

You mentioned the debt back in Georgetown that had prompted his flight from Guyana to the States. Hadn't you taken care of that for him?

Yes, you had, he agreed. But that was decades ago; he had paid you back tenfold, in loyalty, in service.

"Who is it?" you demanded. "Berger, Mandelbaum, Greenblatt? What are they offering? I'll double it."

Reggie had proven to be valuable over the years and would be dangerous on the other side.

"Mr. Silver,"—Reggie was always formal with you, even after all this time—"it's nothing like that, I swear to you."

The man was sweating, but it was hot out, August in New York. The windows were open and the AC off. You were overheated too. It was making it hard to think. You had to focus.

"So that's how it's going to be, my friend? After all these years together?"

"It's not goodbye," Reggie said, lulled by your affable tone. "We can meet at the diner. And my daughter's getting married, so you'll come to the wedding, I hope."

You were a little surprised by that. You knew his daughter Juliet didn't like you. She always made a sour face when she saw you with her father. And now he was living with her in her house in Kensington, in a separate apartment her boyfriend, a contractor, had built.

You couldn't allow yourself to be distracted.

"What makes you think Uncle Sam will let you stay?" you asked him. "If the feds knew why you left your country, they would roll up the welcome mat."

The threat had registered. You saw Reggie glance at his phone and knew there was a chance he would call for backup.

You felt for your weapon but it was gone. Had the man disarmed you? You didn't remember a struggle, but there must have been one.

You never went anywhere in Munich without your gun.

This DP was going to give you trouble, you could tell.

He wanted more money and he wanted it to come out of your cut. When you refused, he threatened to report you to the Occupation authorities.

The Gypsy bastard wasn't going to get the better of you.

You grabbed his knife arm and the man parried, pinning you against the concrete abutment. You had one arm free to pull out the letter opener, gripping the swastika handle, which bit into and bloodied your palm. You thrust it at him, once, twice, three times, sufficient to sever the carotid artery, as your training had taught you. Then you passed out.

When you awoke, you were back home with the family without knowing how you'd gotten there. You understood that you were losing track of time and even, in your more lucid intervals, that you were losing your mind. But you had something to do before the end.

You had to recover the murder weapon. You couldn't let them find it under the pier off the Parkway. It would lead back to your family.

You slipped out while the aide was busy in the kitchen, boarding a bus that would take you toward your old meeting spot. It dropped you on Emmons Avenue, so you set off on foot. The wind cut through your jacket. You did your best to ignore it, even as shivering overtook you and your legs gave out.

You dug around in the soft ground where you lay but couldn't remember what you were looking for.

You thought you heard your daughter's voice, and your mother's and your sister's and your wife's: "Pops, Artie—you're home now. Nobody's in the hospital. Everything's okay."

You closed your eyes to rest. If the MPs didn't find you first, there was time enough to return to base in the morning.

❧

Reggie had seen the signs of his boss's illness—forgetfulness, irritability, confusion. But it became impossible to ignore that day on the Shore Parkway, when he told Mr. Silver that he was going to retire (he was sixty-seven, after all) and the man became agitated, threatening him with deportation, raving about displaced persons and army contraband. War stories. He had even gotten physical, flailing away at Reggie with his bony, age-spotted hands, their skin paper-thin and bleeding from where his wild punches had landed on the pier's concrete pilings. He did what he could to placate him and dropped him off at home. He immediately phoned the daughter, who had asked him to alert her if there were any incidents.

Mr. Silver's decline was swift. A few months later, he left his house (which Ellie had put on the market in preparation for moving him to a nursing home and her mother to nearby senior housing) while the aide (a woman Juliet had recommended, so Reggie felt responsible) was preparing his meal. He must have taken the B4 bus, because there were sightings of him on Emmons Avenue. Then he vanished. The police eventually found him off the Shore Parkway. He had died from exposure: hypothermia. It was cold, the end of November, and the old man was just wearing a thin jacket.

It was a shame what had happened to him in his dotage, his mind wandering in the wilderness of the past. There was no safety, no comfort in old age if you constantly had to refight battles you had already won.

He went over to Ellie and offered his condolences. She had phoned him herself to tell him about her father's passing, inviting him to the funeral and to sit *shivah* (which he discovered was a kind of Jewish wake) at their house. And she had helped his son Joseph get a job at her law firm.

"Is there anything I can do?" he asked.

"You've done so much for him. You were a good friend," she said. "I thought you might want something of his."

He had helped them clear out the storage floors when they sold the Emmons Avenue building. What was left of Mr. Silver's past was a box stored in the basement, waterlogged from flooding during the storm.

It was true that his daughter Juliet had never approved of their relationship, but she didn't understand.

The man had told Reggie his stories and Reggie had told him his. They shared the details of deeds they had never revealed to the females in their lives, the wives and daughters. These were things the women couldn't know: what a man had to do to ensure his future, to protect his family.

While Reggie had entered the U.S. on a tourist visa and stayed on when he met her mother, what his daughter didn't know was that he was fleeing a criminal gang and corrupt policemen back home. His involvement in a gambling ring had necessitated a working relationship with the police. But when a rival gang gained official favor, he had to abruptly flee the country.

Before he did, he took care of a cop who knew too much, who would have made it difficult for him to start fresh in America. He sometimes regretted garroting the father of a family now that he had one of his own, but it couldn't be helped.

That was a different life, a life that had made him effective in Mr. Silver's business, a fact known and appreciated by him.

Mr. Silver and he had each done things that, in hindsight, were perhaps overkill.

A man acted and was sometimes wrong about the perceived threat.

But failure to act was unforgivable.

There was one thing he wanted from that waterlogged box that would serve to cement the memory of his relationship (he couldn't really call it a friendship) with Mr. Silver, something even more meaningful than the expensive watch Ellie had offered him.

It was a piece of memorabilia that the young Lt. Silver brought home with him from the war, a letter opener with the Nazi insignia.

Each of their people in every generation had their own battles to fight against hatred and prejudice. This was a reminder of one that had been victorious, if at great cost.

Like the old man always said, you can't let the bastards win.

SUBURBAN SPRAWL

Her Daughter's Bat Mitzvah: A Mother Talks to the Rabbi

Adam D. Fisher

We have to have my side of the family and his side and with all the blending we need a Cuisinart to put it together. Oh, and I almost forgot, I'll never forgive myself, that dear aunt of my ex. Come to think of it, she snubbed me at her husband's funeral, but of course she was upset. Upset? Bullshit, pardon my French, she probably killed the old guy who was better off dead—well, maybe not, but you know, anyway, on second thought leave the bitch out. So where were we? Like I was saying, we're having this Bat Mitzvah, well actually it is my daughter, Carly, but you know what I mean, like I feel that it is mine since I couldn't possibly have a daughter old enough and then just look at her, she isn't even developed yet and she's supposed to be a woman. Now come close I want to whisper this, she wanted a training bra, but I told her, baby, you don't have any boobs to train yet, but she said all the girls have them and she feels like a freak, so would you believe, I went over to Macy's and bought her a couple, and then I told her that I hoped she wouldn't have big bazooms like mine because they are one hell of a weight to carry around all the time, but of course at her age, what does she know, she wants boobs, and when people ask me what they can get her for her Bat Mitzvah I want to tell them, "boobs, big boobs," but of course I don't, except, well, I did to my sister and we had a good laugh about it. So there we are. Rabbi, you don't know me. I don't go to services and I'm not religious but I'm proud to be Jewish. One day at work, this guy started talking about someone who tried to "Jew him down." Boy did I give him an earful. I was ready to scratch his eyes out. Nobody, but nobody gets away with that shit around me. Actually come to think of it, I do come to the High Holy Days—well I do at least come to *yizkor* for my mother and I always light the Hanukkah candles and celebrate Passover— we eat matzoh and gefilte fish. Isn't that what it's about? You know when I was a child my brother, the family saint, the prince of Rodney Street, went to Hebrew School and had a big Bar Mitzvah. They must have figured girls weren't important. Bullshit. Sorry. Maybe I wasn't important. Bat Mitzvah? Fuggedaboudit—I didn't even have a sweet sixteen and boy was I sixteen—big bazooms already. My father treated my mother like she was a maid or something. Except a maid would have given him the finger and left. I think the asshole, excuse me, felt the same way about me. Fortunately that bastard died and my mother had a few good years without that putz. Sorry. But that's what he was, plain and simple, a putz. Today's kids would call him a dickhead. Now, what did you say I need to do at the service? Oh well I don't know any Hebrew, but wait, you want to me to learn? Me? I couldn't even learn to say *buenas días* properly after five years of Spanish and you expect me to pronounce Hebrew correctly? You may not realize it, but you are talking to a real dunce. Yes, I mean it, I barely graduated high school and then I married her father. Boy was that a mistake, well I don't know, I had no choice, and okay, I was pregnant and I didn't see anything else I could do, so we had to get married. That's what you had to do those days. Today, well it's a whole different story. A girl gets knocked up and it's no big deal. She has an abortion or keeps the baby and no one says boo. Back then it was a *shandeh*, big time. Well, things were okay for a time and then the baby came and he seemed to lose interest so I went to the gym and got myself a terrific figure but that didn't work. I even sent Carly to her grandparents, planned a dinner with candles, wore a filmy negligee—I looked sensational, but that didn't work either. And then maybe I lost interest in him, well maybe if I had tried harder, I don't know, but that bastard, excuse me, he could have tried too, but I have to admit he was a good provider. He's paying for most of the Bat Mitzvah, even hired this big time DJ with kazillion-watt speakers and a Viennese table to boot. This will be the dream Bat Mitzvah. Flowers from Fancy Arrangements, a dress from Elaine's, invitations from Invitations Galore, holding it at the Seaside Country Club. The whole nine yards—costing a fortune! My so-called friends will have their tongues hanging out and Carly's friends will really be impressed. Hell, we don't want her to feel cheap or unimportant. I haven't got a pot to piss in but one thing, maybe the only thing about my ex, is that he isn't cheap. Even after the divorce he kept up the payments and saw Carly all the time and when he came I always put on a nice dress, something that showed off my figure and made sure my makeup was perfect and I invited him in and made sure Carly saw her grandparents. My ex-mother-in-law is a real bitch. But then he remarried this girl fifteen years younger—a fucking, sorry, cradle robber—and that was the worst day of my life and now we have this Bat Mitzvah and there is just me and then there is him and that new wife of his and Rabbi, you're supposed to know these things, tell me, how the fuck, sorry, am I supposed to get through this?

Sucker's Game

Michele Lang

"You're the people killed Christ. Right?"

I was already having a rotten time in third grade, and this gigantic, sweaty clown on my bus home from school wasn't helping. He smelled like onions and coffee, a weird combo for a sixth-grader. Way in the back, my more bohemian comrades were smoking grass, obliterating the misery of the day. The bad kids, Mafia kids like Falcone and Gravano, but at least those guys left me alone.

I stared straight ahead at the back of the seat in front of me as the bus ground its gears and the giant kid sitting next to me shifted in his seat.

The metal back of the seat said Superior. I muttered SuperOR under my breath, like I could curse the guy away.

No dice. "Right?" he asked again, fake joviality oozing from his pores. The kid was enormous. The size of Nebraska.

We went over a big bump down by Four Corners right then, and the boy reached out, grabbed my left shoulder, and slammed me back into my seat. I gritted my teeth. The bastard was escalating.

I stared straight ahead. SuperOR. Super OR.

"I'm gonna tell you something straight, you stuck-up little bitch. You talk so grown-up, like some fancy kike lawyer or something. I don't like you. You don't belong in this neighborhood. I'm not gonna let you forget it."

The bus swung sharply to the right. Hallelujah, it was the beefy kid's bus stop. Maybe there was a Supreme Deity after all.

We lurched to a stop. The kid smacked my left shoulder with the back of his hand, and then he spit on my bookbag.

"See you in the morning," he whispered in my ear.

And then he lurched to his feet and swaggered off the bus. I watched him go, tears stinging the back of my eyes—no way was I ever going to cry in front of that jerk.

He was right. I was the only Jewish kid on the Catholic side of the lovely suburban town of Crestwood. And nobody was going to forget it, not him or any of the other nouveau riche, miserable kids who all had something to prove.

※

I'd been in the neighborhood for exactly one month, and had made exactly one friend. One friend made a big difference, and Edie was a hell of a friend. But me plus one friend wasn't enough to negate a whole busload of enemies.

My stop was the last one. I exchanged a glance with the dyspeptic bus driver, who managed to survive his bus driving life by pretending we passengers didn't exist. He looked through me, his filmy eyes focused far away, on something else, something beautiful from the past, something better than me and my fellow brats, something better than the Darwinian nightmare of Long Island in the '70s.

I didn't know what faraway memory put a glimmer of hope into that bus driver's eyes, but it sure as hell wasn't me.

I clomped off the bus, still shaking all over from my encounter with Alphonse. No wonder he was a bully . . . probably when he was my size everybody in the vicinity was beating the crap out of him, just for having a name like frickin' Alphonse.

But Alphonse wasn't my only problem.

I tried the front door. It was unlocked.

I took a deep breath, braced myself, and tiptoed inside.

I hoped against hope that my dad had come back from Argentina, but I knew full well he wasn't coming back for a long time. A damn long time.

I looked for a sign of him . . . his beat up Samsonite suitcase, covered with stickers like he was the star of some 1930s movie. His porkpie hat, his cigars. Nope.

I chewed the inside of my cheek looking around, then I dropped my spit-on bookbag with a sigh, rubbed at my shoulder where the straps had dug into my skin. I considered hiding out in my room and skipping snack time, skipping dinner, skipping everything forever.

Because I knew, deep in my bones, that "Grandma" was waiting for me in the kitchen. And I didn't have the stomach for dealing with her right now, not after Alphonse.

"Grandma" was a lady who showed up right before my dad left for Argentina three weeks before this. She wasn't any grandma that I'd ever met before, nobody who existed in the faded black-and-white pictures my parents had humped over from the old country, from before the war.

"Grandma" was here because she needed help. That's what my dad told me, right before he left for Argentina for "business."

That was a big load of bullshit, and we both knew it. "Grandma" was here now because this time, my dad wasn't sure he was coming back at all. And while I was pretty damn sufficient for a nine-year-old kid, even my dad wasn't going to leave me in the house totally alone forever.

My mom was dead and I was an only child, and while the homework would get done and I'd keep the place at least somewhat decent, I was too short to drive by myself to the supermarket and all I knew how to cook was eggs.

"Grandma" was there to feed the illusion.

That was fine, I got the deal without my dad having to spell everything out. That didn't mean I had to like it, or that I had to relate to "Grandma" like an actual grandma or anything. My dad called her Frieda so that's what I called her when I was trying to be polite.

I wasn't trying to be polite now. My rage boiled over in me, a hot, ugly, bubbling cauldron of tar. I clomped into the kitchen, headed for the fridge. Ignored the tiny, hunched-up lady sitting at my dad's place at the kitchen table near the window.

She looked like the Velveteen Rabbit, like her fur had gotten all rubbed off and her eyes fell out and got drawn back on. But it wasn't love that had worn her out like that, no. It was war, and fear, and battle to the death that had left those scars on her.

I ignored her like my life depended on it, and I reached into the deli bin for the liverwurst.

"Anna. You had eh good day?" she asked, her accent so thick and indeterminate that it had taken me a couple of weeks to learn to decode her speech.

"I had a horrible day."

I shuffled over to the linoleum counter with the liverwurst, grabbed the rye bread out of the breadbox. My left shoulder still burned where Alphonse had smacked me.

"Any day you still live is a good day."

I grabbed a butter knife out of the silverware drawer and tossed it on the counter. "You don't know what you're talking about," I hissed through gritted teeth. "You just can't understand."

"Is that boy bothering you again?"

I snorted and ignored her. I picked up the liverwurst and began smearing it all over the slice of rye bread I had slammed on the counter.

Out of the corner of my eye I watched her rise to her full height of four feet something. "You know what your father would say, yes? That you are blond, you have blue eyes. You can pass. Why do you not simply pass?"

I concentrated on the liverwurst, smearing it so hard that it broke through the bread. How could I explain it to this lady? I grabbed a paper towel, slapped my sorry-looking sandwich on top. Folded the bread over, took a big, savage bite.

I chewed and swallowed like nothing in the world was more important in this moment than getting this bite of liverwurstian glory. I glared at her, shuffled to the table with the rest of my sandwich, and sat down.

She glared back, her arms crossed over her scrawny chest.

"I can't pass," I said finally. Sighed and began ripping an elaborate design into the edge of the paper towel. "It doesn't matter what I say is my last name, it doesn't matter how blond I am, how well I play sports. They know what I am, I know what I am. Trying to pass is a sucker's game. I'm not going to even try to play it anymore."

She smiled then, uncrossed her arms. "For a little *pisher*, you think straight, you know. I know your father, he would try to pass. But he does not even realize what the other people see, when they look at him."

When they looked at any of us, she meant. We were a pretty sorry pretend family, and we stuck out in this fancy Long Island neighborhood like a rabbi at an Irish wake. Alphonse and his kind could see right through me and my efforts to fade into the background. I tried, but he wasn't going to let me pass as something else, a fake version of one of them.

So what was the point of trying to pretend?

I took another bite of liverwurst sandwich, swallowed hard to force it down. I shrugged. "Why talk about it?"

"Let me get you some drink," she said. "Don't choke."

Ack, I hated when "Grandma" was nice. I knew she was putting on an act to get my guard down, and I knew that I was a sucker for going for it. My greatest fear was being a sucker, being played, being tricked and robbed and abandoned. I knew that was "Grandma's" intent, yet I fell for it, every time.

She brought me some seltzer in a chipped scotch glass. "Drink it."

I tossed it back like it was straight scotch instead of water. "I wish my dad came back already," I said instead of thanking her.

I put down the scotch glass, gently, slowly. "Where is he?"

"Argentina. On business."

She was lying. Oh, maybe factually she was on the level, but the truth hid somewhere in the spaces between her words.

My name for now was Anna Sterling. My father had started out as a Schwartz and worked his way up to silver. I guessed next we would be Gold. Crestwood was the fourth or fifth place we moved to after my mom killed herself. The first couple of times, I thought we were playing some kind of long game, but it got clear pretty quick that I sucked as a grifter. Every bully in this town could see right through the artifice to what I really was. Somebody who didn't even know the rules of the game, somebody who was running away for her life.

I didn't even know the details of why we had to keep running, let alone the secret rules I kept breaking. All I knew was what I was supposed to pretend to be.

And the business? My jovial, sad-eyed dad pretended to be a working *zhlob*, but even at nine years old I could tell he was also trying to pass. If it wasn't even working for me, I doubted that anybody else around us was fooled either.

Only "Grandma," Frieda without even the artifice of a fake name, stayed real, in that beat-up, terrifying, Velveteen Rabbit kind of way. I think that's why she drove me nuts on a daily basis.

I sighed and gave up trying to pry information out of her. Instead I got up, tossed the rest of the liverwurst sandwich in the trash, knowing this wanton waste of food drove her crazy, but doing it to get the perverse satisfaction of getting on her nerves for a change.

"I'm going for a walk," I said. And without waiting for her answer I slammed out the kitchen door and into the yard that led to the woods.

I used to play partisan out in the woods, all alone. It was my deepest secret . . . I would pretend I had a pistol in my pocket, create lean-tos where I could hide from the Nazi bastards, and I would sometimes creep close in the underbrush behind my neighbors' houses, spying on them like they were enemy bases.

I climbed my favorite tree, which stood at the edge of a clearing hidden in the woods. Nobody could get me, all the way up here. I could hide from the Alphonses of the world, and I could scan for Nazi patrols that got too close to our partisan outpost.

I sat up there until my heart stopped its pounding and my breath came out less ragged. I swayed in the wind, disappeared among the branches, and finally I stopped waiting for my dad to come back. I was alone but free.

A rustle of dead leaves sent me into a silent panic. I froze against the side of the tree trunk, wished bitterly I had worn something more subtle than purple paisley pants for my sojourn in the wilderness.

The man walked out of my worst nightmares and through the woods. He wore brand new, stiff-looking dungarees, a brown plaid shirt tucked in and buttoned all the way up to his skinny neck, and worst of all, weird-looking European shoes that didn't belong in the Long Island woods of 1976.

They belonged on the streets of Berlin. In 1943.

I disappeared into the forest, so still that a bird landed on the branch next to my face. I gave that bird such a look, willed it not to sing and accidently give me away.

I knew to the marrow of my bones that this was a bad man. Somebody who had malevolent intent. Somebody who sneaked through the woods instead of ringing the doorbell and announcing his intentions openly.

It was the shoes that convinced me. The man was a fraud and an interloper. Hey, it took one to know one.

He marched steadily through the woods, never looking up. He edged to within three feet of the uncut brambles at the border of our property. Inch by inch, I turned my head and looked under my left arm to see what he was going to do next.

He squatted down, intent on remaining unseen. He tilted his head, looking this angle and that, framing the house in his fingers like he was some film director or something, some cinema auteur who had just gotten hideously lost.

But he was not lost, no. He had appeared out of the underworld for a specific mission.

The man rose from his haunches and stretched to his full height. He was not a tall man, but something about the spareness of his form suggested a compact, muscular brutality. I didn't know how to pray, but in that moment I wished I had any kind of relationship with my Creator.

And then he turned back into the woods, and the spell of immolation was broken. He retraced his steps, trying to walk quietly, but I could hear every footfall, every pebble getting pushed deeper into the dirt under his pointy oxfords. I froze again, my head still tucked under my left arm looking back at the house, and this time I didn't even dare to move to track him as he left.

Only when I did not hear his footfalls did I dare to move my head.

But he wasn't gone. He was directly under my tree.

He was looking at me.

Crap.

I held on for dear life so that I didn't fall out of the tree, and I got a good look at his face. Skinny and hungry and scared looking. "Little girl," he asked. "Could you tell me who is living in that house?"

He had an accent like "Grandma's," thick and raspy. He looked familiar, somehow. In the back of my mind I was thinking, he was one of us. He was just stumbling through the woods like I was. I wanted him to be a partisan, trying to fit into a world that didn't want him.

But for some reason instead of telling him the truth, I shrugged and smiled, a goofy fake little girl smile. I took comfort in the fact that I was up too high for him to grab me and pull me down. "I don't know. Some family that looks like the Brady Brunch," I said.

I could tell from his expression that he didn't get the TV reference. A low wind picked up in the trees, and the branches over my head swayed and released a shower of golden leaves.

He craned his neck to look up at me, and I knew he was reading me as intently as I was trying to read him, a thick book with tiny lettering in another language. But I had the advantage of youth, very blond hair, and being up in a tree. At least for this guy, I thought I could pass as something other than I truly was.

After another moment, he broke eye contact and scrubbed at the back of his skull with his hands. "Very well then. Thank you." And without saying goodbye, he tromped away through the piles of leaves, into the scrubby woods that ultimately led to the reservoir behind the Murphys' house.

I watched him go, squinted at the center of his back like I was looking through a rifle sight. And with a final flash of dark blue dungarees he was gone.

I hugged the tree trunk so I wouldn't fall out. A squirrel climbed up the tree next to mine and screeched at me in that hilarious bizarre way that they do sometimes. I was sure I was messing somehow with his acorn stash.

But for the life of me I couldn't get down, at least not yet. I was so dizzy I was afraid that I would fall if I made the attempt. Instead, I tried to ignore the squirrel's vulgarities and focused on reminding myself to breathe. And confirming that the guy was in fact gone and not ambushing me instead.

It was getting dark when I finally climbed down like a crab and fell out of the tree about four feet from the ground. A big pile of orange and brown leaves cushioned my fall, which was good because I had gotten so stiff up there I was a total klutz coming down.

Ow. I welcomed the pain for zapping me back into the present, into the reality of where I really was. I half-ran, half-limped back into the house. The sunset reflected in the back windows, setting the living room and dining room on fire with a golden glory.

I shaded my eyes with my hands until I made it to the back patio. Slipped into the house, my shoulders shivering in the dying light, and tried to sneak into my room without being detected.

No luck.

"Grandma" blocked the doorway, her tiny hands balled into fists and planted on her hips. "You were certainly gone for a long time. Where were you?"

I gulped. "In the woods, walking around."

We stared at each other for a while. I considered a fast retreat and going back out there, though I was secretly afraid of getting eaten by a stray dog or a bear. Or grabbed by that guy.

"Did you see anybody?"

What a strange question. Nobody wandered around in the trees between properties . . . other kids, maybe, but not after dinnertime.

I didn't trust her before that question. But now, I wondered how much she knew about the man with the stiff, brand new dungarees and pointy European shoes. Maybe he was her accomplice. In something devious and horrible that I didn't understand.

So I lied. I shrugged, said, "Well, I saw the neighbors' dog Wally . . . he's getting fatter day by day. At least he's friendly."

Frieda wasn't born yesterday. "I mean a person. Did you see any persons in the woods?"

I folded my arms across my chest. "No."

I could tell she thought I was lying. Her face changed and she turned and stalked away without another word. At the time I thought that she was mad at me now, that I had finally made an enemy out of Frieda.

I was wrong. My inability to lie convincingly saved my life at about three the following morning.

※

I went to bed without supper. No overt punishments were discussed; I had no appetite and for once Frieda didn't force her sweetbreads or fried chicken gizzards into me.

So I tucked myself into bed, hid under my flowery quilt, shut off the light, and stared, sleepless, at the shifting shadows on the ceiling. My spit-on bookbag now sat in the corner next to my white princess desk under the far window, unopened.

Homework was a problem. I liked to do it on the bus, at the very last minute before it was due so I didn't waste my time on school any longer than necessary.

However, Alphonse and his gross attentions had destroyed my commuting time, so I had to come up with something else.

I had zero desire to do homework now, and nobody in my life who gave enough of a rip to enforce it. But the bag pulsated with promises yet unkept, demands unfulfilled.

The bag, not the guy in the woods, stalked my nightmares. Again and again, I jolted out of sleep, covered with sweat, imagining mold growing over the bag where Alphonse had hocked his loogie.

Each time, I'd lie back down, stare at the shifting shadows, listen to the rustle of the leaves against the windows. And drift back asleep. Only to bolt awake again when I dreamed of my teacher forming a firing squad at dawn. For homework-less me.

Guilt has its use, or else why are we sometimes riddled with it?

I woke again, to hear a branch scraping against the screen window opposite my bed. Except there was no tree by that window.

I didn't think. Didn't freeze. I rolled off my bed, landed as lightly as I could, then slid under the bed. Afraid that whatever or whoever was scraping the screen could look inside and see me. But knowing I didn't have the time to run away.

The scrape turned into a long ripping sound as the screen got peeled away from the window frame. My heart beat so loud I was sure that whoever it was breaking into my room would hear me. A telltale heart under the bed.

I didn't want to admit I knew who it was, breaking into the house. It had to be the guy with the Nazi shoes hiking around in the forest. Silently I cursed my pigheaded stupidity, not telling Frieda about the guy when I had the chance.

I tried to convince myself I was safe with the dust bunnies and random books that had ended up under the bed with me . . . I'd left my blanket on the bed, and any intruder naturally would assume I'd just wandered off for a late-night tinkle down the hall or something.

But it was creepy. The guy had chosen my room to make his entry. Why? The whole house was ridiculously easy to break into, not that I had ever given the matter a thought before this moment.

Was it me? Was the guy breaking in specifically to steal me?

And if so, what for?

Somebody climbed onto my princess desk, which was placed just under the window, making a perfect step down into my room. The desk creaked in protest, then the matching painted-white chair. Then the heavy whump of feet hit the bare wood of my bedroom floor.

I squinted in the near-darkness. A pair of European pointy shoes, the laces of the left one untied. Standing right next to my bed, presumably staring down at my empty covers in the moonlight.

I held my breath.

I knew he knew I was under the bed. In a rush, I suddenly understood. Just like in the forest, this man had been watching me, not the house. I was his target. His only, or at least primary, target. But why?

I knew he was going to bend down and haul me out from under the bed in another second. And I knew I had no defenses, nothing, no way to protect myself or run away. I kept my eyes open so I'd see his hands, and I silently grabbed the back foot of the bed to make it harder for him to drag me out and slit my throat or whatever other awful plans he had for me.

Right before his knees started bending, I heard a shout from the doorway to my bedroom, a scratchy German barrage.

Instead of crouching, the shoes turned around to face the doorway. A fusillade of German curses shot back to the door. To where "Grandma" was screaming at the stranger, daring him to do his worst.

I wished desperately that I understood German and what the two of them were yelling at each other about. It sounded like a continuation of an argument these two had been having since the dawn of time.

A half dozen steps of the pointy shoes, the sounds of a scuffle.

Then, a single gunshot.

Silence.

A body slamming into the floor.

More silence.

I was dead meat now. One of the two was dead, and no matter who it was, the survivor was coming after me next. And I doubted the killer wanted me hanging around as a witness.

Fast footsteps to the bed. Scuffling around the bedclothes, sounds of the bed getting stripped.

Then, "Grandma's" face peeking under the bed, looking for me.

"You are safe. Good."

She looked calm, amused even.

I just stared back at her, amazed that she could see me with her wizened little eyes, to where I stayed hidden in the deep shadows. Even with the moonlight I could barely see her.

"Come out. You will be fine."

I gulped and grabbed onto the back of the bed harder. My brain chewed on what had just happened, a tough piece of steak that threatened to choke me. From what I could make out, Frieda had just shot the guy who broke into my room.

Wasn't I next?

I didn't say anything.

"*Liebchen*, we have time but not very much. You have nothing to fear. Come."

I looked at her again. She was smiling, but it was a grim sort of smile. Fierce. Deadly.

I had to make a basic choice. Trust this little old murderer or hide under here until my dad came home, the next of never?

I took a deep shuddering breath, the first one I had taken in quite a while.

I slid out from under the bed. My pulse pounded in my ears like a tide coming in.

"Good," she said, gently. "Very good. Come."

I stood up and smoothed out my flannel nightgown. The intruder was crumpled in a heap by the door to my room like a pile of unwashed laundry.

"Who is that?" I forced out. My voice sounded huskier than hers.

"Never mind. Come out from here first. And we will talk a bit."

She grabbed me behind the left elbow and ushered me, a little too quickly, past the dead guy and down the hall. Once we made it to the kitchen and the wall phone, she switched on the lights.

That was the first time I saw her weapon. She laid it to rest in the center of the kitchen table like a strange artifact on an altar.

It looked to match the guy dead on the floor in my bedroom. A piece that had time traveled from the war into my 1970s New York world. I knew nothing about guns, but the patina on this one suggested to me that it was very old.

Old as the serpent. Old as time itself. Almost as old as Frieda.

"You were waiting for that guy," I gasped, staring at the gun instead of her.

She sighed. "It was only a matter of time."

I turned to face her. "Am I next?"

There. I asked it. No point in pussyfooting around with this lady. That guy who tried it was cooling off down the hall . . . if she wanted me dead, that was it.

"Ach, no. Did your father explain nothing?"

I turned around to look at her. Her little fists were balled onto her hips again, and she looked disgusted. At my father or me, I could not tell.

"He went to Argentina for business. You know . . . import-export."

She pursed her lips. Obviously he hadn't told me the details of what that business entailed . . . evidently the downsides included assassins from the old country showing up to kidnap, mutilate, or otherwise dismember his daughter.

"His business is very serious."

"How do you know?"

"Let us say that I am his partner. And we are working on a deal with high stakes."

"What does that have to do with that guy? The guy who . . ."

She cut me off before I could finish the sentence: the guy who broke in. The guy who came to kill me or worse. The guy who obviously knew Frieda and spoke the same language.

She waved away my words. "Let us say simply that the man in your room wanted you as collateral. Or perhaps . . . he was a person who refused to stay in the past."

That made absolutely zero sense to me, but I didn't bother to ask. I just watched her face and I listened.

"You need not trouble yourself about this."

Yeah, right. That gunshot was going to haunt my nightmares for the rest of my life. I already knew that for sure.

"All you need to know is that you mustn't worry. Your father called me here to watch over you. He loves you that much."

That pissed me off. Love had nothing to do with it and she knew it. "He didn't love me enough to stay here with me and protect me himself."

The words shot out before I could call them back, and I knew as I said them they were the wrong ones. It meant my life to remember how dangerous Frieda really was. Her disguise—"Grandma"—was designed to conceal, and it worked damn well. If I ripped that disguise away to reveal the truth of what was going on here, who knew the price I'd have to pay?

She looked at the ceiling then, her nostrils flaring. "You do not understand this today. Perhaps you never will. But the truth is, your father loves you enough to leave you behind here. In America. In the easy place. Where if every sacrifice is accepted, you will grow up ignorant and happy."

It was my turn to roll my eyes. "Nobody asked my dad, or you, or my mom, anybody, to be a sacrifice for me. I was lucky enough to get born too late. I didn't do that on purpose."

She smiled then, sadly. "You think the danger is in the past. But the danger is here, it will never go. And despite your father's business in Argentina, any sacrifice he makes may still not be enough."

Whatever my father's business was, it had the effect of awakening dormant monsters, stirring them up like hornets. I wasn't sure if it was the past or the present that was the bigger danger.

I let her change the subject, let the mystery of my dad's absence, the dead guy's presence, to remain. I pretended not to care. "As long as I'm not the burden my dad is carrying, I guess I can handle it."

"We must call the police now," she said. "Say nothing. I will speak only."

I nodded, watched her knobby arthritic fingers dial 911 on the rotary phone on the wall. She explained the situation briefly, factually. Left out every important detail.

Replaced the receiver into the cradle with a gentle click. "They will be here in a few minutes. Remember, say nothing."

"Thank you for saving my life," I finally said. "I'm sorry I said such nasty things." Just being careful, just a little insurance against the next night I would be spending alone with Frieda in a house full of secrets.

She pushed her glasses up the length of her nose. "You said nothing."

I got the message loud and clear. None of this happened. Her explanation, the truth, the silence around the truth . . . all an illusion.

My job was to pretend to be a scared, innocent little blond girl. I could play that part to perfection. So I did.

❦

The police spent a surprisingly brief amount of time investigating what had happened. They made me look at the body to see if I recognized the guy.

In fact, I did. They turned on the light in my room, and I got to see his face without having to worry whether he was going to kill me or not. And I remembered.

My mother had still been around. It was about two or three summers before, a hot, humid Ohio summer in a rented house. Moving around even then, but not running away. Not yet.

Her brother came to visit us, a man dressed like a Hasid, with long side curls and a scruffy black beard. Except I'd noticed when we sat down in the yard that the beard was fake. Glued on, and the glue was getting a little melted in the humidity.

My parents talked to him for a long time, behind a closed door and in a foreign language. And then soon after that, my mother was gone.

Staring at the stranger now, clean shaven and dead, I realized that he wasn't my uncle. And with a sudden painful jolt of clarity, I realized that my mother hadn't killed herself after all.

It was this man. I was supposed to be next.

So I made the most of the moment. I burst into tears, cried like I couldn't when I was alone. I'm sure I was very convincing to the authorities . . . and it was a luxury for me to fall apart. So I did.

The cops asked me if I knew who he was. I shrugged, sniffled, and said no.

They didn't take either of us in. By the time they collected their evidence and got the body out of my room, it was time to get ready for school.

Even Frieda thought it was a good idea for me to take a day off. "You earned it," she said.

We regarded each other in the kitchen, wary but with mutual respect. I favored her with a smile. "I did good," I acknowledged. "But I better go today."

After a minute, I took a deep breath, decided to take a chance. "Are we leaving this place?"

She pursed her lips, considering, then shrugged. "That man is dead. There is no reason to run away anymore."

I didn't really believe her but I still had to deal with my life. Not the past, but this morning. "Well, if we're staying here, then I have to get on that bus. Or else I'll never go back there again. You know?"

She favored me with a smile back. Frieda wasn't a big one for smiles, so that was significant. "I know. You are a tough little *pisher*."

"I'll take it. Hey, I'll call you Grandma and mean it."

She didn't hug me or anything like that . . . it wasn't Frieda's style and to be honest it wasn't mine either. But she fried me a whole kielbasa and made me hot chocolate besides. This was like three days of food in her world.

I ate the whole thing. And fortified, I sat back and watched the sun rise over the police cars still parked outside.

Frieda cleaned everything up, another covert sign of respect. "You are sure about school? Stay here and rest."

I appreciated her offer. But I said no. If I stopped long enough to think, I was going to lose my mind. So I washed my face, tried to calm down my puffy, bloodshot eyes, and got dressed.

The cops had done a great job cleaning up my room and getting most of the traces of the guy out. But I would always see him there, crumpled up by the door. I tried to ignore his specter and got dressed, in Billy the Kid blue jeans and a button-down gingham shirt.

I waited for the bus in a light drizzle, not bothering with a slicker or an umbrella. The cold wet washed away the artifice, the last vestiges of my desire to get along and convince the people in my world somehow that I belonged in it.

When the bus showed up, the police cars were still in the driveway. I was the first one on the bus, so the bus driver was the only one treated to the spectacle of the law doing its business. He looked at me, his eyebrows levitating. I just nodded, unwilling to acknowledge the police lights setting off the inside of the bus like fireworks.

Exhausted all of a sudden, I turned around and sat in the front seat, right behind the driver. If Alphonse wanted to come get me I was going to make it hard for the big bastard.

The bus filled up fast. Alphonse made his appearance and started right in on me. "Hey, you're the people killed Christ. Right?"

I turned to face him. "Damn straight. You wanna be next?"

I was dead serious. The kitchen knife I'd slipped into my backpack would be plenty enough to do the job.

Some instinct warned him to cool his jets. He shot a glance at the bus driver, who glared at him through the rear view mirror and shook his head in disapproval.

Another kid sidled up to us from the back of the bus. I stifled a gasp. It was Joey Falcone, a sixth-grader and son of the Mafia royalty, one of the bad kids. That kid's family was made, and everybody on the bus knew it. He didn't concern himself with petty rivalries or the daily bloodshed on the bus. I'm sure he had more important issues to worry about.

So everybody on the bus, including the driver, took note of his progress to where I sat, to where Alphonse was doing what he always did.

"Hey, Al, shut the fuck up and leave the girl alone."

I looked at Falcone. Alphonse looked at Falcone. Every set of eyeballs on the bus looked at him, riveted by his every word.

He nodded at me, a noble acknowledgment indeed. "She just wacked a guy broke into her bedroom last night. Heard it on the police scanner over my Wheaties. Back off, Alphonse. You stupid mook."

Falcone turned and strolled back to his seat, holding on to the tall puffy seat backs to stay balanced on his orange Keds.

Alphonse edged away from me like I was radioactive. I kind of was.

The thing was, I didn't want him to back off. I was sick of him and I wanted to end the game he was playing, me the mouse to his cat.

The only way to win a sucker's game is to stop being the sucker.

And I was done playing charades.

"So you were saying? My people killed Christ? Yeah, we did. You know why? Because he wouldn't shut up."

I was goading him now. But Alphonse glanced back at Falcone. He wasn't going to take the bait, not now. So my victory was empty . . . unlike Frieda who got to finish the job I had to watch Alphonse slide away from me, slink to the back of the bus in disgrace. Humiliated by a pissed-off third-grader with nothing left to lose.

The bus rumbled and chugged on its way to school. I figured two things . . . one, my dad was either coming home right away or never again, and I'd be okay either way. I was finished with waiting. And two, I'd managed to impress Frieda. The first thing of note I'd ever done.

Either way, I was done running away. Lucky or not, this was where I had landed, and now I was making my way in the world, following my own set of rules and keeping score with my own system. I was the only Jewish kid on the Catholic side of the lovely suburban town of Crestwood. And I wasn't going to let anybody forget it.

Jewish Easter

David Liss

The last day of school, before spring break, our science teacher had us go around the room to tell the class about our family's Easter traditions. This was the late '70s, and while there was probably some general understanding among educators that not every student necessarily had to be Christian, none of them really gave a crap.

When it got to be my turn, Tim Killian and Kevin Hanson, in the back of the room, started laughing and making those fake sneezes—*Jewboy!*—which Mr. Reece handled deftly by giving them a stern look and saying, "Come on, guys. Al is telling us about Jewish Easter."

I guess that's how a couple of rednecks like them learned what a Passover seder was. I didn't go into all that much detail, because everyone looked bored out of their minds except Tim and Kevin, who continued to lob anti-Semitic sneezes and the occasional ball of paper. They were the reason I said as much as I did. They were both big guys—Tim was muscular and Kevin just fat. They both kept their hair shorn in humorless military cuts, one in imitation of the other. Tim had a face red with acne, like he'd been scoured with steel wool. They were both rumored to have had trouble with the law, and they were widely feared around their trailer park and our school. So I looked at them, smiled, and kept talking.

I'd had to deal with those two since the third grade. Sometimes other kids would move in and out of their orbit, but Tim and Kevin remained at the center. I'd lived in a very Jewish New Jersey suburb before the family moved to Florida, and back there I'd never encountered Jew-haters. I hadn't even known they existed, but my Jacksonville middle school was full of them. Lots of places in south Florida have plenty of Jews, but they were further south, in Fort Lauderdale and Miami. I was the first non-Christian a lot of kids, and even some of their parents, had ever met.

So, third grade was the first time I'd had the shit kicked out of me for being a Jew. Fourth grade was the first time I kicked the shit out of someone for pushing me too far. I beat Tim Killian until his teeth were stained red with blood. I knocked Kevin Hanson down and kicked him until he cried for his mother. They were both taller and heavier than me, but I was fast and could take either of them, and I'd done it enough times for there to be no doubt about it. I couldn't take them both at once, though, and so they stuck together and tried to get under my skin and acted like I was the coward because I tried to avoid them ganging up on me.

This was the eighth grade, so I figured this would be the last year I'd have to deal with them constantly. Once we got to high school, there would be more kids to thin out my exposure. I would head into the honors program, they'd be tossed into the pit of remedial classes and shop. There was still the problem of the bus to and from school, but eventually we'd all learn to drive and the day would come when I could go days at a time without having to cross paths with either of those assholes. I wasn't afraid of them. I wasn't afraid of fighting them. I wasn't even afraid of them getting the drop on me. It happened a couple of times a year, and I could take it. I just didn't want them around. I wanted not to see them or hear them or remember that they existed.

For the time being, I would have to content myself with spring break, though things at home weren't so great either. My sister, already in high school, had shifted her position toward me from benign indifference to hostile contempt. My mom and stepfather were having problems again, which meant he was more impatient than usual, and she was hitting the sauce pretty hard. It wasn't the screaming or my mother's drunken tears or my stepfather's door slamming that got to me. It was more philosophical. We'd moved to Florida because of *him*. *He* was the one who had wanted to be here, for reasons that—all these years later—were not clear to me. If the two of them couldn't even get along, then what were we even doing in that wasteland?

Lou's business, as near as I could tell, could have been conducted anywhere. He ran some kind of import-export operation in which the actual goods beings imported and exported were, as far as I could tell, entirely notional. He never appeared to cross paths with any shipments, he never visited a warehouse, and he never visited a dock or airport. I'd long since accepted that the details were vague and unlikely to change. Maybe I should have been suspicious from the beginning, but when you're little, everything is plausible. Then the years go by, and it just seems like the way things are.

When I was younger, I'd imagined Lou spending his days sitting at a cluttered desk, filling out inscrutable customs forms, his half-moon-shaped reading glasses sliding halfway down his nose, but the older I got, the less I believed it. I'd been to his tiny office a couple of times, located in rundown building very near, if not actually in, a part of town best avoided after dark. I hadn't been there since I was in fifth grade, but on the few occasions I'd been parked there—school holidays when my mother needed him to watch me for a few hours—I hadn't seen him do much besides make cryptic phone calls and leaf through magazines.

"Your stepfather is a drug dealer," my friend Gus told me earlier that year when I was complaining about his weird job. "How can you not know that?"

"Lou? Are you kidding? He doesn't have it in him."

"I'm telling you," Gus insisted. "My brother and his friends smoke, like, a ton of weed, and they heard all about him. He's got some connection in Jamaica or something. He brings it in and then ships it out to distributors—like gangsters, not street dealers. He's pretty high up the food chain."

I didn't believe it. Not that I thought Lou could never do something crooked, but because I didn't think he had the balls to sell drugs. On the other hand, we lived in a pretty nice neighborhood, had expensive cars, and never seemed to be short of cash. You don't get that kind of money from looking at magazines in an office and listening to phlegmy coughs through the thin walls.

Later, after Gus had told me all that, I looked at Lou like I'd never seen him before. A little on the short side, skinny, with a big pot belly, a long face that I guess could have been handsome once, but now just looked slack and irritated. Could this guy be a criminal? I didn't think so, but I wondered if that was because accepting what Gus said would make him seem somehow more impressive.

There were also the plane tickets, which Lou paid for. My father wasn't on the scene, and if he had been, he wouldn't have been able to afford buying much of anything. My sister and I flew up north to visit our grandparents several times a year—including for Passover when it coincided with spring break or a weekend. We would have gone that year, but my grandparents decided to take the previous seder's "next year in Jerusalem" seriously, and they were spending the holiday with a distant cousin off Ben Gurion Street. My stepfather had been grumbling for days about having to run the seder, and all the signs pointed to the tension, cheerlessness, and eruptions of anger that were the hallmarks of holiday dinners over which he presided.

Then one thing I could count on was brevity. I liked the long seder when my grandfather ran it. He had been in sales most of his life, and he had a gregarious theatricality about him. When I was over at his house, I found myself absorbed by the rituals, by the holiday foods, by the once-a-year strangeness and the comforting familiarity. At our house, with everything that had been going on, the best I could hope for would be a race to the finish through the Maxwell House *haggadah*.

To make matters worse, Lou's mother, Nana Anna, had been living with us for a couple of months now. She was in her late seventies, thin, and pale—a Holocaust survivor who still spoke with a faint German accent. Her health had been falling apart over the past year, and she probably should have been put in some kind of facility, but Lou didn't want to pay for that, so when her neighbors found her wandering naked down the street of her Teaneck neighborhood, Lou had decided to relocate her to our guest room and put my mother in charge of her care. "What the hell else do you have to do?" he reasoned.

Even when she'd been sharp, I'd found her to be a woman who disliked children in general only slightly less than she disliked her own offspring. In the past, her visits had often coincided with my birthday, which she made no secret about resenting. She would generally slip me a dollar bill on the table in front of me and say, "Here. You happy now?" This year she'd ignored my birthday entirely, and she fell asleep while my mother lit the candles on my cake and made me sing "Happy Birthday" along with her because my sister and stepfather refused to join in.

The good news was that we were making our way through the seder with record speed. *Karpas* to the four questions was a blur. My sister glowered at anyone who dared to look at her, let alone ask her to read. Meanwhile, my step-grandmother was humming softly to herself and my mother perked up only during the mandated wine drinking. She'd been thin and pretty when Lou had married her seven years back, but she'd put on weight, mostly from drinking, I supposed, and she now wore big, shapeless dresses and looked a good ten years older than her thirty-eight years.

Less than half an hour after starting, we were at the part where my stepfather read, "Let all those who are hungry come and eat." In the spirit of the holiday, he turned to me. "Move your lazy butt, and open the door."

I pushed my chair back along the white tiles of the dining room floor, maybe a little grateful for the break, however short lived it would be, from the table. I opened the door, expecting to see nothing but the dark of our quiet street, and it took me a moment to recognize the shadowy forms lurking on the porch as people.

Tim Killian and Kevin Hanson were standing kind of bent over, like they'd been pressing their ears to the door, listening to what was going on inside. I stared at them in shock. Maybe nothing but confusion, and possibly embarrassment, came over Kevin's fat features, but Tim was nothing but pure defiance, like he was daring me to make him explain himself.

"Well, I'm hungry," Tim said. He pushed past me and stepped into the house. Kevin hesitated for just a beat and followed behind him.

A vortex of unreality swirled around me. These guys lived in a trailer park not two miles from my house, but I'd never seen them in the neighborhood before. They had no reason to be here. They had no reason to want to be here, but they were in my house, and there was a kind of terror in that. They were breaking the most basic rules that governed the truce between middle school kids and adults. The pact, as I understood it, said that the Tims and Kevins of the world could be as cruel and as violent as they wanted as long as they did not force teachers and parents to pay attention to them. Somehow, when no one was looking, these two had declared war on the entire system.

My stepfather did not get it. He had his reading glasses on, propped on the middle of his nose as usual. He ignored the intruders and looked at me. "Al, this is no time for your friends to come over."

There were a lot of things going on here, many of which I had trouble processing, but not least among them was that my stepfather might imagine that these two guys were somehow my friends. I never brought my friends to the house. I hadn't had a friend over in maybe three years. My mother and stepfather never seemed to notice this, just like they carefully avoided noticing when I came home with a black eye or my clothes torn from fighting.

Kevin was lagging behind, not quite sure what to do, but Tim was operating in full hooligan mode. He stepped forward, shedding any fear of consequence, inhabiting the moment heedless of what might come next. It was electric and terrifying. For a thirteen-year-old to walk into a stranger's house, full of adults, and command the room with his heedlessness was strangely beautiful. It was like watching thousands of years of social order destroyed with the strike of a match.

"You know," Tim said, "after Al told the class about your Jewish Easter, and I got kind of curious, so I went to the school library and did a little reading. I learned all about that funny bread you eat and that wine drinking, and how you have to let anyone who wants have dinner with you."

Lou was staring at me. They all were, like this was my mess and it was my job to clean it up. I had nothing to say. I was still standing by the door, trying to fit these chunks of reality together like mismatched Lego pieces. For want of anything useful to do, I closed the door.

Tim, meanwhile, was advancing to the sideboard.

"Roast beef, huh? I like mine rare."

Nana Anna had her head down, but she was smiling, mumbling to herself, lost in some sort of fantasy. Everyone else was looking at my step-father, expecting him to resolve this crisis. And why not? He was the man of the house. He always liked to tell us this, as though it were a conferred title, like being a baronet. It *was* up to him to fix this.

More than that, I had a feeling this had less to do with Tim's sudden fascination with other cultures than it did with Lou's office on the wrong side of town and those rumors about his business.

Lou stood up and faced Tim. He looked perplexed but also annoyed, which was his default. It was simply a more intense version of how he'd looked all night. "We're having dinner," he said. "You boys need to go home."

Tim folded his arms and rocked back on his heels. "I heard you say that anyone who's hungry should come eat. I'm hungry. I want to eat."

"You're not hearing me," Lou said, and his voice was strangely authori-tative. It wasn't the annoyed tone of exasperation that he used around the house. There was some heft behind hit. This was the voice of a guy who wholesaled drugs, of a guy who had contacts in Jamaica and clients who had done jail time. He was no longer a kvetchy asshole but something far more dangerous and powerful. "I don't know what you think you know about me, but I'm giving you a chance to walk away."

"So, what you said," Tim pressed, "doesn't mean anything? The part about hungry people being invited inside? Is that what you're telling me? That you're a liar?"

"Tim," Kevin cautioned, but Tim wasn't listening.

"It's just a stupid ritual," my sister said, sighing.

This was, of course, a mistake. You don't ever ask someone like Tim to notice you, particularly not when he's already in a social-compact-breaking tailspin. He now looked up and smiled at my sister. "What's your name, honey?"

My sister flipped him off.

"That's not very nice," Tim told her. To Lou, Tim said, "My father says Jews are born liars. I always thought that maybe it's true, maybe it's not. But you said if I was hungry I should eat, and now you're telling me to go away, so I guess that pretty much answers my question."

"I'm not hungry," Kevin said, shoving his big hands into the pockets of his jeans. He was clearly unable to see an ending of this story that didn't involve police cars, public humiliation, and his notorious cruel father holding a belt in his hands.

"Well I am," Tim said.

He moved a little closer to my stepfather, swaggering like a gunslinger. He was big and muscular and every movement radiated the kind of twitchy power that comes with not giving a damn about what happens next. Now was all that counted, and the idea of *consequences* was as alien to him as particle physics. Lou must have seen it too, because whatever tough guy bravado he'd managed to summon crumbled. He blanched and he took a step back.

I heard myself groan. I'd been facing off with Tim for six years, and I knew how he operated. He was like a cat staring at a wounded bird. He was all twitch and instinct, and backing down or showing weakness were stoking the fires of his animal brain.

"We don't want any trouble," my stepfather said.

Tim laughed. By this point in his life, he knew too well that only people who were already in trouble ever said that. Wanting was out of the picture. "Me either. I just want some of that roast beef."

My mother stood up. "I'm calling the police."

"You sit on down, big lady," Tim drawled, lazily, like it was a suggestion, even an invitation, but there was no mistaking the command in there. "What are you going to tell them? You invited me in to eat, and when I expected to get some food, I was breaking the law? Is that what you're going to tell them?"

My stepfather was standing stock still now, pale and uncertain. He was a good six inches taller than Tim, and he probably had a hundred pounds on him, but Tim was wiry and feral, a weasel of a boy, and you only had to look at him to know you didn't want to mess with him.

"You got something to say?" he asked my stepfather.

My stepfather didn't answer, but saying nothing, in this case, was kind of what Tim wanted.

"Then move your lazy ass over there and cut me some roast beef. And then we'll talk about what else you might have for me."

This was the decisive moment, I knew. Lou could push back here and now, make Tim show his cards. Given that Kevin wasn't on board with this insane stunt, it seemed like the right play. I was ready to get in there and help to bring him down, but it didn't feel like the first move was mine to make. This seemed like a job for adult authority. I was backup.

"Look, I'll get you some food, and then you'll go," Lou said.

Tim grinned. "Get me some food," he said, "and then you can get me a package of something for dessert."

Lou suddenly looked alarmed. "If you think that I keep goods in my house . . ."

"We can go for a drive," Tim said. "That's fine. For now, get me some food. And try not to touch it with your filthy Jew hands. My daddy says you people are animals, and the last thing I want to taste is your nasty filth when—"

That was as far as he got before he toppled over. Nana Anna stood over his body, her steak knife sticking out the back of his neck. Tim lay on the white tiles of our dining room floor, blood pooling out, pumping into the cracks and flooding over.

"Nazi *mamzer*," she said, her voice strangely calm, like she'd spotted a favorite species of bird.

❧

Several things now happened at once. My sister screamed. My stepfather fainted. He actually fainted, falling down to the tiles in a neat heap, like a human Slinky. Nana Anna returned to her seat and began mumbling, like none of this had ever happened. My mother, in a clear display of priorities, began to pour herself another glass of Manischewitz. And Kevin, with perhaps the most level-headed reaction of any of us, began to run for the door.

In the clarity that comes with hindsight, I should have let him go. Tim had come into our house, had threatened us, and while we had been attempting to deal with this situation calmly, an addled old woman had reacted out of blind, and understandable, instinct. What were the cops going to do? Send Nana Anna to prison? This was a terrible outcome, but no one was really to blame except Tim himself, who had taken his youthful exuberance too far and had met the same fate as countless other adolescents who had crashed and burned when they'd flown a little too close to the sun.

This all came to me clearly later on. At the moment, all I could think was that I couldn't let Kevin get away. I was on him before he knew what had happened, tackling him around his waist and bringing him down. My sister screamed again as Kevin landed, his head making hard contact with the tiles, cracking one of them in a lightning bolt pattern. Kevin lay there, motionless, and we were two-for-two with rednecks. A moment of pure joy coursed through me, but it only lasted a second before I realized that I had just completely fucked things up by making it seem that these two middle school kids had just been attacked by a family of psychos, the head of whom was a guy I was now sure was a big-time dope dealer.

❧

My stepfather hadn't hit his head, and he wasn't out long. In a few minutes, he was up and suddenly in command. "Get a sheet to wrap up that body," he said to my mother.

She finished her glass of wine and moved, strangely focused in her motions, like maybe this wasn't the first time they'd had to get rid of a body. Part of being thirteen years old is feeling like you don't really know your parents, but I was getting a double dose of that.

"Is the fat kid still alive?" he asked me, gesturing at Kevin.

I looked down, and I could see the rise and fall of Kevin's chest under his checked shirt. I didn't know how hurt he was, but he was breathing. "Yeah."

"Then we need to tie him up."

"We should call the police," my sister said.

"And tell them what?" Lou demanded. "That a couple of kids came in here and we had to kill one of them to protect ourselves?"

"Nana Anna didn't know what she was doing," Laurie said.

"If they'd stop with her, that would be one thing," Lou said. "But they won't. They'll want to ask questions."

"Call the cops," Laurie repeated. "Let them ask their questions. Are you afraid of them finding anything out, *Lou?*" She said his name like it was an insult.

"We're not calling the cops," he told her. "We don't have a choice. We have to get rid of the bodies."

As if to underscore exactly what Lou was saying, Kevin let out a small cough and shifted.

My mother was now standing over Tim's body, a limp sheet in her hand.

"Don't just stand there," Lou said. "Wrap him up."

"You do it!" she snapped.

"You want me to get my fingerprints all over that thing?"

"You want me to get mine?" my mother answered.

"Yours aren't in the system."

My mother sighed and spread the sheet over Tim and then began to roll him up. My sister, meanwhile, had fetched some towels and was beginning to mop up the blood. I went in search of some twine I could use to bind Kevin. I grabbed the twine and then rummaged around in a kitchen drawer until I found a folding knife I could use to cut it. I slid the knife into my pocket and headed back to the garage.

It seemed like we were finally doing something together as a family.

❧

We loaded up the El Dorado in the garage. Tim, wrapped in sheets and then in garbage bags, was in the trunk. Kevin, with his hands and feet tied together with kitchen twine, was slumped in the back seat.

Lou turned to me, holding out the keys. "Just take New King's Road until you see swamp. Make sure both sink, and then come straight back."

"I don't know how to drive," I reminded him. "I'm thirteen."

"Are you going to be babied all your life?" he shouted.

Setting aside the issue of whether or not I should bear the blame for not knowing how to drive two years before I was eligible to get my license, I thought I'd point out the more obvious issue. "I don't know that it's a good idea for me to teach myself how to drive while I've got Tim in the trunk."

"Fine." He held the keys toward my mother. "You take him."

"I can't deal with this, Lou. You've got to do it."

"You want *me* to do it?" Lou demanded, as though the absurdity of the suggestion required no explanation. "It's your son's friends who got us into this."

"Just take care of it," she said.

"So you can stay here and get drunk?"

"First I am going to mop the floor," she said. "Then I'll get drunk."

"Great," he said, like they'd been squabbling over whether or not to change the bag in the trash compactor. "Get in the car already!" he said to me.

We drove through the dark. It was going to take at least an hour to get to a part of the swamp deserted enough to dump a body. The weight of that time pressed on me. The time there and the time back, alone with my stepfather, furious at me for reasons that were still not exactly clear.

"Why do you let these kids push you around?" he demanded at last.

"I don't," I told him.

"I didn't see you stand up to them."

I decided not to point out that I was the one who had tackled Kevin. I also decided not to point out that he had cringed when Tim was ordering him around, not me. In fact, there was really nothing much at all to say, so I kept quiet.

"This is your fault," he said after a few more minutes, nodding to himself, talking himself into believing it.

I thought it would be better to put him back on the defensive. "I still don't understand why we couldn't call the police. Nana Anna wouldn't go to jail."

"I have reasons, and they put food in your mouth and clothes on your back while your father is off doing who the hell knows what, so don't give me shit."

In the back, Kevin moaned.

"What are we going to do with him?" I asked.

"He's going into the swamp."

I didn't say anything, but it must have been obvious what I was thinking. It's one thing to dump a body, but it's another thing to actually produce one.

"Look, we're not going to kill him," Lou explained. "We're just going to put him in the swamp. If he dies, that's not our doing."

This was pretty much like saying that all Nana Anna had done was put a knife in Tim's neck. If Tim had died from the wound, that was his choice.

Lou eventually pulled off the main road and started following a dirt road into the dark of the swamp. I watched the thick foliage pass as it brushed our car, making an uneasy hissing noise. Lou seemed to know exactly where he was going, which bothered me. How many bodies had he already dumped, exactly?

Finally he pulled into a clearing. "I'm going to go look for a good spot," he said. "Wait here."

Lou got out of the car holding a flashlight and disappeared into the darkness. I sat there listening to chirping of frogs and crickets and the louder bellowing of what might have been distant gators.

"You're not really going to let him kill me, are you?" Kevin asked.

I turned around. Kevin was awake now in the back seat. He was slumped against the side of the car, but his eyes were open, and he looked scared.

"I'm sorry about what Tim and I did, and he got what he had coming, but you heard me. I didn't even want to be there."

"But you were," I said.

"Come on, man." In the dark I could see the whites of his big eyes. They were wet with tears and maybe frustration. "There has to be a way out of this."

I looked back at him. "My stepfather isn't going to let you walk out of here."

"Then you have to help me stop him. He wants to kill me. That makes him a bad guy, doesn't it?"

"I don't know," I said. "I mean, he's family."

"I'd say he's pretty crappy family," Kevin said.

It was hard to argue with that.

"You have to do it," I said. "I'm not good with stuff like that."

"You tackled me pretty good," he said resentfully.

"If you want to walk out of here alive, you're the one who's going to have to take him down."

Kevin thought about this. "Yeah. Okay. I can do that, but you'll have to get me a weapon."

"I'll find something," I said, "and then it's up to you, because I don't think I can hurt someone in my family, even if he deserves it."

Lou came back a few minutes later. "Is he still out?"

I nodded.

"Okay, let's dump the body, and then you can take care of the fat kid."

So Lou expected me to deal with Kevin. He expected me, a thirteen-year-old boy, three months shy of his Bar Mitzvah, to commit murder so he wouldn't have to. I was suddenly feeling a lot less guilty about the deal I'd cut.

We opened the trunk and before grabbing hold of my half of Tim's body, I found a tire tool and slipped it into the back of my jeans.

Lou looked at me quizzically.

"For Kevin," I said.

"I'm glad to see you're finally taking some initiative."

I grabbed the feet end and he grabbed the head. It was still heavy, and I suspected Lou was, literally, not holding up his end, but it was only about a hundred feet to the edge of the swamp. We stood there while Lou counted to three, like this was all a game, and then we tossed the body into the water. There was a splash, and the sounds of animals scattering and a brief break in the ambient noise. Then the frogs and crickets started up again, and everything was as it had been.

We got back to the car, and Lou held back, like this was my problem, and he wasn't going to do more than watch. I reached in and cut Kevin's ties with my knife ands then dragged him out of the car. Lou was standing back, watching to make sure I didn't mess things up, but distant enough that Kevin couldn't get the drop on him if something went wrong.

I slipped the tire tool into Kevin's hand.

"Distract him," Kevin said, "and I'll get him from behind."

I nodded, and Kevin vanished into the darkness. I wondered if he was just going to leave me there, but we were miles away from anything, and I had to think that helping me with Lou was going to be a better deal than facing snakes and alligators.

I got to the edge of the swamp and found a large rock, which I picked up and dropped a few times, which I hoped would sound like a struggle. Then I tossed the rock in the water.

"It's done!" I shouted. Then I waited about a minute. "Holy crap! Come here, Lou."

"If it's not important, forget it," he called back.

"No, really. I think you'd better see it."

Lou came over to the edge of the swamp, where I was staring into the water. Just as I'd hoped, Kevin crept up behind him and struck him hard in the head with the tire tool. Lou cried out, though weakly, and fell into the water. It wasn't as deep as I would have liked, but I didn't see that it much mattered. I had no plans to stick around.

"Shit," Kevin said. "That was easier than I thought it would be. I never killed anyone before, but it's not so hard."

"Good to know," I said, and I stabbed him in the back of the neck with knife, just like Nana Anna had done.

Kevin stared at me in surprise as he staggered back.

"You're still an asshole, Kevin," I said. It was enough of an explanation for me.

I pulled the knife out of his neck, dipped it in the water, and got back in the car. He was right. It wasn't that hard.

It's true I didn't know how to drive, but I figured every adult moron in Florida could do it, so I ought to be able to figure it out. I'd already done more difficult things that night. And if I didn't know where I was going, that was okay too. I had a car, some cash, and now I had job skills. Things, I decided, were looking up.

The Golem of Jericho

Jonathan Santlofer

I remember it all, everything that occurred during those first few months of Long Island living in the biblically and ironically named town of Jericho, a mid-island development built on the site of a former potato field, flat and devoid of character, still a few years away from malls, multiplexes, and Jews.

I was ten when my parents moved us out of an apartment in the city into a split-level home, the postwar dream (theirs, not mine), maybe a hundred or so houses cheek-to-jowl on streets named for famous admirals—Dewey, Nimetz, Leahy, Halsey—all worthy seafaring men I'm sure, though I had no idea who they were at the time. Our split-level was on Seaman Road, one more thing to be teased about though I had no idea why until much later. I knew so little then.

But I know what happened and what I brought on, something unimaginable and unspeakable, which I am about to tell you, actually admit for the first time, and I hope you will understand that I didn't mean for it to happen.

❧

"Jew boy."

I am in the playground of the Robert Seaman Elementary School, on the first day of third grade, recess on a hot September day, two older fourth-grade boys strutting toward me. The bigger one, though they are both bigger than me—a fleshy kid with straw-colored hair and a pug nose—pokes me in the chest hard enough to knock me back a few steps.

"Jew boy," he says again. "I'm Roy, and this is Johnny."

"Hi Roy," I say.

"Shut up," he says and pushes me again. "Don't use my name."

I struggle to stay on my feet but as I teeter his friend, Johnny, skinny with hair pomaded into a pompadour, slams his hand against my chest and I go down, the two of them laughing and rocking like cartoon meanies. The other kids in the playground look over though no one moves. A few yards away, a teacher in a baggy beige suit loosens his tie and tugs at his collar, glances at us then turns his back.

I try to get up but Roy, the fleshy one, plants his foot on my chest.

"You like Elvis?" he asks.

I try to process this question: *Is liking Elvis good or bad?*

I notice the skinny one, Johnny, has the Elvis-style pompadour and quickly say, "Yes."

"Fairy," the fleshy one says, and the skinny one says, "Elvis don't need no Jews."

"No, he doesn't," I say, quick to collaborate with my Jew-hating enemies. "Why would he?"

They exchange looks, furrowed brows, mouths twisted. Then Roy says, "We're gonna beat you up after school."

I am still on the ground, a dozen kinds of fear ping-ponging in my brain, trying to think what I've done to deserve this.

"Jewww," Roy says, rolling the word around in his mouth like a sour ball.

But how do they know? I am not a particularly Semitic-looking kid with my fair hair and hazel eyes. My nose, which will grow at puberty, is still on the small side and I won't get the black-rimmed Buddy Holly glasses, which make me look more like Lenin or Marx than Buddy Holly, until seventh grade. Someone must have told them. *But who? And why?*

A few of the other kids now mosey over and stare and then the teacher ambles over—no one's in a hurry—and he says, "That's enough," without much heart, and the two boys shrug like they have no idea what he's talking about, but as I get up Roy leans in and hisses, "After school, you're one dead Jew."

The rest of the day I am in terror, my mind filled with images of them beating me to death—the punches, kicks, bones breaking, teeth bashed in, choking on blood, all of it real and vivid.

As an adult, I read that a successful torturer holds off inflicting any actual pain for as long as possible because once the physical pain has started, he's lost his power. But what did I know then?

When I leave school, the bullies are nowhere to be seen. Still, I run home.

❦

My mother asks, "How was your first day?"

"Okay," I say,

"Just okay? And your teacher?"

"Okay," I say.

"So *everything* is okay." My mother puts down the raw meat she is forming into meatloaf, wipes her hands on a dishtowel, and gives me a pointed look. "What's going on?"

"Nothing," I say.

She continues to stare at me then shakes her head and goes back to forming the meatloaf as I slip off to my room where I try to work on a half-finished model airplane, my hands shaky, the smell of glue making my head light.

At dinner, I can't think of anything to say, my mind consumed with fear of my future beating.

"Are you sure you're okay?" my mother asks. "You're not yourself."

I want to say, I am exactly myself, *a Jew boy*, and I am furious at her and my father, who is still at work in the city, for moving us to this Jew-hating town but I don't say anything because I can't quite grasp the reality of the situation, or what it means, or even my own fear-driven anger. I glance over at my sister, who is two years older, eating her peas one by one and wonder if anyone at school has called her a Jew girl. But she's already said she likes her teacher and seems fine, though she is shy and quiet and reveals little, so it's hard to know.

That night I lie in bed with a question buzzing in my brain: *How did they know I was a Jew and why do they hate me for it?* The seeds of my self-loathing anti-Semitism inadvertently sown: if those boys wanted to hurt me for being a Jew there had to be something wrong with me, and with being Jewish.

꙳

The next day at recess I spy the bullies at the edge of the yard, their heads close together, whispering and throwing me hate-filled looks. I stay as close to the teacher as possible, asking him inane questions, to which he mumbles halfhearted answers. If I had to guess now, I'd say he is probably in his midthirties, soft-looking with a quarter-inch crew cut and pale colorless eyes. When another teacher, a pretty blond woman in a sleeveless summer dress, waves him over from the school entrance he bolts, and the bullies waste no time. Suddenly beside me, they grab hold of my arms and walk/drag me into the trees that border the field and playground. We are barely out of sight when the fleshy one, Roy, punches me in the stomach. I crumple to the ground and he says, "More later, after school," and the skinny one with the pompadour, Johnny, snarls, "Yeahhh," and they walk away chuckling and shaking like toy clowns.

The rest of the day my fear is like an electric wire cut loose inside me, flickering in my gut, my head, my chest, the tips of my fingers alternating hot, cold, or numb.

This time, when I leave school, they are waiting for me.

The afternoon is sultry, summer hanging tough with an electric buzz of insects, or maybe it's that wire in my gut. I clutch my books and walk skittishly from the school into the street. Seaman Road is not far, past a small dairy farm, then five suburban blocks, but I am as scared as I have ever been, heart racing, mouth dry and metallic-tasting. I look back, and see them, following me, slow and determined. I move faster but do not run; even at ten I realize that showing my fear will fuel them. At the farm, twenty or thirty black-and-white cows lumber on the other side of a low wire fence, chewing grass and ears of half-rotten corn that litter the ground. The smell of manure is harsh and acrid, intensified by the heat, and one of the cows looks at me, large sad eyes blinking away flies, and then the boys are beside me whacking the books from my hands, tugging, poking, jeering. They knock me down and one sits on my arms, the other on my legs and they start punching me, slapping me, both of them huffing and snorting and cursing, faces red and blurry in close up. I close my eyes and go limp and they punch and pinch me a little more until one of them says, "Shit, is he—dead?" The other one says, "No way, the little coward," and they get up and I hear them dusting themselves off but I lie still. One of them nudges my side with his shoe and says, "Look, his chest, he's breathing," and the other one says, "You can stop playing dead now, Jew," both of them breathing hard, but I lie still and wait. Another shoe nudge, this one closer to a kick then I hear them shuffle away through the tall grass though I remain perfectly still a few more minutes before opening my eyes to a white-hot sky.

Grass and weeds are stuck to my clothes and skin. My khaki pants are dusty with dirt, and when I rub my nose there is blood on my hand and my gut feels that same hollow shame that almost, but not quite, cancels out the pain.

I gather my books and head home. I slip in fast and dart upstairs to the bathroom. I splash cold water on my face. I lift my T-shirt—there are red marks from the punches and pinches, one where the skin has been broken, a trickle of blood down my side. I clean it off with wadded toilet paper and flush away the evidence.

In my room, I change clothes, the whole time my mother is calling from the kitchen, "Is that you? Are you home?"

I yell back, "I have a lot of homework," and hide in my room until dinner, which is the usual trio: mother, sister, me. Though my mother never eats; she waits for my father who is rarely home before eight or nine.

I am usually jokey and funny, the one who keeps everyone in a good mood, but tonight I am sullen, head down, hardly eating.

"What's on your face?" My mother puts her hand on my chin and lifts my head. "Is that a black eye? What on earth—?"

"I don't know."

"You don't *know*?"

"I tripped."

"Where?"

"Near the cows. I stopped to feed them and tripped over a rock."

"Why were you feeding the cows?"

"I like them." I'd never seen cows before, close up, never realized how big they were, and they made me feel happy and sad all at once.

"Stop feeding them. You'll get in trouble."

The cow discussion—to feed or not to feed them—goes on for a while. Then my mother says my nose looks swollen and I say it must be from the fall and ask to be excused and she says, "But I made chocolate pudding, instant, the kind you like, with no skin." I say I'll eat it later, that I have a lot of homework, and my mother, eyes narrowed with suspicion, says, "Really?" But I don't answer. I go to my room where I try to read an Earth Science book but can't concentrate, the words blurring on the page as I picture that sad-eyed cow and myself on the ground.

I examine a bruise on my chest and one on my leg starting to turn purple. I go to the bathroom and see that my mother is right: I have the beginning of a black eye and my nose is slightly swollen.

I want to tell her the truth but I don't dare. I know her. She will race up to the school. She will threaten the principal. She will ask to see these boys who are persecuting her son. She will confront their parents. And then the boys will surely kill me.

It's close to my bedtime when my father, who has been working all day in Manhattan's garment center dealing with *shysters* and *liars* and *ganefs*, gets home. He sits heavily on the edge of my bed. His jaw clenches and unclenches. His five o'clock shadow is blue-black at nine thirty.

"Your mother thinks you've been fighting."

I shake my head without making eye contact.

"You know," he says, "it's okay to fight if someone picks on you."

He *knows*! But how?

"*Did* someone pick on you?"

I shrug.

"If you stand up to them, you'll be okay. Don't let anyone bully you. Punch back! Punch first! That'll end it." He shakes a fist.

I want to say, *But there are two of them and they're both in fourth grade and bigger than me*, but I don't because I want my father—a tough guy from Queens, the kind of guy no one would ever bully—to be proud of me, and who would be proud of a coward?

My father pushes himself up wearily from the bed. "Remember," he says, "throw the first punch! That'll stop them."

I don't tell him it's too late for that.

I read a Superman comic under my blanket with a flashlight and wish I had superpowers and can't stop thinking about more beatings and my inability to throw the first punch.

❧

The next day they are there, at recess. But one push, one shove, and they've had enough, more interested in getting back to a game of volleyball that I have not been invited to play. I think they are bored with me and that perhaps I am safe.

But they are there after school and chase me for two blocks, yelling and laughing though they give up when I outrun them. At least I am fast. I consider this a success until it sinks in: only cowards run away.

For a few days the bullies ignore me and I think it will be okay but near the end of the week they are waiting for me outside of school, and they follow me. This time I'm smarter, I start talking to a girl in my class, and we walk together in the direction of her home, the opposite of mine and she says, "Isn't your house the other way?" and I say, "Yeah, but I feel like walking 'cause it's a nice day," and she looks at me like I'm crazy because it's raining. I walk her all the way to her house sneaking peeks over my shoulder—they're still there, hanging back but following—and when she's gone I cut between two houses and dart across a backyard, then another sprint toward the narrow lane that separates two rows of houses, a shortcut to Seaman Road, and I'm pretty sure I can outrun them. I am flying over freshly mowed lawns and manicured bushes, a mix of terrified but newly confident, my breath coming fast but steady when I see the construction fence twenty feet in front of me, eight feet high, tall wooden slats side by side, nothing to grab onto, no way to scale it and no way out. I think I must have gone the wrong way. There was no fence here yesterday. Or am I dreaming? Either way I am trapped in a thirty-by-forty-foot backyard.

Are the people home? Can they see what's going on? Will they hear me if I call out? All of this going through my mind as the boys tackle me, worked up from the run, sweating and panting and punching, when I hear someone yell, "You boys—cut it out!" and a woman has come out of the house, moving toward us, shaking a finger, and the boys take off.

"Are you okay?" she asks.

She looks about the same age as my mother, in a billowy maternity top and shorts.

I tell her I'm fine.

"You don't look it."

"I am, really."

"Boys," she says, and pats her belly. "I hope I have a girl!" She laughs. Then serious, "Do you live around here?"

I point to the newly erected fence. "Right on the other side, on Seaman Road."

"Oh. Wait a minute. I met your mother the other day. Edith, right? We exchanged numbers, we're backyard neighbors after all. I'm Beverly O'Connor. Bev. Come on," she says. "I'm taking you home."

"It's okay," I say, backing away.

"But your nose is bleeding."

I touch it and my fingers come away red. "It does that," I say. "It's okay."

She plucks a tissue from her pocket and hands it to me then plants a hand on her swollen belly. "Why don't I drive you home? With that fence they've just put up—squeezing a new house in here somehow—you'll have to walk all the way around."

I insist I'm fine and thank her and wipe my nose and start walking before she can insist.

"Say hi to your mom for me," she says as I head down the narrow path between her house and the next, praying the boys are not waiting for me. But there's only a man mowing a lawn and a kid on a bicycle.

My mother is standing outside the front door as I reach my house.

"My God. Beverly O'Connor just called. You were fighting in her backyard? Are you okay?" She is kneeling down beside me, patting me, looking me over, her face pinched with worry.

"I'm fine," I say.

"*Fine?* Young man," she says, "you will tell me what's going on right now." She stands, hands on hips, waiting.

I tell her about the fighting and being picked on but not the "Jew boy" part.

"But *why?*" she asks. "Why would they do that?"

"Because I'm the . . . new boy."

"I'm going up to that school right now! I'll put an end to this!"

I tell her that will only make things worse.

"You want to wait till they break your arm or give you a concussion?" She exhales a sigh. "How about I pick you up from school at the end of the day."

This, I am certain will solidify my status as a coward. I tell her no, that I can handle it.

"Obviously not," she says.

"If you try to pick me up," I say, "I won't get in the car."

That night, the family piles into the car and heads for the Bronx, dinner with my grandparents, Sam and Minnie Brill, in their sprawling tenement apartment, a weekly event I always look forward to. The Brill family is large, my mother the only girl with five married brothers each with two kids. (I was a ringleader among them, and something of a bully, to hear my cousins tell it today.)

Minnie was old world, her English mixed with Yiddish, but my grandfather was a modern man with an omnipresent smile, who adored his kids and his grandkids and we all adored him. He was the father I dreamed of, kind, sweet, funny, a natural storyteller. We would gather at his feet for made up tales of horror and dismemberment that filled us with awe and terror and hilarity. Though on this particular night I am glum, and he pulls me aside after his story.

"What's the matter?" he asks, "and do not tell me nothing, because it is on your face written, not to mention the black eye I see. I am not blind yet!"

I tell him about the fighting and the name-calling. I tell him everything and he listens, rolling a nonfilter cigarette between his thumb and forefinger, taking long puffs as I talk. I show him the bruises on my body and he gently touches them with the tips of his tobacco-stained fingers. His eyes shine but no tears fall.

When I finish he hugs me to him, his stubble against my cheek, enveloped in a cloud of Old Spice and cigarettes. "You are a great kid," he says, "with a great mind, and a great artist one day you will be." Then he adds, "And we will take of it."

I have no idea what he means but there is a look of determination on his face that stops me from asking *How?*

Later that night it is decided that I will sleep over, something I do on occasion and love, on the floor beside my grandparents' bed on a thin mattress with lots of blankets.

In the middle of the night, my grandfather awakens me with a soft touch and leads me to the kitchen at the far end of the apartment, the whole time a finger to his lips to indicate I should not speak.

In the cramped kitchen, redolent with the smells of last night's chicken, he makes us each a cup of coffee—his black, mine a quarter coffee and three-quarters hot milk with sugar. The room is dark, a neon sign blinking outside the one narrow window casting the room in flashes of garish orange.

We sit at the table and drink our coffee, then my grandfather lights a cigarette and sits back in his chair.

"There is something," he says, "from where I came, some*one* for help to call on."

"Who?" I ask, watching him, orange neon winking in his eyes.

"The *Golem*," he says, the word whispered.

"What's that?"

He gets two small books from a drawer, sets them on the table, then finds a yarmulke and places it on his head. He was never ostentatiously religious but said a prayer at dinner and my grandmother lit candles on Friday night and he always said he was looking forward to my Bar Mitzvah, something he would not live to see.

He opens the first book and recites something in Hebrew, which I do not understand. Then he turns to the other book. "This is the *Sefer Yetzirah*, the Book of Creation. In here, of the Golem it tells and . . ." He stops to take a deep breath, ". . . how to make him."

He snatches a potted plant from the window ledge, tugs the plant out by its roots, then pushes our coffee cups aside to make room and dumps the dirt on the plastic checkerboard tablecloth. He fills a glass with warm water and adds some of it to the dirt, then finds a sack of flour and sprinkles some in. "Because I have no clay," he says, gathering the mass together in his hands. "You must help," he says, "you, the artist of the family. Together, we will make this."

"What are we making?" I ask.

"A man. A strong man."

And we do. With the donation of another plant's dirt, more water and flour we soon have a large mass of dirt from which we begin to form a crude body.

"The head," he says, "it needs to be big."

I have never seen him like this, so lost in concentration, so determined, face drawn, lips clamped down hard on the cigarette, which drops ashes into the mud and flour.

I add more of it to the head, dip my fingers into the water to smooth one area, then another. I have, for several summers, been the star Arts & Crafts camper and it is paying off.

"How should he look?" I ask.

My grandfather thinks a moment, searching for the right word and finds it: "Fierce."

I have no idea why, but it doesn't matter. We are in this together, whatever it is, and I am working by instinct.

"I need a knife."

My grandfather hands me a butter knife. "Careful," he says. "I don't want you should cut yourself."

I use the knife to shape the arms then begin to carve crude hands.

"Make them big," he says, "and strong."

While I carve them, my grandfather finds a bag of white rice in a cabinet.

"For eyes," he says.

I pluck two kernels from his palm and squish them into the mud-man's face.

"Give him a mouth," he says.

I carve into the mud like I would a pumpkin's skin, creating a wide rectangular mouth then I use the other end of the knife to make shallow lines for teeth.

"Such talent you have," my grandfather says, nodding and smiling. In the blinking orange light his grin appears demonic.

I carve and smooth, carve and smooth.

"Good," he says, "good," again and again, encouraging me.

When I have completed the hands and mouth and smoothed the mud he says, "Good," in a way that means *stop*. Then he hands me a toothpick. "Here," he says, "I want you should write something on the head. Three short letters that together form a word."

My grandfather says something in Hebrew and I stare at him.

"What?" he asks. "You don't understand?"

I shake my head no. And he shakes his.

"What are they teaching you in that Hebrew school?"

I tell him there is no Hebrew school in Jericho and he lets out a long sigh. "Okay," he says, "I will spell it out. In English. First word, A-L-E-P-H."

I carve each letter carefully.

"What does it mean?" I ask.

"*Aleph* is the first Hebrew letter, to begin, to create. Now write *mem*, M-E-M. Now . . ." He takes a deep breath, the orange light flickering over his face. "*Tav*. T-A-V."

I ask the meaning again.

"Tav is the last letter of the alphabet, also it is a sign, a cross, perfection it is."

I have no idea what he's talking about but I add bits of mud to the letters then smooth around the edges with the butter knife to make them stand out.

"Perfect," he says, and we both sit back and stare at what we have made.

It is reminiscent of pictures I've seen in *National Geographic* of statues made in faraway primitive cultures, places I've never heard of, but different too. For a while my grandfather says nothing and neither do I. We sit together in silence looking at what we have created.

Finally, he says, "Wash your hands."

And we do, in the sink, then dry them with a kitchen towel that smells of food and grease.

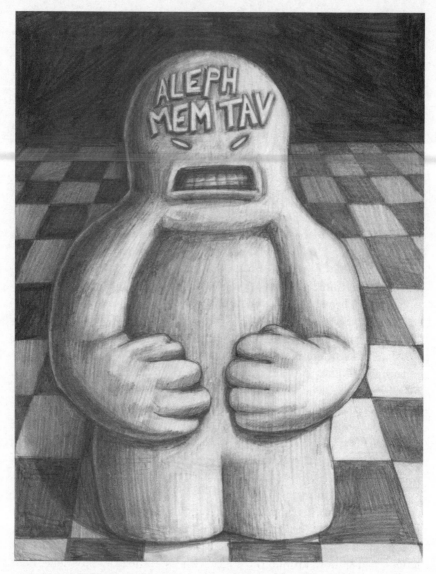

My grandfather takes hold of my hand and gently tugs me up from the table, which he slides from the wall then leads me in a circle around it as he recites something in Hebrew, a prayer or incantation.

I ask what it means but he shushes me and we continue to circle the Golem and he keeps up his soft chanting. Then he stops.

I stare at the mud-man. Nothing about him has changed. But what did I expect, for him to grow huge and come to life? Yes, a part of me did.

"It didn't work," I say, trying not to sound as disappointed as I feel.

"Shh," he says. "Do not say such a thing."

He recites his incantation once more then wraps the Golem in wax paper and carries him down the hall into the bathroom where he hides him under the sink behind a clutter of bottles and boxes, Vitalis, Phillips Milk of Magnesia, Barbasol Shave Cream, Miss Clairol.

Back in the kitchen he takes the tugged-out plants and puts them back into their pots. He shakes half the dirt from two other potted plants into the empty ones and adds water. "No need to tell your grandmother," he says. "Tomorrow I will get more dirt from the street. Like new they'll be."

Then we quietly traipse back down the hall.

My grandmother, a short, stout woman, is on her side, snoring, and my grandfather slides in beside her while I get into my makeshift bed on the floor.

He leans over and pats my head and I curl under my blanket feeling safe but sad because the Golem had not come to life.

☙

I spend the next day glued to my grandfather's side, happy to help out at his laundry shop, taking in wash and talking to customers.

"My grandson," he says to everyone who comes in. "A genius like you shouldn't know from, and like an angel he draws."

I am embarrassed but proud.

The next night I check under the bathroom sink and the Golem is still there, lumpy and inert under the wax paper.

A waste of time, I think.

☙

A day later I am back at school. At recess, I look for the bullies but they're not there and I'm relieved. I play on the monkey bars with a couple of classmates who dare to talk to me since the bullies aren't around.

☙

It isn't until the next day that the news breaks and the police are at the school and we are all sent home, parents at the school entrance in idling cars or standing with worried looks on their faces.

"What's going on?" I ask my mother. The police and teachers have said nothing.

"I'm not sure," is all she says.

"Is it the Mad Bomber?" He'd been all over the news with his bombs in movie theaters and libraries and Penn Station and Radio City Music Hall.

"No, the bomber's been caught," she says "Thank God. No need to worry about him anymore."

☙

The next day there is a school assembly. The principal, a dignified white-haired man tells us in a halting voice that there's been an "accident," that two boys have been "hurt." He adds, "But you are all safe—there's nothing to worry about."

I am still baffled.

⁂

Nobody really knew what had happened to those boys. The first reports said it had to be wild dogs, a whole pack of them from the shape of the bodies. But no wild dogs were ever found in the area. Then, for a while, it was suspected that it was a pair of sadistic pedophiles but the autopsies showed no sexual assault. This was not in the newspapers but a classmate's father was a doctor at Syosset Hospital where the boys' bodies and body *parts* were taken and his son overheard him discussing it on the phone and he told everyone at school and it was all anyone talked about, the tearing off of limbs, one boy supposedly decapitated, not with a knife but with brute force—someone or some*thing* had actually torn his head off!

⁂

The next Thursday night my family makes the usual pilgrimage to the Bronx.

After dinner I manage to get my grandfather away from the crowd.

"What's the matter?" he asks, reading me as he always does.

"It happened," I say.

"What happened?"

"They're dead."

My grandfather sucks in a breath. He seems to understand me without further explanation.

Later, he somehow convinces my parents to let me stay over. My father protests about missing school but my grandfather, always persuasive, wins.

⁂

That night we sit in the kitchen waiting for my grandmother to finish the dishes. When she does she tells us not to stay up late but we ignore her.

My grandfather wants the details and I tell him what I know.

After a long pause he says, "They had it coming." Then mutters something in Hebrew, then still muttering, practically a whisper, he says, "God forgive me," and quickly adds, "About this, you had nothing to do."

I see the lie on his face. I want to say, *Grandpa, we did it—the Golem did it—we are murderers!* But I don't say a word because it is too late.

We creep down the hall to the bathroom.

The Golem is still there under the bathroom sink behind the Phillips

Milk of Magnesia and Miss Clairol. My grandfather carries him into the kitchen where he unwraps the wax paper and places him on the kitchen table.

It isn't possible, I think, looking at the crude mud-man we'd made with our hands. One of the rice eyes has fallen out, giving him the look of a mushy Cyclops.

"He couldn't have done it," I say.

My grandfather lets out a deep sigh. "The Talmud says that two rabbis, Rav Hanina and Rav Oshaya, used the *Sefer Yetzirah* to make a calf, and long ago the famous Rabbi of Prague, he too made a creature, a Golem, to protect the Jews, so persecuted in his country." He lays a hand on my shoulder. "*Mayn kind*," he says, the Yiddish words for *my child*. I have heard the phrase often. "There is magic here."

"And you believe it, grandpa?"

He sighs again, heavier this time. "I have in my life seen many things— things I never thought I would believe." Then he slides the table away from the wall the way he did before. "We used God's name to bring him to life. Now we will use it to undo life."

He takes my hand but this time we walk backward as he chants.

"He looks the same," I say after we've circled the mud-man twice.

"Again," my grandfather says and we do our backward stroll one more time as he recites the Hebrew words.

I stare at the Golem for any signs of change, but see none and say so.

My grandfather consults the *Sefer Yetzirah*, flipping pages, stopping here and there to read something, his thin face rapt in concentration. Finally, he reaches out and with his finger smudges the carved word *aleph* off the Golem's forehead until it is gone, the dirt smooth. There are two words left, *mem* and *tav*.

"Does that mean anything, Grandpa?"

He nods. "Now it means . . . death."

I am not only startled by what he says but the way he says it, his usual smiling face taut and severe.

"What do we do with him?" I ask.

"Maybe, for now, we keep him," he says and rewraps the wax paper then marches the Golem back to his hiding place under the sink. It is clear that my grandfather is afraid to destroy this thing we have made from dirt, flour and water. And I am too.

After that, I saw my grandfather differently. He was still, and always, the kindest of men. But I knew something else about him now; I knew that he had power.

Back at school, the talk has not died down. There have been no arrests, not even a suspect so far as anyone knows. There is another assembly as many kids are shaken by the murders. At night, my parents talk about it in whispers.

ℜ

At some point there was a story about Roy and Johnny in the local newspaper with their pictures, Roy looking fleshy, his mouth half open, Johnny with an Elvis sneer on his lips.

My mother catches me reading it.

"Terrible," she says, shaking her head.

I mumble, "Uh-huh."

"Did you know them?" she asks.

I picture the Golem figure crammed under the bathroom sink, a mud-man stripped of his power.

Would things have been different if I hadn't told my grandfather about the incidents with the boys? But I had to tell him; no one else would have understood. I learned then what I know now, that there is a price to pay for telling your secrets.

My mother is waiting for an answer. "No," I say, "I didn't know them at all."

Your Judaism

Tasha Kaminsky

In the interest of being honest, I didn't kneel down first. I sort of just tapped him with my foot. I didn't kick him. It was a nudge, and when I think back on the moment I vaguely recall saying something along the lines of: "Man, you can't sleep here. Have you considered checking out our library?" That's not a direct quote, that's just how the story has come to be framed after telling it to a series of different St. Louis police officials. I didn't feel good about nudging a dead man, who wasn't really a man. Human and male yes, but man has a certain connotation of life experience and the like, and I've had enough time to learn about the guy and he just wasn't a man. He was a guy at best, and a kid at worst. I'm sorry that he's dead.

When you tell a story enough times you embrace a pattern. Doesn't matter if the story is about discovering the corpse of a twenty-two-year-old in a synagogue lobby. Any narrative can become mechanical. So here is the story as it stands to this day:

I got to work at 7:56. I know it was 7:56 because I was annoyed with myself that I was at work at 7:56 when I didn't actually need to be there until 8:30. I don't believe in Jewish Standard Time. That's complete bullshit and part of an agenda to advance the interests of inconsiderate assholes who can't keep time. Not to mention I resent the stereotype implied. Jews are no better or worse at keeping time than any other ethnic group. Don't laugh nervously and say *Oh, well, you know, Jewish Standard Time and all*, as you walk into the staff meeting fifteen minutes late. That's not a thing.

I was definitely in the building before 8:00 because it doesn't take more than a minute to walk from the parking lot to the building. I was also the first one in the building as far as I could tell. I have my own key code to get into the building. The security system isn't what it should be, but it's there. You either have a code or you need to be buzzed in. You can, in theory, be followed in because the lock is triggered by motion from the inside. That means once you're inside, if you approach the locked door it automatically opens so you can exit uninhibited. That also means that if you've just entered, if someone is close behind you and you stop to take off your coat or wipe your shoes on the mat, they can just walk right in too.

I went directly to the front office, which naturally is in the back of the building. Because I was the first one in, I unlocked the front office door, and that was when I saw the deceased. I approached him while announcing myself, and then yes, I nudged him with my foot. Once I nudged him, I realized that he was not sleeping and he was unresponsive and that is when I called 911. I only touched the body when prompted by the dispatcher and when I did I observed it was cold.

So that was a fun first day on the job.

My first day had been delayed due to a series of setbacks. I don't want to call it bad luck but upon further introspection I'm opening myself to the idea that maybe the universe isn't indifferent and it's actively against me. I spent the summer staffing a trip for Jewish teens to tour Israel. Not Birthright, but not propaganda-free either. We made the regular kibbutz rounds and heard the speakers talk about the wars. Nationalism at its finest, but harmless. For the most part we saw the sights. I saw the kids to the airport and spent an extra two weeks in the Holy Land touring on my own. Just enough time for a military incursion to break out. At regular intervals throughout the day, a siren would go off and people would shout, and then silence. When a rocket explodes miles away, you can feel it in your chest.

I still feel that hollow sensation in my chest when I'm lying down, ready to sleep. And after the first day of work I started to see that guy, that boy.

His name was Jonathan Silverman. He looked nothing like the picture on his Missouri driver's license. He had an angular face that was offset by a smattering of light freckles and prominent eyebrows. His clothes were too big for him, and the beginnings of a gingery shadow had started to fill in on his gray face. I found him on Facebook. We had nine friends in common and a mutual respect for the art of Tupac Shakur. He was one of those people who kept his entire page open for the world and prospective employers and college admissions officers to see. I could trace the timeline of his online life back to his high school years and even caught glimpses of his childhood. Occasional images of a full-faced toddler with brown eyes like glass buttons sitting in the lap of a slightly older girl swirled between posts critiquing different rap releases. Rebecca Silverman seemed to delight in sharing pictures of her baby brother from the time he was a baby but as far as I could see there were no pictures of them together as adults.

Jonathan was born in St. Louis, Missouri, in 1990. He went to Clayton High School. He went to NYU. He dropped out. He moved back to St. Louis in 2012. He died on August 28, 2014. More than half of his Facebook friends were black hats, deeply Jewish with beards and conspicuous names like Chayim and Mordechai. They called him Yoni, and they were primarily the only people who commented on his statuses or wrote on his wall. Messages ranged from Shabbat dinner invitations, to holiday greetings, to concerns and support. "Too violent for my tastes. You should come around for *chavurah*, Yoni." That was the message Yitzhak Spielberg left on April 7, 2014, on a posting of a Hoodie Allen rap video. Come study with us, he said to a college dropout whose cover photo proclaimed: "Fuck bitches, get money." Yoni didn't buy into the Tupac-Biggie rivalry.

His family buried him by his grandmother the next day. The eulogies focused on what Jonathan was like when he was younger. "When he was a child," most of them began. I caught allusions to a more recent time between the lines and toward the end. "Jonathan struggled with depression," his father said. "He was fighting demons." I focused on the girl I recognized as Rebecca Silverman. She didn't speak at the funeral. Her brow was deeply furrowed and her cheeks were blotchy and red. She gritted her teeth. "It's a shame," a white-haired woman said under her breath to the man next to her. "A smart boy like that. It's a shame they didn't get him help."

Shivah was crowded with a balanced mix of young and old. I slipped in, silently taken for a friend of Jonathan's though I didn't mingle with the rest. Instead I found the bathroom. The sink had a stick of Adidas deodorant, a bottle of Old Spice spray, and some sort of styling wax. This was his bathroom. I peered down the hall and crossed over into an open bedroom. An overweight black cat was sprawled on the blue plaid comforter. I offered it my hand to smell. It promptly batted it away. "All right then," I said.

The room was surprisingly clean. Someone had evidently made it presentable, stashing away what I imagined must have been heaps of dirty laundry, sheets of music, and maybe one or two posters of bikini models. All that remained was an incensed cat and a shelf of books. Jonathan had a collection of Tanakh and Talmud, printings that I remembered receiving at my own Bat Mitzvah, and unfamiliar copies too. He had something like the Jewish version of Gideon's Bible. A printed and bound handout from an organization called Aish. One of those jams where Orthodox

Jews found nonpracticing Jews to return to the fold. The same idea as Chabad but without the worshipping of a dead man. In college, I attended a Shabbat service and dinner at Chabad. I was nineteen and poured a liberal glass of wine and then was offered schnapps at the meal. It was a solid racket. Free drinks and all I had to do was go along with the segregated seating plan and the no-women-reading-Torah policy. I didn't really care about alcohol all that much, though I knew I was in the minority.

"I think the cleaning lady literally shoved everything in the closet."

I dropped the Aish Bible and a business card fell out.

"Didn't mean to sneak up on you."

I pocketed the business card and replaced the Bible on the shelf. "No, I'm sorry. I shouldn't have been in here, probably," I said as I looked up and saw Rebecca closer than before. She seemed about my age.

"I don't mind. Were you a friend of Jon's?"

"Not exactly. Sort of like a friend of a friend. I'm really sorry for your loss. Ah, and you don't have to say anything to that. I know it's weird when someone is like, I'm sorry for your loss, and you're all, what do I say next? Because it's not like I caused it and it's not like anyone really caused it or—It's weird. But I'm sorry for your pain. "

"Thanks."

"Uhm, I'll get out of his room. That was rude. I shouldn't have—I just saw it was open and I was curious. I wanted to see what he was like so I could remember him the right way."

"He was murdered. So technically someone caused it."

"I know."

"You know?"

"No, I mean, uhm. Okay, I guess I know. No, I know. I, uh, boy. Okay, I was the person who found him, in the synagogue. That was me. I'm—I really don't know him at all, like even a little. I'm not even from St. Louis."

"That was you?"

"Ahhhh. Yeah, I feel gross now, for being here. I just felt bad and I didn't know what to do so I thought I'd just. I don't know what I'm saying."

"That's why you keep making those faces."

"What? No. I'm not making a face."

"No. You're making a face."

"It's not a bad face."

"No. It's like a judgmental face," Rebecca said.

"I'm not judging anyone. I just, I feel bad that I couldn't help him."

"He was using. The police think it was just a drug thing. One of his shitty friends or a dealer."

"I didn't know that." All right, I had figured that out but I think I sold my ignorance well.

"Sorry I snapped. You are making a face but I don't think you're being judgmental."

"I make a lot of faces I don't mean," I said.

"I'm Rebecca."

"Miriam."

⁂

I wouldn't have thought much of the business card if it weren't for the barely decipherable scrawl on the back. "If you need anything, just call." The business card was for a synagogue community organizer, Rabbi Ornetzkey. Not the synagogue I found Jonathan in either. There's a stretch of road in St. Louis that has something like ten synagogues on it. This particular synagogue was near the east end of the stretch.

So I decided to go for a Shabbat service. The building was infused with multipurpose add-ins, each wall on hinges, able to collapse or expand. Each flight of stairs accompanied by a ramp. It was a clever use of space and a clean, bright presentation. The skylights were above, and a pristine tile floor was below. I liked this synagogue, the newness of it, the perceived efficiency of its design.

Flashes of color peeked through uniformly black outfits. Pins with green and red stones, or a practical pair of purple flats. I had donned an ill-advised jewel-toned blue dress, more focused on the sleeve length (past my elbows) and the skirt length (past my knees), and now people were repelled from me by three feet in any direction. What did Tupac enthusiast Jonathan find here?

"I love your dress."

A middle-aged woman, who wore no makeup but had a soft and even face, had broached the three-foot buffer. "Thank you!"

"Is it your first time at Or Chadash? You'll have to forgive me if it isn't. I just didn't recognize you."

"No, it is. I just moved here and a friend recommended I try services here."

"That's so nice to hear. I'm Miriam," she said.

"I'm Miriam too. What a world. It was either that or Sarah, Rebecca, Rachel, or Leah, am I right?"

The woman smiled but didn't respond and I pursed my lips together.

"Come sit," she invited me after a healthy awkward pause. I liked this other Miriam. She had an authenticity about her without any pretense. I had pictured myself sitting alone through this service and then standing off to the side while I drank my lemonade and nibbled on cookies, but that wasn't what was happening.

The sanctuary was divided into two uneven sections. Down the middle of the room was a *mekhitzah*, a raised wooden wall on wheels. The light oak had images of menorahs and lions carved into it, and at the very top was a frosted glass trim. I sat beside the other Miriam in the noticeably smaller section. Women on one side and men on the other. The service began although that went unacknowledged on the women's side. A low chatter continued as the chairs filled and then overflow began to stand. Each person had at least one other to speak with and embrace. I felt like I did at my family reunion nearly ten years back. I wasn't sure who these people were but they all seemed to be excited to see one another. I wasn't sure where I fit in with all of them, but I wanted to feel more a part of them. Whatever was happening on the other side of the wall didn't interest me. There was enough material here to keep me meditating on how great human beings could be in all their different layers and labels. Other Miriam waved to those who approached her, but kept her prayer book open and her lips moving. As warm and buzzing as the space was, I felt bad for her. She deserved silence and breathing room.

⊱

"This is Miriam," Other Miriam introduced me to a circle of indistinguishable women. All pleasant to look at, all dressed identically. Their wigs were more appealing than any natural hair I had seen, all shiny, smooth, and auburn.

"Oh, another Miriam!" They laughed, and I laughed. My parents had given me the ultimate in. A severely Jewish name can open just as many doors as it can close.

"So Miriam, do you have a husband? Children?"

"I like—I do not, hm!"

"You're so cute and thin though. We have boys we can introduce you to."

"Oh, thanks. That's really kind of you."

I like women. Well, yes, I like women. I also prefer women. In friendship and in bed. I didn't really feel an obligation to explain this to anyone at Or Chadash though.

"How did you hear about us?"

"Miriam has a friend who sent her here," said Other Miriam.

"Who's your friend?"

"Jonathan Silverman."

If the circle of conversation had been a cymbal, then the drummer had just placed a hand on top of it. Other Miriam put an arm around me and patted my back. "Poor Yoni," she said. "How did you know him?"

I was in the right place. There was Jonathan and there was Yoni. Jonathan the addict. And poor Yoni of Or Chadash.

"We met in New York while he was in school. Before, you know, everything happened."

"Such a sweet boy. My Yitzhak just adored him." A woman across from me spoke up.

"It's silly but I miss him, I haven't seen him in years," I said. "I'd love to talk about him with someone who knew him."

"Come, I'll introduce you."

❦

That was how I ended up having dinner at the Spielbergs' home.

❦

Yitzhak was rigid in his stature, and wore a well-tailored black suit. The uniformity in clothing was normal and I only felt acutely aware of it because I was clad in an unsuitable blue. I should not have gone to this dinner, but I had it in my mind that if I befriended this Yitzhak he would open up to me about the guy he had known as Yoni. Which came first? Jonathan or Yoni? That was what I most wanted to know. How did a Yoni end up using? Or was Jonathan using and found Yoni only to revert back to Jonathan?

While I ate bland chicken soup it occurred to me that there was no reason that anyone at this table would be above using drugs. Orthodox Jews used drugs. All people used drugs. Just because Jonathan was Yoni for a time didn't mean he stopped using drugs or didn't start while he was Yoni. This was my own prejudice that I was going to have to overcome. The same way I was shocked as a child to learn that Jewish people also committed wretched crimes and went to prison for them, I had to keep in mind that I had not just sat down to dinner with people above reproach because they were more literal about interpreting what the Talmud had to say about keeping the Sabbath holy.

"Miriam was a friend of Yoni's back in New York, may his memory be a blessing," Mrs. Spielberg said. "I thought you might be happy to meet a friend of his, Yitz."

Yitzhak looked at the food on his plate and spoke quietly. "May his memory be a blessing. He was a good man, a good Jew. I know he struggled, but who doesn't struggle? I wish he had shared more of his struggle with us. Maybe he would still be here. Only *Hashem* knows."

Well, this probably wasn't going to get me anywhere.

"Are you all right, Miriam? You're . . . you look unwell," Mrs. Spielberg said with genuine concern as she gazed at me.

"Oh no, I'm fine. I make a lot of faces I don't mean. I'm not sure why I do it."

"A guilty conscience perhaps," Yitzhak suggested.

I made a face that I did mean.

"Stop that. How can you be so rude? We're welcoming a guest. He's still upset about his friend, forgive him."

"We grieve in different ways." I said.

"How did you know Yoni?" Yitzhak asked.

"We met in New York."

"Yes, but how?"

"In person?"

"I think Miriam is being coy," he said.

I thought the implication was a romantic one so I immediately felt compelled to dispel it.

"I didn't understand the question. We met at a Shabbes dinner in Brooklyn, one of those meet-up groups that they do. We got to talking about St. Louis."

"Makes sense," he said as if it were the opposite.

"How did you know Yoni?" I asked.

"Or Chadash. We studied together. He was *baal teshuvah*. Returned to Judaism. I was helping him with that. Rabbi Ornetzsky set us up in a *chavruta*, told me to keep an eye on him, but it was a good match. Yoni was an old soul. A good man, a good Jew."

Everyone kept using this term "man" for Yoni and I couldn't see it. He struck me as a kid trying to find a place.

"He had good taste in music," I added.

"He had unhealthy pastimes that brought out anger," Yitzhak countered.

"I thought he was happy when I met him."

"And I thought he was ready to lead a healthy life when I met him. Maybe we were both wrong."

Given that I had never met Jonathan Silverman, at least not while he was living, I decided to quit while I was ahead or at least stop trying to argue that he had been a happy person at any time. How happy could he have been if he was an addict?

Some Jews saved all their guilt up for Yom Kippur and starved it out of their bodies. I preferred an uncomfortable Friday night dinner approximately once a month to keep me humble and grateful. By ten thirty I had dropped every conceivable hint that I needed to be anywhere but there, and by a quarter to eleven, Yitzhak took pity on me and said, "Miriam wants to leave, Ma." Which was more like passive aggressiveness than pity, but whatever.

"You're making a face," he added.

"Am I?" I asked. I was. It was directed at him.

I still had to walk back to the synagogue and then another two blocks where I had parked my car. Far enough away that no one would know that I had driven on Shabbat.

In the entry hallway, next to the decorative menorah, Yitzhak paused. "I'd like to see you again."

"Uhm . . . okay?"

"You're not Orthodox are you?"

"Not particularly," I admitted.

"Were you into all that with Yoni?"

"Not even a little." Also true.

He handed me a business card. His cell phone number already scrawled on the back. He was prepared. "*Shabbat Shalom,*" he said, closing the door behind me.

I flipped the card over. He was a lawyer. Of course.

❦

Rebecca looked a lot like her brother. The same small brown eyes. The same freckles. The same chin. She had a stoniness to her that I never picked up on in pictures of Jonathan. Word associations led me to adjectives like seething, bottled, and pissed. Her hair was swept back into a bun, and she seemed to have made little effort to appear anything but plain, and I supported that.

"You know how it's easier to open up to someone you don't know? Like you can just say things to a stranger that you can't say to your mother?"

"Sure," I said. "There's an anonymity there. I get it."

"I don't want to cry on your shoulder or anything."

"I didn't think you did."

"But they're saying they caught the guy. Some dude named Cheese."

"Wait. Cheese?"

"It's like some stupid nickname. One of Jon's lame friends."

"Yeah, that is a stupid nickname," I said. What else could I say? Sorry your brother chose the company of an addict named Cheese? That sucks.

A lull crept over us and I peered into my iced tea. The indentations of the chair were pressing into the backs of my exposed thighs and the early September heat was a wet one.

"Was he really strangled?" she asked me quickly and casually, her tone high-pitched but steady.

"I'm not sure. Maybe."

"I don't understand how that happens."

"Theodicy or . . . ?"

"No, literally. Think about it. How does some skinny junkie named Cheese overpower a twenty-four-year-old man and strangle him to death?"

I didn't want to tell her that I was pretty sure that sort of thing happened often enough. It was too hot outside for me to feel comfortable patting her hand. I stayed quiet. I let the silence linger. This was about stages of grief. She was in anger. I could respect that. Nothing made sense and she wasn't going to let it go, but I felt weird enough. I didn't want to try and talk her into believing that her brother made perfect statistical sense.

"He had one of those addictive personalities," she said after a lengthy pause.

"One of those?" I asked.

"Like he could never do something halfway, and he could find the most asinine thing to be the be-all and end-all of life. It was always a phase with him. He had the German phase where he was going to learn German and move to Germany and that was all he would ever fucking talk about. Then he had his New York phase where he was going to be a musician. Then the crack phase. Then he had this Aish cult phase where it was all about purity and God and repenting. And then when that didn't pan out for him it was the crack phase again."

I looked up at the mentioning of his Aish cult. "You mean Or Chadash?"

"That place is messed up and it messed him up too. I'm not saying he was great to start but they knew about his problems and they preyed on that."

I blinked. I hadn't felt preyed on, but I had felt that there was something significant happening there. A completely unfounded feeling, but one that I had just the same.

"It seemed kind of standard to me. They were all about that welcoming the stranger. I get the appeal. I'm not into the women on the right, men on the left deal, but to each her own."

"It's not standard. They told Jon some really messed up and crazy shit," she said through her teeth.

"All right, like what kind of crazy shit?"

Rebecca leaned in, dragging the iron patio chair across the concrete. Not for polite company to hear. I leaned in as well and met her gaze as best I could from behind sunglasses. I had been avoiding making a face that I didn't mean, or at least getting caught while doing it.

"This rabbi brings in young guys, teens and twentysomethings. Does group study with them, checks in on them, fills the dad role in all the ways they wish their dads actually filled the role. With Jon it was like several calls a day, invites to all these events, one on one attention."

"Sounds nice."

"Sounds creepy. It was creepy. He gets Jon confiding these really private things about our family to him. Just the things our parents fought about and even like who I'm dating. Private stuff that isn't his business and then this rabbi gets Jon on this kick. This holy kick. We aren't holy enough for him. We're holding him back from reaching his true holy potential."

"We?"

"Me. My family. Jon told me the things he said. Jon was just not one of those Jews. He starts lecturing me about the clothing I wear, how I'm sending some sort of message. We had some big fights, we all did. Really nasty ones. He said some awful things but that wasn't him. He wasn't a judgmental person, not at the heart of it."

"So you think he was brainwashed?" I asked.

"Yeah, basically. He got out though. He just snapped one day and he was done with it. Really done with it."

"When was that?"

"He had been with them for maybe six months? A little more? They even talked him into moving out of the house, which fucking broke my mother's heart by the way. He was living with some other lost boy, and then he showed up at home. Crying. Apologizing. And we forgave him. He was so . . . miserable. He was a mess and when I think back to it I know he was using by then. Something happened there. It got him started again."

"What happened?"

"I don't know and he didn't want to talk about it. We didn't want to push it. I was mad but I didn't want to scare him away. You have to remember he's sick, that's what our dad said, and I feel like that's the only way to understand it. But he started telling me some of the things that rabbi said, and it was—it's hard to explain."

"You don't have any theories about what happened?"

Rebecca tensed up like she had been stung. I replayed what I had just said in my head, and it did sound accusatory.

"The rabbi just stopped talking to him. Stopped checking on him. Cut him off. I think it hurt him. Or I think maybe Jon hurt him? But to go from someone being that involved in your life, choosing where you live, telling you what to eat, what to say when you pray, picking out your clothes, to nothing? Just radio silence?"

"Sounds like an unhealthy paradigm." I took a sip of my tea to at least keep up the image that this was a casual conversation. "I don't want to cross a line and you don't have to answer me, but you said Jon had some stories about this rabbi. What sort of stories?"

"I don't know. Okay, no, I do. It's just—it's weird and gross but at the same time maybe harmless. And I don't want to come across as, well I'll just say it. I don't want to come across as homophobic, but that's not what this is about."

"All right, I'm listening, not judging."

"They would have study time, all these younger dudes. They would get together with the rabbi, and according to Jon, one of those dudes was definitely gay. Nothing weird about it. He just was gay and that was the way it was. He was Jewish and he really was buying into this Aish method of reaching God so he was digging deep to find a way to be that kind of Jew and still be attracted to guys. Jon felt bad for him. He wasn't the type to care if someone was gay. So this guy would always ask questions about temptation and what the line for temptation was, which is so painful and personal, but that was the kind of space they built. It was like you told this rabbi everything, all your hang-ups, and then he told you what to do. Everyone knew the guy was gay and they were accepting enough of it. Like they weren't kicking him out. And he wasn't overtly drawing attention to it either, the way Jon talked about it, it wasn't like everything had to be about him being gay. But the rabbi talked about it a lot and was always bringing up the worst parts of Leviticus. The whole abomination business. And there was this one story that sticks out to me. The rabbi told this poor gay kid, in front of everyone, that if he could masturbate with his hand he could masturbate with a vagina. What the fuck."

I was beginning to see how this constituted a cult. I was also making a face that I meant. "Was this Rabbi Ornetzsky?"

"Yeah, it was."

א

In certain circles of the Orthodox world, dating is a myriad of rules and propriety. Parents need to be contacted, blessings need to be given. Maybe a grandparent would vouch for my good character. I read an article about a call-in system in New York where Jews are assigned a PIN code. You call in, enter your code, enter your potential date's code, and an automated voice tells you the likelihood of whether your child will be born with Tay-Sachs Disease. Better to cancel your date than potentially fall in love with someone who couldn't make you a proper Jewish baby.

Yitzhak had his work cut out for him given that my parents were happily living in Florida under the impression that I was going to marry a fantastic woman who would make us all better someday. I also had no living grandparents to vouch for me. And I was pretty set on adopting children so my Tay-Sachs status was more or less irrelevant.

"I'm an orphan," I said.

"Is there anyone I can call?"

"I'm a twenty-five-year-old consenting adult willing to meet you in a very public space and keep my hands to myself. I'll understand if this is too compromising a set up."

"Stop. People will talk."

"Not if we go to a barbecue restaurant."

"You don't keep kosher?"

"Uhm, no, I do, sort of. I don't really eat meat so that more or less takes care of the issue."

He might have really believed I was an orphan and that was why he agreed to meet me at the Botanical Gardens. I felt bad about that, but I felt worse that I was letting him waste his time on me since this was going nowhere from my point of view. But Yitzhak was good at wasting time. He spent it with Rabbi Ornetzsky.

"I thought you would be late," he said flatly, squinting either because the sun was too strong or he hated the dress I was wearing. Maybe it was something else. I shouldn't have presumed.

"That's rude. Why would I be late?"

"Jewish Standard Time," he said.

"No. That's not a thing. That's called being rude and inconsiderate."

"It's a thing," he said.

"No, it's not, and you're part of the problem for perpetuating the myth. You are disgusting."

"Wow."

"I'm not joking. I'm serious."

"I believe you," he said.

I should have been more accommodating but I wasn't ready to commit to this fraud in its entirety. I wore a dress that had short sleeves and came above my knee. That was my fair warning to him about how this was going to be. We walked the path of the garden, keeping a respectable distance from one another.

"I thought you didn't like me," I finally said.

"I don't not like you. I didn't like what you were talking about."

"Yoni?"

"It's a sore subject."

"I heard he had a falling out with Rabbi Ornetzsky," I said.

"Where did you hear that?"

"His sister."

"Yoni had some family issues, I'm sure the Silvermans are good people, but they were leading him down a path that wasn't right for him."

"And the Aish path was right?"

"You sound like you've made up your mind about this," he said harshly.

"About what?"

"About Aish and the rabbi and Yoni."

"I just think, from what I've heard, you don't seem like the kind of guy who would be mixed up in all of it."

He stopped walking. "What kind of guy do you think I am? You don't know me."

"You are a gainfully employed lawyer. You have a sense of self and a strong connection to your family. You are sure of your faith, but you are not dogmatic. You are comfortable with asking questions and questioning yourself because of your faith. You actively sought out my company, so I know enough to make an educated guess."

I was met with silence.

"Rabbi Ornetzsky has made Judaism accessible and relevant to Jews in a way no one else in this city is. Read any article and it says modern Judaism is dying. Young people aren't joining synagogues. But Rabbi Ornetzsky is reaching people who need to be reached."

"Okay," I said. "That's kind of irrelevant to our conversation, but sure. In certain sects of Judaism, young people are less likely than ever to join an institution. Statistically, millennials prefer to be engaged in ways that the modern synagogue is struggling to replicate in a sustainable system. That's less about Rabbi Ornetzsky's ability to make Judaism accessible and more about him discovering that young men are incredibly prone to loneliness and depression, desperate to feel validated in a way that other demographics aren't. I'm sure he's got a great personality though."

"You're judging something you don't know and haven't experienced. Don't dismiss this community as desperate. They're good people. What do you have? The word of a drug addict?"

I felt this tenuous connection that I had found for myself already slipping away. I wanted to know what happened to Jonathan Silverman. Not how he died. I knew that now. His friend had killed him. Probably over money. Maybe over something even stupider if it was possible. In a drug-induced fit, one kid strangled another kid and there was nothing to show for it. Just an abandoned Facebook page filled with links to the compositions of Tupac. I wanted to find some indication that Jonathan had been happy or secure, maybe not for long, but for a time.

"I know and have experienced Judaism. I have not experienced your Rabbi Ornetzsky's boys' club. I know what Yoni experienced bothered him enough that he left."

"Just by the way you're speaking, the language you're using, I can tell this isn't going to be a useful conversation."

"What happened to the gay kid?"

"What?"

"There was a gay kid who started coming around Or Chadash the same time as Yoni. What happened to him?"

"There is no gay kid. I don't know what you're talking about."

I knew there was a gay kid, and he had stuck out to Jonathan. According to Rebecca, the kid left an impression, and potentially drove Jon away. So I wanted to know who he was and if they were friends. Rebecca couldn't remember the kid's name so I sent her a list of potential candidates I had garnered from cross-referencing Jonathan and Yitzhak's friend's lists. Avram Levine was the winner.

And Avram Levine was a newlywed. He had married at the height of summer, sweat overcoming him in the pictures with his bride. She, however, was miraculously matte, immune to humidity. Her hair was suspiciously smooth and strawberry blond. I didn't know her and I already knew Racheli deserved better. Not that Avram wasn't good enough to be loved, but I liked to think she had aspired to be something more than a vagina to masturbate with in her marriage.

The gay kid had stayed, and Yoni had left. One drug for another and back again. That feeling of perfect belonging and greater service to God was enough to make you forget you were a pile of chemicals and organic materials.

"Did he ever tell you why he left?" I asked Rebecca.

We ambled along in cutoff shorts and sneakers. The Loop is a section of Delmar Boulevard and regarded as one of the most walkable neighborhoods in the country. What used to be a densely Jewish neighborhood became a black neighborhood as Jews integrated and pushed out into the suburbs. And lately the Loop was an urban Disneyland, bought up and polished by the same business mogul who owned the honored music establishment Blueberry Hill. Hints of a Jewish and black presence remain. Stars of David etched into the cornerstones of buildings, a mural of Chuck Berry. Whispers of one hundred years of history funneled down a corridor of college bars, boutique hotels, and a Korean-Mexican fusion restaurant.

"It wasn't just one thing. He didn't come home in one day. It was a lot of days and a lot of things. He wasn't stupid. I know you think someone has to be stupid to get themselves in that situation but he was smart. Really smart. Way smarter than me."

"I don't think he was stupid."

"My parents are—whatever. You know? They weren't terrible. They were mostly good. But the kind of pressure they put on him, it didn't make him thrive like it might have for another kid. It just made him sad. But Jon and I were a team when we got past our fighting phase. We talked pretty much every day and because of those people and their fucking brand of crazy, I lost time with my brother." She speedily wiped at her eyes.

"They took his phone?" I asked. It didn't seem outside the realm of possibility.

"No. It wasn't like that. It's just what I said before. They told him that we were holding him back. That I was holding him back. That I didn't really want him to get better. That I didn't want him to have a good relationship with God because I was scared of God, which is—I'm not scared of God. God should be scared of me."

"He left because of you."

"Eventually. He knew what he wanted for himself, but he knew what I wanted for me, and in the end I think it was more important to him that I got what I wanted."

"What did he want?"

"I don't know what Jon wanted. I guess to fill some hole. He just felt like he wanted something. It was like that from the time he was little. He told me all the time that he wanted something but he didn't know what he wanted. Like from the time he was a toddler. And he just never stopped feeling that way. Ever. He found things he thought would help and maybe they did for a little while but the feeling would come back."

We crossed the street where the sidewalk was blocked and a set of luxury dorm rooms had been installed by Washington University. "I can't even remember what used to be here," Rebecca said distantly, one brow raised much higher than the other.

"And what did you want? Or what did he think you wanted?"

"To not feel like I was going to miss out. I used to be so, I don't know, anxious? Maybe just sad."

"Yeah?"

"The best parts of my life were the parts when I was a kid with my family and we were celebrating Shabbat. It was all of Friday night. Sitting in my dad's lap, and Jon was in my lap, and we were singing in synagogue. And it was lighting the candles with my mom and Jon tearing the bread. And I thought I could only have that if I got married and had a family that looked like our family. I didn't know how it could be done any other way. I just had no idea. No one ever told me that it could look different. I didn't know any Jewish kids with two moms."

I knew that hole that Jon wanted to fill. Not as intimately as he did, but I was aware of it. I can't be sure but I think most people are aware of it. I fill my hole with service to a community. Scheduling every moment. Helping other people fill their holes. Teaching children the best ways I can think of to keep that hole filled.

From what I can tell Jon tried all kinds of things. He really did try. He tried school and he tried music. He tried religion and he tried God. He tried family. I think the world disappointed him. That's probably more on the hole that was in Jon than it is on the world. He was a handsome enough boy, smart too. He loved his sister more than he loved his sense of belonging.

※

Rabbi Ornetzsky is the worst part of your Judaism. Miriam, your Miriam, Or Chadash Miriam, is the best part of your Judaism. Your frat should meet regularly with her.

Yitzhak took a week but he e-mailed me back.

It's not a frat, but I hear what you're saying. Shabbat Shalom.

Shabbat Shalom, I replied.

KAFFEE MIT SCHLOCK

Who Shall Live and Who Shall Die

Charles Ardai

> **On Rosh Hashannah it is written,**
> **On Yom Kippur it is sealed . . .**
> **Who shall live and who shall die.**

Rain swept across the stained-glass windows to either side of the *bima*, hammering the panes in a dull, irregular rhythm. The sound provided a droning accompaniment to the prayers of the eleven men who stood before the open ark, nodding their heads as they spoke.

Shema yisrael, a dozen voices murmured. *Hear, O Israel.*

A pair of Torah scrolls stood upright in the cabinet, tilted against a wooden panel painted orange and gold. The temple's third Torah lay open on the podium, a silver fescue in the rabbi's hand pointing its outstretched finger at the first words of the reading for Yom Kippur.

The rabbi faced the ark along with his congregation until the prayer ended, then laid the pointer down and pulled the doors of the ark shut. The other men took their seats in the half-empty pews of the sanctuary; the rabbi returned to the Torah. A small lamp clipped to the dais cast a yellow pool of light onto the parchment of the scroll. The rabbi found the beginning of the passage and began to chant.

His voice filled the chamber with the story of Jonah, son of Amittai, who fled the Lord rather than carry His message into the world. The other men listened in silence, their eyes turned inward.

Beneath the drumming of the rain and the rabbi's chant, sounds intruded from the street outside: cars passing on the slick asphalt, honking their horns as they went; voices, in midconversation, raised to be heard over the rain; angry winds, whistling down the canyons formed by the buildings of lower Manhattan. But as the rabbi finished, holding his final note, the sounds of the world outside seemed to grow quiet.

With an effort, the rabbi lifted the heavy Torah above his head. "This is the Torah that Moses brought down from Sinai," he intoned, "to fulfill the word—"

The doors at the rear of the sanctuary suddenly sprang apart, slamming against the walls on either side. A man, drenched from head to foot and carrying no umbrella, staggered in. The doors swung closed behind him. He bent over, his hands on his knees, panting heavily.

"—of Adonai," the rabbi finished. Of the Lord. He carefully put the Torah down.

Still doubled over, the man looked up. His face was flushed. "Please—"

He wiped some water out of his eyes with the wet sleeve of his overcoat. "Please help me. Someone's trying to kill me."

❧

The man straightened, pulled off his hat and shook it, throwing water off on the floor. Then with shaking hands he unwound the long scarf from around his neck. His hair, as white as every other man's in the synagogue but lacking a yarmulke, was dry. "I don't know if he saw me come here. If he didn't, he may not think to look here. But if he did—" He shook his head. "If he did, he'll be here any minute. And even if he didn't, he might check every building . . ." His voice shook. "Please, is there anywhere I can hide?"

The rabbi stepped down, descending the three steps to the floor of the sanctuary. He took the trembling man by the shoulders. "Who? Who wants to hurt you?"

"Please, there's no time," the man said. "He'll be here soon. Don't you understand? He'll kill me."

"This is a synagogue, no one's killing anyone," the rabbi said.

"You're wrong. He's out of his mind with rage. You've got to hide me."

"Hide you?" the rabbi said. He waved a hand around him. It was a small room. "We'll help you, but there's nowhere to hide you."

"Oh, God . . ."

"Listen," the rabbi said. "You have to tell us what's going on."

"All right," the man said, his breath still coming raggedly. "All right. My name's, my name's William Karoly, I'm a, I was a . . . oh, Jesus, I'm sorry—"

"Calm yourself," the rabbi said.

"Okay," Karoly said. "Okay." He looked down at his hat and his gloved hands and a violent shiver shook his body. "Nineteen years ago—My wife and I went to the theater, okay? Just a night out, her and me. But she didn't feel well, so she left at intermission, and afterward, I was walking home . . ."

The rabbi waited, the other men waited.

"I was walking home, on Ninth Avenue, and I saw a man get shot. Murdered."

Karoly cast a look back over his shoulder, but the big doors remained shut. The rabbi turned to one of the men beside him—they were all on their feet now. "Benjamin," the rabbi said, "please lock the doors."

Karoly had already gone on: "He walked right up to him, pulled out a gun, and bang, just like that, two shots in the back. Then he saw me, I was standing there, maybe twenty feet away. I couldn't move. He pointed the gun at me. That was it, I was going to die, I knew it. Only then we heard a siren, and he ran. He ran away."

Karoly shook his head. "I should have run too. Before the police arrived. I could have run away. But instead I stood there, and when the police came I told them everything. What I'd seen. I described the man who pulled the trigger, and later, at the trial, when they asked me to testify against him, what could I do? Tell me that. What could I do?" He didn't wait for an answer. "The bastard went to jail, and seven years later they executed him. Gave him an injection."

"Then who—"

"His *son*," Karoly said. "God help me, his son. We've moved, we changed our telephone number, but somehow he found me. Now, after so many years! Just this morning I got a phone call from his wife, crying, saying he was on his way to my apartment, to kill me. Because he blames me for his father's death. And he's right to."

"You said his father was executed for murder."

"His father's dead, and I'm the reason. I can't pretend otherwise. And it wouldn't matter if I did." Karoly wiped his eyes once more. "Well, this time I ran. Hung up the phone, grabbed my coat, and ran. Like I should've done nineteen years ago. But he saw me coming out of my lobby. He was waiting across the street. I made it to the subway, got on the first train I saw, but I there's no way he didn't follow me. He could be right outside now—"

"That's why we locked the doors. If he's outside, you're fine. You're inside."

"One way or another he's going to—"

"We don't know what he is going to do," the rabbi said. "Maybe he's outside, maybe he isn't. Maybe he saw you come in, maybe not. You can stay here with us until sundown, and then we can call the police. When they come, you tell them what you told us. All right?"

Karoly said, "Why do we have to wait?"

"It's Yom Kippur," the rabbi said. "On Yom Kippur we do not use the telephone."

"But I'm not Jewish."

The rabbi shook his head. "Not our phone. I'm sorry."

"It's my life we're talking about."

"Right this moment, your life's not in danger. If that changes—"

Karoly looked in the eyes of the men around him. "You don't understand. A locked door won't stop him. You won't stop him. If you don't let me call the police, he'll shoot me dead, right at your feet."

"In a synagogue," the rabbi said, "in front of all of us? I don't believe that."

"You didn't see him. He is obsessed. This is nineteen years of obsession, since he was a kid. His wife called it that. The man's *wife*."

The eleven men faced Karoly with pity in their eyes. Outside, the drumming of the rain against windows and walls seemed very loud, the keening of the wind piercing.

And in that moment a knock came, quite clearly, at the door.

No one moved.

The knock was repeated. The doorknob rattled. Then a pounding began.

"Who is it?" the rabbi called out.

There was a pause during which the pounding ceased. The voice, when it came, was a young man's voice, an angry young man's. "My name's Hank Garton. Ask Karoly who I am. He knows."

Karoly whispered, terrified, "It's him."

The rabbi glanced around. It was too late to call the police now; the only comfort being that it would have been too late a minute earlier as well. Meanwhile, there really was nowhere to hide Karoly. Under a pew? Behind the doors of the ark? He would surely be found.

"You'd better open this door," Garton shouted. He started pounding on it again.

"Rabbi?" one of the men said.

The rabbi held up one hand.

"I'll count to three," Garton shouted through the door. "Then I'm shooting the lock."

The rabbi grabbed Karoly's hands, looked at the gloves, turned them over. "When he saw you, from across the street, were you wearing all this? The gloves? The coat, the hat, the scarf?"

Karoly nodded.

"One!"

The rabbi pulled open the buttons of Karoly's overcoat. "And it's raining—he doesn't know what you look like."

Karoly said, "My photograph was in the paper. When his father was tried."

"Two!"

"That was twenty years ago," the rabbi said. He reached into the pocket of his robe and pulled out a spare yarmulke.

"What are you doing?"

"I'm hiding you," the rabbi said.

※

The doors smashed inward. Immediately the rain came in and began to collect in a pool on the floor. Hank pocketed his gun. He hadn't even needed to use it. A couple of swift kicks had been enough.

The doors wouldn't close properly with the lock splintered and the hinges bent, but Hank pushed them halfway shut with his hip, hitched up his jeans, and unzipped his rain-drenched hoodie. The right-hand pocket hung down from the weight of the automatic. His father's gun.

He walked down the center aisle of the synagogue. There was room for twenty, maybe twenty-five, people, Hank guessed, but only a dozen were there, all of them old, white-haired men wearing skullcaps. Five men in the left pews, six in the right, their noses buried in their prayer books. Old men—men who hadn't been robbed of the chance to grow old. All pointedly not looking at Hank. And up at the altar was the rabbi in his black robe, his skullcap, his prayer shawl. He, at least, was looking at Hank—trembling, but looking him right in the eye.

Where was Karoly? Had they stuffed him away in some corner? Was he cringing behind the podium the rabbi stood at? Hank looked around the room, searching.

"You didn't have to break the door," the rabbi said.

"You didn't want it broken, you should have let me in."

"We would have," the rabbi said, "but not to kill a man. Not to commit murder."

Hank advanced down the aisle, scanning the rows left and right. "It's not murder. It's punishment."

"Killing a man is murder," the rabbi said. His voice shook.

"Oh, really," Hank said. He shifted his gaze from side to side, straining to catch a glimpse of Karoly. "Tell that to the men who killed my father. Tell them they're murderers. Oh, they'll disagree with you. But twenty years ago a nearsighted old man told them my *father* was a murderer and that was enough for them. Suddenly it's not murder to kill someone—suddenly it's the justice system."

Hank took the gun out again, swung it in a loose grip to cover all the men in the room. "You know what I want. Tell me where Karoly is."

The rabbi gripped the edges of the podium. "Don't," he said.

"*Where is Karoly?*"

"He's not here. We turned him out." This came from one of the seated men in the first row, a man with small, tired eyes and a gray goatee.

Hank turned to him. He brought his gun up and pointed it at the man's face. "I don't believe you."

"Look around," the man said. His voice was surprisingly steady. "Do you see him?"

Hank looked around the room once more. He climbed up to the dais and looked inside the podium. Karoly was not there.

Hank approached the ark, pulled open the doors with his free hand.

"Don't you dare!" The man from the front row was on his feet now. "You come into our temple on the holiest day of the year, you desecrate our worship with a gun and a threat of violence—"

"Shut up." Hank reached into the base of the ark, beneath the shelf on which the Torah scrolls rested, and pulled out a wet overcoat. Then he pulled out a crumpled hat and a scarf. He threw them into the first row. They landed at the old man's feet.

"Don't lie to me again. Don't tell me Karoly isn't here." Hank turned to the rabbi. "He's here. Tell me where."

"You have no right to harm him," the rabbi said.

"My father is *dead*," Hank said. "Because of him. I have every right. Isn't that in your book? Eye for an eye?"

The rabbi closed his eyes and shook his head. "He doesn't deserve your hate."

"What do you know about it?" Hank shouted. "He deserves what I say he deserves." He wheeled to face the men in the pews. "Why are you protecting him? He's not even Jewish!"

"We know what it means to be hunted," the man in the front row said.

Hank's eyes narrowed. Twelve old men. Each wearing one of those Jewish prayer caps, but how hard was it to slap a cap on someone's head? What would Karoly look like with a cap on? Like one of these men.

He suddenly knew where Karoly was hiding: right in front of him. Oh, they were clever, very clever.

But which one was he?

Hank stepped down to the sanctuary and picked up the hat that lay at the old man's feet. "So you know what it means to be hunted," he said. "Maybe recently? Maybe today?"

The old man shook his head.

"I think maybe you're Karoly," Hank said.

"I?" The man laughed. "I am Nathan Weiss. And I have been hunted by worse than you. In 1944, in Austria—"

Hank waved him to silence. "I don't want to hear about 1944. Maybe you're not Karoly. But one of you sure as hell is."

From his pocket he pulled a laminated newspaper clipping. He looked from the clipping to the faces of the men in the sanctuary. None looked similar to the photograph in the clipping—a fifty-year-old man standing in front of the courthouse under the headline "Garton Trial Continues." Not similar enough. Any of them could have been Karoly, or none of them. Hank put the clipping back in his pocket.

He handed the hat to Nathan Weiss. "Put this on. Then pass it along. Each of you is going to try it on."

"What will that tell you?" Weiss said. "Many people have the same size head."

"Shut up and put on the hat."

Weiss put the hat on. Its damp brim hung down over his eyes.

Hank shook his head and waved his gun at Benjamin. "You next."

Weiss passed the hat back over his shoulder to Benjamin, whose hands shook as he tried it on. It was too big for him as well.

"You next," Hank said.

Each congregant tried the hat on in turn. It fit some less poorly than others, but in its current condition it fit none of them well.

When the hat returned to Weiss, Hank snatched it and threw it back on the floor. Then he wiped his hands on his pants. The damn thing was still wet—

And suddenly, Hank had his answer. He knew how he could find Karoly.

Karoly would still be wet.

Not his clothes, maybe, because the coat and scarf had protected them. Not his hair, not his face, not his hands—maybe. But Karoly had not been wearing rain boots. His shoes, at the very least, had to be wet.

"I've got you," he said, to everyone in the room. "Damn it, you son of a bitch, I've got you."

❧

At gunpoint, the congregants stepped out into the center aisle and filed past him one by one. Each man put his feet up, one by one, on the seat of one of the pews in the first row. Hank checked each man's shoes carefully.

Impossibly, none was wet.

"Damn it!" he said. "Which of you is Karoly?"

No one spoke.

"I'll kill you all," he said in a quiet voice. "One by one, I swear, if that's what it takes. I don't have anything to lose." The hand holding the gun trembled, his finger tight on the trigger. "I'm not going to jail. Not going to let them inject me with the stuff they gave my father. I'm taking care of this, and then I'm checking out. Only question is how many of you come with me. You understand that, right?" His voice almost sounded pleading, almost sounded reasonable. "If you don't tell me, you're all going to die. You don't have to. But you will."

"No," the rabbi said. Hank spun. "You won't kill eleven innocent men."

"I won't if you just tell me—"

"It's not so easy, is it?" the rabbi said. "A roomful of old men all look pretty much the same to you. You can't say which one of us you saw on the street only a little while ago. You could make a terrible mistake." The rabbi stepped down from the pulpit and approached Hank. "Let's put this in your terms. You shoot one of us. All right. The rest will get that gun out of your hands before you can shoot any more. Who knows, maybe you manage to shoot one more—two out of twelve, those aren't good odds. You probably won't get Karoly, and then the police *will* get you, and they will inject you, and Karoly will walk free. Are you willing to risk that?"

"I can get more than two," Hank said, but his hand was shaking worse than ever, and he was squinting, fighting back tears.

"Don't do it," the rabbi said simply. "Put the gun down."

Hank seemed to be considering it. But his hand didn't budge.

"Please."

Slowly, finally, in increments of a millimeter at a time, it tipped down.

"Thank you," the rabbi said.

Hank spoke in a whisper. "You're going to call the police."

"No," the rabbi said, "just go home. I'm sure Mr. Karoly will forgive you."

Something caught Hank's eye as the rabbi spoke. The gun swung up again.

Without lowering his aim, he knelt and touched the rabbi's shoes.

The rabbi's hands clenched into fists.

Hank stood up. He wiped his hand on his pants.

Hank and the rabbi stared into each other's eyes for a long, awful moment. Then Hank pulled the trigger.

❧

Nathan screamed, lunging forward as the rabbi collapsed onto the floor. But he didn't grab Hank or the gun—he dropped to his knees and lifted the rabbi's bloody head, cradling it in his lap.

No one else stood.

The echo of the gunshot rang in the walls and faded slowly.

"You thought you were so smart," Hank said. "It wasn't enough for you to hide him as one of you—no, you dressed him up as your *rabbi*! Who'd ever suspect? Who'd even imagine that the *rabbi* might be the faker? Well, it didn't work."

"You're wrong," Weiss said, from where he knelt on the ground. "This wasn't Karoly."

Hank turned slowly. "You're lying."

"His shoes," Weiss said, "were wet because he was wearing Karoly's shoes. He knew you might think to look for them, so he wore them himself."

"No."

"He couldn't turn away a man who needed help," Weiss said. "And this is how he is repaid for it."

"You are lying!"

"No, he's not." A man came forward—a man slightly taller than the others, a man with stooped shoulders and shaking hands. "I am Karoly. I can't let this go on."

"No," Benjamin shouted. He stepped forward. "That's not Karoly, I am—"

"You're lying," Hank shouted, "both of you. I killed Karoly."

"You killed Meyer Landau," Weiss said. "You killed an innocent man."

Outside, under the sound of the rainstorm, a pair of sirens wailed. Not so close, but not so far.

"You made me do it," Hank said, weeping. "You tricked me."

He raised the gun once more, but turned it toward his temple.

"Don't," Nathan Weiss said, and reached a bloody hand toward him.

"I'm sorry," Hank murmured.

When the police came into the sanctuary, it was as though the echo of the second gunshot could still be heard.

Errands

Gary Phillips

Delicately I bit the head off the yellow chili pepper, earning two mildly hot seeds on the tip of my tongue for my effort. I spat those out and shook the pepper's juice on the temporarily topless pastrami burger. This is a concoction that is exactly what it sounds like, slices of steamed lean pastrami layered on a charbroiled patty. Heaven.

Putting my lunch back together, I took a healthy bite, savoring the mélange of tastes. Wiping my mouth with a paper napkin, I happened to glance at the other cat sitting near me at the side counter. He was sitting slightly sideways on his stool. Something piqued his interest and he swiveled around to look toward Adams Boulevard behind us, parallel to the outside counter of Johnny's Pastrami.

Turning to also take a gander, I spied a late-model oxblood red Mercedes SLK 55 glide to an empty space at the curb. Frowning, I took another bite, smaller this time, and again wiped at my mouth as I chewed and swallowed my food. Sure enough, Alicia and her significant other Markie got out of the car and walked toward me. Alicia looked as she always did, rockin' some sort of designer skirt and shirt, heels audible across the cracked sidewalk, a Hermès bag or its dupe, tucked neatly under her arm. Markie, the butcher one, was dressed as usual too, in worn jeans, flats, and an Oxford cloth button-down shirt.

"Your girlish figure is going to go all to hell eating like that," Markie cracked.

"You two come to put my claim to the test?"

Markie snorted. Alicia frowned, then her pretty, alert face composed itself again. "Oh right, that time you said the pastrami here was better than at Canter's."

"What can I do for you, ladies?" Me and Alicia were related but it wasn't an obvious thing. An eavesdropper on our infrequent phone conversations probably wouldn't have a clue as to how. The fact she'd tracked me down and not called me told me something was up, something she needed me for and was pissed at herself because of that.

"Can we talk?" Alicia nodded toward her car.

"Okay, hold on a sec." I got off the stool and got a paper bag from the lady behind the sliding window screen where you got your orders at the stand. Wrapping up what remained of my sandwich, I bagged it and walked over to the Mercedes. I had to hand it to Alicia. For a chick who rarely journeyed east of La Cienega, she didn't look the least discomforted leaning against her ride here in the 'hood.

Conversely Markie would be relaxed at a pit bull fight. Alicia now stood apart from us as I leaned against the Mercedes, having placed my bag on the roof of that sweet sled just to get a rise out of her. A tic twitched at the side of her mouth but she didn't object. She must really need me, and got right to it.

"Stu is meeting with Kleener Lockhart tonight." Alicia stood close to me, a hand on her hip.

"Why?" I made no effort to hide my irritation.

She leveled her patented "how retarded are you" glare on me.

"Specifics would be helpful."

"I can't say for sure, but the point is what good can come of it?"

My partially eaten lunch gurgled in my stomach. "Great, you want me to try and stop him?"

She hunched a shoulder. "I already tried that."

Like a direct attempt from me would be useless was her implication—being only the half-brother. But we both knew that was bullshit. She'd been worked since middle school that Stu and I were close. But why prick at that now? I took a different tack. "How do you know this is going down, Alicia?"

A lowrider '67 Impala rolled west on Adams and the eses in it wolf whistled at her, ignoring Markie. Alicia almost grinned wearily. "He bragged about it to me, of course."

He would if they were having one of their arguments. As our old man stepped further back from the business, each of them made more aggressive moves to show they were the one to inherit. It sure as shit wasn't gonna be me. "Where's the meet?"

"I don't know that either."

"Shit. Why not put the bag over my head and let me loose in the room with knives sticking out of the walls."

Markie muttered something but I didn't catch it.

"Come on, Ellis, don't be like that. You're the only one that can find out."

"Yeah and to quote the sage, that's why black men tend to shout."

She gritted her uneven yet appealing front teeth. "Really, we're going there now?"

A dry chuckle escaped my throat. "You doing this for the righteous reason or just to knee-cap Stu?"

"I can't believe you talk to me like that."

"He's a grown-ass man, Alicia. This might be his chance and you want to make sure the works get gummed up."

She gave me the finger and the two of them started to get back in her Mercedes.

I gave it a beat or two. "Okay, I'll see what I can find out. Then what?"

"Could you, you know, spy on the meet?"

I made a face. "It depends where it's going to be."

"Do what you can."

Shit, she knew I would. I wouldn't let Stu sit down with that big bad wolf without watching his back. Still. "If this goes south, you're riding this beef with me."

"Naturally," she smirked.

Alicia got behind the wheel. I moved to let Markie into the passenger seat. We exchanged a nod and for the briefest of moments, she seemed to be considering saying something but didn't. She got in the car and they drove off, probably to their shop I figured.

Thereafter I returned to the store. It's one of a chain of eight Kingman Mattress stores that stretch from the Los Angeles area to San Diego and Palm Springs. We sell a good deal of mattresses to the gays and old folks out that latter way. I sometimes daydream various scenarios as to why that is. But today is not the day for such speculation. The one I manage is on La Brea in a strip mall not far from Rodeo where further south past that you got into middle-class Baldwin Hills. The street was pronounced like what you'd call a horse event. Not Row-Day-Oh like that other street, the tony one in Beverly Hills. We occupied a big space and took up a corner of the shorter end of the ell shape of shops. Next to us was a nail salon and in the long part of the shank a rent-to-own.

I came in and waved at a couple of our deliverymen bringing in a shipment of the new memory foam mattresses. They were selling like we had billboards up of Miz Beyoncé rolling around butt naked on them. Now that would be an ad. I made for Lola Estrella's office. She was our finance person, among other talents. Like all of the Kingman stores, there were a few staff members who walked in two worlds—the civilian one and the underground economy. I supposed if things kept going the way they were, Wall Street shafting Main Street, those distinctions might disappear altogether when it came to folks trying to keep beans and bread on the table. I knocked on her door, which was ajar.

"Negro, you just have yourself there at eight, understand?" She stopped speaking and I assumed she was listening to the man on the other end of the line. I was pretty certain who it was from her tone and words. "Uh-huh, never mind all that drama," she soon said. "I don't care nothing about that silly twist you think is in love with your old ass. Be there on time." With that she cradled the handset and said, "Come on in, El." Her window looked out partially on the showroom and she'd seen me coming.

I did so and closed the door behind me. I sat opposite, my serious face in place.

Lola, in a silky rayon top, a hint of her ample cleavage in evidence, transmitted a wary look and placed both her hands flat on her desk top. Her silver-colored nails damn near pulsed under the overhead fluorescent lights. She was a Chicana by way of Pico Rivera and had kids by two baby daddies.

"Yes," she said.

"You still seeing that dude, Alonzo?" He was not one of the baby daddies.

Her eyes narrowed. "What's up, Ellis?"

She used my full name to show her displeasure at where she knew my line of inquiry was heading. "Would you mind asking a favor of him?"

"He's out of that now."

"It's not that kind of favor. No errand on his part. I just need a little info."

She was not in the mood. Why couldn't I have gotten to her before her call with Melvin, one of her kids' fathers? Mel was black, well, half-black like me and more light-skinded, the kids say, than me. 'Course we were both black enough when the cops stopped us. The other cat she had a kid by was a *carnal* from Michoacán who no one had heard from or seen around in some three years now.

I told her what was up. "I've got to get a line on the meet without, you know, tipping off the parties. I don't want to come at Stu direct on this less he gets his hackles up."

"And I don't want Alonzo running in those circles no more," she said with conviction. I could understand she wanted to keep him away from me, from whatever nefariousness might arise from dealing with Kleener Lockhart. I guess it was kinda cliché, but maybe she figured if she could save Alonzo, she could save herself.

"This one's a keeper, huh?"

"I look to make him so." The tension in her upper body finally abated. "Look, let me see if I can make some calls for you, El." She snapped her fingers. "Like what you call it, discreetly."

"I appreciate that, Lola." I smiled as I walked out but didn't think her getting on the phone, if she did, would amount to much. I'd wanted to get to Alonzo because he used to be a kind of high-end drug dealer, supplying his candy to upper-tier rappers, B movie actors, producers, and such. Among them was this knockout would-be starlet who liked running with bad boys—specifically one of Lockhart's main arm-twisters, Tony Bones, real name Tony Bennett. Yep, just like the man who left his heart in San Francisco, only this Tony was six-four and built like a mobile meat locker. It was a good bet that he'd be with Lockhart doing bodyguard duties at this meet. My idea being if I could get to her through Alonzo, I might sweet talk something useful out of her.

That plan was bust but there was another move to make. If I couldn't get to an ally of Lockhart, there was always a rival. Her name was Sylvia Hayden and once upon a time she'd been married to the Kleener. I took care of the paperwork in my In box then drove over to her place of business, a funeral parlor on Vermont not too far south of USC. The Hillman-Hayden Mortuary, nicknamed the Double H, was where luminaries like local city council and state assembly members were laid to rest. When LA native, rhythm and blues great Jack "Jump" Thornton passed, his service there had folks lining up three blocks deep to see him lying in state in his silver and gold coffin.

One of our commercials was playing on my Dodge's stereo. It was the one where pop is a genie and grants the wisher the miracle of sound sleep. "You shall slumber like no other," his voice echoed assuredly, his accent a cross between a Lou Costello bit and what white actors would do playing an American Indian on a TV western. He loved doing those ads. I got to the mortuary and went upstairs where the public isn't directed.

"Mr. Culhane. Long time no see."

"Good to see you too, Edie." I gave the older lady a peck on the cheek. "Could you buzz the boss to see if she could give me a few minutes?" Sylvia's office was located in the rear of the second story. It was last decorated in the eighties but was of the sort of understated furnishings one expected of this sort of outfit. The alluring aroma of a stand of fresh flowers in a vase buffeted the room.

"Yes, okay," Edie Colliers was saying into her phone's handset. She cradled it gently, the diamond on her finger complementing her tailored outfit. "Go on in, young man."

I thanked her and stepping past her, opened one of the darkly varnished double doors into Sylvia's inner office. Here the decor was of a more modern slant with chrome and leather and a built-in bookcase. The proprietor was up from behind her large desk at the other built-in, the wet bar.

"Cream soda, Ellis?"

"I'm good, thanks." She was pouring herself some into a coffee cup. Her favorite beverage, I recalled. She was a handsome woman in her forties who once was svelte, but a few too many cream sodas over time had added some weight. In a gray business skirt and Donna Karan blouse, she had what my pops would call a *zaftig* quality.

She sat lightly on her couch and I joined her there. We made a little with the chit-chat, then I got down to it. "I'm trying to find out what your ex is up to with my brother, Stu."

"Hmmm," she proclaimed. "And you came to me why?"

"I don't have time to play coy, Sylvia. We both know you keep tabs on what Kleener does."

"Not always." She had another sip of her soda and placed the cup on a coaster with the mortuary's name on it.

"If this is happening I can't believe it wouldn't have appeared on your radar."

"Is your brother fronting for Jacob?"

I shook my head to indicate negative. "This is his initiative."

She held up a finger. "But unlike him." She regarded me with her heavily made-up chestnut colored eyes. "And not turn to his little brother for help on the black tip in forging the cross town alliance . . . if that's what it is."

She tantalized with that hint while also holding back. That's why I hadn't been all that eager to come here. It wasn't about money. She liked to horse trade. "Okay, what's the *khesed*, the favor you want me to do?"

Her grin was like what a lioness must display closing in on an antelope. "I thought you Jews only did favors asked at weddings?"

"Teachings talk about putting yourself out for others." Not that I was an adherent of such. "What do you want done?"

She feinted with her hand in the air as if listlessly swatting at a fly. "There is a dear friend of mine, we go back many years. She has this wayward niece of hers. Meth head, tweaker I think they call them." She fixed me with a look. "Just the other day I was commiserating with her about this. Very sad."

Already the muscles in my stomach were doing the watusi. "Those types can't be helped until they want to help themselves."

"This is so. But if she could be extricated from her present circumstances, the niece might be afforded the opportunity to get on the right path again. My friend has some means."

Then why the hell didn't this friend go and get her? But I said, "What's the boom?"

"The boom?"

"What is it about her present circumstance that presents the obstacle?"

"Ah," she said, as if it just occurred to her at this moment that there was danger involved in this retrieval. "My friend has good reason to believe the niece, Gladys, is at a house where these sort congregate. Out there near Lynwood off the MTA line."

I almost cursed aloud. "That would be Four Trey Dalton territory."

She nodded her head. "I believe so."

Kleener Lockhart before he parlayed his drug monies into semi-respectable white-collar gangsterdom had been a Four Trey Dalton. Was this just coincidence or had I been led by the nose by my willful sister to this exact situation? That seemed like too many moving pieces, but at this stage I was hooked anyway. I had to see how it played out. I got as much detail as I could from Sylvia, including a couple of snapshots of the wayward twenty-two-year-old sent to my smartphone, and left the Double H.

On the way to the meth house on the Watts/Lynwood border, I made a stop at a hardware store to make a few purchases. I then got over there and first drove past the crib to give it a look over. It was one among countless 1940s era California Craftsman to be found in the poorer parts of the Southland. This part of town had been mostly black back when and was now majority Latino. The house needed a paint job but it wasn't dilapidated and the lawn was dying but not overgrown or trashed up.

But as I feared there was an indication that not just faded-out meth heads were inside. There was a late model white with gold flake trim Lincoln Navigator that screamed attention parked in the driveway with expensive rims. That meant some Four Trey shot caller was in there getting his freak on with one or more of the female druggies. He got to sex 'em up in exchange for some tina, the shaboo, or whatever the hell they were calling it these days.

My first idea had been to set the back of the house on fire and grab a hold of Gladys when she ran out with the rest. But meth heads tend to be in stupors when they're on the downside of the shit, so burning up a few of them might not be a loss to humanity but still, I was no psycho. The good news was, having had some experience with meth users, I knew they came and went at all hours—some to go rip out copper wire from street lights to sell for more drugs or otherwise get their hustle on.

I got my purchases together and stepping to the Lincoln, let the air out of one of the tires by pressing the point of a key into the valve stem. Two middle-aged women, one of them pulling an old-folks type of wire basket cart full of groceries, walked past speaking in Spanish. They didn't eyeball me, knowing better than to involve themselves with whatever foolishness was about to go down with this house. I then went onto the porch and listened for a moment at the door and sure enough, the latch gave when I pressed it.

Inside was gloomy and dank; musty body odors and the air heavy with layers of past fried food. A dude sitting in an easy chair looked over at me then back to the Dodger game playing on low over a portable radio atop an upturned plastic milk crate. He glared at it as if visualizing each play being described by the announcer. There was some activity in the kitchen through the open door at the rear, I heard two male voices arguing. To my right was a large padded chair next to an entrance to a hallway. Being over six feet and not lacking in the shoulder department helped me to not get challenged—at least just yet.

At the doorframe to the hallway, a noise startled me and looking behind me first, saw no one charging. I then looked down at the padded chair. Due to the semidark, I'd assumed it was empty. But I could now discern a form curled up on its wide seat, seemingly folded in on itself. It was a woman so I bent down and turned her head some. She was a pretty Latina, but not Gladys, who was black. The girl moaned and I left her to her narcotized dreams.

Down the hallway I peeked into a room. A man with one leg and half the other rested on his back on a bed damn near buried among junk from compact appliance motors to plastic garbage bags stuffed with who knew what. His prosthesis sat upright on a nightstand.

"Hey, what the hell are you doing in my house?" he demanded.

"Inspector," I said, but not too loud. I'd heard a baritone coming from what I figured was the house's other bedroom. Coming from in there was a deep male base rumble of pleasure. I grinned. I'd been known to make that sound my damn self. At the door I took in a breath, held it, then barreled inside, the door giving away to my hurtling body.

"The fuck," the Dalton exclaimed. His pants were down around his ankles and he was standing at the rear of a bed in his woven Ralph Lauren boxers. The girl on it, Gladys I was happy to see, had been polishing his knob with gusto, I lasciviously imagined.

He whipped around and bent to reach the Glock he'd put atop a mini-fridge. Fortunately his pants situation impeded his movement just enough for me to reach him and crack him on the skull with the Mag flashlight I'd bought earlier. It was the type the cops used to open up a fool's cranium; made that more efficient what with the D batteries I'd also bought and loaded in it. He sagged some, getting his arms around me, cursing a streak. He smelled heavy of marijuana. I hit him again on the head. This time he dropped like a Kardashian on a free diamond.

"Come on, Gladys, your auntie sent me." She was fully dressed so there was that too in my favor.

"Okay," she said. I liked that about meth heads. They could be reasonable and compliant depending on what phase of their high they were in.

Deny the addict their want, now that was a different matter. Naturally I had the concerned homeowner to deal with back in the hallway.

"What the fuck's going on here?" He was using a crutch to get around. Where the hell had that come from?

I beamed the light on his haggard face. He might not have been older than me but it was hard to tell. "Didn't I tell you I was inspecting?"

Before he could get further I took hold of the crutch and yanking it from under his arm, upended the man. I then hit him with his implement a few times, busting it apart. Yeah, what a motherfucker I am, beating on the handicapped. But I didn't have time to be PC.

"I'm'a get you, nigga," he whined but didn't get up as we hurried past him.

Nobody else messed with us as the curious invaded the hallway. We got outside and back in my car. I had duct-taped over the plates, my other purchase at the hardware store. There might have been an energetic druggie up in here and I didn't want to tempt fate. We blew out of there. A few blocks away, I stopped, took off the tape so as not to draw a sheriff deputy's ire—as they patrolled this part of the county—and got back in my car.

"Can we get some spaghetti? I haven't had any in a long time." That was the first words she'd said after sitting in the Challenger for several minutes.

"Sure, we can get some spaghetti, Gladys." And we did. I also delivered her to Sylvia and the grateful aunt—who turned out to be a well-known state rep, a congresswoman who was a leading member of the Black Caucus. Not an hour later, I was on the other side of town as rush hour arrived. I parked at a meter near the modest storefront of Carthy Watch Repair and Sales on Beverly Boulevard a block and a half west of Fairfax Avenue. This was the edge as it were of the Fairfax District, the traditional Jewish section of Los Angeles. These days, not too many miles south on that street it became the Little Ethiopia section. Too, the Farmer's Market and the conjoined Grove were nearby. The former was an old school establishment of open-air stalls ranging from kosher butchers and Mexican eateries to wine and beer bars. Old timers and hipsters would gather in the middle near the tables and chairs to eat and shoot the breeze. The Market led into the Grove. It was one of those sprawls of numerous anchor stores, paeans to consumerism. Their facades had the look of small-town America by way of Disney, made complete with a trolley that tooted past the stores.

Stepping to the shop, I reflected that over the years I'd heard of the proprietor, Mort Weisinger, now and then but hadn't met the man. I'd also heard his mother had been among the six thousand or so Lithuanian Jews that had been saved in World War II by the Japanese ambassador to that country, Chiune Sugihara. Apparently, defying his government's orders, he and his wife had put in all-nighters for a period of nearly a month in 1940 as the Nazis took power to fill out exit visas for as many of that country's Jewish population as they could. Over in Little Tokyo, there was a life-sized sitting metal statue of the cat. What else I knew was Weisinger didn't expect or desire a statue, plaque, or proclamation about his accomplishments. He liked to remain behind the scenes. Rumor was he owned this whole block of buildings through dummy fronts. The only reason he'd agreed to the meet was because Sylvia vouched for me.

"I'll have it for you by next Tuesday, Mrs. Ramirez," the seventysomething Weisinger was saying to a customer, a handsome heavyset Latina, as I entered. A clock like what you'd see on a crowded mantle under a glass dome was next to them on the shop's glass counter. All sorts of timepieces were inside the counter on display. Unexpectedly, I heard no clocks ticking anywhere, even though there were more along the walls and shelves, all running silently.

She thanked him and left. I stepped over to the counter as he extended a knobby hand. "You must be the other son of Jacob Kingman."

"Ellis Culhane." We shook hands.

"Hold on a second." He moved from around the counter and in the middle glass of the front door, turned over one of these plastic signs that have a clock dial with plastic watch hands on it. This announced to passersby he'd be back in twenty minutes. He came back toward me, pointing at a curtain behind the counter.

"Let's have some tea."

I followed the spry older fella in his baggy pants behind the curtain into a softly lit back area where there was a cot, a workbench, tools, clock pieces, and the like. There was already a kettle, which looked to be of another era vintage, heating on a hotplate that was so battered and worn it was a wonder it hadn't shorted out and caught the place on fire. He steeped the tea in the kettle and poured the liquid over sugar cubes suspended across old world–style tea glasses in metal holders. He handed me one and took a seat on the room's only chair, me sitting on a stool he'd dragged in.

I said, "I appreciate you seeing me, Mr. Weisinger."

"Did you know I know your mother? Knew I suppose since I haven't seen her once she retired to Vegas."

I was genuinely surprised. "I did not."

"Me, her, Sylvia, we were part of that fabled collation that brought Bradley to office."

"I'll be damned." Tom Bradley had been the only black mayor of Los Angeles. He was first elected in 1973. Well, second if you counted the partially black Pio Pico from way the hell back.

"Oh yes. Black folks out of the Ninth and Tenth Districts mobilizing, and us raising the money on the Westside." He sipped, a faraway melancholy enwrapping him momentarily.

"You ever drop around to her club?" I placed my tea glass on a nearby shelf.

"I did now and then. Great place."

Mom had run a joint called Hill's Hideaway where the likes of Redd Foxx would drop by to hear Ernie Andrews or Jimmy Witherspoon sing. There had been a husband, Hilly Bledsoe, but he'd dropped dead unexpectedly from a heart attack one day while stacking cases of beer.

"Did you know Hilly?"

"We went back a long way. When we were kids, we ran errands on the east side for the Solly Davis crew."

Solly Davis had been a lieutenant of Mickey Cohen.

He went on. "When it came to it, I'm the one who brokered the investment package for the club. No white bastard banker on Wilshire was going to give a brother like Hilly a legitimate loan. Shit," he sneered. "Now this was before he met your mother," he added.

Jake Kingman hadn't been an investor. But he'd dug that kind of music and journeying into the "jungle" made him never no mind back in the early eighties. I was the product of their affair together, even though dad was married at the time. I wound back to the present. "That's why you agreed to see me."

"Yes, among other reasons."

He didn't elaborate and I didn't press it. "I believe Sylvia mentioned I'm trying to find out if Kleener Lockhart is making moves to create his own off-the-books brand of the black-Jewish alliance."

"With whom?"

I told him and had more of my tea. It had cooled to tepid.

Weisinger was quiet for a time. He had one leg folded over the other and held his glass of tea in a relaxed manner. He finally spoke. "I do not believe this is so. Oh, I know Kleener is a man with vision, of that you and I will agree. But, and this is no offense to you and your family, young man, but he would not be doing such with Stuart Kingman. I suspect you know this too, deep down."

He spoke with the certainty of an oracle. Maybe he wasn't, but he'd convinced me. "You suggest I question the source?"

He stared at me evenly, crinkles appearing at the ends of his eyes. Those lines were like glyphs etched into his face before Pluto went cold. "More tea?" he finally said.

I had another cup and back outside I first called Stu's number. It buzzed but didn't pick up nor went to message. I next dialed Alicia's number. That went to voicemail and I didn't leave a message. I called her shop, the inner line, and also got no response. I called yet another number. Alicia and Markie, with seed money from our pops, had an enterprise that currently resided in Koreatown. It was a swap shop, one of those no-name places you had to know somebody who knew somebody to know where it was—as by necessity the secret location changed from time to time. They sold knockoff Kate Spade and Louis V bags, belts, scarves, and those sorts of accessories. They used quality material and seasoned craftspeople. They sold stuff like that Hermès bag sis was sporting this morning. The real ones went for twenty grand and they sold theirs for a few grand and still made bank.

Kingman Mattress trucks had been known among a select few to move contraband around, sometimes hidden in the goods. And now the daughter was making that contraband. There was something synergistic about that, I mused.

"Deedra, it's Ellis," I said when the line connected on my fourth call.

"What up, dog?" Deedra worked the swap shop along with Alicia and Markie.

"Have you seen Alicia around?"

"About an hour ago she was here. We had a new shipment of Oscar D to go over. But she left after that."

"Any idea where she was heading?"

There was a momentary pause. "Yeah, she talked to Markie over the phone about picking up something from Canter's and meeting at her father's house. Oh, I mean—"

"That's okay." Being the bastard son elicits awkward responses sometimes. "Thanks, huh?"

"Sure."

Our pops lives in a modest house on a narrow street in an area that's not quite West Hollywood and not the Fairfax District either. His wife, Rosie, passed more than two years ago and except for the commercials he still enjoyed doing, he wasn't involved too much now in the day to day of the Kingman Mattress empire. The street is permit parking and it was full up anyway. I parked a couple of blocks away and walked back. I heard female voices from the kitchen as I eased along the shrub-lined walkway toward the rear of the house. I came through the unlocked rear door. It wasn't like I didn't have a key.

"What are you doing here?" Markie snarled at me.

"Kiss my ass." I glared at Alicia. She held a plate with a pastrami sandwich on a kaiser roll set on it. The take-out container from Canter's was on the kitchen table. A small mound of coleslaw was heaped next to the sandwich.

Markie moved toward me. "Go home, Ellis."

Alicia looked from her to me. She swallowed hard. What was wrong with this picture? The dutiful daughter bringing dinner to her old man. Buttering him up, sure, that made sense.

Markie had her hand on my chest. "Didn't you hear me, motherfuckah?"

"Be cool," Alicia said.

Markie was efficient in the roughhouse department. She'd been an MMA fighter once upon a time before she got too banged up and became an EMT. But something about her trying to give me the rush rankled me. Too, we never did get along much. Before she could get that other hand on me and put me in a headlock or kick my shins out from under me, I took out the pistol from under my Calvin Klein windbreaker. The one Alicia got me last Christmas. The roscoe was the one I'd liberated from homeboy at the meth house.

I cracked her on the head with it, twice. I was getting to be a good head whupper. Sheeet.

"Dammit," Alicia said, sliding the plate onto the kitchen table. Markie had taken a knee, her elbow on the table for support.

"You guys okay in there?" our dad said from the front room.

"It's just me, pop."

"Oh, hey, Ellis."

"We'll be right in," Alicia said.

"If you try anything, I'll be happy to shoot you," I said to Markie stepping past her and taking a piece of pastrami hanging from the sandwich. They both stared at me as I ate it. I didn't think my sister would try and poison the old man outright. But this is where the bit about Markie being an EMT kicked my imagination into overdrive. Maybe they looked to give him a heart scare or something. Sprinkle a little digitalis or what have you on his chow. Hurry up his exit from the business so they could take over.

I didn't fall over or cough or anything like that once I swallowed. I did though take a couple of strips of the meat and put them in a plastic baggie. I'd have them analyzed later at a lab. I put the doped pastrami in my pocket. The other hand still held the gun. I figured just as they'd come up with a cock-and-bull story to keep me occupied, they'd told Stu some wild tale to keep him chasing his tail as well. They didn't want one of his sons dropping by tonight unexpectedly to say hi.

"Dad," Alicia called out. "They messed up the order. I'll have to get it redone."

"Sure, honey."

"I'll visit with you till they get back."

"I'd like that a lot, Ellis. Seems to me you and I haven't talked, really talked, like we should in some time."

A sullen Markie was at the back door and I took Alicia by the upper arm and squeezed hard. I leaned in and breathed, "From here on out, the old man gets the sniffles and I'm looking at you two. And don't think just 'cause we're related that will stay my hand."

For the first time in her life, Alicia saw me for who I was.

They went to get him untainted food while my dad and I had a real nice talk.

Doc's Oscar

Eddie Muller

The *mishegas* really started with the cat, but my version begins with Daphne's boobs.

Since this might be the last story I ever tell, I'm going to do it my way. After all, with thirty-eight pictures under my belt, millions in box office receipts, and a career that spanned more than four decades, I know a thing or two about what sells. You don't start with the cat, never with the cat—not when you can begin, believably, with a pair of nice, big tits.

Ever since I've been relegated to this *khazerai* wheelchair, Daphne has taunted me with her breasts. They practically smother me when she gets me dressed, or ties on the bib when I eat. She knows what she's doing and I'm not complaining, mind you. Far from it. Her bosom is something this wheezing old fart can look forward to each day. Sometimes I drop stuff on the floor, purposely, so I can get a bird's eye view of the Grand Canyon. That said, I dread the days she shows up with too many buttons undone. It usually means she's going to ask for more money.

"Mr. King, I've been working for you for two years," she said, the day the whole thing started. "Isn't it about time I got a raise?" It wasn't the first time she'd asked.

I replied with a variation on the spiel I've been using since the forties, when I produced a slate of pictures that made Majestic the most profitable studio on Poverty Row: "Listen, honey—you're here two years, still doing the same things I paid you for when you started. Am I right? Is it my fault I'm not falling apart any faster? I could live to be a hundred. If I gave you a raise now, for doing what you've always done, where do I get the money to pay what you'll cost once I have to be fed through a straw and have my diaper changed three times a day? When you've got more responsibilities, then we'll talk about more money. No offense, but what you're suggesting is what ruined this country—people expecting a raise just because they show up for a job they should be lucky to have."

I was about to tell her—for the hundredth time—about how my brother Maury fought professionally to keep food on the family's table during the Depression after our father died, but she was in no mood for it. "Your dinner's in the fridge," she said coldly. "I moved the microwave so you can reach it yourself. I'm leaving early."

"Look, don't be mad at *me*," I told her. "It's the facts of life. I gotta preserve what little time and money I got left."

She sighed, so deeply I thought she might pop another button. She stalked toward the front door. "Where's Jinx?" I called after her. "Did you already let him out?"

"I'm not paid to look after the cat, remember?"

"I'll call you if I need you."

"Don't bother. I've got a date." She banged the big front door behind her.

I like Daphne. She can get as moody as my late ex-wife and on certain days—like this one—she can be a pouty bitch. But mostly she's a great caretaker, full of good humor, clean and conscientious, and a damn good cook. She makes devilled eggs that are to die for. I'd trade my worthless brother in a heartbeat to have Daphne as my real family. Herman, the rat bastard, he's all I got left since Maury died ten years ago. I haven't seen Herman since then, although he sends the occasional card. Truth is, the older I get, the more Daphne seems like my nana—which makes it tough to hold the line on her salary. But I have to keep the budget in order, damn it.

When she started, Daphne thought she'd hit the jackpot. Caring for a rich old movie mogul, one of hundreds, if not thousands, who'd moved to Palm Springs to play out the string once the creative juice dried up. Living alone in a house that has panoramas of the desert and mountains in every room, big tiled swimming pool, lots of fancy-ass art, a ridiculous fountain running the length the entryway—it seems impressive at first glance. But all this shit's been here since I bought the place in '68—before I lost the Midas touch. Trust me, dicking around in the stock market is no substitute for counting a new picture's box office take on opening weekend. Not even close.

※

Daphne's dinner was good, as always. A couscous and vegetable thing, not too spicy, but with flavor. A decent piece of fish, too, if a little small. I used to eat nothing but buttery steaks and big desserts. That's over with. It's pitiful to reach my age and have to watch your weight. But if I get too fat to fit in this wheelchair, I'm finished. Given how much it cost, I intend to get every last nickel out of the damn thing.

I left the dishes in the sink and motored out to the living room. Jinx appeared, mewing to go out. He's been my buddy since wandering out of the desert five years ago, skinny and mangy and barely breathing. Now he's furry and fat and loves to go outside at sundown, when the air has cooled but the rocks and cement are still warm. He hops up on the ledge of the pond, eyeballing the fish in there as he trots along beside me. For both of us, it's the same routine, every day. I barely get the front door open before he bolts out, chasing some bird or lizard.

Suddenly, the door was shoved open, smashing my hand against the wheelchair. I yelled and jerked the chair forward but couldn't keep this lanky young guy from squeezing inside.

"Hey, wow—sorry if I dented your wheelchair," he said, almost laughing. "Holy shit. How do you like that? Wow, check out this place!"

He was in his early twenties, maybe younger. His clothes were lived-in and he needed to get reacquainted with soap and water. Otherwise, he looked like any young kid you see wandering the streets these days, even Palm Canyon Drive.

"I don't remember inviting you in, son. If you need something, let's discuss it outside."

"Nah, that's okay. I like it better in here. It's air-conditioned."

The squirrely eyes and twitchy movements reminded me of junkies on Hollywood Boulevard, back when we had an office right off Ivar. He ambled around, scoping the place. I motored after him. First chance, I'd call the cops.

He stood in the middle of the living room, examining the place like a prospective buyer.

"Okay, what's your story?" I asked. "Whatd'ya want?"

He thought for a moment before answering. "I'm living across the road, down in the arroyo. You can't see my tent from the road. Been here a couple weeks. Every night you let the cat out at exactly the same time. So, I figured I'd come over and say hi. Meet my neighbor, you know?"

"So you're only passing through. But before hitting the road again you decide to touch up the fat old guy in the big house for some spending money."

"Aw, man—c'mon. I'm only being neighborly."

"Can the bullshit, kid. You got a knife. In your pocket there. Right? You don't strike me as the gun type."

"Wow. You get right to it, don't you?"

"You broke in my house, kid. Let's not pretend this is a cordial visit."

"Man, you're cocky for dude in a wheelchair."

"Just don't do anything stupid. How much you need to get back on your way?"

"Hard to say. Not sure where I'm headed yet."

"Listen, I don't keep big money around the house. I got five hundred bucks in cash, that's it. It's in the bedroom, I'll go get it."

"No, no, no. You stay right where I can see you. I'm not stupid."

"That remains to be seen. For example, what exactly are you gonna spend this money on?"

"I don't know. Just living. Getting me to the next place, you know. Keepin' on."

"So . . . dope. Right?"

"Maybe. Some." He chuckled. "Maybe, yeah."

"If I was in your place, know what I'd do with five hundred bucks?"

He eyed me like I was a loon, even though I was about to offer him the best advice of his miserable life.

"I'd go to one of those outlet stores off the highway, where they sell the brand-name factory rejects. I'd get a nice black suit and a pair of decent dress shoes. That's what I'd do. Ever think of that?"

"And, uh . . . why would I do that, exactly?"

"A black suit gets you in anywhere. Any restaurant or club, you can walk right in—"

"In case you hadn't noticed, man—I got no money, not for that kind of shit."

"Well, listen, with a black suit you get a leg up in any job interview. You seen the way kids dress these days—even in service jobs? It's ridiculous. Black suit—you're hired. They're gonna pick you over anybody who shows up in jeans and tennis shoes. I guarantee it."

"Is that your pitch? Really? Are you kidding me, man?"

"How 'bout this—let's say you get killed breaking into somebody's house. You're wearing a black suit—*boom*—they can bury you in it. Your mother won't get stuck paying for new clothes you're only gonna wear once."

"Shit. You are some piece of work, man."

"Yeah, I've been told. Many times. Now, if you don't mind, how about getting the fuck out of my house."

"Aren't you afraid I might kill you?" He finally pulled the knife out of his pocket. A stupid little jackknife. He'd been squeezing it since he barged in.

"Why the hell would you kill me?" I scoffed. "You seem to think there's a bunch of loot in this place. Kill me, you don't even find the five hundred. Five hundred that I'd probably just give you anyway. Seriously, kid, you're kind of fucked-up. But you don't strike me as stupid enough to kill somebody. Not over a few hundred bucks."

That shut him up. He wandered around for a few minutes, looking at all the photos on the walls. I don't think he recognized anybody, but he got the drift.

"You were in the movie business?"

"I'm a retired Jew in Palm Springs. Go outside and throw a rock—you'll hit a Jew producer. A *former* producer."

"You make anything I maybe seen? It musta been a real long time ago, right? Like *Jaws*. You didn't make *Jaws*, did you?"

"No, that was another Jew. And I didn't make *Star Wars*, either—since obviously that was gonna be your next guess."

"George Lucas made *Stars Wars*. Everybody knows that."

"You ever see *Stranger's Serenade*?"

"Never heard of it."

"It was nominated for Best Picture."

"No shit! And you made it? How long ago?"

"Before you were born."

"You ever win one? An Oscar?"

"I got one right over there." I pointed. It stood out from the other awards on the mantle, as well as all the pictures of me and Maury and Herman, and the big portrait of our mother. The kid loped over and grabbed it.

"It's hella heavy! Best Screen Story, 1957 . . . Franklin Fuller. Hey, that ain't you, man. I'll bet this ain't even yours, is it?"

"The winner gave it to me. Meant as much as if I'd won it. Put it back, would you?"

He clutched it over his head, like he'd just won it. "I want to thank all the dumb schmucks I fucked over to get here," he said, grinning ear-to-ear. "I couldn't have done it without ripping off the whole bunch of you. Thank you all!"

"Don't jerk around. Put it back."

"I'll bet this is worth a lot of money, huh?"

"Now you *are* being an idiot. You're gonna steal my Oscar and sell it? How stupid can you be?"

"It ain't *yours*. It's Franklin Fuller's. Maybe he'd like it back. Maybe he'll pay for it."

"There is no Franklin Fuller, dumb-ass. That's an alias Doc used when he couldn't put his name on anything. I'm the guy who kept him working all through the fifties."

Dumb-ass looked dumbfounded.

"You never heard of the blacklist?" I asked.

"Nope. Don't care, either. Before my time."

The kid was starting to piss me off, acting like a tough guy. Dangling

Doc's Oscar, swinging it around like it belonged to him. I steered slowly toward him.

"No, you wouldn't know nothing about that," I said. "Why would somebody who's never worked a day in his life give a damn about something like that? C'mon—hand it over. That belonged to the best writer in the business."

The little shit twirled away, laughing. "Well, it belongs to me now."

I banged the chair into the coffee table turning around too fast. He laughed some more.

"Is this really your life, kid? Traveling around sleeping on the ground and stealing money to get high? That's it? That's a life? The guy who won the trophy in your hand wrote three novels and ten screenplays by the time he was twenty-five. Can you imagine? He supported his entire his entire family just by telling stories. Like fucking Hercules with a typewriter. And then a bunch of worthless shits decide he can't work anymore 'cause they think he's a commie—and a Jew, of course. But he kept making a living for his wife and three kids, signing phony names to the best scripts in town. So guys like me could go on making money, paying him while we had to pretend he didn't exist. Seriously, kid—put it down. You don't even deserve to touch it."

Oh, yeah—that hit a nerve. He stopped laughing and glared at me.

"You know what, you fat old fuck? Nobody gives a shit. About any of that. Nobody cares at all—except you. So if you want your fucking stupid statue back—pay me for it."

"Put it on the table. Put it on the table and I'll give you the five hundred. Then you can get the fuck out of here. Go buy your dope."

"Lemme see the money. Five thousand. That's what I want. Five thousand."

"Fuck off. Put it on the table. Right there. Then you'll get some money."

He set Doc's Oscar down. I motored closer. He opened the knife, as a threat. He looked surprised when I pulled five hundred-dollars bills out of my shirt pocket. Old habits die hard; I've carried five C's on me every day since April 30, 1945. He tried to snag the money, but I dropped it.

Dumb-ass went down to a knee to grab the bills off the floor. I hit him in the head with Doc's Oscar, hard as I could. The first blow just stunned him, but he lost his balance and fell into me. I moved my chair back about six inches, to get a better angle. The second shot, above his ear, made a crunching sound and the base of the statue actually sank into his head. He toppled onto the floor. I turned Doc's Oscar every which way, making sure it wasn't damaged.

Then I stared at the kid, in a heap, on the floor, not moving. The shock suddenly hit me. I couldn't believe it. He'd managed to fall with his head on my white berber carpet. Six inches the other way and he's bleeding on a tile floor. Easy as hell to clean. But this asshole falls so as to leave a huge goddamn stain that'll never come out. This fuck-up couldn't even die right.

I steered into the kitchen, Doc's Oscar still in my lap. I ran warm water over it to get the blood and gunk off, then dried it with one of the dish towels she always left hanging on the oven door.

About five minutes later I did the only thing possible in my situation. I called Daphne.

She burst in about twenty minutes later. To say she was stunned would be a huge understatement. When she saw the body she collapsed into the big leather recliner and sat there, silent, for almost five minutes. But she didn't freak out or start screaming, which was as a good sign. She finally said, "What happened?" and I told her.

"Write it down," she said. "Like you just told me. Put it all in writing, every detail. That way there will be some kind of statement in case you need it later. He was trespassing. You had a right to defend yourself inside your own home."

"Okay, yeah, I'll do that. In the meantime, what are we gonna do about *him*?"

"Do you want to bring in the cops?"

"Not really. What's the alternative?"

"I make him go away."

❧

That statement has been locked in Ben's safe for the past two years. I decided to take it out and read it while sitting *shivah*. I took care of him, all day, every day, since that night. At a certain point, his emphysema got so bad we had to attach the oxygen tank to the wheelchair. Around that time is when I moved into the guest room permanently. I became his mother, wife, and daughter, all in one. Think what you will.

Ben died on August 12, 2002. Chevra Kadisha of the Desert had him in the ground two days later. About twenty people, every one a show business old-timer, attended the graveside service. Maybe half of them knew Ben. The rest just show up whenever an old Hollywood Jew gets laid to rest. It's a tribal thing.

The *Los Angeles Times* ran Ben's obituary; I could hear him bitching—it wasn't nearly a big enough item for a man of his accomplishments.

Three days ago his brother Herman showed up. Turns out he was living all this time in Oxnard, just a few hours away. He was eating his third devilled egg when he finally got to the point of his visit. He managed to make it sound as dirty as possible:

"I guess there was nothing you didn't do for Ben," he said, "and that's why he left you everything."

"We became very close during the past four years, that's true."

"I'm impressed with how fast you got the estate settled. Very tidy work."

"We had an understanding. Ben was a very grateful, very generous man."

"Yeah, *right* . . . I suppose I shouldn't have expected anything, anyway. After all, to use Ben's own words—I was the good-for-nothing brother."

"I had one of those once. Although I have to admit—in the end, he was good for something."

About twenty yards away, in a slim bit of shade cast by the saguaro, Jinx dozed on a warm, flat rock. It covered the makeshift grave where I'd buried my brother, a kid so utterly worthless he couldn't even rob a fat old man in a wheelchair.

Herman squinted across the desert, then back at me, seeing nothing, understanding less. Before leaving, he helped himself to more devilled eggs and a few unsubtle ganders at my chest.

Just like his big brother—may he rest in peace.

Everything Is *Bashert*

Heywood Gould

**Don't count on your warhorse to give you victory—
for all its strength, it cannot save you.**
—Psalm 33

The rabbi vanished after the fourth race. One second he was there, a blue vein pulsing in his forehead, screaming, "Run, Handsome Harry, you *mamzer*, you *farkakter ferd*!" Larson was doubled over the rail, pleading, "All you gotta do is show, baby . . ." Franny had gone fetal under the chair, hands over his eyes. "I can't look . . ." Then Larson was jumping around like a kangaroo. "We won. The rabbi hit the trifecta . . ."

"It's a miracle, *Baruch Hashem*," the rabbi shouted.

Suddenly, no rabbi. It was as if he had run out from under his voice. "Where'd he go?" Franny asked.

"Maybe to cash the ticket."

Franny's sparse red hair was dark with sweat. "How much did we win?" he asked.

"We gave him twenty bucks," said Larson. "It'll be ten times the posted payoff." And poked Franny so hard his belly jiggled. "Didn't I tell ya we should hook up with him?"

They had been watching the rabbi for weeks. He was always first in line for the special train that left for Aqueduct every morning. Black suit, fur hat, even on the hottest days. Tall and scarecrow skinny with a scraggly beard and a bent back like an old man but he couldn't be more than thirty, tops. Always reading from a little black book, lips moving, swaying. Everybody else had their noses in their iPads or smart phones, on their handicapping apps. The rabbi just sat in the back mumbling over that book. At the end of the day he'd be first in line waiting for the train back to Brooklyn. People telling the day's sob stories, not him. "How'd you do, Rabbi?" somebody asked. He shrugged. "I'm still alive, *Baruch Hashem*."

The rumor spread that he was a huge winner. That he sent shills to collect for him so as not to draw attention.

"This guy's on a streak," Larson told Franny. "We gotta jump on his bandwagon." Next morning as they got on the line, Larson warned, "Don't spook him." He tapped the rabbi on the shoulder. "Good morning, Rabbi." The rabbi looked around like he was checking the weather. "Yes, it does seem to be a very fine day . . ."

They followed him to the back of the car. "These seats taken?"

He blinked like they were total strangers. "I couldn't say." They slid in across from him. Tried to show their expertise, talking about which horses were good in hazy weather, how the odds would change if it started to rain and how the jockeys would adjust. The rabbi listened politely, but seemed indifferent. Then, hurried off the bus without the traditional "good luck."

They hung around the two-dollar window to see what horses he was betting. He wrote his picks on a piece of paper and slid them to the clerk.

"Like he's slippin' 'em a stick up note," Franny said.

Larson laughed and poked him. "You oughta know." Then got serious. "He won't do business with losers. Flash some cash like you just collected."

Next morning the strategy seemed to have worked. The rabbi was beaming as they walked up. "Good morning, gentleman, a good day for the races, no?" This time he sat across from them. "So what is the sure thing for today?"

"The sun'll go down," Franny said.

The rabbi laid his finger across his nose. "Only if *Hashem* wills it, if you remember the story of Yehoshua Ben Nun . . ."

They got real friendly on the trip out. Larson knew which horses had won over the last few days and acted as if he had bet on them. The rabbi was impressed.

"I'd like to hear your ideas," he said. "Maybe we can pool our knowledge."

"I thought religious people weren't allowed to bet the horses," Larson said.

The rabbi stroked his beard and cleared his throat as if he were about to give a speech. "Our Talmud permits gambling if the person has a trade or a profession or another means of earning a living. Gambling is permitted on holidays like Hanukkah, where children spin a top for candy and gifts . . ."

"Roman soldiers shot crap for our Savior's clothes," Franny said.

Larson pinched Franny's handles so hard he almost jumped off the seat. "Wrong pew, bozo," he whispered and asked, "Can the Bible tell the future, rabbi?"

"Oh yes," the rabbi said. "*Hashem* has determined everything that will happen to us until the end of days. Like the sages say: Everything is *bashert*."

"Including horse races?" Larson asked.

"Yes," said the rabbi, "it is all ordained."

This was too much for Franny. "You tryin' to tell us you got the names of every horse that will ever win in that little book?"

The rabbi laid his finger across his nose again. "Not the names. The numbers. You see since *Hashem* contracted his essence to make a world for mankind he doesn't keep track of the comings and goings of every human soul. He controls everything by numbers, Gematria, we call it, and if you know the system you can see what his plans for the future are . . ."

"So you can tell who's gonna win the first race."

The rabbi studied the form for a second, then nodded. "Oh yes, but I can't bet. I'm waiting for a man who owes me five hundred dollars for some advice I gave him yesterday . . ."

"We'll front you a fin," Larson said.

Now it was Franny's turn to do the kicking. "You crazy?"

Larson pushed him aside. "Give you 20 percent commission."

The rabbi shrugged like he was apologizing "I prefer to be partners if that's acceptable . . ."

Larson conceded. "Can't blame a guy for trying . . . Yeah, sure fifty-fifty, partners . . ."

"So . . ." The rabbi studied the form, lips moving, then looked up. "Honest Injun," he said. "When translated into Hebrew the numerical value of his name equals fifty-four, which is a multiple of eighteen, which means life . . ."

Franny hooted. "Big deal, it's the favorite, goin' off at three to five."

"So what, favorites don't always win," Larson said. He handed the rabbi a crumpled five. "Go for it, Rabbi . . ."

The race was neck and neck all the way and ended in a photo finish with another horse, Popular Mechanic, finishing first. Franny scoffed. "Looks like even God can't deliver a sure thing." He was about to rip up the ticket when the announcement came over the PA. "Judges have reversed the results. The winner is Honest Injun."

The rabbi seemed surprised. "Did our horse actually win?"

"God corrected his mistake, rabbi." Larson said. "Wanna double down on the next race?"

"If you don't mind I'll take my share now," the rabbi said.

The horse had only paid $3.80 so Larson had to get change to make the rabbi's $1.90. The rabbi jammed a dollar in his right white athletic sock and dropped the change into his pocket.

"Who do you like in the second, Rabbi?" Larson asked.

The rabbi studied for a moment. "Tell Me No Lies," he said. "The numerical value of generosity and charity." Larson gave him another fin. The horse went off at 11 to 1, and ran away from the field, paying $56.50.

"Didn't I tellya," Larson said. "The guy's golden."

Franny still wasn't buying in. "If he could really do this every day he'd roll with a Ferrari and two strippers."

"That's how you would roll," Larson said. "Maybe he just gets off puttin' money in his socks."

The rabbi was poring over the form, pulling his beard. Finally, he took a breath and decided. "Seventy. This is a holy number in the Torah. The seventy names of God. Jacob took seventy souls when he fled Laban. Hebrews were chosen among the seventy nations to celebrate the seventy holy days. Septuagint is the . . ."

"Race is about to start, rabbi," Larson said. "Who you pickin'?"

"Gregory the Great."

Franny checked the form. "This horse has never run in the money . . ."

"He wasn't bushed, right, Rabbi?" Larson said.

"*Bashert*," the rabbi corrected.

After one false start, Gregory the Great bolted out of the gate, almost throwing his jockey, and was jammed against the rail in seventh place. On the far turn he worked his way to the outside and started to make his move, the crowd chanting "Go Gregory . . . Go . . ." Franny got a nosebleed at the rail and had to sit in the corner with his head between his legs. He waited until the race was over to look up.

The rabbi was shaking his head in wonderment. "Maybe it's because I said Kiddush for my father this morning."

"I've never won three races in a row," Franny said.

"Me neither," said Larson. "I used up all my luck gettin' back from Iraq."

The rabbi went off with his book and was back a minute later with a wild look. "The sages say signs are for fools, but I believe this race is a message to me." He held the form in front of him like a proclamation. "There are three horses whose numerical values represent victory and the power of faith and the blessing of Jacob on his sons . . ."

"Three horses!" Larson said. "Think you got the trifecta?"

"*Baruch Hashem* . . ."

And then the race was on. Their one and two horses jockeyed back and forth for position. Larson kept shoving Franny into the rail. "Go, go . . .

That's it . . . Yeah!" The three horse fell back, struggling—"I knew it was too good to be true," Franny groaned—but then with a burst of speed came out of nowhere to finish third. Larson hugged Franny so hard he had to push him away. "You're breakin' my ribs . . ."

"It was bushed, baby," said Larson. "Let's get our money."

There was a commotion at the twenty-dollar window, bettors waving tickets, track cops pushing them back. An ambulance, moaning and blinking, nosed up the ramp "Step aside, give 'em air," a cop shouted. The crowd parted. Franny grabbed Larson's arm.

"Jeeze."

The rabbi was on the ground. His black hat had rolled off, leaving his gray hair matted to his head. A ribbon of dark blood trickled out of his nose onto his grizzled beard. Larson, who had been a combat medic, shook his head.

"This is not good news."

The rabbi's arms were outstretched, the fringes of his prayer shawl spread under him like wings. Eyes wide open, staring at the heavens. A kid in a Yankee cap was telling anyone who would listen, "He was reachin' down into his shoes. Then he looked at me like I was gonna jack him. He's like, 'Are you Malcolm Movers?'"

"*Malekh hamoves*, it's Yiddish," an old man said. "He thought you were the Angel of Death."

"He grabs my hand like he's trying to say something. Then his eyeballs go up in his head and he drops like a tree."

A paramedic was giving the rabbi CPR, pounding on his chest, while another hooked up a defibrillator.

"Can they save him?" Franny asked.

Larson shook his head. "Nah . . . They're just grandstandin'."

A couple of jolts from the defib and they bent to speak to him. The rabbi didn't seem to hear. His mouth drooped and his eyes widened.

"I've seen that look before," Larson said.

Franny tugged on Larson's arm. "Did he cash the ticket?"

"Couldn't have. They just posted the results . . ."

"So he's still got it on him." Franny pointed to the board. "Trifecta paid forty-nine hundred and forty-three fifty. What's ten times that?"

"Round it off, fifty G's," said Larson. "Twenty-five G's for us. If he'd just waited twenty minutes to stroke out we'd be rich."

Franny shook him. "We are rich. We own half . . ."

"Who says? We don't know this guy."

"We backed him."

"Go tell the cops two deadbeats like us were partners with a rabbi. They'll laugh in our face."

Larson watched the paramedics lifting the rabbi onto a gurney and turned to Franny grim with determination.

"We gotta steal that ticket."

One who fell and died instantly, if he was injured and is bleeding and if the blood came into his clothes we bury him in his clothes and shoes.
—*Shulkhan Arukh*, laws concerning burial of the dead

The tailgate was slammed and the ambulance took off.

"These guys move fast," Franny said.

"They don't wanna hold up the betting," said Larson said. He grabbed a passing track cop. "A friend of mine got sick. Where's the dispensary?"

"There's nothin' here," the guard said. "Try Jamaica Hospital."

They found a gypsy cab outside. "How much to Jamaica Hospital?" The driver scratched his head under his turban.

"Stop tryin' to figure out how much you can take us for," Larson said. "We'll give you forty bucks. Forty-five if you get us there in fifteen minutes."

The driver peeled out, throwing them against the back seat. Franny banged on the driver's window. "Slow down . . . What's the hurry?"

"We gotta beat the vultures to the punch," Larson said. "The track cops'll toss him, then the ambulance guys'll turn his pockets out. I'm hopin' they'll be happy with chump change, but once he gets in the morgue they'll take off his clothes and find the ticket in his socks . . ."

They made it to the hospital in ten minutes. The ambulance was still parked outside the Emergency Room. Larson jumped out of the cab while it was still moving. "Pay the guy," he told Franny.

The ER was a chaos of squalling infants, tottering oldsters, nodding junkies, harried nurses calling names in the bedlam. Larson went up to a massive black nurse at the triage desk. "Friend of mine just came in here. A rabbi?"

She gave him a *say what?* look. "Friend of yours?"

"Good friend, yeah. We don't think he made it."

She went back to her computer. "Then he's in the basement . . ."

Larson took off, Franny huffing behind him. "Slow down you'll give me a heart attack."

They clattered down a flight of metal stairs into a long corridor, dodging wheelchairs and patients on gurneys, nurses and orderlies yelling, "Where you think you're goin'?" Then they hit a quiet stretch, past blank green walls, ending in a frosted glass door.

The morgue. No one at the desk, the room was empty. Larson ran to a bank of lockers built into the far wall and started pulling open drawers.

A young black man in a bloodstained hospital smock. A young woman, eyes bulging, mount agape in a silent scream.

"She looks scared," Franny said.

"People die with their last thoughts on their faces," Larson said. He yanked open another drawer. An emaciated old man, rheumy eyes, staring into emptiness. Franny drew back. "I can see why they close the eyes . . ."

Another drawer opened and there was the rabbi, hands folded. "Jeeze," Franny said, "with the beard and little smile he looks like our Lord and Savior."

The rabbi's pockets were turned out. "Tolya," Larson said, "they already searched him." He pulled up the rabbi's cuffs. The white athletic socks were still high on his calf. There was an unmistakable green bulge in the ankle. "Jeeze," Franny said. "We caught a break."

Shouting outside, rushing footsteps. The door burst open. "Stop!"

Larson slammed the drawer shut and stepped back, whispering. "Don't say nothin'."

The room was full of Hasidim, old and young, all in black, high hats, beards, braided sidelocks, jostling, muttering, with cries of "*Baruch Hashem.*"

A Hasid with a thick black beard, burning black eyes, belly bursting the buttons of his gabardine, came in, giving orders in a strange language. The young men started to fling open the drawers and found the rabbi. A gurney appeared. Another growled command and a few of the young men lifted his body.

"Where do you think you're goin'?" Larson said.

The Hasid bumped Larson with his paunch. ""We have a release from the Health Department to take the body of Eliezer Straubing," he said. "No offense to you, but for us this is not a clean place for our departed souls. No one can perform an autopsy on this body. No one can even touch him but *khevreh kadishe.*" He waved a piece of paper in Larson's face. "Just sign the release and it's out of your hands."

Larson shrugged. Nothing he could do. He signed. "Many thanks my friend," the Hasid said. He pressed a folded bill into Larson's hand. "And for your associate . . ." He dropped another bill in Franny's shirt pocket. Then took a closer look. "Are you Jewish by any chance?"

"No," Franny said, startled.

"Maybe a distant relative. You should check."

Franny watched glumly as they pushed the gurney, wheels squeaking, out of the morgue. "Knew it was too good to be true," he said.

"Ain't over yet . . ." Larson pointed to a note on the release. "Contact: rabbi Ezra Schuster at the Zemelman Funeral Home, 9950 Avenue Z."

"We got one more shot."

**It is a great mitzvah to visit a mourner, and is a kindness
to the relatives and to the deceased whose soul is also in
mourning.**
—Talmud, concerning the burial of the dead

Larson put five gallons in his mom's Civic. Zemelman Funeral Home was
an old taxpayer, crumbling brick, tattered awning on Avenue Z, so close
to Coney Island they could smell the ocean. Larson parked in front of a
fire hydrant. "Fifty-dollar ticket," Franny warned. Larson jumped out. "No
time to cruise around looking for a space."

Franny stopped him in the middle of the street. "Tell the truth, do I
look Jewish?"

"I seen fat redheaded Jews who look like you, come to think of it,"
Larson said.

Hasidim were milling in the lobby. Startled looks. Franny stepped
back, but Larson plunged into the crowd, "Rabbi Schuster, here?" Franny
tugged at his coat. "We're not welcome," but he pulled away and disappeared in a sea of black.

Around Franny, people were complaining, "He was a heretic."

"A *shnorrer* is what he was. He took all my money with his stupid system."

"Stole from my uncle in the 99 cent store."

Then Larson was back, followed by an old Hasid with a hunchback
and a long white beard. "This is my colleague, Mr. Quigley, Rabbi," he said.

Rabbi Schuster offered two black yarmulkes. "Please, put these on."
He led them through the hostile crowd. "This is very unusual you under-
stand for outsiders to come to our mourning," he said. "Not even other
Jews."

"Well, we were good friends with the rabbi," Larson said.

"Don't refer to him as *Rabbi*. It will cause much distress." More muttering men were clustered at the door of the reposing room. An old woman,
black kerchief over her head, was prostrate on the floor, moaning, "*Lazele,
mayne Lazele . . .*" Men with prayer books were rocking back and forth. A
chubby kid with tight red side curls sat kicking his legs against the chair
and crying bitterly. Two little girls in long black dresses, tears streaming,
were trying to comfort him. A young woman in a black headscarf with a
fussing infant on her lap, called "*Shloimele, Shloimele, kim tsu mir . . .*"

The little boy ran to her. "Mama, mama . . ."

"That's his widow," Rabbi Schuster whispered.

"Those kids, his?" Larson asked.

"Yes. Eliezer left no money. No one to take care of her . . ." He took
Franny's hand and walked him over to the widow. "Sima, look who came.
Friends of Eliezer to pay their respects . . ."

She was a kid herself, twenty tops. Delicate oval face like in Franny's grandma's cameo brooch. Like the Madonna and child, he thought. Tried to take her hand, but Rabbi Schuster pushed him back. "No touching please . . ."

"But I just want to offer my condolences," Franny said.

"You cannot speak to a mourner. Only if she speaks to you first."

"I'll speak to them, rabbi," the young widow said. The men moved forward, protesting; "Sima, you can't . . ." But she waved them away. "You were friends of my husband?"

"The ra . . . I mean your husband was a very good friend of ours," Larson said.

"From where could you get to know him?" she asked.

The old lady at the coffin turned with a piteous cry. "Oy, Sima. From the horses, where else?" She pointed an accusing finger. "You gambled with my son. Took the bread from my grandchildren's mouths . . ."

"It's not their fault, mama," the widow said. "They are afflicted with the same disease as poor Lazer . . . Aren't you?" she asked Franny.

Glittering blue eyes, he was speechless in the radiance of her gaze. Larson elbowed him. "Yeah, yeah, I'm afflicted," he said.

"Look how the babies cry for their papa," she said. "Doesn't that prove he was a good man?"

"Definitely does," Larson said. "Oh yeah, you can definitely see that."

She turned away from Larson like she knew he was a phony. "He was a very good, very kind man, but this thing was *shlekhtik*, an evil urge inside of him." she said to Franny. "He couldn't eat, couldn't sleep, ran out first thing so he wouldn't miss the train. He believed he had found the secret in Kabbalah. I told him: Eliezer, *Hashem* doesn't raise a man to wealth above the others with gambling. He said he had discovered the secrets and not even *Hashem* himself could stop him. That was a sacrilege, I know, but . . ."—she sobbed so piteously, Franny felt tears welling up in his eyes— "he didn't know what he was saying. He was sick like a drug addict . . ."

Rabbi Schuster took her arm. "Not now Sima . . . It's a *shandeh* for the *goyim*."

She shook her head, doggedly. "They suffered, too. They understand . . ." She turned back to Franny. "He went every day to the horses. Lost everything . . ."

"Lost?" Franny looked at Larson in astonishment.

"Still he went," she said. "He would find people to give him money, I don't know how with that crazy story. You gave him, didn't you?"

Larson jumped on it. "Yes, we gave him all our money." Turned to the widow for sympathy. "He promised we would win."

"I'll pay you back," the widow said.

The room erupted. "Sima, what are you saying? Think of your children . . . You are not obligated . . ."

The widow pointed accusingly. "You were happy to let him take the sin of sorcery upon himself, when you thought it would make you rich." The men shrank from her look of disdain. "These men were his friends. I want to make up for what they lost . . ."

"You don't owe us anything," Franny said. "We wo . . . Ow!" He felt Larson's iron grip on his arm.

"We could never take money from you," Larson said. "Your husband's friendship was more than enough, wasn't it, Mr. Quigley?"

"Ahhh . . . More than enough."

Larson pulled Franny out of the room. "Our condolences, if there's anything we can do . . ." Outside, he slammed Franny against the wall. "You nuts, blabbin' about winnin'? They'll search the body . . ."

"I can't steal from a widow," Franny said.

Larson slammed him again. "We're not stealin', moron. We're recoverin' lost property."

It is forbidden to open the coffin after earth has been placed on its lid. However before the earth is placed it is permitted to open.
—*Shulkhan Arukh*

Larson pulled Franny down the hall.

"We find an empty room and hide until closing," he said. "Come back and open the coffin."

"That's grave robbin'," Franny said.

"How many times I have to tellya? It ain't robbin' because that ticket belongs to us."

They passed rooms of mourners. Children everywhere. Boys with sidelocks, little girls in long dresses, toddlers underfoot. "They have big families," Franny said. "Like the Irish."

"That redheaded kid looks like you," Larson said. "Maybe you are a Jew."

At the end of the hall an elevator door opened like it was waiting for them. They slid in next to a plain pine casket. "Push B," Larson said. The elevator creaked and wobbled and opened onto a pitch-black hallway. Larson hit the flashlight on his iPhone. They followed the moted beam along the walls to a door. "Let's duck in here." A dank, musty room. Larson sniffed. "Uh oh . . ." Franny stumbled into something cold. Reached out and touched a shoe. "Jeeze!" Larson played the flashlight onto a porcelain slab. It was the rabbi, suit dusty, beard still clotted with blood. Franny crossed himself. "That won't work here," Larson said. "Check his sock." Franny rolled up his pants. His shin was bony and cold. Franny recoiled. "I can't do it." Wheels squeaking. Larson pulled him back. "Somebody's comin'..." He turned the flash on a coat rack in the corner, white shrouds stirring like ghosts. They ducked under it as the door opened and a white pine casket on a cart with a red plush cover rattled in pushed by two old men, gray scraggle, baggy suits. Larson shook his finger vehemently at Franny, mouthing "shut up." A work light sputtered over the slab. An old man walked to the rack and took a white shroud off a hanger.

"*Gut, gut,*" the other man said. They raised the rabbi off the slab and slid him into the shroud. Smoothed it down. Picked up the rabbi and laid him in on a white sheet in the coffin. Wheeled the coffin out, stopping to turn off the light. The wheels squeaked going down the hall. Their voices faded into silence.

Franny got up, "We're committing a mortal sin . . ."

"Not our first," Larson said. "Might as well be rich doin' it . . ."

One may not sleep in a house alone.
Whoever sleeps in a house alone is seized by Lilith.
—Babylonian Talmud, Tractate Shabbat, 151b

Larson opened the door and looked out. "Coast's clear . . ."

They followed the flash down the hall. The elevator bounced to a stop and opened. "Did you push the button?" Franny asked.

"No," said Larson, "did you?"

Franny backed up. "I'll take the stairs."

Larson pulled him in. "If you go a different way you'll get lost in the dark. Push two."

The elevator creaked open on the second floor. So quiet Franny could hear waves breaking in the ocean a few blocks away. Splashes of light rippled outside the rooms. Candles were burning at the heads and feet of the coffins.

Larson walked down the hall, counting "one-two-three," and stopped in a doorway. "This is it." He tiptoed to the coffin and raised the lid. The candles cast flickering shadows across the rabbi's face, making his expression seem even more peaceful. Larson lifted the bottom half. "Good carpentry," he said. "No nails, all dowels." He shoved Franny. "Whaddya waitin' for?"

Franny rolled the right sock down the rabbi's cold, blue shin. The roll of bills was folded around the orange ticket.

"*Halt!*"

"Jeeze!"

A little man came out of the darkness, pointing with his prayer book, screeching:

"*Shotan . . . Shotan gey avek . . .* Liebel . . . Mendel . . ."

Franny turned in a panic. "Where he'd come from?"

Two more old men ran into the room. "*Vos iz geveyn . . . Oy gevalt!*"

Larson lowered his head and flapped his arms like a giant bat. "Rrrrr . . ."

"Oy . . . Oy . . ." An old man fell backward, taking a lamp down with him. Another waved a prayer book, shouting, "*Shlekht gayst, aroys, aroys!*" Franny tripped over something in the hallway. Another old man, hands and feet flailing. "*Oy, mayn hartz . . .*"

They took the stairs running. Franny missed the last step and went down hard, twisting his ankle. Larson yanked his arm. "On your feet, soldier . . ." He lifted the iron bar off the door, pulled up the police lock and ran across Coney Island Avenue, Franny limping after him. "Wait up . . ."

In the car Larson was wheezing with laughter. "Didja see that guy go down? The guy with the book was so scared I could see his eyes in the dark."

"Fell over a guy," Franny said. "Hope I didn't hurt him . . ."

"They musta thought we were ghosts," Larson said.

He who is partner with a thief hates his own life.
—Proverbs 29:24

The guys at the Park View Bar and Grill couldn't figure it. Franny Quigley was usually the life of the party, chugging beer after beer, telling stories. He had a way of seeing the funny side of life, they said.

Not tonight. He had switched to vodka on the rocks. Sat at the end of the bar staring into his glass. Someone asked if he was okay. "I'm celebrating, can't ya see?" he said and they left him alone. After closing the porter found him passed out in a booth in the back and called Larson to come get him. "I never seen Franny like this," he said.

"He took a beating at the track," said Larson.

He shook Franny like a rag doll. "C'mon champ, wake up." Took him home and threw him into a cold shower with his clothes on. Franny came to, choking. "Hey whaddya doin'?"

Larson pushed him back under the spray. "You crazy gettin' loaded like that?"

"Don't worry," Franny said, "I didn't tell nobody nothin'."

"Hope not," said Larson. "I owe money all over the neighborhood. This gets out they'll all be around with their hands out."

They took the subway to the train. "Act like it's a normal day," Larson said.

"Hear what happened?" someone said. "That rabbi dropped dead yesterday. They found him with his pockets turned out."

They went to the twenty-dollar window to collect. The clerk ran the ticket through a machine. Asked for SSN and ID and ran their cards through another machine. Squinted at the ticket again.

"You act like it's your money," Franny said.

"He just hates to see anybody win," said Larson.

The clerk counted out four hundred and ninety hundreds, a few twenties, and some change and slid the envelope across the counter. "You'll give it all back," he said.

"Not to you, pal," Larson said.

They crowded into a stall in the bathroom to divvy it up. Larson snapped a Benjie. "Crisp . . . Right outta the mint."

"Never seen this much money before," Franny said.

They each got two hundred and forty-five hundreds. "Flip for the chump change?" Larson asked. Franny called heads and won. "Today's your lucky day," Larson said, grudgingly forking over the $45.75. "Wanna put a C-note on a coupla longshots?"

"Nah, I'm quittin'," Franny said. He wedged the cash into his right sock. "See if I can do somethin' useful with the money."

Larson poked him. "Better tell me what you're gonna do. Just to make sure it ain't conspicuous."

Franny went to the door. "Don't worry, nobody'll know . . ."

Larson grabbed his collar and twisted it around his throat. "Better tell me . . ."

Franny boxed Larson's ears. Gouged his eyes. Put two hands against his chest and pushed hard. Larson slipped on the slimy floor and had to grab a sink to keep from going down.

"Krav Maga," Franny said. "I seen it on YouTube."

If you steal you sin not against things but against the invisible human spirit that hovers over them.
—Samson Raphael Hirsch, *Choreb*, Chapter 49

The ride to Coney Island was long enough for Franny to suffer over every petty chisel he had ever pulled. Boosting candy from the grocery store, grabbing a drunk's backpack in the park, putting twigs in a bag and telling some kids it was marijuana. Stealing an old lady's purse while she dozed trustingly next to him on the subway, that was the worst . . .

Zemelman's Funeral Home was dark, door locked. A card in the door window gave an address in Crown Heights for "Eliezer Straubing."

Franny took the train to Utica Avenue. He was Brooklyn born, but this neighborhood was like a foreign country. Reggae music coming out of "jerk" cafés. African women in vivid print dresses and headscarves. Hasidim were a black-and-white stream flowing through this riot of color. Gesturing, bickering, carrying prayer books and little blue bags with gold Hebrew letters. Mothers and little kids tagging behind.

He found the building on Rogers Avenue. The Puerto Rican super followed him to the elevator, lobby, keys jangling. "I'm paying a condolence call on the Straubings," he said.

"Elevator don't work on Shabbat," super said. "Six E."

He had to stop twice on the stairs, sucking wind, his heart pounding. Funny if I dropped dead like the rabbi with the money in my sock, he thought. Voices behind closed doors, weird smell like disinfectant. The door to 6E was ajar, but he tapped timidly. Rabbi Schuster got up from a couch in the living room, shaking his head. "This is the Sabbath, we don't receive visitors . . ."

He put his foot in the door. "Rabbi, look, I know I caused a little disturbance yesterday, but I have to speak to Mrs. Straubing . . ."

"Absolutely impossible. She is having a difficult time . . ."

"I got a way to make it a lot easier," he pleaded. "Trust me, Rabbi. Give me a minute alone with her, you'll see I'm telling the truth."

Was that a smile? The rabbi seemed to understand. "Come with me . . ." Franny put his finger to his lips and touched the mezzuzah on the door. The rabbi watched, eyebrows raised.

"The people who lived in my apartment before me were Jewish," Franny explained. "I always kiss it for luck . . ." He found the yarmulke from the day before in his pocket and put it on. The few mourners looked up in surprise as he followed the rabbi through the living room to the bedroom. The widow was sitting by the window, sun glowing on her tear-stained face. He took the envelope out of his sock. "Mrs. Straubing, I know nothing can make up for the loss of your husband, but please accept this . . ."

She dropped the envelope like it was a hot potato. "My God, no!"

"It's okay, Mrs. Straubing," Franny said. "It's the money your husband won at the track yesterday. Twenty-five thousand dollars."

"We can't touch money or even talk about it on the Sabbath," Rabbi Schuster said.

"My bad . . ." Franny put the envelope on the dresser and dropped on his knees in front of the widow. "Please let me try to explain this to you," he said. She looked away then turned, her eyes searching his. "They say horse-playing is a science, but it's pure luck. Most people win just enough to keep their hopes up. But when you go for years like your husband—like my friend and me—without picking a winner, you start to believe that God, is punishing you. It's bad enough if you're a loser in life, but if even God is against you what chance do you have?"

"He's right," she said to Rabbi Schuster. "This is the way Lazer felt."

"But God gave your husband much happiness, yesterday," Franny said. "He picked every winner, even a trifecta. It's like God was saying, I haven't forsaken you, Eliezer . . ."

She shuddered and covered her eyes, tears trickling through her fingers. "Was he happy? Was my Lazer finally happy on his last day?"

"He was overjoyed, Mrs. Straubing. You should have seen him. He spread out his arms like an angel . . . It's a miracle, he said. *Baruch Hashem* . . ."

The widow squeezed Franny's hand in a febrile grasp, her eyes big. "Evil spirits tried to take his soul last night, but the *shomrim* defeated them with prayer. Everyone says this proves he was a *lamed-vovnik*, one of the thirty-six righteous men . . ." She shone with pride. "In death my husband finally has found honor . . ."

**Praise the bride's beauty and the groom's piety.
It is permitted to stretch the truth and exaggerate so
they will be more beloved to one another.**
—*Shulkhan Arukh*

On their way out, the widow called to Rabbi Schuster. "*Er hot a yiddishe neshumah.*"

"What did she say?" Franny asked.

"She says you have a Jewish soul. And I agree. But don't be too righteous. Take a reward for yourself. Ten percent . . ."

"Nah, I'll just put it on a horse," Franny said. He shivered in a cold sweat of shame. "I gotta make a confession, Rabbi."

"Too many ears," the rabbi said. He walked Franny out into the hall, away from the apartment. "So . . . Confess . . ."

Franny swallowed the hot lump in his throat. "Those weren't evil spirits last night. It was me and my friend. We broke in and took the winning ticket out of Eliezer's sock. Almost gave some guy a heart attack. Didn't wanna hurt nobody, we thought the place was empty. "

"We never leave the departed alone," Rabbi Schuster said. "Keep a *shomer* or a watch-man to say prayers and protect. These are the men you saw. They are heroes today . . ."

Franny choked back a sob. "We're not bad people, Rabbi, I swear. But we desecrated the dead and stole from a widow. I know I must confess this to her . . ."

"*Sha, sha* . . ." Finger to his lips, the rabbi drew Franny onto the landing and lowered his voice. "Why add suffering to one who is already bereaved? This young woman believes that pious men fought off evil spirits to save her husband's soul. This is a better story . . ."

"But it's not the truth," Franny said.

"The truth! Every time I hear that word I know pain will follow. The truth is that you fought off the evil spirit within yourself to bring solace and wealth to a widow. The truth is what God put in your heart at the very beginning of time. The good deed he chose you to do."

It was like when he was a choirboy and would get chills when the voices rose up around him. "Yes, I see, rabbi, now I see," Franny said. "Everything is *bashert*."

The Drop

Alan Gordon

The van pulled up and parked three blocks up and one over from the club. The side door opened, and a young man jumped down to the curb and immediately started walking, never even acknowledging his ride. He wore a black blazer-hoodie combo over a burnt-orange tee with "SHALOM BITCHES" emblazoned on the front. Rocco jeans, skinny tight but broken in. Wouldn't stop him from dancing. Wouldn't do his balls any favors when he did.

He looked like a bastard child of Uniqlo and Express.

And then there were the LeBrons. Vintage, from his sneakerhead teens and the Cavalier days, but he busted them out again when LeBron re-signed with Cleveland. Air Zoom LeBron II's, mix of oranges and black, "FO SHIZZLE" on the back. Bought with money he made from dealing X in high school, hidden deep in his closet so his mom wouldn't ask how he could afford them. They were worth more now than most of his clothes put together, but no way he would ever sell them.

The club was on Steinway, converted from a long-gone factory. There was a line to get in. He pulled his ticket out along with his ID when he got to the door. The bouncer, a refugee from the Gold's Gym down the street, gave a long look at the ticket, which was legit, and a perfunctory one at the ID, which was not.

"Cool LeBrons," said the bouncer, tearing the adhesive off a wristband and wrapping it on him.

"Thanks," he said, and he went inside.

He guessed, no, he knew he wasn't the only one in there with a fake ID, but he also guessed he was the only one in there using it to make him seem younger. Twenty-three, it said. Twenty-three. Wasn't so long ago. Seemed like forever.

He paid too much for a plastic tumbler with too much ice and not enough Grey Goose, then wandered over by the dance floor, checking out the girls. The club owners had torn out most of the flooring, punching a jagged two-story pit into the basement, the stage at the lowest level. Smoke machines belched clouds which floated over the bouncing and writhing ravers. Lasers pierced the fog, changing colors and criss-crossing, strobes pulsed in sync with the synthesized bass drum. The DJ, a local guy on the rise, danced behind his fortress of consoles, headphones around his neck, conjuring forced euphoria with his index finger.

He sipped his drink slowly, watching the DJ and the crowd bouncing in the pit, then scanned the perimeter, looking for a likely target. There. Leaning against a column, also watching. She glanced at him, then looked away, then back again. The eyes he was searching for. Bright, and a little glazed.

He tossed back the rest of his drink, then walked straight at her, his eyes never leaving hers.

"You need to dance with me," he said, keeping the accent slight.

She gave him the once-over, lingering on the Roccos.

"Does that line work on other girls?" she asked.

"There are no other girls," he said, holding out his hand.

She cocked her head and held for a beat, playing the delay, pretending that her decision hadn't already been made, then placed her hand in his and allowed him to lead her into the pit.

Green fishnet top. All but the biggest fish would have escaped with ease. Underneath, the main event—a brightly colored bra with a field of stars emerging from orange, yellow and red clouds of cosmic dust, the whole affair trimmed incongruously with lavender roses. Slight, soft bulge in the stomach, not helped by the tight, black high-waisted shorts that made his Roccos seem roomy in comparison. Day-glo pink wig. And the inevitable Camel gogo boots.

"Like the outfit," he said.

"Thanks," she said. "Found the top online. The picture's from the Hubble."

"The what?"

"The big telescope in space?"

"Oh, the Hubble. So that's what?"

"It's stars being born. Get it?"

"You're a star being born."

"Gonna be," she said. "Rachel."

Maybe, he thought.

"Avi," he replied. That was a lie.

"Israeli?" she asked.

"Yah." That was true. Once. "How about you?"

"Hills," she said.

He gave her the once-over.

"Not Bukharian," he said. "Russian?"

"Good call," she said. "Born here, but my parents came from there. Back when everyone came over. Where you live?"

"Flushing." Lie. Keep them coming.

"Where do you go?"

"Was in Queensboro," he said. "You went to Hills?"

"Yeah. Going to New Paltz. Gonna get my Ed. degree."

"Went to a party there once. Knew a girl."

"Who?"

"Karen something. She graduated last year. I think. We didn't stay in touch."

"Oh," she said. "Got a girl now?"

"I'm hoping by the end of this dance," he said.

"Right," she laughed. "I'm not that easy."

"Never said you were," he said. "Boyfriend?"

"No," she said. "Not looking for one tonight, thank you very much."

"Maybe you'll change your mind."

"Come on," she said. "Let's just dance. No pressure, okay?"

"Fair enough."

But she did nestle into him more.

The music came down low, the bass hitting every other measure, a shimmering of tuned popping noises repeating over it.

"You know the DJ?" he asked.

"I saw him at Amazura over spring break," she said. "And he did a set at Electric Daisy last year. At Randall's Island. You go to that one?"

"Yeah," he said. "All three days. That was epic. At least until the cops busted everyone."

That was actually true. He was there for all three days. But he was wearing a different outfit then.

"Yeah, my girlfriend got caught in that," she said.

"She okay?"

"Probation, has to finish rehab to get clean. Usual shit. I felt bad."

"Why?"

"She was carrying my stuff. But she didn't give me up."

"Good friend."

"Yeah," she said. "The best. They won't let me visit her. Said I'm a bad influence. Sucks."

"Sorry," he said.

The lights dimmed and the lasers shut down. Near them, a group of girls' bras started flashing in the darkness. Rachel looked at them enviously.

"Mine's supposed to light up," she sighed. "But it isn't working."

"I could fix if you like," he offered. "I know about electronics."

"Could you?"

"Probably a loose connection," he said. "Of course, I must examine it closely."

"You just keep coming up with lines, don't you?" she giggled.

"Seriously, I could fix if you want, sometime when you're free."

"How do you know about electronics?"

"I work for my cousin. We do high-end sound systems. Installations in all those McMansions. Bukharians and Russians, mostly. The Albanians don't use Israelis."

"You do that one on Jewel Ave?"

"Which one?"

"The one where they put in the pink brick driveway."

"Oh, I know the one you mean. No. Wish we had, that place is fucking huge."

"You make a lot doing that?"

"Not really. My cousin pays cash, so I'm off the books. I'm trying to save for school. Want to go for business ad."

Like everyone else was, he thought. Everyone but him.

"My parents would like you," she said.

"Is that good or bad?"

"They're always telling me to find a nice Jewish boy. An Israeli would totally make them jump for joy."

He leaned over and put his lips by the pink polyester strands covering her ear.

"I'm Jewish," he said softly. "But I'm not so nice."

And that was the truest thing he said all night.

"Where in Israel?" she asked, pushing him back.

"Tel Aviv," he said. "You been?"

"No," she said. "I was gonna go with Birthright last year."

"What happened?"

"I was supposed to go with my girlfriend. Then she got busted. I have to wait until Probation says she can travel again."

"You must visit me when you do," he said. "We got great clubs in Tel Aviv. Raves, trance, everything, make EDC look like county fair."

"I thought you were staying here."

"Student visa only good if I'm in school," he said. "If I don't make enough for next semester, I have to go back."

"Maybe I'll have you come fix my bra for me," she said, and the idea sent her into a fit of giggling.

"Yeah, could be very lucrative new sideline for me," he laughed. "I'll do all the hot girls with electric bras."

"I'm not a hot girl."

"I disagree. Very pretty. Amazed you were alone."

"I'm not pretty," she said.

They danced in silence.

"I'm sorry," she said finally. "That was a shitty thing to say. You were being nice."

"Being accurate."

"Stop," she said. "It's okay. I'm not ugly, but I know I'm not pretty. Don't tell me what I'm not."

Then she staggered for a beat. He caught her.

"Thanks," she muttered.

"Starting to kick in?"

"Yeah," she said. "I tried to time it so it peaks with the Drop."

"How do you know when the Drop is?"

"The Drop always happens around midnight in this club," she said. "It's a thing."

"X or molly?"

"Molly," she said.

"Got any left?"

"No," she said. "Bought what I needed and took it. Didn't have enough to buy extra. I go up, I come down, it's over and I get a cab home. Cops can't search for what I don't have."

"Smart," he nodded. "I was looking for my guy, but he didn't show tonight."

"Who's your guy?"

"D-Mob. Also Israeli. Blond with pink streaks last time I saw him."

"Yeah, I buy from him sometimes. Used to. Heard he got busted."

"Shit!" he exclaimed, although he already knew that. "When?"

"Maybe a week ago?"

"Is he in?"

"I guess. He's not here. Maybe Immigration got him."

"Looks like I'm gonna need a new guy. You know anyone here?"

"You want molly or X?"

"Molly."

She chewed on her lower lip, looking at him. The music started to raise in volume.

"The guy I bought from wasn't my regular guy, and he took off," she said. "My regular guy I haven't seen yet. He's supposed to show, but I'd have to introduce you. And I don't know you."

"I don't need any right away," he said. "And I don't want to cause any trouble. So, fuck the molly. Get to know me."

"For real?"

"For real. I'm having great time dancing with you. I don't need anything else."

She smiled up at him, and it was a genuine smile.

It would have broken his heart had he given a damn.

"I could take you to him later," she said, wrapping her arms around him. "After the Drop. Just for the intro."

"What's his name?"

The DJ chose to land a particularly heavy chord at that moment. She said something. Sounded like Mel.

They swayed together. It was all they could do, all there was room for. The music kept building, and more dancers swarmed onto the floor, forcing everyone closer together.

The DJ had skills, he had to admit. The build was not too fast, not too slow, and had enough things happening to keep you wanting more. He liked trance music—that wasn't part of the act. It made him feel the way doing Ecstasy used to. It took away his anger when all he wanted was to lower his head and charge against every wall the world put up. Trance, when it was good, when it was done right—it was ocean waves rolling across a beach, and he was a pebble, rocking gently with each wave, never rolling too far away, feeling the rough edges get smooth.

He let the music carry him. In the middle of the crowd, in the smoke, in the lights, he was safe. His old crew not likely to be here, not likely to make him in the crush and the distractions, and even if they did, they'd think, Oh, he's back. He slipped back into it again. No surprise there.

His old crew. Transplanted Israelis keeping old connections going, breaking their promises to the Promised Land by coming to the New Promised Land. America, the land of milk and honey, his grandmother used to say, but she stayed in her apartment and watched the Hebrew and Russian channels because she was afraid to go outside. He wasn't. And when he was, the little yellow pills would make the fear go away. Yellow or blue or pink, some stamped with butterflies or eagles or anything that flew. The older boys recruited him when he was still in middle school, babyfaced cutie. It's no big deal, they told him. Cops don't care about the club kids, they're too busy busting crackheads in the projects. He'd carry the stash in his violin case, under the fake velvet padding.

No one looked inside a violin case carried by a nice Israeli boy.

His crew. Some went back, some joined the Black Hats, some went legit. And one died, Sasha, and that's when he fell apart and got put back together in rehab.

There were Israelis here tonight. That was the tip. Someone was bringing major weight, and he was going to find him, just like he found D-Mob, and he was going to make a new friend. Nothing else.

So, all he had to do was just dance, dance, dance. He didn't even have to pretend he was enjoying it. Not a bad deal, go dancing in a good club, decent DJ, a pretty enough girl pressing her barely dressed body against you, waiting for the Drop.

More than pressing, he realized, as she began to grind slowly against him, back and forth, the high-waisted shorts getting better acquainted with his Roccos. A standing lap dance. Well. He was using her, so why not? Fair play all around. The crescendo kept building, incrementally, inexorably, sudden bursts of machine-gun snare, and she was rubbing against him faster, harder, her breath ragged and irregular, the skin on her back hot through the fishnet, no one cared who could see it happening, and you could sense it was going to happen, happen to all of them squashed into the pit, a collective moan rising into a scream on the dance floor as the bursts of snare shot around the room, ducked in and out of different speakers, linked, coalesced into one last, long acceleration and the lights bathed the dancers in a purple glow and she looked up at him in a moment of vision and clarity and stillness and mouthed something, he was pretty sure the second word was "Coming," but whether it was "I'm coming" or "It's coming" he never knew and never found out because the Drop hit, a shift in the bass drum through the mass of giant subwoofers that reverberated through their bodies and she started convulsing in his arms, her eyes rolling back in their sockets, her head flopping back until it faced up to the lights that she could no longer see.

A woman's voice keened through the loudspeakers, an oddly ancient sound in a language he didn't know. Greek? Turkish? People were howling around him, but Rachel had gone limp, only the occasional spasm shuddering through her. They were jammed in on all sides. No room for her to fall. She was sliding down his body and the only thing he could think to do was to hoist her up and throw her over his shoulder.

He had to get her out of the pit, but there was no give in the huddled masses, no easy paths through the labyrinth. He pushed through, trying to protect her as they were buffeted about, his free hand scrabbling for his cell to hit the panic button but there was no signal, he was in a basement and the panic button was no good to him, no good to her, so he used the free arm to make a hole and claw his way through until he found a ramp, then steps and he carried her up to the bar and this time the panic button worked but even as he screamed, "Someone call 911!" he knew it was too late for Rachel, if that was her name, because the last spasm had already happened while he was still on the ramp and the breathing had stopped after that.

"What happened?" shouted the bouncer charging toward them.

"OD'd," he said. "You got something for that? Adrenaline? Anything?"

"This ain't no *Pulp Fiction*, bro," said the bouncer, but he made the effort, pounding on the poor girl's chest, blowing air into her lungs.

The savvier club kids were already slipping out, but then a swarm of blue uniforms shoved them back. He faded back into the circle of people watching the bouncer work, some somber, some cheering him on, counting the rhythm of the CPR like it was just another beat.

Someone must have told the DJ to shut it down, because the music abruptly cut off, triggering howls of frustration from the dancers below. Then a middle-aged white guy walked onto the stage, greeted by the soft clattering of pills and blunts littering the dance floor.

"I am Detective Walton of the 114th Precinct," he announced. "Nobody goes home until they talk to us. Get in line. Anyone tries to run or throw anything now, we charge you with all the shit we find on the floor."

After a period of shoving and confusion, two lines formed, snaking toward the offices that had been commandeered.

"Cell phones away!" shouted the cops herding them. "You can tell your mommies what happened when we're done."

"You can't do this!" screamed one girl. "We have rights!"

A cop stepped forward, grabbed her by the dyed faux-fur collar of her jacket, and shoved her face into the face of dead Rachel.

"She has rights, too," said the cop. "More than you got right now. So shut the fuck up and get back in line."

There was no more dissent after that.

He stood with the rest of them, back to the wall, waiting his turn. The guy next to him was sweating.

"Shit, shit, shit," he muttered.

"Keep it down," advised Avi. "You don't want to attract attention."

"Think they're gonna search us?"

"Maybe. They're not supposed to, but they're cops, so they don't give a shit right now."

"Shit. I am so screwed."

Avi glanced at him. Saw a version of himself from a few years back, wearing a thin, black Asos bomber jacket over a paisley shirt. He took a chance.

"I'll hold it for you while you're in there," he offered.

The other guy looked at him suspiciously out of the side of his eyes.

"Hold what?"

"Whatever."

"What makes you think—"

"Forget it. Go get searched. I don't give a shit."

"How do I know you won't keep them? Or take off with them?"

"Because I'm going in after you. I can't leave before you. I'll pass them back when you get out. That way, we're both covered."

"Why would you do this?"

"Don't like cops. Don't like how they're acting. Up to you."

The guy gave him a look.

"What's your name?" he asked.

"Avi."

"Israeli."

"Yeah."

"Where?"

"Holon. Near Tel Aviv. You know it?"

"Heard of it. I'm David. Keep it tucked into your waistband, right side, under the jacket."

Avi felt something pressed into his hand. He slid it under his jacket. He had been expecting maybe a couple of pills. What he got was a black vinyl pouch the size of a hero.

Score.

"Make some space," muttered David as he went into the office.

Avi nudged the girl on his other side.

"Wanna go ahead of me?" he asked. "I'm in no rush."

"Sure, thanks," she said, sliding by him.

David came out five minutes later. The girl went in.

"Hey, see you outside," said David, bumping chests.

He removed the pouch like a pickpocket working the subway at rush hour and sauntered out. Avi didn't bother checking which way he went.

The girl came out, looking relieved. Avi went in. Walton sat behind a desk covered with headshots of performers.

"ID," he said.

Avi slid it over. Walton looked at it, then held it up to the light.

"Gotta say, this is the best fake I've seen all night," he said.

"It's real," said Avi.

"I know who you are," said Walton, pulling out his cell. "I am now going to call someone. Watch the numbers that I use."

He punched in a number. Avi nodded when he got to the end. Walton put it on speaker. Someone answered on the first ring.

"Go ahead," said a voice Avi knew all too well.

"Got your boy here," said Walton. "Want to say hello?"

"I'll say hello when I pick him up," said the voice. "Full cooperation, understood?"

"Yes, sir," said Avi.

Walton disconnected.

"He's okay," said the detective. "Coordinated with him when I was with Narcotics. Good call sending you in here—I never would have made you for DEA."

"That's the point, isn't it?" said Avi. "Send in the guy who passes. No one expects an Israeli to be an undercover. At least, not outside of Israel."

"Okay, what can you tell me?"

"I'm going in long-term, trying to hook up with the Israelis running the club drugs over. They've been using Black Hats, Birthright kids, every crazy route they can come up with."

"And the girl was with them?"

"She was just a buyer. I was looking to get to her dealer. Then she OD's on me."

"Any line on who she was? All she had was fake ID and cab fare stuck in her bra."

"Said she was Rachel from Forest Hills, went to SUNY New Paltz and had Russian parents."

"Okay," sighed Walton. "That's a start, assuming the name's for real. May have to wait for Mommy and Daddy to start calling before we find out for sure who she is. Was. She wasn't with anyone? No crying girlfriends stepping forward."

"Not that I saw. Single girl out for a good time."

"Did you get her dealer's name?"

"Not sure, but you got the pedigree on the guy who was two ahead of me?"

"Why?"

"He had weight on him."

"Not when I saw him."

"He passed it on to me."

"You have it now?" said Walton, sitting up.

"Gave it back when he came out."

"I'm gonna send a squad to pick him up."

"Negative," said Avi. "Then he'll think I ratted him out. He may be my way in."

A momentary expression of disgust crossed the detective's face.

"He might have been the one who gave Rachel Anonymous her last dose," he said.

"Don't think so," said Avi. "She said the guy she got it from took off. Probably wasn't molly or X, the way it went down. So, some other guy was selling bad shit, maybe PMA, maybe a mix, and she couldn't handle it. You can't connect it to this David guy. All you get on him is weight, and that's probation if he's a first-timer."

"If it was bad shit, we could match the chemistry," argued Walton. "I could hold him until the ME gives us a tox report."

"Still can't prove it came from him," said Avi. "Anyway, he's ours. I found him, I'm gonna work him. Don't worry, he'll get lots of Fed time when I'm through."

"And what does that do for the dead girl?"

"Nothing can be done," said Avi. "We take down the network, we accomplish something."

"Until the next one comes along," said Walton. "Okay, I've kept you in here long enough. Here's that guy's address and number."

Avi copied them into his cell.

"Nice meeting you," he said. "You covering the Electric Zoo?"

"We'll be there."

"May see you there. Act like you don't know me. Okay?"

"You got it. Be safe."

"Do my best."

He walked out, looking like a guy with nothing to worry about. The stretcher with Rachel's body was gone, off to the autopsy. He hoped they let the ME know she was Jewish. Just in case the parents were religious— you never knew with the Russians.

As he turned the corner, there was a low whistle from an alleyway. He turned. David was standing there.

"What street in Hodon?" he asked.

"Fuck you," said Avi. "I'm done answering questions. I'm tired, and I'm going home."

"Hey, hey, hey, don't be like that, I'm sorry," said David quickly. "You did me a solid. I owe you. Need some product? On the house."

"Needed it at the beginning of the night," said Avi. "Don't want to carry anything now. Cops everywhere. I get caught, me and my visa get to fly home forever."

"Next time then," said David. "Let me give you my number."

They swapped info.

"How am I gonna know it's you?" asked Avi. "I know like a million Davids."

"It's Dahveed, actually," said David.

"What neighborhood are you from?"

"Bayside."

"You know what I mean. Back home."

"Jerusalem. Old City."

"You don't sound it."

"Been here since I was six."

"So, how am I gonna know it's you?"

"It comes through as Melech," said David. "King David, Melech Dahveed. You know any other Melechs?"

Melech. Mel. Rachel's guy.

"You're the only one," said Avi. "Cool. I'll give you a call when I go out again."

"Anytime, anywhere, I'm twenty-four seven," said David. "See you around. Cool LeBrons."

"Thanks," said Avi.

They pounded fists, then separated. Avi kept walking until he was certain he hadn't been followed, then doubled back to the van. The door slid open. He stepped inside and closed it. The van drove off.

"Well, that was a colossal waste of time," said his boss, sitting by a bank of monitors.

"I salvaged something at the end," said Avi.

His boss listened intently as he described his encounter with David.

"All right, I feel better now," said his boss. "You want the cover apartment or your real place?"

"Don't need the cover tonight," said Avi. "Don't have anyone to bring home."

"No love for you," agreed his boss.

They rode on in silence.

"What's eating you?" asked his boss finally.

"Girl died in my arms. We were dancing, having a little fun, and she was dying the whole time and didn't even know it."

"Guess we all are, kid," said his boss. "Right, home sweet home. Get some sleep. You can report in at eleven."

"You're a mensch," said Avi, yawning.

He jumped out of the van and went into his building. No one was in the lobby. It was 3:00 A.M. He went up to his room, tossed his keys onto the table and hooked his phone to the charger. Then he went into his bedroom and stripped down, hanging up the blazer-hoodie and the Roccos neatly, tossing the tee into his hamper. He put the LeBrons on a towel and wiped them down carefully.

It wasn't his fault she was dead. Rachel wasn't David's fault. Rachel was Rachel's fault. Just like Sasha was Sasha's fault, not his fault. He shouldn't have dug into his stash, shouldn't have taken so many, shouldn't have taken any without knowing what they were or how many was too many.

But try telling that to a ten-year-old who worshipped his big brother.

It wasn't his fault, but it was. And it wasn't David's fault, but it was, and there was a moment in the alley when he wanted to take the asshole's stupid head and smash it against the pavement until it split open.

He finished wiping his sneakers and put them into their box and closed the lid.

"Shit," he said out loud.

They were never gonna make it right for Rachel. And there was no number of dealers he put away that would make it right for Sasha. But there was no other course that would stop the anger. Well. There were two, but one was in pill form and the other came with a closed casket.

There was one thing he could do for Rachel in the meantime.

"*Yit'gadal v'yit'kadash sh'mei raba,*" he chanted.

He wasn't so nice. But he was Jewish.

Twisted *Shikse*

Jedidiah Ayres

Eighty years after Charlie Birger kicked the Ku Klux Klan out of his corner of Southern Illinois I got the swastika tattoo on my chest artfully reworked into a rose. Or a vagina. Or whatever the fuck it was. It wasn't a swastika any longer. Pop told me once that I was named after the tough old Yid and it felt like a betrayal to have put that shit on my body in the first place. I'd been a scared kid just trying to stay alive when I did it and it seemed like a good idea. Never did fit in with the peckerwoods in Jefferson City, but I never had much trouble from them either. Originally I thought I'd have it refashioned into a six-pointed star when I got out, but I decided that was pushing it.

When Kate asked me what the blocky, ink design on my chest was, I told her "cubist." When I asked her why she'd pawned my bubbe's Kiddush cup to buy crank, she told me it was "obvious."

She sang for an outfit called The Taoist Cowboys who were a regular attraction at Carl's, the bar where I'd been working for five years. When they'd take the stage all eyes would be on Saint Kate as she shook her skinny, Scotch-Irish ass and tossed her hair in ropey, red braids to the shitkicker stylings of the band the RFT had once described as Aerosmith reincarnated as a cow-punk cult fronted by the banshee of Haley Mills.

Don't think about it too hard.

The first time I noticed how turned on she was by violence she was sucking blood out of my nose. Wasn't busted, but that third turd from the left outside Carl's had landed a lucky elbow before turning to run. I'd reeled back, pulled my pea-shooter, let it spit, and winged him as he was turning the corner. He gave a comical yelp and his retreating form canted to one side, but he didn't go down.

Kate had her own bruise from the skirmish rising among the freckles beneath her right eye, and at the Cowboys' next gig she looked like a raccoon dressed as Courtney Love for Halloween, but damn if she didn't work it—compensating for the indistinction of the lyrics by forcing them through her puffy lips with gale force. The quartet of punks making a grab for the Cowboys' equipment outside Carl's hadn't expected the level of resistance Kate'd put up and all they got away with was a guitar. And a gram or three of amphetamines in the case.

"Whoa, whoa, whoa, nice shooting, Tex," she'd said, reaching for my pop-gun. "Lemme see that thing."

"Uh-uh," I snatched it away from her grasp.

"Well, I'd say you tried to miss him," she beamed, "but didn't quite. That was awesome. What do you pack?"

"Well," I said, trying to tuck the damn thing away again, "it's no Desert Eagle great big ol' pistol, I mean .50 caliber."

She didn't miss a beat, "No, but you're still a badass Hebrew."

I did a double take of both her recognition of the song and my tribe.

She stood on her toes, ran her hand between my legs and licked the blood trickling out of my nostril into my beard. "What kind of Jewboy likes country music, anyway?"

Her tongue in my orifice and hand on my crotch were equally exciting and off-putting. There was no denying the tightening of my pants, but I didn't entirely care for the implications. "What, you never heard of Kinky Friedman?"

That night she'd wrecked my bed. And in the morning kicked me in the head. Metaphorically. That Kiddush cup wasn't worth much to anybody else. I noticed it was gone about an hour after I noticed that she was.

But the cup held sentimental significance for me.

When I had gone down for selling crack to an undercover policeman, bubbe Malmon was the only family I had left. Mom split when I was a kid, Dad had died when I was in high school, and bubbe had taken me in. She was an old-school conservative and a good woman, but her progeny had given her plenty of reason to be ashamed. She'd hired me a good lawyer who got me a short sentence, and she'd tried to visit me in Jeff City, taken a cab all the way from the Delmar Gardens retirement community she'd moved into when her health declined, but I wouldn't see her. I was too frightened of somebody else making more of my ethnic heritage than I ever had.

She wrote me letters. Prayed for me. Died a month before I was released. I didn't get to attend her funeral, but I'd had that Nazi abomination on my body obscured before I visited her grave. The cup was all that had survived of her, especially for me, and I walked out of the lawyer's office holding it—the entirety of my earthly estate. My spiritual one as well.

If I didn't suspect Kate would get off on it, I might've hit her. Instead I just said, "Show me where," and followed her directions to the pawn shop where I paid more to get it back than it was really worth.

At their next gig, I helped myself to an amplifier and nobody said shit. They'd just borrowed one from those Hooten Haller boys and knew better than to complain. Still—they worked a cover of "Choctaw Bingo" into their set that night, and Kate'd shot a finger pistol at me from the stage during our verse. I was angry all over again.

Of course that had me worked up enough to want another go at her, but that night she'd brought another date. Big guy with a spider web tattoo on his, I shit you not, neck. I seethed a bit, but steered clear, satisfied to post the amplifier on Craigslist and wash my hands of her.

Right.

She was leaning on my car when my shift ended. Neck Tattoo was heeled behind her. "Hey, Charlie Malmon, I think you've got something that belongs to me."

"That how you see it?"

Neck Tattoo straightened up and joined the adults' conversation. "You want to give it back, or shall I just take it?"

Before I could answer, he dropped a cinder block through the rear window and was reaching inside. He claimed the amp and stood holding it while Kate shot me with her finger gun again.

She backed out of my way while I fished the keys from my pocket and opened the driver's side door. She spoke to me in a self-satisfied, taunting voice. "Charlie, love, you still want to fuck me?"

Neck Tattoo's eyes pinballed in his skull.

I did. "I do."

Her eyebrows arched as she licked her fingertips and slipped them down the front of her jeans.

God damn it.

I grabbed the tire iron under the front seat and snapped the asshole's jaw with a single swipe. I opened the passenger side door and she climbed in. We left Neck Tattoo where he'd dropped next to the amplifier. They both looked broken.

Not gonna lie, it turned me on too, but I didn't take her back to my place.

She still liked it rough.

Agony separates itself from ecstasy pretty clearly with a few hours' remove, but her scrapes and bites and tiny fists beating on me felt indistinguishable from her kisses and licks and probes in the moment.

Ten miles north of us the local government was showing its ass to the world in the second act of a totalitarian PR clusterfuck as cops in full army drag maced and shot rubber bullets at citizens assembled to express shock, hurt and anger over the shooting of an unarmed black teenager by a white cop, but it wasn't anything we were paying any attention to.

Instead I awoke several hours later on her futon surrounded by the cast of *Walking Tall* looking like they'd run out of cousins to fuck. The leader of the pack, a six-foot, shiny-domed, cut-off sleeved Hazelwood hick with pickup truck testicles, I have no doubt, gave me the stink eye and asked if I'd been fucking his little sister.

"Sorry, were you not finished?"

I didn't even see the kick, I heard it. Right in the nose again. I hope that at least I got some blood on his boot.

Through blurry eyes I spotted Kate in the corner of the room clenching her hand between her thighs.

When her brother looked over, Kate stopped touching herself and straightened up. "What do you want, Bryce?"

Bryce looked at me pointedly and acted cagey. Kate rolled her eyes, "What? Just say it, he's okay."

"I want you to go stay with Mom and Dad for a while."

"Well you can want in one hand and shit in the other."

Bryce wasn't hearing any of it. He told his crew to pack her some clothes and toiletries and they hopped to like good little toadies while Kate screamed at them that they'd better not touch any of her fucking stuff. Bryce grabbed her wrist and steered her into another room to talk in private. "You're going to. It's not a discussion. It's not safe in the city."

They were both yelling at each other within seconds and through the walls I picked up the broad strokes in Technicolor. Turns out the civil unrest of the night before had sparked a panic that the darkies were going to burn the city down, and every clear-eyed Christian should read the signs and flee to the southwestern borders of suburbia without looking back lest they be turned to salt.

"Are you fucking kidding me?" Kate said coming back into the room as I was pulling on my pants. Her refutation of the good sense her brother was preaching made me smile, which Bryce didn't like. He was right behind her and glared at me dressing in his sister's room. Kate looked in my eyes and addressed her brother with her back to him, "Be sure to tell Dad, I'm staying here 'cause I like kikes and niggers to eat my pussy."

Shit.

She had a thing, I guess, and getting me involved in violence seemed to be a big part of it. But fighting three big dudes at ten in the A.M. through a whiskey and cocaine hangover is a young man's pastime that I'd left behind in my twenties. To boot, as Bryce, or as I came to know him, Officer Schloegel, put it so succinctly, were I not to fuck off right the fuck then, I'd never fuck anything else ever again. The badge on his hip now visible and the butt of the Glock that his palm rested on inclined me to accept his plan.

I looked at Kate and said, "Let's not do this again," grabbed my shirt and walked barefoot to my car with the busted out back window and drove away, calling Kareem to come meet me before things could get worse.

א

"The hell happened to you?"

"I got laid," I said, wincing as I gingerly examined my once majestic, now probably broken nose.

"You got laid out."

"Yeah, well, that's a damn fine hair to split."

My friend laughed, but his eyes were sad. "I think you're doing it wrong."

"I've been told that before."

I'd met him before he was a righteous ex-con activist cabbie. Back then he was just another backslid-Baptist, rock-slinging, Florissant-cracker named Brad. We both did our time at Missouri State Pen, but, as he puts it, he came out belonging to something, part of a movement, and a friend of Allah while I was born with roots, ties to ancient traditions, a chosen people, threw it all away, and came out with nothing. Somewhere along the way Brad became Salami or Salih or Ali and I had to get that damn swastika wiped off my skin.

Somehow we're still friends.

Ahmed picked me up in his red cab at the garage where I left my Cavalier for repairs, and took me to the gyro place on South Grand for sustenance. Afterward he gave me his keys and wallet and we left his cab at his grandparents' house. Then he picked up the keys to their beige PT Cruiser and told them not to worry.

Overnight the eyes of the world were on our back yard, Palestinian activists on the other side of the world were Tweeting advice to St. Louis citizens for dealing with tear gas and police thugs—#Ferguson—and Abdul and his imam organized peaceful protests on the streets every night and staying on the lines through the chemical weaponry and skull-crackings, never raising a hand in violence or even defense and landing in jail anyway. My part was to drop him off at night and pick him up at the jail in the morning.

Part of me felt guilty each night for not being arrested right alongside my friend, but another part of me felt smart every morning for waking up in bed. I'd bring coffee and breakfast burritos and drive him back to his grandparents' home where he'd crash out for a few hours of sleep.

On our third time through this routine we caught a police tail leaving the station and the day after that there were strangers sitting in parked cars across the street from his grandparents' home in shifts. White-power activists started calling his job trying to get him fired, and harassed his family, following the elderly Baptists to the grocery store, to church and to bingo.

Hakeem quit staying there out of respect for the good people who'd raised him (though the intimidation tactics continued), and that's how my Tower Grove apartment became his new crash pad. Truth be told, I kinda hoped some of those "I am Darren Wilson" T-shirt-wearing dipshits had the sand to set up camp on my block so I could stop by and say hi, but a daylight drive by was all they ever dared.

Till that night.

𐤟

Kate was there. Of course. The *meshuge* cunt had just firebombed her own brother's house. That's the way the story was told anyhow. She'd shot a flare gun through the window panes of his kitchen window and it had started a fire that left some smoke damage, but was overall a pretty chickenshit little blaze. It wasn't the only attack on cops' homes in the area that week, but it was the only one that brought me any personal blowback.

She'd tried to burn his shit down while he was out upholding the Constitution and no one had been hurt, but a rag-tag group of self-appointed minutemen had been vigilant in their neighborhood watch and had followed her car all the way to my place.

I still can't decide if I think she knew.

She told me, she'd done it in retaliation for the coffee shop full of tired marchers the cops, her brother among them, had tear-gassed, forcing the panicked patrons into the blacked-out basement or out the back door into handcuffs. Shooting out her brother's window had gotten her pretty horny and she told me the story of her revolutionary actions in a feverish bout of reverse Taoist Cowgirl that chapped my hips.

I had the presence of mind to grab bubbe Malmon's Kiddush cup and secure it under a blanket with me before I passed out.

In the morning she was still there, and I felt a twinge of affection for the crazy bitch as she lay innocent in sleep. God knows it wasn't lust. I hadn't been this sore since the days of dry humping Reveka Weiss in junior high. Grinding my crotch into her ample thighs until I'd orgasm in my underwear, I'd often wake in the morning to find scabs on my dick where I'd bloodied it against the zipper of my jeans. No, she wasn't getting to me through my poor abused genitals now. Must've been my poor abused brain.

When I picked up Faruq he looked damn near beat. I got him into the car and when I tried to hand him his coffee he ignored it and shut his eyes, clutching his kidneys. "Just let me get some sleep."

"Listen, man, why don't you take a night off? Let me go in your place tonight."

Saddam did something then that I'd never seen him do. And he wasn't weeping, but a tear escaped the outer corner of his left eye. I didn't say another word the whole trip. I opened the passenger side door for him and helped him out and he put his arm around me for the walk to my front door, but we didn't get there.

They hit us three feet from the curb and had bags over our heads before I even knew they were there.

※

They rang my bell pretty good and drove around with us on the floor of a van. Somebody's foot was resting on my head most of the time. When they took the hoods off of us we were inside a parking garage and the side door of the vehicle slid back to reveal a cadre of grim, red-faced members of the Westboro Baptist farm team. Officer Schloegel front and center.

His eyes narrowed when he saw my face.

Toadie #1 noticed that. "You know this piece of shit?"

"Fuck yeah," Toadie #2 chimed in, "This guy knows his sister."

Toadie the First looked closer and recognition began to dawn.

The Grand Dragon spoke up. "What do you want us to do, Bryce? You want to have them arrested?"

Officer Schloegel thought about it for a moment. "No. Not going to be worth trying to prosecute some bullshit arson charge. No fun anyway. I'm insured. But I don't ever want to see these two again, you hear me? Teach 'em a lesson for me, would you, fellas?"

I tried to speak in our defense, but it was one of the faculties I was bereft of.

Officer Schloegel got in his car and when the sound of his squeaky brakes faded out, the junior G-men went to work.

※

They didn't kill us, but I, for one, wished that they had a couple of times. I could get dentures I supposed, but I'd never play piano again. Hell, I might not manage picking my nose. Busted mitts, swollen testicles, incontinence, broken ribs and a knee that would never bend again, but there's nothing like the loss of an eye to get your attention. Not like it fell out of my skull, but it never worked again. The light just went out. It was like God saying, "No more of that, dickwad. Straighten up. Fly right."

And Brad. Shit, Brad. He was in a coma for three weeks. Brain damage. Paralysis. I never saw him again. I just asked after him. His grandparents and some members of their church were usually around, praying for him. Waiting by his bed for him to open his eyes.

It was a month before I walked again, and the limp was conspicuous. But I'd had time to think. Time to weigh things. I saw faces when I closed my eyes. Eye. Brad's, Kate's, bubbe Malmon's, my father's and even the smiling mug of ol' Charlie Birger on the way to the gallows.

Charlie was the last legally hanged man in the state of Illinois and he's buried in Chesterfield, a twenty-minute drive my father took me on once on the day he told me about my namesake. Charlie was accompanied up the gallows by a rabbi and insisted on wearing a black execution hood rather than a white one so he'd bear no resemblance to a Klan member.

As much as I admired old Charlie's style, ours were not the same.

During the fall while the city, county and country held their breath for the grand jury to return with a decision on whether or not to indict a member of the power structure for performing his job with what some folks would say looked like a little too much enthusiasm, I bided my time, kept my head shaved to the scalp, and got a new tattoo.

Another swastika. On my neck.

I went to see the Taoist Cowboys one more time. Kate looked terrific, but I didn't. Nobody knew me. I'd cut all ties and was living off the pittance I made selling my possessions. Bubbe's Kiddush cup helped pay for the tattoo. And the grenades.

I started hanging around the shitkicker dives on the east side and deep South County until I spotted Toadie #1 one night at the Beaver Cleaver in Sauget. I got some information out of the bouncer and knew when to expect him the next week. Turned out his name was Charlie, too. Huh. We had some drinks and I threw the last of my money around and talk turned to the situation across the river and what troublemakers and thugs were gonna do when the grand jury decision came back not to prosecute.

We agreed, it was going to be bedlam.

I told him about my neighborhood watch initiative. Told him how I reported suspicious vehicles and neighbors all the damn time, but how the cops didn't seem to take me seriously. Nobody took a gimp with an eye patch seriously, I told him. He told me I ought to meet some friends of his and come out to their pre-Thanksgiving meeting, and I thought that sounded swell.

The next day I wrote two letters—one to Kate and one to Brad. I told Kate what her brother had done. I figured if it meant anything to her then she'd probably do something pretty fucked up in retribution, but I also suggested that she seek some professional help for her whole life.

In Brad's letter I told him that he was my hero, the man I wished I could have been and that he was right, I'd scorned my birthright and threw away every good thing I'd grown up with, but I that I finally had my own chosen people and that he was chief among them.

I threw both letters away.

※

Charlie picked me up where we'd agreed and he drove me out to a special meeting place in a barn on somebody's farm way the hell out in Pevely. It was a small group—six men in all. Bryce was not among them, but Toadie #2 and The Grand Dragon were both present, and after the Pledge of Allegiance and a prayer that I didn't know they took turns reporting their week's activities and observations.

When they came around the circle to my turn to contribute to the group, I struggled to stand on my gimp leg, but they waited for me respectfully. I told them that I was there on behalf of a friend of mine named Brad, only I used his Muslim name. I hope I got it right.

For a moment it was quiet enough in there to hear a pin drop.

All of them actually. I opened up my jacket and let the pins fall from the half dozen grenades I had strapped across my chest.

"*Shabbat Shalom*, motherfuckers."

All Other Nights

Jason Starr

When I arrived home from work I knew tonight wouldn't be like all other nights. Sarai usually had dinner waiting for me, the house smelled like brisket or flanken, and I heard the sounds of the children's laughter. But tonight there was no table setting for me in the kitchen and the apartment was silent.

"Sarai?" I said, walking down the long hallway, passing the children's room. "Sar?"

Now I heard my daughters' giggling from beyond the door to their room. We had nine beautiful children. My oldest son Moishe had a good job as a computer programmer in Manhattan, and his wife was pregnant with their first child. My oldest daughter Leah had married a good man, a jeweler like me, and had given me three healthy grandchildren so far—all boys. My other seven children lived at home with Sarai and me in a three bedroom on East Sixteenth Street near Avenue M. Three boys shared one room, three girls shared the other. The baby, Ellie, slept in a crib in our bedroom.

I went into the bedroom and saw Sarai was in her street clothes—long denim skirt, a gray blouse, white sneakers. This was strange because she usually changed into a nightgown by this time of the evening. I'd known Sarai since she was a teenager and she was my first and only love. She was thirty, okay forty, pounds overweight, and had crooked teeth and brown hair that was too long and too frizzy. I guess there was nothing special about her, but who was I to talk? A *zhlobby* jeweler from Midwood? I seemed to go up a new pants size every birthday, and I was forty-seven. Besides, Sarai was the mother of my children and I couldn't imagine life without her. Was not being married to a beautiful woman the most awful thing in the world? My father had been a complicated man, but he had a simple saying that I never forgot. He often told me, "Never complain to

Hashem about your life, because your life could always be better, but it could also always be much, much worse."

I sat next to Sarai on the bed, rested a hand on her soft shoulder, and said, "What is it, Sarai? What's wrong?"

She was sobbing so hard she couldn't speak. Her mother had been ill, had recently had surgery for diverticulitis, but the doctors had said she'd make a complete recovery.

There was no dinner prepared so I knew something awful must've happened.

"Is it your mother? I hope not," I asked.

She tried to speak, couldn't get enough breath, then said, "N—no . . . No."

"*Baruch Hashem*," I said. "Then what is it then, Sarai? Not something with the children, I hope."

She cried harder. Now I was seriously scared. Oh God, may Your name be blessed, hurt me, but please don't hurt my children.

"Who?" I wanted to shake her to make her stop sobbing. "What happened, Sarai? You must tell me. Right now."

"It's . . . it's Jacob," she said.

If my heart didn't stop, it almost did.

"Jacob . . . ?"

She nodded, sobbing.

I rushed into the boys' room. I knew I'd seen Jacob, but my panicked brain had to make sure. Thank God, Jacob was at the foot of his bed, studying for his Bar Mitzvah.

Maybe no father should have a favorite child, but I'll admit it, Jacob was my favorite. He was the boy I wished I had been at twelve years old. So kind, so considerate, such a mensch. My quietest child, but also my brightest. He was brilliant in math, at the top of his class at the yeshiva, and I expected him to work on Wall Street or in banking someday. I joked, what do I need with retirement funds? I have Jacob. I was happy Jacob was okay, but now I was angry at Sarai for causing such tumult.

Back in the bedroom I said to her, "What's the matter with you, causing such tumult? You almost scared me to death."

Still sobbing, she said, "You . . . you don't know."

"Don't know what?" I was annoyed. "He seems fine. Please, what is this, Sarai? Why are you causing such *mishegas* after I come home after working so hard all day? You nearly scare me to death, telling me something is wrong with my favorite son, and then I see that the boy's fine? Why do you do that to me, Sarai? Why?"

She stopped crying, glared at me, and said, "He is not fine, Izzy." She waited, then repeated it slower, "He is not fine."

"Look," I said, "I don't know what this craziness is about. I just saw him, in his room, and—"

"I saw blood in his underwear, Izzy."

Of course I knew what she meant, what she was implying, but I said, "Blood? What do you mean, blood?"

"There was blood. I saw it."

I stared at her for a long time, wondering if this was just her imagination, or if she was crazy. Women, they have so many complicated emotions, they couldn't be trusted sometimes.

"Okay, so you saw blood," I said. "Maybe he wiped too hard."

"I asked him, Izzy," she said. "He told me what happened."

"Told you? Told you what?"

"He said it happened at his Bar Mitzvah lesson this afternoon," she said, "when he met with Cantor Schwartz."

I already felt it in my *kishkes*. I'd known Meir Schwartz for years, knew his family so well. My children, they were friends with his children. I'd been selling jewelry to the family for years.

"You're imagining this," I said.

"He told me, Izzy. He said the cantor made him take off his pants and underwear, bend over his desk and—"

"Stop!" I yelled.

Ellie, startled, started crying in her crib, and Sarai went to hold her.

I knew if Jacob had said it had happened, it had happened. He was a good boy, he didn't lie. Did I feel anger? Of course I felt anger. Who wouldn't feel anger when hearing such a thing about his son? Did I feel guilt? Of course I felt guilt. After all, it was I who paid for the lessons with Cantor Schwartz. How could I not feel guilt for sending my son to the house of a pervert, a maniac, a monster?

But, mostly? Mostly I felt shame.

When Sarai was through quieting the baby she said to me, "We have to do something, Izzy. Meir Schwartz is a criminal, he hurt our child."

I had been sitting on the bed with my head in my hands. But now I looked at her and said, "You didn't do something foolish and call the police, did you?"

"No, of course not," Sarai said. "I'd never do such a thing without talking to you first. I was going to call you at work when I found out, but I thought it would be better to tell you in person, when you came home."

"You did the right thing," I said, and kissed her on the cheek. "*Baruch Hashem.*"

"But we have to do it now, right?" She was shaking with hysteria. "We have to call the police."

I grabbed her by her arms, below her shoulders and said, "Sarai, calm down." Then she turned toward me and I looked right at her teary, bloodshot eyes and I said, "You know we can't call the police, we can't call anybody. You know that."

Like me, Sarai had grown up in a strict Orthodox community in Brooklyn, and she knew what happens to people who make accusations, especially accusations against a beloved cantor. Cantor Schwartz was a Kohen, no less; he came from one of the most respected families in all of Judaism. People who make such accusations, they're shunned by their community, that's what happens. I knew my boy and knew he wasn't a liar, but no one would believe the word of a boy over the word of a respected Kohen. We couldn't go to the police; we couldn't even go to Rabbi Pearlman. I had worked for years to build the life I had—build a business, provide for my children, be part of a wonderful Jewish community. Did I want to ruin it all with a phone call?

"But . . . but we can't let him get away with it." Sarai was crying.

"We have to talk to him," I said. "Who knows the stories children make up?"

"You know Jacob doesn't lie."

"Maybe he doesn't think he's lying. Maybe Cantor Schwartz hugged him or did something else. Maybe it was misunderstood."

Sarai was shaking her head, sobbing.

I left our bedroom and returned to the boys' room. Jacob, his lips moving as he silently read the word of *Hashem*, looked fine. I wanted to believe he was fine.

I asked the other boys to leave us alone and when they were gone I sat on the bed next to Jacob.

"Jacob," I said. "Your mother tells me such a terrible story, but I know it's just her imagination, isn't it?"

I laughed a little, trying to make it into something funny, but I was feeling no humor.

Jacob was looking at his book, not at me. The behavior wasn't normal. He was always such a respectful child.

"Please, please look at me," I said.

When he did, I said, "This isn't true, right? Nothing really, right?"

"It happened," he said.

All I could think about was going to *shul* on Friday night, having to shake Cantor Schwartz's hand.

I stared at Jacob without blinking for several seconds, then I grabbed his shoulders and shook him, saying, "It didn't happen. Tell me it didn't."

Jacob, remaining remarkably calm during my outburst, said, "I'm so sorry, father. I couldn't stop him. I tried, but he was too strong."

"Maybe he just hugged you."

"No, he put his penis in me."

Still, he was very matter of fact, didn't seem at all frightened, but I knew he was telling the truth. I snapped out of my rage and felt nothing but love, compassion for my child.

Hugging him tightly I said, "Okay, okay," and then I stood up.

"What are you going to do, father?" he asked.

Leaving the room, I didn't answer.

❧

I walked to East Nineteenth Street, to Cantor Schwartz's house. Although he only lived about five blocks away, it was a cold night with a harsh wind, and when I arrived my face was numb and my nose was running.

Lillian, the cantor's wife, opened the door. I wondered if she knew what type of man she was married to, or if she believed the lie like the rest of us.

"Is Meir home?" I asked.

"Yes, please come in," she said.

Several of the cantor's children were milling around. The house smelled like boiled chicken, reminding me that I hadn't eaten dinner yet and I was starving.

Meir came to the door and said, "Izzy, what brings you here?"

Meir was stocky, gray, about sixty years. I looked into his eyes and saw the guilt.

"I have to talk to you about something."

"I'm in the middle of dinner right now, Izzy. Can't it—"

"No, it can't," I said.

Lillian was nearby, overhearing.

"Fine, okay," the cantor said, and led me downstairs to the office in his finished basement.

The cantor sat at his desk, but I remained standing.

"Is this about the bracelet I bought from you last month?" he asked. "I know I said my wife thought it was too big, but we had it resized here in Brooklyn."

"It's not about the bracelet, it's about my son."

Again I saw the guilt evident in his eyes.

"Oh, yes, Jacob, such a smart boy," the cantor said. "He's doing so well. And what a great natural voice. He could be a singer if he wanted to."

"He told us what you did to him today," I said.

"What I did?" he said. "I don't know what this means."

"My son is not a liar," I said. "If he says you raped him, you raped him."

Meir stood angrily and said, "Are you some kind of crazy person? Coming in here and talking to me with such disrespect?"

I hated him, as much as I hated Hitler himself. But I also knew there was nothing I could do with my rage. I was a good Jew. I didn't believe in an eye for an eye. Besides, he was a Kohen.

"You know there's nothing I can do," I said. "But I'm warning you, if you touch him again, I will do something. And for what you did already, the damage you've done to my family, *Hashem* knows about it, and you will have to live with that for eternity. That will be your punishment."

I left the cantor's house and walked home in the cold.

When I entered our bedroom, Sarai asked, "Did you take care of it?"

"There's nothing to take care of," I said. "It's in *Hashem*'s hands now."

For the first time in twenty-four years of marriage, my wife spent the night on the couch.

⌀

The next night, when I returned home from work, again no dinner had been prepared for me. This time I wasn't surprised.

I had a can of tuna fish and the leftover macaroni and cheese from the children's dinner.

While I was eating, Jacob, in one of the black suits he wore to the yeshiva, came to the table and said, "We need to talk."

"Okay, talk," I said, wondering what this was about.

"In private, right now," he said.

By his tone, I knew this was related to what had happened with Cantor Schwartz. Had the cantor ignored my warning and molested my son again?

I went with Jacob out to the hallway in front of our apartment and said, "Tell me, what is it?"

"Not here, father, outside."

It was another cold night and neither of us were wearing overcoats, but we went out in front of the building anyway.

"What?" I asked. "Before I freeze my *tukhes* off."

"I killed him, father."

I stared at him, then looked around to make sure no one was nearby. Then I said, "What? What are you talking about?"

He pulled up his suit jacket and showed me the blood on his shirt.

"I brought a knife to Bar Mitzvah studies today to protect myself," he said. "And when the cantor tried to pull down my pants again, I stabbed him."

"No." I didn't want to believe it. "You didn't."

"Yes, I did," he said. "He's dead, in his office at the *shul*."

"Please," I begged him. "Please tell me this isn't true. That blood, it isn't real. It's ketchup from the kitchen."

"No, it's blood," he said. "Cantor Schwartz's blood."

I wanted this to be a nightmare. I wanted to wake up in my bed screaming.

"Why, Jacob?" I asked. "Why?"

"I didn't want him to hurt me again."

"Do you know what's going to happen to you now? Do you know what's going to happen to *us*?"

"I'm sorry, father."

I slapped his face so hard my hand stung. He barely flinched.

"In the *shul* they'll find him, if they didn't find him already," I said. "The murder of a cantor, a Kohen, they won't ignore. They'll want justice. Did anybody see you?"

"I—I don't know, father."

"You probably left fingerprints, your hairs," I said. "You'll go to jail, we'll be shunned by our whole community, my business will be ruined. Why did you do this to me? Why did you do this to us?"

"I'm sorry, father," he said and ran back into the building.

Sarai still wasn't talking to me, which was a good thing. I couldn't imagine how upset she'd be if she knew what her son had done. I had to think, figure out what to do, and I couldn't be around her hysteria.

With Sarai sleeping on the couch in the living room, I had the bedroom to myself. I watched the news on TV, bracing myself for a big story about a murder of a cantor in Brooklyn. The rabbis dealt with most crimes in the communities on their own, but for a murder they would involve the police. It was possible that Jacob had shut the door to the cantor's office when he left, but wouldn't the cantor's family wonder why he didn't return home from work?

The next day was Shabbes. I checked the news on my phone all day during work in the Jewelry District in Manhattan, but there was still nothing about Cantor Schwartz. Was it possible that the body hadn't been discovered? What if Jacob only thought he had killed the cantor, but the cantor had survived?

I left work early and, before sundown, walked to the *shul* with my whole family. I had no idea what to expect at *shul*, but I knew it would be some kind of nightmare.

Right away Sasha Weinberg, a man about my age, approached me and said, "Hear the news?"

I braced myself, asking, "News? What news?"

"I'm surprised you didn't hear about it," he said. "It's Cantor Schwartz. He died of a heart attack last night."

"A heart attack?" My shock was real.

"Yes," he said. "Isn't it terrible?"

The whole *shul* was buzzing, mourning the cantor. During the service, Rabbi Pearlman had prayers for the cantor. I looked over at Jacob several times, but he was staring straight ahead, or looking at his *siddur*, obviously ignoring me. Sarai was behind the *mekhitzah* with the rest of the women so I couldn't see her reaction to the heart attack news. Meanwhile, I couldn't focus on the service at all, too absorbed in worry and fear.

After the service, I just wanted to get outside, for some air, when Rabbi Pearlman came over to me and said, "Can I have a word with you please?"

It was very unusual for the rabbi to ask to speak to me alone on Shabbes.

He led me to the back, to a secluded area of the *shul*, near some offices, and then asked, "Do you know what happened to Cantor Schwartz?"

I paused, thinking, then said, "What happened? He had a heart attack, right?"

"So then you don't know anything of this?" he asked.

"I'm sorry," I said, bracing myself. "What do you mean by this?"

"Your wife murdered Cantor Schwartz yesterday," he said.

I was stunned, of course, as this wasn't what I was expecting to hear. "Excuse me?" I asked.

"She was seen leaving his office," he said. "She stabbed him many times in the chest."

Was this possible? Had Sarai done it, and Jacob had lied to protect her?

"That's . . . that's crazy," I said.

"It's true," he said.

"But . . . but you just told everybody in the congregation that it was a heart attack."

"Listen, I know why she did it," he said. "But she's crazy, going around stabbing people. You have to talk to her, get her a mental evaluation, make sure this never happens again. And you have to keep this a secret now or your wife's going to jail, you understand?"

"No, I don't understand," I said. "If this is true, if my wife did this, why wouldn't you call the police? Why are you—"

"There were others," he said. "Let's just leave it at that."

"Wait," I said. "You mean you knew this was going on and you—"

"Listen, you're lucky your wife isn't going to spend her life in jail," he said. "You're lucky the community doesn't know what she did. Do you realize how lucky your whole family is right now? I'm doing you a favor by not making this all public."

"No, actually, I think you're doing yourself a favor," I said. "What about Cantor Schwartz's family? Do they know the truth?"

"They know nothing," the rabbi said. "He's already in the casket. They'll never see the body."

"So what's this?" I asked. "Your idea of justice?"

"Your wife killed a Kohen," the rabbi said. "She's the one who will have to face God."

"And what about you?" I asked. "Will you be facing God?"

I watched the rabbi walk away.

❧

At home, when the kids were asleep, I confronted Sarai in the kitchen, telling her what Jacob had told me yesterday and the rabbi had told me today.

"I'm so sorry, Izzy," she said. "I was so angry, I've never felt such anger. He did this to my child, my baby. I couldn't just sit back and do nothing."

"How did Jacob get blood on his shirt?" I asked.

"He saw me when I came home," she said. "I was so upset, he hugged me, told me it would be okay. He's such a mensch, after everything he went through, to care more about me than himself. Trying to protect me and telling you he did it, that's a real mitzvah. I didn't care if the body was found, if I went to prison."

"Do you realize what could've happened to us?" I asked.

"But it didn't happen," I said. "The rabbi said it was a heart attack. We got away with it."

I imagined Sarai, going into the cantor's office, stabbing him like some crazy person. This was my wife? The mother of my children?

"Murder's against Jewish law," I said, and went to slap her face but she moved and I hit her right in the nose.

Blood gushed but she seemed strangely calm, at peace.

"I'm sorry, I didn't mean to do that so hard," I said. "Can I get you some ice?"

"No, don't get me anything," she said. "I did a horrible thing in the eyes of God. I don't deserve comfort. I deserve punishment."

"Punishment is nothing," I said. "But guilt . . . guilt, Sarai . . ."

I didn't have to finish the thought because she knew what I meant. She knew.

❧

At Shabbes dinner, after the prayers, we ate the leftover flanken with cholent and *lokshn kugl*. Sarai was silent, her eyes bloodshot, her nose swollen. The children must've known why her face was swollen—they were smart children, and they'd heard all the arguing, all the fighting—but they didn't ask anything and pretended not to notice. Jacob didn't speak at all, looking at his food.

I missed the talking at the dinner table, the laughter. I just wanted more nights at home like all other nights.

I had two pieces of pound cake with vanilla frosting for dessert.

"Do you want some more?" Sarai asked.

"No, I'm full," I said.

I left her with the dishes.

I knew what I was going to pray for in *shul* tomorrow morning. God had always been there for me in times of trouble and tragedy. Tomorrow? Tomorrow I hoped He'd at least be willing to listen.

Something's Not Right

Dave Zeltserman

I could start this with when I first decided to kill Malcolm Pratt, but the problem is that I'm not exactly sure when that was. The obvious moment would be when I first received his letter, but I don't think that was it. I'm not saying his letter didn't have me seeing red. It did. And yeah, I'll admit that if he had been in the same room with me when I read it, I probably would've beaten him to death before I realized what I was doing. But even still, I think it was years later before I consciously made the decision to kill him. I might've at times found myself fantasizing about doing awful things to him if I had the chance, but those were really nothing more than harmless daydreams.

Even when I started sneaking away to a shooting range four towns over, I don't think I was seriously planning to kill him. Not even when I bought a 9mm pistol from a gangbanger in Bridgeport, Connecticut. I can't tell you why I did either of those things, but I'm pretty sure the idea of hunting down and killing Pratt was still only a farfetched thought floating around in my subconscious and not something I seriously planned on ever doing.

Maybe it was at the awards banquet last year. Pratt had sought me out to congratulate me for the success I'd been having, and when I looked into his round pink-scrubbed face, the lower half covered by his meticulously groomed facial hair, and saw the way he smiled at me in his innocuous, clueless way I realized he had forgotten about the letter he had sent me twelve years ago. Something about that bothered me far more than if he had remembered doing it. It was as if I was too insignificant for him to care about the torment he had caused me and he could just send me that letter and forget all about it as if it were nothing. I think it was then that the idea of killing him, actually killing him and not just fantasizing about it, took hold and became something real. But again, I can't be completely sure that was the exact moment.

Some of you reading this are probably familiar with my short stories and novels, and are naturally going to draw conjectures about me from them, and you'll think you have some clue about why I did what I did. You'll be wrong, but that's still your prerogative. Others of you who aren't previously familiar with my writing are probably going to assume I'm little more than a deranged psycho. I could be deluding myself, but I don't think that's the case.

I guess it's not too hard to figure out that I'm a writer, given that this story is sitting smack in the middle of a Jewish noir anthology. Of course, the other stories surrounding this one are fictional works, while mine is something very different. For now let's call this a piece of creative nonfiction, although that's not what it is. Some of you might be thinking I've written a confession, but you'd be wrong. Badly. If you have enough patience to read on until the end, you'll understand what this really is and why I needed to write it.

Since it may help to explain why things happened the way they did, I should tell you that me ever ending up as a writer was a long shot, at best. It wasn't that I didn't read a lot as a kid, I did, sometimes a book a day, although they were mostly pulp fantasy or hardboiled crime novels. Even with my interest in books, from early on I showed a strong aptitude in math and, later, computer science. My future seemed pretty well mapped out for me to major in computer science in college and then get a job in the industry, which is what I did. But I've always had the writing bug lurking inside me, and at some point I started fooling around writing short stories. It started out mostly as a lark. During those early days I never thought I'd get published. I mean, I was a math and computer science guy with an engineering degree who was only able to fit three English courses into my college curriculum. How was I going to compete with the more literary-minded English majors who lived and breathed this stuff and could quote esoteric writers I'd never heard of? I had no training and really no confidence that I could ever write anything worthwhile. But then something happened. Something very unexpected. I found my voice and started writing stories that I believed could be published, and when I submitted them I had a small amount of success.

All of my early stories, and really my first six novels, fit under the noir genre. These days publishers like to call every piece of watered down mystery and crime fiction *noir*, even when the story has a happy ending. They do this because they think noir is hip, and that if they slap the noir label on a novel it will help with its marketing. But there are no heroes or happy endings in noir. And there's certainly no hope. True noir is about the alienated, the hapless, the broken. Things start off bad in noir fiction and only get worse. Moral lines are crossed that can't be uncrossed and characters fight a losing battle to keep from tumbling into the abyss. The irony is that these very same publishers who are only too happy to hype any book with the slightest hint of darkness as noir wouldn't touch a true noir novel. And there's a good reason for that. Most readers want happy endings. They don't want to be bummed out by following a noir protagonist to his doom. And the last thing they want is to get into the head of a borderline psychotic narrator.

You might be thinking that whatever drew me to writing noir is relevant to what ended up happening, and I guess you could be right, at least somewhat. To be clearer about my situation, I wasn't just writing noir but a darker and more twisted version of it called *psycho noir*, in which the protagonist's perceptions and rationalizations are just off-kilter enough to damn him to hell. Maybe that information could also be useful. I don't know.

Since this is a book of Jewish noir, I could also try to explain how my being Jewish allows me to better empathize with the alienated and disenfranchised, which are frequently characteristics of a noir protagonist. There might be a tiny kernel of truth to that. It's not much of a stretch to say that it can be hard to grow up as a Jew in a predominately Christian country and not feel like an outsider at times. But that would be a trite rationalization at best. I grew up in a nice neighborhood and was raised within an upper-middle-class family where there was never any question about my going to college, and while I might've occasionally run into people who hated me simply because I was Jewish, I certainly didn't suffer any deprivations or hardships because of it. No, my being Jewish had little to do with my attraction to noir. And when I talk about being Jewish I'm talking only culturally, because I haven't been in a temple since I was Bar Mitzvahed, which was twenty-nine years ago. The few times when someone has asked me what religion I am or whether I believe in God, I don't tell the person I'm Jewish. Instead, I say that I'm an agnostic, which is a white lie I tell because I don't want to appear to be an extremist by admitting that I'm an atheist. But that's what I think I've always been, even as a small child. The only thing that I believe that's waiting for any of us is a cold, endless abyss, and maybe that's a small part of noir's appeal to me.

Without being too convoluted about it, let me explain what really attracted me to noir, which might also give some insight into why I couldn't just forget about Pratt's letter.

When I first started getting my noir stories published, my cousin would always call up to make sure my wife was okay. Of course, he was only joking around, and I'd laugh it off with the big joke being that I must be as twisted and fucked up as my noir protagonists to be writing the stuff I was writing. And my wife would also always laugh it off when friends of hers would call up worried. She would explain to them that it was only fiction, and that I was a decent, gentle guy with a wild imagination, and I'd play along and pretend that that was all it was. The reality, though, was something different. I was able to write those noir characters as believably as I did because I identified with them. I understood them. As much as I'd like to pretend otherwise, they were a part of me that I was able to keep well hidden. They were who I could become if I wasn't careful enough. I know that something about me isn't quite right and that my cousin's jokes weren't as funny as he might've thought.

But enough of all that. It's about time I got back to Malcolm Pratt and the letter he wrote me.

As I mentioned earlier, I had some success right away with the short stories I was submitting, but my novels were a very different matter. I had a long, hard road with them where it took me nine years to get my first novel published. I would eventually see them all published, and once that happened they ended up getting a good amount of critical acclaim, but those early years were brutal. If I hadn't sold those short stories, I probably would've lost faith and quit entirely. As it was it was pretty dispiriting.

And now for how Malcolm Pratt fits into all this. After four years of my first novel collecting a thick stack of rejections, I read an interview with Pratt in a literary magazine where he raved about the noir author Jim Thompson, who in the 1950s and '60s wrote arguably the greatest psycho noir novels ever written. Pratt was a senior editor at the prestigious New York publishing house Harleston Books, and I got excited as I read his interview and thought I found a kindred spirit. I wrote him a letter telling him that I shared his sentiments regarding Thompson's writing, and asked if he'd be willing to take a look at my first novel. He wrote back to tell me sure, send the book over, that he was always looking for a good noir read.

This is what I got back from Pratt less than two weeks after I mailed him my manuscript (and yes, I've recreated his letter from memory, which wasn't hard since every word in it was permanently burned into my brain the same as if a branding iron was used):

> After your earlier letter I was expecting at the least a diverting read, and not the excruciatingly hackneyed and clichéd disaster that you sent me. Your inane plot plodded along at a pace that made me want to drive sharpened spikes through my eyes, your characters barely qualified as cardboard cutouts, and your dialogue was what I'd expect from a failing eighth-grade creative writing student. The only thing that kept me reading your "masterpiece" to the bitter end was my fascination over how shockingly bad it is.
>
> I know you must be disappointed that I cannot offer even a

single word of encouragement, but I can offer advice. Please, for the love of God, never put pen to paper again unless it is to compose a suicide note. Even that, I'm afraid, would end up as an unreadable mess.

Best of luck in your future career as a busboy or another such endeavor for which I'm sure you'll be eminently qualified.

Yours sincerely,

Malcolm Pratt

My wife knew within seconds that something was wrong. She must've read the letter over my shoulder. (I must've been sitting down at the time, although I can't remember that part of it. I'm six feet tall while she's only five feet two, so it would've been impossible for her to read it over my shoulder if I was standing.) At some point I became aware of her breath against my cheek, and then her calling Pratt a fucking asshole. I wasn't kidding before about seeing red. I was too enraged to talk and couldn't have responded even if I had wanted to.

"You should rip up that letter," my wife said.

I think I shook my head, although I can't say for sure. My wife commented how it would be counterproductive for me to ever look at that letter again. "He's a miserable human being," she said. "He has to be. You can't let someone like him make you feel bad. That's what he wants. Please, dear, just forget about it and let me throw it away."

I somehow found my voice again and heard myself telling her that I needed to keep the letter for motivation. I still remember how odd and tinny my voice sounded, almost like it was echoing out of a cave, as I told her, "Every time I feel like quitting, I'll read that letter."

That left my wife stymied. Even though I'd been able to hide the part of me that I needed to hide from her, she still intuitively knew that me holding onto Pratt's letter was a mistake, but she really couldn't argue with what I'd said. After all, she had always been my biggest cheerleader, and if I was claiming that I could find motivation in that letter, how could she argue with that?

"Promise me you won't dwell on it. Please?" she asked.

I promised her. And I knew better than to ever mention Pratt's letter to her again. Over the years whenever I felt bile rising in me because of that letter, I'd swallow whatever rant about Pratt I was dying to unleash, and I'd leave the room so my wife wouldn't see my face muddled with rage. A few times she caught me, though. Lost inside of my hatred toward Pratt, I'd hear her asking me what was wrong, and it would surprise me when I'd look up and see her face pinched with worry. It would make me wonder how successfully I'd been hiding that other part of me. I would always tell her that I was only working out the plot of the latest novel or short story I was writing, and somehow she'd believe it. Or maybe she didn't. Maybe she only badly wanted to believe it.

When I think back on it, I must've made up my mind very early on to kill Pratt, even if I wasn't aware of doing so. That must've been what happened, because I never told any of my friends about that letter, nor did I ever mention Pratt to any of them. That had to be because I didn't want any of them connecting me to Pratt's death, although there never would've been any logical reason for them to make that leap. It's funny how the mind works, because I swear I wasn't consciously aware of making that decision back then, even though early on I'd started plotting Pratt's murder.

Of course, I convinced myself that my plotting his murder was only a writing exercise and that the information I was learning would be used in my later crime fiction. That doesn't explain the extraordinary caution I took. Since I was working as a software developer back then, I knew that while I could scrub my computer clean of any history of web searches, those searches could still be maintained by my service provider, and so I did all my searches on computers at libraries several towns away from mine. I learned a lot about Pratt's routine and his background. If he had been Jewish, or maybe even another minority, I might've given up the idea of killing him, even though I hadn't consciously realized that I'd made that decision. But he wasn't Jewish, and he wasn't part of any minority. Instead he was from a wealthy, privileged family. He went to Yale, as was expected of him since four previous generations of Pratts went there before him, and since he had a trust fund he was able to join Harleston Books after graduation and not worry about the pittance that they paid him. What made my blood boil was when I read how he viewed it not only as his sacred duty to keep those that he decided were unworthy from being published but to do whatever he could to crush their spirits.

I soon found that it would be easy enough to kill him. Well, killing almost anyone is easy if you don't care about getting caught, but with Pratt I figured out how I could do it and get away with it.

Thanks to his grossly inflated sense of importance, Pratt had started what he called an Algonquin Roundtable for the twenty-first century, where he cherry-picked other *great literary minds* so that they could meet once a month for lively discussions. It probably would've made me gag if I had to witness these blowhards in action, but it gave me a window of opportunity every month to kill Pratt. Instead of meeting at the Algonquin hotel, they met at a restaurant on a quiet street in the SoHo section of Manhattan, and their oh-so-lively discussions would break up around two in the morning. While the other great literary minds would take cabs from the restaurant to wherever they lived, Pratt would walk to his apartment three blocks away. Once I started getting books published, I'd arrange for book events in New York so they'd coincide with these monthly meetings, and later those nights I'd find a quiet place to park along the route Pratt would use to walk home, and I'd wait for him. I could've killed him each of those nights except for two problems. First, I needed a car that couldn't be connected to me. As quiet as the street seemed at that hour, there was still a chance I could be caught by a hidden surveillance camera. And second, I had other things in mind for Pratt than a quick death on a Manhattan street.

The car issue turned out to be easily solved. Using a dark and secretive part of the internet called the Deep Web, I found what amounted to a matchmaking site for owners who wanted their cars stolen for the insurance money and people like me who needed a car to either chop up for parts or to use for a crime. The owner leaves the keys in the car and agrees to wait a day before reporting it stolen, while the thief agrees to make sure the car no longer exists after twenty-four hours. All this is arranged without revealing your real identity. The second issue of needing time to do what I wanted to do with Pratt resolved itself six days ago when my wife needed to go to Florida for two weeks to take care of her mom. At least I think it was six days ago. It's hard to keep track of time where I am now.

The timing of my wife's trip worked out perfectly as two days ago (assuming I've been able to keep track of the days correctly) was Pratt's last roundtable and I was able to arrange on the Deep Web site to pick up a car that same night in Hartford, Connecticut. The bitter cold weather and the snow were also perfect for what I had in mind. I left my home in Boston at seven o'clock and by ten I had my car parked in a garage in Hartford. By eleven I was behind the wheel of a beat-up Ford Taurus sedan and heading to New York, and by one I parked on a SoHo street that was along the route Pratt took to walk back to his apartment. I settled in to wait for him.

As much as the cold and snow worked into my plans, there was a chance that Pratt had cancelled his roundtable because of the weather, and I felt a knotting in my stomach as I worried about that. Yeah, I know, logically it shouldn't have been that big a deal if he didn't show up since I'd always be able to try it again. But that wasn't quite true. I would need my wife to leave town again on a night that coincided with one of Pratt's roundtable nights, and that might not happen for years. And before that could happen again, he might disband his roundtable meetings for good, or he could end up dying on his own. As I sat in the car worrying about all this, I realized how much I needed to be the one to end his life—and not just end it, but make sure he knew why I was going to kill him. I couldn't possibly describe the sense of elation I felt when I looked in the rearview mirror and saw him trudging down the sidewalk, his head bowed to protect against the cold and snow.

Even with him wrapped up in an overcoat, and a big Russian-style fur hat covering his lowered head, I knew it was him. He never saw me as I sneaked out of the car and crouched behind it. When I struck him on the back of the skull with the gun, I held back with the blow because I didn't want to crack his head open, but because of his furry hat all I did was stagger him. It didn't matter. He let out a soft *murrh* noise and took several drunken steps away from me before I caught up to him again. This time I knocked off his hat before hitting him a second time. Again, I hit him only about half as hard as I could've so I wouldn't kill him, and this time I mostly knocked him out. He was still making whimpering noises, but otherwise he wasn't moving as he lay face down on the snowy sidewalk. I used a plastic zip tie to bind his wrists together behind his back and then flipped him over so I could make sure it was really Pratt. His eyes were half open and glazed, and his mouth continued to move as he made his soft mewling noises, but otherwise he was out of it. I dragged him by his feet to the back of the car. He was a small man and it was surprisingly easy to lift him up and dump him into the trunk.

It took no more than thirty seconds from the time I first hit Pratt until I had the trunk closed on him. I gave a quick look around and the street was empty. Even if a surveillance camera had caught me in the act the police wouldn't be able to identify me. Even my wife wouldn't have been able to identify me with the getup I had on. Ski mask, bulky snow parka, ski pants, thick rubber snow boots. She'd never seen me wearing any of these items before. But even if I didn't have my face covered by the ski mask and that massive parka draped over my body, a surveillance picture wouldn't have done the police any good given the snow flurries and how dark it was.

I have to admit that for the first ten minutes my heart was beating like crazy in my chest over worrying that someone might've looked out a window and called the police, but by the time I reached the Holland Tunnel I'd calmed down and was feeling only a grim satisfaction with how things had gone. I still had a long way to go before I was going to be done with Pratt. A five-and-a-half-hour drive deep into the Adirondack Mountains and then several more hours of hiking, but the trickiest part of it was done. It was possible that Pratt could expire during the drive. Even if I hadn't knocked him mostly unconscious, he was sixty-eight and to me seemed like a frail man, and he was going to be spending all that time bouncing around in the frigid trunk. If that were to happen it would be too bad, but it wasn't worth worrying about. At that point it was out of my hands.

The drive to upstate New York went by faster than I would've imagined, especially with how much the snow was picking up. It wasn't blizzard
conditions, but it was still coming down at a good clip. It was funny how
these large lapses of time seemed to pass by without me being aware of it.
One minute I'd be driving through Poughkeepsie and the next it was as if
I was just entering Albany, and it seemed to go on like that the whole trip,
almost as if my mind was blanking out on me. Like I was numb and on
automatic pilot. Whatever the reason it made it an easy drive, and fortunately I had enough presence of mind to pull over for gas when I needed
it and to pay for it with cash instead of a credit card. I couldn't afford to
have anyone trace me to where I was heading.

It was a little after seven thirty in the morning by the time I reached
the spot that I had decided on months ago. The snow had picked up and
had made the roads treacherous, but it hadn't slowed me down. I guess I
must've been driving recklessly, as if I didn't care about anything anymore.
It was an odd way for me to be feeling. I already suggested how much distress Pratt and his damn letter had caused me over the years, but I didn't
mention all those nights when I'd wake up seething in my hatred for him,
or how for months I'd been obsessing about taking care of him this way. I
couldn't understand the sense of regret I was feeling. Maybe it was because
I had a premonition of what was going to happen. I can't say for sure.

Pratt's skin had turned gray, kind of like a corpse's, but he was still
alive and was fully conscious. He must've been both cold and scared out
of his mind with the way his teeth were chattering like one of those old
novelty items. I pulled him out of the trunk, dumped him onto the side of
the road, and then pulled him to his feet.

"Start walking," I ordered. As added incentive for him to head off
into the woods, I shoved the barrel of my 9mm pistol against the back of
his head.

He moved in a slow pace, which was probably all he could manage
with his hands bound behind his back and the snow already halfway up to
his knees with more of it coming down. With his Italian leather shoes and
the tuxedo he wore under his overcoat, he certainly wasn't dressed for the
hike in the woods that we were going to be taking. His shoes must've been
ruined and soaked through within seconds of trudging through the snow,
and he had to be absolutely miserable. Even though this is what I thought
I wanted, I found myself feeling a mix of regret and remorse. Before too
long I started trying to think of some way out of killing him. We hadn't
walked that far from the road yet, no more than half a mile. He didn't know
who I was and had no way of ever knowing, and it was doubtful he paid
any attention to what type of car he'd been thrown into. If I left him where
he was, he'd have a good chance of getting back to the road and having

someone pick him up, and by the time that happened I'd be long gone. I had just about decided to do that when he came to a stop.

"I'm not taking another step," he stated, his voice surprisingly strong given what I'd put him through. "If you want to shoot me here, go right ahead, but I think you're too much of a coward to do that."

I couldn't back down then, not with him challenging me. In a way it would've been so easy to just shoot him and get it over with, but I wasn't ready to make that decision. Not with the buyer's remorse I was feeling.

"This was only supposed to be a kidnapping," I said. "There's a warm cabin two miles further into the woods where I was planning to stash you, but fuck it, I should be able to collect the ransom whether you're alive or dead."

I lifted the gun as if I was going to shoot him in the back of the head, and even though he was facing away from me, he must've sensed my action given the way he cringed. In any case, what I said must've made sense to him because he asked me not to shoot him, and he started walking again, albeit in a slow crippled pace.

Even though my heart was no longer in it, I couldn't give it up, at least not then. Maybe after we hiked another mile I could, but not then. We didn't go very far before he commented how my voice sounded familiar. "Do I know you?" he asked.

I have to admit I felt my chest seize up when he asked that. The idea of him being able to recognize me from my voice was ludicrous. We talked once a little under a year ago, although he was in attendance at the awards banquet when I gave my acceptance speech. Still, how could he possibly recognize my voice given the conditions? Not only did I have a ski mask covering most of my mouth, but with the snow and wind howling about it shouldn't have been possible. Logically, I knew he couldn't have known who I was, that at any time I could still turn around and I'd be safe leaving him alive. But even understanding that, when I barked at him to shut up, I made my voice lower and more gravelly than normal. That seemed to amuse him. A short time later he asked if I was from Boston.

"I told you to shut up!"

The damn question kept me from turning around like I wanted to. I had decided I no longer wanted to kill him. I could accept that the suffering I'd caused him over the last six and a half hours was a fair trade for all the rage his damn letter had inflicted on me. As long as I could be sure he hadn't recognized me, I could just walk away from this. The odds were good that he'd be able to make it back to the road and that someone would pick him up. Maybe he'd suffer some frostbite and hypothermia, but that would only enrich the story he'd be telling over and over again at his monthly roundtable. And if he didn't make it out of the woods, well, that would be an act of God, even if I didn't believe in any sort of God. All I needed to do was convince myself that he couldn't have recognized me, and I would've ended this without him dying. Or those others either. I had almost reached that point when he turned around to tell me he knew who I was. And then he told me my name.

"What is wrong with you?" he demanded. "I've been an advocate of yours. Chrissakes, I've been recommending your books to other editors I know. I told you this when I met you last year. So why in the world would you do this to me?"

My spine turned into ice when he mentioned my name. Now, though, as I stared at him it was as if my skin was burning up.

"You're a fucking liar," I said through clenched teeth. "An advocate, huh? What about the letter you sent me?"

"What are you talking about? I never sent you any letter!"

"Sure you did. When I sent you my first book."

"I don't know what you're talking about." He shook his head sadly at me. "I caught up with all your books last year ago, and I thought your first one was a solid debut."

I laughed at that, although it came out as something strangled deep in my throat. "Yeah? That's not what you wrote in your letter." I had his letter tucked away in my inside coat pocket, but I didn't bother taking it out as I recited it to him. As I'd already mentioned, I had every word of that damn letter forever burned into my brain.

He gave me this odd look as he shook his head. "That must've been years ago," he said.

A red glaze covered my eyes. I could barely see past it. "Twelve years ago," I forced out, hating how my voice shook.

Even though his hair, eyebrows, and carefully cropped beard and mustache were encrusted with snow and ice, there was no mistaking the look of pity and contempt that he gave me. "I didn't read your book back then," he said. "That was a form letter I used to send out as my way of helping to separate the wheat from chaff, so to speak. The writers with true talent wouldn't let a letter like that discourage them and would find a way to persevere. But if that letter could help encourage the vast majority of wannabes who were bothering me to quit writing, then good riddance." He paused for a moment, his eyes turning every bit as icy as the weather. "I suggest strongly that you take me home now before you get yourself in even worse trouble."

He shouldn't have used that patronizing tone with me. He should've known full well by then that something wasn't quite right with me, and he should've been smart enough not to do that. If he hadn't used that tone, it was still possible that I would've let him live, even with him knowing who I was. But that tone ignited all the dormant rage inside me to once again boil up the same as when I first read that damn letter, and before I fully realized what I was doing I fired two bullets into his face. I think the first one hit him in the eye. I'm not sure where the second one hit him, but there was no doubt he was dead before he ever hit the ground. It was only after I fired those shots that I noticed the two hunters who were standing ten feet off to the side of me.

I had no idea how long they'd been standing there. I hadn't heard them approach, but I wouldn't have been able to in any case with the way the snow and the wind was blowing about. They were both only in their twenties, and they both wore these odd half-frozen smiles, as if they thought they might've wandered over to where a movie was being shot, or maybe that this was only a bizarre practical joke for a TV show. The way I looked at them snapped them out of their stupors, and their goofy half grins quickly changed into something fearful and grim. Before they could raise their rifles, I fired two shots directly into the chest of the one on my right. When I turned my gun on the other one, my first shot missed wildly because of how he dropped to the ground for cover. The split second I got off my second shot, I saw the end of his rifle barrel spitting fire at me, and then it was as if I'd been kicked in the stomach by an angry mule.

For a half hour, maybe longer, I lay on my back expecting to die. The snow was still falling at a heavy rate, and although my world had become a white haze, I saw things with a clarity of thought that I hadn't had for a long time, and I accepted that what happened had to happen. If I had been a different type of person I would've simply been pissed off by Pratt's letter and days later be able to laugh it off. But I wasn't that type of person. He shouldn't have indiscriminately sent out those letters. By doing so, eventually one of them was going to go to someone like me. What happened to him was inevitable.

At some point I realized I wasn't going to die, at least not then. Shortly after that I also realized that I could move. At first I just wanted to stay where I was and let the snow bury me. It hurt like hell and it would've been so easy to just let myself be buried under the snow and die out there. But I found that I couldn't just do that. Slowly, gingerly, I rolled onto my knees, and once I did this, I realized why the other hunter hadn't finished me off yet. My second shot had taken off the top of his head. Even though he was covered by a half inch of snow, there was still enough gore left behind from the shooting to make it obvious that was what had happened.

At first I was crawling on my hands and knees. I was trying to retrace my path and head back to the car, but the snow had covered up the tracks Pratt and I had made and given my state of mind, I doubt I was going the right way. But still I kept crawling, and when I could I got to my feet and staggered along. I tried not to think about the bloody mess my stomach had been turned into, and I certainly tried not to catch even a glimpse of it. At some point I fell back to my knees and crawled along the ground as long as I could keep moving. And then everything went black.

When I woke up next the world had become painfully bright, like I was directly under a searchlight. I had the sense that there were a bunch of people bent over me, but I couldn't really see them because of how bright it was. I didn't feel any pain in my stomach then, only a tugging sensation. Someone shouted, "He's come out of it! Put him under!" and as if a switch had been thrown everything went black again.

I found out later that a snowmobiler found me and called for a rescue crew, and while it was touch and go during the three-hour surgery, the doctors ended up saving my life. By five o'clock the very same day that I shot Pratt and those other two men to death, I was lying on a hospital bed in the intensive care unit, the middle of my body wrapped in thick bandages, my mind just barely alert enough to make sense of what the doctor was saying as he explained to me what had happened. While my mind was fuzzy and I was having trouble keeping my focus on what he was saying, one thing that struck me was how uncomfortable he appeared. I knew outside of him there was a nurse in the room, but there had to be someone else also. I could tell that from the way this doctor's gaze shifted momentarily to where this other person must've been standing. Even without that, I would've felt this other person's presence. After the doctor finished filling me in, he cleared his throat and told me the local sheriff wanted to ask me a few questions, and asked if I was up to it. I shook my head and closed my eyes, and let the morphine drift me back into unconsciousness.

It turned out that the sheriff was determined to speak to me that day. I know that because a nurse whom I later became friendly with told me that he camped out in my room waiting for me to wake up from my morphine-induced sleep, which didn't happen until after nine that same night. He was a big rawboned man in his fifties with short-cropped salt-and-pepper hair and a ruddy complexion. He introduced himself as Dale Grandy. As he stared at me, a hardness settled over his face and not a drop of sympathy showed in his expression for the near-fatal injury I had suffered. He asked me if I remembered what happened. I nodded and told him in a voice that was barely a croak that I was shot in the stomach.

His eyes glazed when I said that. I knew right then that if he could've gotten away with it, he would've poked a finger into my bullet wound until I told him everything he wanted to know. But he couldn't get away with it. All he could do with the doctors and nurses hanging around was ask me questions. I could lie right now and say I didn't understand the reason for his outward hostility toward me, but I understood it fully, which I'll explain later. What I didn't know at that time was whether those other bodies had been found yet. They hadn't been, which made sense since the snow would've covered any bloody trail I might've left back to them, but I didn't know that then.

"Do you know who shot you?"

I shook my head, and croaked out that I was guessing a hunter did it. "He must've thought I was a deer. I didn't see him."

"You're from Boston?"

I nodded.

"That's a long way from here. What are you doing in our neck of the woods? Did you come up here just so you could take a rifle shot to the belly?"

I think he was trying to make a joke with his last question, as if he were trying to establish a rapport with me, but there was no hiding his true feelings toward me. In any case, I just told him it was a long story.

"I've got all night," he said, his lips twisted into a thin, harsh smile, another halfhearted attempt on his part to show me we could be friends.

"I think it was last night when I was driving to New Haven? I don't know how long I've been out of it, but I think it was last night—"

"What day was it?" he asked, interrupting me.

I told him the day that I left to kill Pratt.

"It was last night," he said.

"Okay. I was driving to New Haven and like an idiot I stopped to help out what I thought was a stranded motorist outside of Hartford. It was a setup. I don't know whether he was out to kidnap me, steal my car, do perverted things to me, or all of the above, but he forced me at gunpoint to get into the trunk of his car—"

"What type of car was this?"

I squeezed my eyes tight as if I was trying to remember it. Of course it wasn't too hard to figure out that the car had already been found. "Something old, beat-up and brown. I think it was a Ford Taurus?"

He nodded, letting me know I got the answer right.

"He must've driven all night with me in the trunk. When the car finally stopped, he pulled me out of the trunk and made me march into the woods. But he wasn't the one who shot me, because he was behind me, and I didn't see who it was in front of me. So it must've been a hunter."

My story was a doozy. That's what I do for a living. I make up stories, and in this case I did the best I could with what I had to work with. Just so you don't get the wrong idea, I didn't make it up on the fly right then and there. I started thinking about it when I woke up after the surgery. It confused Grandy enough that I could see doubt enter his eyes. I wasn't sure what he'd been thinking I had done, since I was the one who was shot and I was convinced from his questioning the other bodies hadn't been found yet, but he still had had me pegged as someone who came to his town with bad intentions. Now he didn't know what to think. Before he could ask me anything else, I forced a couple of weak coughs that were even weaker than the voice I'd been using, and a doctor who must've been standing off in the background quickly stepped forward and ushered a reluctant Sheriff Grandy out of the room, insisting that I had answered enough questions for one night and any more would put my health at risk. Grandy didn't like being chased out of there, but there was nothing he could do about it at that moment.

Once I was alone I thought about the story I had given and whether it could possibly hold up once those other bodies were found. I didn't know. There were several ways I could see of poking holes in it, and I was sure if I studied it more I'd think of others. One obvious way was that I had stopped at two gas stations during the drive up, and if either of the attendants that I paid cash to could identify me, then I'd be sunk. But how could they? I was wearing a ski mask at the time so there wouldn't be any photos from surveillance cameras, and at some point while I was staggering away from the murder site I'd lost the mask—I was feeling feverish, and vaguely remember ripping it off and tossing it. It wasn't going to be found. Not in that snow. So how could either of those attendants identify me? I knew once those other bodies were found, Grandy would know my story was a lie and that I was involved in those deaths, but could he prove it?

Whether it was the morphine or because it fully exhausted me answering Grandy's questions and later worrying whether my story would save me, I drifted off again, and when I woke up the next morning, Grandy was waiting for me. The hostility he had shown me earlier was back, maybe double what it was before. Before he could question me any further, though, he had to wait for the nurse to take care of some things, and then for the doctor to examine me, and while this happened I prepared myself. He didn't bother with any niceties and instead jumped right into it, asking me to describe the guy who kidnapped me.

"A white guy. Late twenties, thin, long hair. Bad teeth that were kind of brown," I said, as I gave him a description of how I imagined a typical meth user. "That's all I can remember. I really didn't get a great look at him."

"Tell me again why you stopped?"

"He looked like he needed help. I'd been having some good luck of late. I thought it would be a good karma kind of thing to do." I did a bit of acting then, making a pained face as if I were suffering from a toothache. "I didn't expect what happened next."

He didn't buy a word I was saying, but I wasn't going to let him know

I knew that. Instead I shook my head angrily over what my imaginary kidnapper did to me.

"Why were you going to New Haven?" Grandy asked.

"Research. I'm a writer. I've been working out an idea for a new crime novel that takes place in New Haven. I headed out there somewhat for inspiration but mostly to work out some details that had me stumped."

He didn't like my answer at all. Again, if there weren't any doctors or nurses around he would've forced me to give him a different one. I could see it in his eyes. But since he couldn't do that, he asked me why I was dressed the way I was.

"Snow pants, snow boots, heavy parka, extreme weather gloves," he said with a harsh smile. "That's all stuff you'd be wearing to go hiking in the woods. I wouldn't think you'd be wearing that to New Haven."

"It was cold and snowing, and I expected to be outside a lot. That's why I dressed the way I did. I had a wool cap also, but lost it somewhere along the way."

"What about your car? You had your car keys with you. Why didn't your kidnapper take them?"

I shook my head. "I don't know. Maybe he was planning to take them later."

Grandy was frowning at my answer. A good-natured frown, though. An act. Like he thought he was about to catch me in a lie.

"What happened to your car?" he asked. "The kidnapper didn't have your keys, yet your car wasn't found anywhere along Interstate 84 like it should've been if you pulled over like you said you did."

I shrugged, while also thanking my lucky stars that I'd left the parking garage ticket in my car instead of keeping it in my wallet. It was pathetic that this was his big gotcha. It gave me hope that I was going to get away with it. "It must've been a two-man operation," I said. "He must've had a partner tow my car. Maybe to a chop shop."

For a long moment Grandy simply glared at me. Then he took two photos from an envelope and showed them to me. These must've been high school yearbook photos of the two hunters I killed, not that that was any surprise. If it wasn't for the morphine, I probably would've started sweating. But as it was I think I was able to maintain a placid expression.

"Neither of them kidnapped me," I said.

A muscle along the side of his jaw tightened. "They're locals. Did you see either of them?"

I shook my head. "You think one of them shot me?" I asked.

He didn't answer me. I don't think he was capable of answering me right then, and I knew why. He suspected those two boys were dead. The only thing that was keeping him from killing me at that moment was he wasn't sure. It was possible that I was shot in a hunting accident like it appeared, and that those two boys realizing it took off to hide and get drunk. Of course, that doesn't explain why he'd want to kill me even if he suspected me of doing what he thought I did. It's pretty simple, really. The first moment I saw Grandy, I could see the strong resemblance between him and one of those boys I killed. The boy could've been a nephew, but the odds were that it was his son.

For the time being Sheriff Dale Grandy was done with me, and as he left I knew where he was heading. Back to the woods to search for his son.

Later, around noon, I was moved out of ICU to another part of the hospital. I guess they decided I was no longer in imminent danger. My new room had a TV set, and it was all over the local news about my being found in the woods shot in the stomach. Nothing yet about any other bodies being found.

The new nurse assigned to me turned out to be a fan of mine and had read all my books. My doctor didn't want me doing anything but resting and recuperating, but I convinced my nurse to get me a pad of paper and a pen so that I could work on a story that I had a deadline for. With her help I also got an envelope for mailing my story, and after giving her my e-mail address and password, she was able to get the address I needed so I could mail this to the editor for the Jewish noir anthology. I'd also arranged for her to mail it for me if I'm gone and she finds it in the night-stand drawer next to me. If that were to happen, as far as she's concerned I was discharged without her knowing about it and I somehow forget to bring the envelope with me. That won't really be what happened. If I'm discharged or arrested, I'll make sure that this so-called *piece of crea-tive nonfiction* that I've been working on like a devil possessed ever since Grandy's third visit will be destroyed and no one will ever see it. The only way this will ever show up in that anthology is if Grandy takes me out of the hospital without anyone knowing about it. Or at least anyone being willing to admit they know about it.

Grandy's third visit was about an hour ago. He asked me about Malcolm Pratt. Of course he found the letter from Pratt that I had tucked away in my inside coat pocket. I told him how I had only met Pratt once and didn't really know him well. He didn't buy that, not with me having that letter. He told me that Pratt was missing in New York. He asked me if I knew where he was. I told him I didn't, and I could tell Grandy didn't believe me.

The reason he hasn't so far dragged me out of here and taken me to a quiet spot in the woods is that he still has a sliver of doubt because he hasn't found those bodies yet. But deep down he knows he's going to, and that's why he hasn't had my gloves or parka tested for gunpowder residue.

He doesn't want to bring other law enforcement into this. He wants me to be able to disappear quietly after he finds his son.

Grandy's going to find all three of them. There's no doubt about it anymore. Not after the weather report I saw on the news minutes after his third visit. Following on the heels of this bitter cold and snow, they expect a warm front to be rolling in, bringing with it heavy rains. If they're right with their forecast, the snow covering the bodies will be gone by Monday. And I have little doubt that that forecast is going to be right.

Now you know why I needed to write this. So that sonofabitch Dale Grandy pays for what he's going to do to me.

Idle Thoughts,
Fifty-Four Years Later

Harlan Ellison®

Had an odd moment of conversation with a very good, trusted friend a couple of days ago; gave me a moment's pause of reflection. Don't remember where the thread began, but at some point he said something like, "I'd like to think there are old girlfriends out there, or girls I fancied, who are sitting somewhere lamenting they didn't hook up with me."

Moment's pause. Conversation whirled past. Much later, my memory went back to that snippet of chat. I tried to think if there were any of the many wonderful women I'd known, married, hung with, fancied, or otherwise cut trail with who, if I considered it at all . . . I'd be condign picturing them as regretting having foregone liaison with me back in some dimly remembered pastel NeverNeverLand. I could not. Not one, of the considerable. Not because I didn't think of them warmly . . . just the opposite. And it led me down a ruminative avenue to thoughts that may inform your reading of this, one of my favorite stories.

Short aside: consider it an *asterisk, and you can look in vain at the bottom of this page for that which I've integrated above. The aside is this: his remark wistfully suggesting that ships who had passed in the night should be—decades later—mournfully tooting their horns in lost remembrance, staved me to realize that I did not have even a shred of ill-wish for those who had saddened, ignored, short-shrifted, or betrayed me in my long past life. Wasn't even moderately smiling to learn that some big-mouth who'd ravaged me in print in 1957 had perished of, ironically, cancer of the typing fingers. Didn't get a whisker of warmth from it. Old girlfriends, ex-wives, movie stars I've seen or been with, desired or otherwise . . . hey, live a great life: *I* have.

Still asterisking. Led me to think about the actual motherfuckers who'd caused me genuine pain, broken bones, loss of revenue, warmth, kindness. Most of them long gone and—here's the warm part—unlamented. I get no smallest quiver of "gotcha" from knowing that one of the four assholes who called me "kike" and beat me up every day in the pickup-baseball-game yard behind Lathrop Grade School croaked as a failed alcoholic some time ago. Yesterday's forgotten yesterdays. Would'ja like a nice piece of coffee cake to go with that cuppa joe? Asterisk complete.

Time magazine interviewed me a few miles back, asked me if, when I looked over my shoulder, there were any things I'd chosen to do then that I'd do differently now. All I could think of, musing long, was that I'd run a continent-length to avoid clutching claw with a certain guy I'd met and had substantial subsequent *tsuris* with, but apart from that single embolism-pretending-at-humanity, I truly could not summon up the minimal steam to twitter a bleat about, I dunno—Hitler, Pol Pot, Alaric the Goth, Ilse Koch, the Grand Kleagle of the KKK, none of the greatest enemies of Decency who had ever disgraced our flawed species with their existence. I was down with it; jiggy; cool, dude.

Then, at that moment, as now, I shrank within myself and thought shamefacedly, "That is a cowardly, evasive way to sum up your righteous animosity of memory after all these years. If I hadn't spent my dwindling life trying in vain to become an iconic much-beloved old curmudgeon, I coulda been a contenduh! I coulda been Jack the fuckin' Ripper, Eichmann, Mme. Defarge. But no, sadly, I have no small spurt of steam even to smile inwardly at their loss, grand or graceless. As is said in Yiddish, "*loyzen geyne*," which I think interprets from my momma as, "Let be what is." Let it go.

It is to weep, this ninth inning faux-Zen luminosity . . . it is not for a nanoinstant that I cannot remember every black eye, every moment of cruel childhood anti-Semitism, every stab in the back . . . I can, I just *don't*. I learned how to vanish every one of them from my universe—like *that*—poof! Gone. No longer exist.

Make no mistake: I am no less a poltroon and con man than ever I have been. I'm still the guy who wrote the disquieting essay on revenge, "Driving in the Spikes," and I can recite the names of each of those four kids in the empty back lot at Lathrop Grade School who beat me bloody, tore off my kike apparel, and left me to crawl home in the slush of an Ohio winter. (Oh, sob for the poor Jewboy.)

To use Nero Wolfe's word for delusion/deception, this is all flummery. (I got my "revenge" on one of that quartet at last, just recently, when the fate I'd ascribed for him appeared in full color, brilliantly rendered by a great graphic artist: had him burning endlessly, again and again, trapped in a moment of time-vortex at the core of an exploding super-nova. Endlessly. Through all time, forever. Right at the instant of greatest anguish.)

This has all been flummery.

Please enjoy my story, and remember how brilliant was the gift of Lenny Bruce.

Final Shtick[*]

Harlan Ellison®

SHTICK: n.; deriv. Yiddish; a "piece," a "bit,"
a rehearsed anecdote; as in a comedian's routine or act.

I'm a funny man, he thought, squashing the cigarette stub into the moon-face of the egg. *I'm a goddam riot.* He pushed the flight-tray away.

See the funny man! His face magically struck an attitude as the stewardess removed the tray. It was expected—he was, after all, a *funny* man. *Don't see me, sweetie, see a laugh.* He turned with a shrug of self-disgust to the port. His face stared back at him; the nose was classically Greek in profile. He sneered at it.

Right over the wing; he could barely make out the Ohio patchwork-quilt far below, grey and gun-metal blue through the morning haze. *Now I fly*, he mused. *Now I fly. When I left it was in a fruit truck. But now I'm Marty Field, king of the sick comics, and I fly. Fun-ee!*

He lit another, spastically, angrily.

Return to Lainesville. Home. Return for the dedication. That's you they're honoring, Marty Field, just you, only you. Aside from General Laine, who founded the town, there's never been anybody worth honoring who's come from Lainesville. So return. Thirteen years later. Thirteen years before the mast, buddy-boy. Return, Marty Field, and see all those wondrous, memorable faces from your oh-so-happy past. Go, Marty baby. Return!

He slapped at the button overhead, summoning the stewardess. His face again altered: an image of chuckles for replacement. "How about a couple of cubes of sugar, sweetheart?" he asked as she leaned over him, expectantly. *Yeah, doll, I see 'em. Thirty-two C? Yes, indeed, they're loverly; now get my sugar, howzabout?*

When she dropped them into his hand he gave her a brief, calculated-to-the-kilowatt grin. He unwrapped one and chewed on it, staring moodily out the port.

Think about it, Marty Field. Think about how it was, before you were Marty Field. Thirteen years before, when it was Morrie Feldman, and you were something like a kid. Think about it, and think what those faces from the past recall. How do *they* remember it? You know damned well how they remember it, and you know what they're saying now, on the day you're returning to Lainesville to be lauded and applauded. What is Mrs. Shanks, who lived next door, remembering about those days? And what is Jack Wheeldon, the childhood classmate, thinking? And Peggy Mantle? What about Leon Potter—you used to run with him—what concoction of half-remembered images and projections has he contrived? You know people, Marty Field. You've *had* to learn about them; that's why your comedy strikes so well . . . because you know the way people think, and their foibles. So think about it, baby. As your plane nears Cleveland, and you prepare to meet the committee that will take you to Lainesville, dwell on it. Create their thoughts for them, Marty boy.

❧

MRS. SHANKS: Why, certainly I remember Marty. He was always over at my house. Why, I believe he lived as much on my front porch as he did at home. Nice boy. I can remember that little thin face of his (he was always such a frail child, you know), always smiling, though. Used to love my Christmas cookies. Used to make me bake 'em for him all year 'round. And the imagination that child had . . . why, he'd go into the empty lot behind our houses and make a fort, dig it right out of the ground, and play in there all day with his toy guns. He was something, even then. Knew he'd make it someday . . . he was just that sort. Came from a good family, and that sort of thing always shows.

EVAN DENNIS: Marty always had that spark. It was something you couldn't name. A drive, a wanting, a something that wouldn't let him quit. I remember I used to talk with his father—you remember Lew, the jeweler, don't you—and we'd discuss the boy. His father and I were very close. For a while there, Lew was pretty worried about the boy; a bit rambunctious. But I always said, "Lew, no need to worry about Morrie (that was his name; he changed his name, y'know; I was very close with the family). He'll make it, that boy. Good stuff in him." Yeah, I remember the whole family very well. We were very close, y'know.

JACK WHEELDON: Hell, I knew him *before*. A lot of the other kids were always picking on him. He was kinda small, and like that, but I took him under my wing. I was sort of a close buddy. Hell, we used to ride our bikes real late at night, out in the middle of Mentor Avenue, going 'round and 'round in circles under the street light, because we just liked to do it. We got to be pretty tight. Hell, maybe I was his best friend. Always dragged him along when we were getting up a baseball game. He wasn't too good, being so small and like that, but, hell, he needed to get included, so I made the other guys let him play. Always picked him for my side too. Yeah, I guess I knew him better than anybody when he was a kid.

PEGGY MANTLE: I've got to admit it. I loved him. He wasn't the toughest kid in school, or the best-looking, but even then, even when he was young, he was so—so, I don't know what you'd call, *dynamic* . . . Well, I just loved him, that's all. He was great. Just great. I loved him, that's all.

LEON POTTER: Marty? The times we had, nobody could match. We were real crazy. Used to take bath towels and crayon CCC in a triangle on them, and tie them around our necks, and play Crime Cracker Cids. Kids, that should have been, but we were just fooling around. You know, we'd make up these crimes and solve them. Like we'd take milk bottles out of the wooden boxes everybody had at their side door, and then pretend there was a milk bottle thief around, and solve the case. We had good times. I liked him lots. It'll be good seeing him again. Wonder if he remembers me—oh, yeah, he'll remember *me*.

There they go, the vagrants, swirled away as the warning plaque lights up with its FASTEN SEAT BELTS and NO SMOKING. There they go, back to the soft-edged world where they belong; somewhere inside your head, Marty Field. They're gone, and you're here, and the plane is coming in over Cleveland. So now think carefully . . . answer carefully . . . *do* you remember?

As the plane taxis up to Cleveland Municipal Airport, do you remember Leon? Do you remember Peggy, whose father owned the Mantle apple orchards? Do you remember Evan Dennis who tried to raise a beard and looked like a poor man's Christ or a poorer man's Van Gogh? Do they come back unfogged, Marty Field, who was Morrie Feldman of 89 Harmon Drive, Lainesville, Ohio? Are they there, all real and the way they really were?

Or do the years muddy the thinking? Are they softer in their images, around the edges. Can you think about them the way they're thinking about you? Come on, don't hedge your bets, Marty Field. You're a big man now; you did thirteen weeks at the Copa, you play the Chez Paree and the

Palace. You get good bait from Sullivan and Sinatra when they want you on their shows, and Pontiac's got a special lined up for you in the fall, so you don't have to lie to anyone. Not to their memories, not to yourself, not even to the Fates. Tell the truth, Marty, and see how it sounds.

Don't be afraid. Only cowards are afraid, Marty, and you're not conditioned to be a coward, are you? Left home at seventeen, out on a fruit truck, riding in the cab right behind the NO HITCHHIKERS sticker on the windshield. You've been around, Marty Field, and you know what the score is, so tell the truth. Level with yourself. You're going back to see them after thirteen years and you've got to know.

I'm cashing in on the big rock 'n' roll craze, slanting songs at the teenagers. The way I figure it, they've exhausted the teen market, and they're going to have to start on the preteens, so I'm going to beat the trend. I've just recorded my first record, it's called "Nine Years Old and So Much in Love." It's backed with "Ten Years Old and Already Disillusioned."

Okay, Marty, forget the sick *shticks*. That's what got you your fame, that's why they're honoring you today in Lainesville. But that's dodging the issue. That's turning tail and running, Marty. Forget the routines, just answer the questions. Do you remember them? The truth now.

You're about as funny as a guided tour through Dachau.

Another bit, Marty? Another funny from your long and weirdie repertoire? Or is that routine closer to the truth? Is it a subconscious gag, Marty, babe? Does it set you thinking about Evan Dennis and Jack Wheeldon and all the rest from the sleepy, rustic town of Lainesville, just thirty-one miles from Cleveland in the so-called liberal heart of the great American Midwest?

Is it the truth, as you descend the aluminum staircase of the great flying machine, Marty Field?

Does it start the old mental ball game, that remark about Dachau, where they threw Jews into furnaces? Does it do something to your nice pseudo-Gentile gut? That gut that has been with you since Morrie Feldman days . . . that heaved on you when you had the nose job done to give you such a fine Gentile snout . . . that didn't complain when the name was changed legally. Does it bother that gut now, and give you the hollow, early-morning-chilly feeling of having stayed up all night on No-Doz and hot, black coffee? Does it bug you, Marty?

. . . ve haff an interesting phenomena in Chermany today . . . you'll haff to excuse the paint under my fingernails; I've been busy all night, writing "Goyim go home" on the doors of cathedrals . . .

Oooh, that was a zinger, wasn't it, Marty. It was a nice switch on the synagogue-swastika-painting bits the papers have been carrying. Or is it just that, Marty? Say, how the hell did you ever become a sick comic, anyhow? Was it a way of making a buck, or are you a little sick yourself? Maybe a little angry?

At what, goddam you, get outta here and let me alone!

Why, at your past, Marty, babe. Your swingin' past in good old we're-honoring-Marty-Field Lainesville.

Is that the axe, sweetie? Is that why you keep swingin'?

Shut up. Let me alone. It's a gig, that's all, just another gig. It's a booking. I'm in. I'm out. I take their lousy honor and blow the scene. There's no social signif here. I'm a sickie because it's a buck. That's it. I'm whole; I'm not a weirdie, that's just my bit. It goes over.

Sure, Marty. Sure, babe. I understand perfectly.

What'd you call me?

Not a thing, swinger. Not a mumblin' thing.

You'd damned well better not call me yellow, either.

Cool it, man. No one's asking you to cop out. The whole world loves Marty Field. He's a swinger. He's a funny man. He was a funny kid. maybe too, but now he's a funny man. Go on, sweetie, there they are, waiting behind the hurricane fence, waiting to greet the conquering hero. Go on, Attila, say something funny for the people.

The banner was raised by two children, then, and Marty Field's face broke into its calculated good humor at the sight of

WELCOME HOME MARTY FIELD

PRIDE OF LAINESVILLE!!!!

❧

It wasn't such a long ride, but then it never had been. Thirty-one miles, past the Fair Grounds, past the Colony Lumber Company where he had played so long before. Remembering the condemned pond, so deep behind the Colony Lumber Company; remembering his birthday, when he had thought there would be no party and he had stayed all day, miserable and wasting time, only to go home and see the remains of the surprise party, held without him. Remembering the tears for something lost, and never to be regained.

Past Lathrop Grade School, where he had broken one of the ornamental lamps over the door. Past Harmon Drive, where he had lived. Down Mentor Avenue, and after a time, into the center of town. The square, and around the square, past what was once the Lyric Theatre, now metamorphosed into an office building. Remembering the tiny theatre, and its ridiculous banner beneath the marquee: *Lake County's Most Intimate Theatre.* Remembering how you had to sit in your neighbor's lap, the movie was so small. Intimate, indeed. Remembering.

Then the hotel, and washing up, and a fresh white shirt with button-down collar, and your Continental suit, so they could stare and say, "He really knows how to dress in style, don't he?"

All that, all so fast, one bit after another. Too many memories, too many attempts to ravel the truth about what really happened. Was it a happy childhood? Was it the way they say it was, and the way you'd like to remember it?

Or was it something else? Something that has made you the man you are . . . the man who climbs into the spotlight every day of his life, takes a scissors and cuts up his fellow man. Which way was it, Marty? Come on, stop stalling.

An honor banquet, and Lord! they never had food like that in Lainesville before. No pasty dry sliver of white chicken meat for Marty Field, no, indeed, not! The best of the best for the man who out-Trendexed *Maverick*. And after the meal, a fast tour of the town—kept open, center-stripe on Main Street left rolled out after eight o'clock—just to stir that faulty, foggy memory.

A dance at the Moose lodge . . .

A late-night pizza . . .

A lot of autographs . . .

Too many handshakes . . .

Then let's get some sleep, don't forget the big dedication of the plaque tomorrow, over at the high school, that's a helluvan honor, doncha know.

Sleep. You call *that* a sleep?

※

"Ladies and gentlemen," the Principal began, "humor is a very delicate thing." He was a big, florid man; his job had been secure for fifteen years, with the exception of the time Champion Junior High had been condemned, torn down, and joined with the new Senior High. Then they had tried to drag in a man from East Cleveland, but the Principal had called on his brother-in-law, whose influence in local politics was considerable. And abruptly, the man from East Cleveland had found his record wanting. The principal was a big, florid, *well-fed*, and *secure* man.

"And like all delicate things," he went on, "it takes a special sort of green thumb to make it flower. Such a green thumb is possessed by the man I'm privileged to introduce this afternoon.

"I recall the first time I ever saw Marty Field," he pontificated, drawing thumbs down into vest pockets. "I was principal of the old Champion Junior High, and one September morning, as I left my office, I saw a thin, small boy hurrying late to class. Well, sir, I said to myself . . ."

Marty Field closed off reception. There it was. Again. The small, short, sickly bit again. Yeah, you were so right, Principal. I was small, and miserable thin, and that was part of it. But only part. That was the part where I couldn't keep up. But that isn't where it began. It went back much further.

Go back, then, Marty Field. For the first time since they contacted you about the honors Lainesville wanted to bestow on you, go back and conjure it up as it really was.

Tell it true, Marty. No gags, no punch lines, no *shticks* . . . just the way it was.

All things are as they were then, except . . .

YOU ARE THERE . . .

Your name is Morrie Feldman. Your father's name is Lew Feldman, your mother is Sarah Feldman. You are the only Jew on your street, the only Jewish kid in your grade school. There are seven Jewish families in town. You go to Lathrop grade school and you are a little kid. At recess time they get you out on the ball diamond, and one of them picks a fight with you. Usually it's Jack Wheeldon, whose head is square and whose hair is cut in a butch, and whose father is a somethingorother at the Diamond Alkali plant. Jack Wheeldon is big and laughs like a jackass and you don't like him because he looks with a terrible strangeness out of his cruel eyes.

You stand there while Jack Wheeldon calls you a dirty kike, and your mother is a dirty kike, and you pee your pants because *all* kikes do that, don't they, you frigging little kike? And when you swing and hit him on the side of the head, the circle of kids magically grows about you, and while you're locked in an adolescent grapple with Jack Wheeldon (who is all the things in this life that you despise because they are bigger than you and slower-witted and frightening), someone kicks you from behind. Hard. At the base of your spine. With a Thom McAn shoe. And then you can't help it and you start to cry.

You fall down, and they begin kicking you. They all kick you very hard, and you aren't old enough or smart enough to pull your arms and legs around you. So after a while everything goes sandy and fuzzy and you know you are unconscious. There's a special sort of pleasure in that, because that's what happens to the good guys in the movies on Saturday afternoons, when they're being attacked by the bad guys. And after a while Miss Dexter with the pointy nose, from the fifth grade upstairs, comes out on the playground, and sees what is happening, and goes back inside to tell someone else. Then, later, the faceless teacher from the third grade, who likes you, comes running out, and lifts you in her arms and tenderly carries you inside.

The first thing you hear when you wake up is one of the kids saying,

". . . dirty Jewish elephant." And you wonder with childish logic why he
calls you an elephant. You don't have a long trunk. That is the first time
they let you know you have a *shonikker* apple between your eyes and your
mouth.

Your name is Morrie Feldman, and you live at 89 Harmon Drive. You
have been away at camp all summer, and now you are back, and your father
is telling you that your dog Puddles was gassed while you were away. Mrs.
Shanks, next door, called the pound while your father and mother were
in Cleveland for the afternoon, and had them take Puddles down and gas
him. Your father tells you he is sorry, and doesn't know why Mrs. Shanks
would do such a thing, but you run out of the house and hide under
the side porch all day and cry, anyhow. Later, you steal Mrs. Shanks's
rug-beater from her garage. You bury it very deep in the soft, amber dirt
behind the garage.

Your name is Morrie Feldman, and you are in junior high school. You
hear something heavy hit the front of your house late one night, and then
something else, and then a half-eaten grapefruit comes crashing through
your front window, and out on the lawn—here in Ohio, and who'd ever
think it—you see a huge cross burning. The next day you learn about the
Anti-Defamation League. You don't tell anyone that you saw Mr. Evan
Dennis from Dennis's Florists, with soot on his face and hands, running
down the street to a car with its headlights out.

The name is the same, and it's later, and somehow you have a girl
named Peggy Mantle, who has blond hair and blue eyes and Anglo-Saxon
features, and you love her very much. Until you catch her doing things she
never did with you. She's doing them in the bushes behind her house after
the Halloween party. She's doing them with Leon Potter from across the
street, whose mother always slams the door when you come on the porch.
You don't say anything. You can't. You're afraid.

You've been afraid for a long time now. When you were smaller, once
in a while you could beat Jack Wheeldon, or convince Leon that he should
play with you. But they've continued to get bigger, and you've stayed small
and frail, and they can beat you with their fists.

So you've learned to cut them up with your tongue.

You've learned how to tear them and shred them and slice them with
your mouth. That's how it started. That's where it came from. That's why
you leave town in a fruit truck, and go to Buffalo, and from there New
York. That's why you go to a plastic surgeon when you've saved the money,
and have your nose molded to look like another nose . . . Leon Potter's
nose, or as close to it as the surgeon's samples came, but you don't realize
that till much later.

That's why you decide to change your name.

Your name is not Morrie Feldman.

Your name is Marty Field.

You're a funny, funny man.

※

"... and so it is my extreme pleasure to introduce the boy we watched grow into a national celebrity ... Marty Field!"

The auditorium caught up the frantic applause and flung it back and forth between the walls. The tumult was like nothing else Marty Field had ever heard. It caught in his eyes and ears and mouth like a great tidal wave, and drenched him with adoration. He rose and walked to the principal, extending his hand automatically, receiving the embossed bronze plaque and the handshake simultaneously.

Then the wave subsided, leaving him washed up on the shore of expectancy, a sea of eyes beyond, waiting to bathe him in love and fame once more.

Fritz, it's cold; throw another Jew on the fire.

"Th—thank you . . . thank you very much . . ."

Tell them. Tell them, Morrie Feldman. Tell them what it was like. Tell them you know them for what they are. Make them realize that you've never forgotten. Show them the never-healed wounds; open the sores for them. Let them taste the filth of their own natures. Don't let them get away with it. That's why you came, isn't it? That was why the conquering hero returned! Don't let them lie to their children about all the good times, the fine times, the wonderful wonderful Marty Field they all loved and helped and admired. Don't let them spew their subtle poisons to their children while using you as an example of what a good non-you-know-what is like.

Let them wallow in their own scum, Marty Field.

So Abie says, "Business is business."

". . . I don't know quite what to say . . ."

Don't let him Jew-you-down . . .

". . . after all these years, to return home to such a warm and sincere . . ."

Kike!

". . . I want you to know I'll always cherish this handsome bronze . . ."

Yid!

". . . means more to me than all the awards I'll ever . . ."

Dirty little Christ-killer!

". . . so thank you very much, again."

You walk off the stage, Marty Field. You hold your thirty pieces of silver (or is that one piece of bronze?) and you leave the high school, and get in the car that will take you back to the airport, and the world that loves you. You had your chance, and you didn't take it. Of course, you didn't, Marty. Because you're a coward. Strike your blow for truth and freedom? Hardly. It's your life, and you handle it for the guffaw, for the belly-buster, for the big exit.

But that's okay. Don't let it wig you, kid. And stop crying; you're not entitled to those tears. Stick with the sick *shticks*, buddy-boy.

Want a tag line? Want a punch line? How's this:

Have you seen the Do-It-Yourself Easter Kit? Two boards, three nails, and a Jew.

Author signifies audience reaction of laughter, applause, and sounds of scissors.

Yeah, you're a scream, Marty.

Contributors

Charles Ardai has received the Edgar Allan Poe Award and the Shamus Award for his crime fiction, as well as recognition as founder and editor of the Hard Case Crime line of novels, whose authors have included Stephen King, Mickey Spillane, Ed McBain, Lawrence Block, and Donald Westlake. He is also a writer and consulting producer on the TV series *Haven*.

Jedidiah Ayres lives in St. Louis, Missouri, and is the author of *Peckerwood*, *Fierce Bitches*, and *A F*ckload of Shorts*. He's not a Jew, but his lawyer is.

R.S. Brenner (Summer Brenner) is the author of a dozen works of fiction, poetry, and award-winning novels for youth. Her crime fiction includes critically acclaimed *I-5* and *Nearly Nowhere* (originally published by Gallimard's Série noire). "Devil for a Witch" is excerpted from a novel in progress. She lives in Berkeley, California.

A native of Berkeley, California, **Michael J. Cooper** immigrated to Israel in 1966 and lived in Jerusalem during the last year the city was divided between Israel and Jordan. He remained in Israel for the next decade, studying at Hebrew University in Jerusalem and graduating from Tel Aviv University Medical School. Now a pediatric cardiologist, he returns to Israel and the West Bank to volunteer his services to children who lack adequate access to care. He is the author of *Foxes in the Vineyard*, historical fiction set in 1948 Jerusalem. A second novel, *The Rabbi's Knight*, appeared in 2015. Website: http://michaeljcooper.net.

M. Dante has participated in NoirCon, Noir Riot, and the Erotic Literary Salon since they began, and IOTA Arlington since 2012. She is currently freelance in Philadelphia, Pennsylvania. Website: http://www.BDC-Lancaster.net. YouTube: http://www.youtube.com/BDCbabe.

Harlan Ellison® has been called "one of the great living American short story writers" by the *Washington Post*; and the *Los Angeles Times* said, "It's long past time for Harlan Ellison to be awarded the title: 20th Century Lewis Carroll." In a career spanning more than forty years, he has won the Hugo Award eight and a half times, the Nebula Award three times, the Bram Stoker Award six times (including the Lifetime Achievement Award in 1996), the Edgar Allan Poe Award twice, the Georges Méliès Fantasy Film Award twice, two Audie Awards (for the best in audio recordings), and was awarded the Silver Pen for Journalism by PEN. He was presented with the first Living Legend award by the International Horror Critics at the 1995 World Horror Convention. He is also the only author in Hollywood ever to win the Writers Guild of America Award for Most Outstanding Teleplay (solo work) four times. He has also been nominated for both an Emmy and Grammy, and according to his own biography he "probably is the most contentious person now walking the Earth."

Rabbi Adam Fisher's short stories have appeared in *The Jewish Spectator* and other magazines. Among the nine books he has published are three books of poems, *Rooms, Airy Rooms* (Writers Ink), *Dancing Alone* (L.I. Quarterly), and *Enough to Stop the Heart* (Writers Ink), as well as *An Everlasting Name* (Behrman House), on the Holocaust, and *God's Garden* (Behrman House), a book of short stories for children. From 2006 to 2014 he was poetry editor of the *CCAR Journal*. He is currently Rabbi Emeritus of Temple Isaiah, Stony Brook, NY.

Alan Gordon is the author of the Fools' Guild Mystery series from St. Martin's Minotaur Books. His short fiction has appeared in *Queens Noir*, *Alfred Hitchcock*, *Ellery Queen*, *Asimov*, and numerous other publications. Alan is also an award-winning librettist and lyricist, with several musicals to his credit. "The Usual," with composer Mark Sutton-Smith, premiered at the Williamston Theatre in Michigan and earned him the prestigious Kleban Prize in 2013. As a storyteller, Alan was featured on "The Moth Radio Hour." When not telling lies for a living, he works as a public defender in New York City. Find out more at http://www.alan-gordon.com.

Heywood Gould was born in the Bronx and raised in Brooklyn. He worked as reporter for the *New York Post* when it was known as a "commie-mockie-pinko symp rag." Later, supported himself through years of rejection working as a mortician's assistant, cab driver, floor-waxer, and bartender.

Gould is the author of eight novels, among them *Cocktail*, *Fort Apache the Bronx*, *Double Bang*, *Leading Lady* (Hammett Award finalist), *Serial Killer's Daughter* (optioned for a minor motion picture), and *Greenlight for Murder*, another Hammett Award finalist! He has written nine movies, including *Cocktail*, *Fort Apache the Bronx*, *The Boys from Brazil*, and *One Good Cop*, which he also directed.

Wendy Hornsby is the Edgar Award–winning author of the Maggie MacGowen and Kate and Tejeda mysteries and many short stories, several of which have been included in editions of The Best American Mystery Stories. History professor emeritus, Wendy lives with her husband in Northern California. Her most recent book is *The Color of Light*, from Perseverance Press.

Tasha Kaminsky is a short story writer and essayist but pays her bills by filling the position of director of Youth Engagement at a Conservative synagogue. She holds a degree in creative writing from Florida State University, and a Masters in Near Eastern and Judaic from Brandeis University. She struggles with Twitter, but you can learn more about her if you follow her at https://twitter.com/tashakaminsky.

Michele Lang writes crime, science fiction and fantasy, and romance. Her short stories have been published by DAW and Running Press, and her Lady Lazarus World War II historical fantasy series was published by Tor Books. Michele's story "Deathmobile" recently appeared in the *Fiction River: Past Crime* anthology, edited by Kristine Kathryn Rusch. A graduate of Harvard Law School, Michele practiced the unholy craft of litigation in both New York and Connecticut. She moved back to her hometown in metro New York City right before 9/11. To learn more about Michele, find her at http://michelelang.com.

David Liss is the author of nine novels, most recently *The Day of Atonement* and *Randoms*, his first book for younger readers. His previous bestselling books include *The Coffee Trader* and *The Ethical Assassin*, both of which are being developed as films, and *A Conspiracy of Paper*, which is now being developed for television. Liss is the author of numerous comics, including *Mystery Men*, *Sherlock Holmes: Moriarty Lives*, and *Angelica Tomorrow*.

Robert Lopresti is a member of Congregation Beth Israel in Bellingham, Washington. He is the author of *Greenfellas* (Oak Tree Press), a comic crime novel with environmental issues, and more than fifty short stories, including winners of the Derringer (twice) and Black Orchid Novella awards. He is also a songwriter and his retelling of the Nakhshon Midrash is sung at some far-flung Passover seders. You can hear it at http://tinyurl.com/nakhshon.

Eddie Muller, known as the "Czar of Noir," is a writer, impresario, and cinema historian. As founder of the Film Noir Foundation, he has restored and preserved such nearly lost classics as *The Prowler*, *Cry Danger*, *Try and Get Me*, *Too Late for Tears*, and *Woman on the Run*. His popular books on the subject include *Dark City: The Lost World of Film Noir*; *Dark City Dames: The Wicked Women of Film Noir*, and *The Art of Noir*. He produces and hosts NOIR CITY: The San Francisco Film Noir Festival, the largest film noir retrospective in the world, which has satellite festivals in seven other U.S. cities. His 2002 fiction debut, *The Distance*, was named Best First Novel by the Private Eye Writers of America.

Alan Orloff's debut mystery, *Diamonds for the Dead*, was an Agatha Award finalist for Best First Novel. He's also written two books in the Last Laff mystery series, *Killer Routine* and *Deadly Campaign* (from Midnight Ink). Writing as his darker half Zak Allen, he's published *The Taste*, *First Time Killer*, and *Ride-Along*. His latest suspense novel, *Running from the Past* (Kindle Press), was a "winner" in Amazon's Kindle Scout program. Alan lives in Northern Virginia and teaches workshops at the Writer's Center in Bethesda, MD. For more info, visit http://www.alanorloff.com.

Gary Phillips, the son of a mechanic and a librarian, draws on his experiences ranging from labor organizing to delivering dog cages in writing his tales of chicanery and malfeasance. He has been nominated for a Shamus and has won a Chester Himes and a Brody for his writing. His books include *The Jook* and *The Underbelly*. Visit his website at http://gdphillips.com.

This year Knopf published *Made in Detroit*, **Marge Piercy**'s nineteenth collection of poetry. Knopf also published *The Art of Blessing the Day: Poems with a Jewish Theme*. Her most recent novel is *Sex Wars*. Schocken published *Pesach for the Rest of Us: Making the Passover Seder Your Own*. Her memoir *Sleeping with Cats* is in Harper Perennial trade paperback. PM Press has published her debut short story collection, *The Cost of Lunch, Etc.*, and the collection *My Life, My Body*. Piercy gives frequent readings and workshops. She was part of the committee that produced the Or Chadash Reconstructionist *siddur*. Her liturgical poems are used by many congregations and *chavurot* here and in England.

Moe Prager is the pseudonym of *New York Times* bestselling author Reed Farrel Coleman, who has published twenty-one novels and novellas. He has been hired by the estate of the late Robert B. Parker to continue his Jesse Stone series and by Putnam to begin a new series featuring retired Suffolk County cop, Gus Murphy. Called a hardboiled poet by NPR's Maureen Corrigan, Coleman is a three-time recipient of the Shamus Award and a three-time Edgar Award nominee in three different categories. He has also won the Audie, Barry, Macavity, and Anthony awards. He is an adjunct English instructor at Hofstra University and a founding member of Mystery Writers of America University. Brooklyn born and raised, he now lives with his family on Long Island.

Travis Richardson has been a finalist for the Macavity short story award in 2014 and 2015 as well as the Anthony short story award in 2014. His novella *Lost in Clover* was listed in *Spinetingler Magazine*'s Best Crime Fiction of 2012. He has published stories in crime fiction publications such as *Thuglit*, *Shotgun Honey*, *Flash Fiction Offensive*, and *All Due Respect*. He edits the Sisters-In-Crime Los Angeles newsletter *Ransom Notes*, reviews Chekhov short stories at http://www.chekhovshorts.com, and sometimes shoots a short movie. His latest novella, *Keeping the Record*, concerns a disgraced baseball player who will do anything to keep his tainted home run record. Website: http://tsrichardson.com.

Nancy Richler's first novel, *Throwaway Angels*, was shortlisted for the 1997 Arthur Ellis Award for Best First Crime Novel. Her second novel, *Your Mouth Is Lovely*, was the winner of the 2003 Canadian Jewish Book Award for fiction and Italy's 2004 ADEI-WIZO Prize. Nancy's most recent novel, *The Imposter Bride*, was a finalist for the 2012 Scotiabank Giller Prize, winner of the 2013 Canadian Jewish Book Award for Fiction, a *Globe and Mail* Best Book of the Year, and a *New York Times Book Review* Editor's Choice. Nancy Richler divides her time between Vancouver and her hometown of Montreal.

S.J. Rozan's novels and short stories have won multiple awards, including the Edgar, Shamus, Anthony, Nero, Macavity, and the Japanese Maltese Falcon. She's written thirteen books under her own name and two with Carlos Dews as the writing team of Sam Cabot. S.J. was born in the Bronx and lives in lower Manhattan. Her newest book is Sam Cabot's *Skin of the Wolf*. Website: http://www.sjrozan.com.

Jonathan Santlofer is the author of the international bestseller *The Death Artist* with four other crime novels including the Nero award-winning *Anatomy of Fear*. He is editor/contributor of the anthologies *The Dark End of the Street*, *LA Noire*, *The Marijuana Chronicles* and the bestselling serial novel

Inherit the Dead. His short stories have appeared in many magazines and anthologies, including *Ellery Queen* and *The Strand*. The recipient of two National Endowment for the Arts grants, he has been a Visiting Artist at the American Academy in Rome, Vermont Studio Center, and serves on the board of Yaddo, the oldest arts community in the U.S. Santlofer's artwork is in such collections as the Metropolitan Museum of Art, Art Institute of Chicago, Newark Museum, and Tokyo's Institute of Contemporary Art. He is currently at work on an illustrated novel for children and an illustrated memoir. He is sorry to say that he was kicked out of Hebrew School, just one of the stories in the illustrated memoir.

Los Angeles Times bestselling author **Stephen Jay Schwartz** spent a number of years as the director of development for Wolfgang Petersen where he worked to develop screenplays for production, including such films as *Air Force One*, *Outbreak*, and *Bicentennial Man*. His two novels, *Boulevard* and *Beat*, follow the journey of sex-addicted LAPD detective Hayden Glass. Stephen was also a judge for the 2012 Edgar and the 2012 International Thriller Writers Awards, and is currently judging the 2015 *Los Angeles Times* Book Prize for the Mystery/Thriller category. His work will be included in a short story collection with T.C. Boyle, to be published by Red Hen Press in 2015.

Yente Serdatsky (1877–1962) was born in Lithuania and immigrated to the U.S. in 1907, where she wrote sketches, short fiction, and one-act plays for the *Forverts* (Forward), *Fraye Arbeter Shtime* (Free Voice of Labor), *Fraye gezelshaft* (Free Society), *Tsukunft* (Future), and *Dos Naye Land* (The New Land), among others. Her only story collection, *Geklibene Shriftn* (Selected Writings) was published in New York in 1913. None of her work was translated in her lifetime, but a handful of her stories have since been translated for publications such as the feminist journal *Bridges* and the anthology *Found Treasures*. This is the first appearance of her story *"A Simkhe"* in English.

S.A. Solomon has published crime fiction and poetry in *New Jersey Noir* (Akashic), *Grand Central Noir* (Metropolitan Crime), and the *Five–Two Crime Poetry Weekly*, and has work forthcoming in a serial heist novel and the anthology *Heroes: Stories to Benefit PROTECT, Vol. 2*. She serves as a regional board member for the Mystery Writers of America, New York chapter. She's working on a noir novel set in Newark and Jersey City. You can find her on Twitter @sa_solomon.

Jason Starr is the international bestselling author of many crime novels and thrillers, including *Cold Caller*, *Twisted City*, *The Follower*, and *Panic*

Attack. His short stories have appeared in numerous anthologies and magazines, and he has written nonfiction for publications such as the *New York Times* and the *LA Review of Books*. He also writes comics and graphic novels for Marvel, DC, and Boom Studios. He is one of several authors who have won the Anthony Award for mystery fiction twice. His latest novels are *Savage Lane* and *Pimp* (cowritten with Ken Bruen). He was born in Brooklyn and lives in Manhattan.

B.K. (Bonnie) Stevens has published almost fifty short stories, most of them in *Alfred Hitchcock's Mystery Magazine*. She has been nominated for Agatha and Macavity awards and has won a Derringer Award and a suspense-writing contest judged by Mary Higgins Clark. Her first novel, *Interpretation of Murder*, published by Black Opal Books, is a traditional whodunit that offers readers glimpses into Deaf culture and sign-language interpreting. Her young adult novel, *Fighting Chance*, is a martial arts mystery for boys, to be published by The Poisoned Pencil. She has also published *One Shot*, a satirical mystery e-novella (Untreed Reads). Website: http://www.bkstevensmysteries.com.

Kenneth Wishnia's novels include *23 Shades of Black*, an Edgar Allan Poe Award and Anthony Award finalist; *Soft Money*, a *Library Journal* Best Mystery of the Year; and *Red House*, a *Washington Post* "Rave" Book of the Year. His latest novel, *The Fifth Servant*, was an Indie Notable selection, a Best Book of the Year according to the Association of Jewish Libraries and the *Jewish Press*, won a Premio Letterario ADEI-WIZO (the Italian chapter of the Women's International Zionist Organization), and was a finalist for the Sue Feder Memorial Historical Mystery Award. His short stories have appeared in *Ellery Queen*, *Alfred Hitchcock*, *Queens Noir*, *Long Island Noir*, *Send My Love and a Molotov Cocktail*, and elsewhere. He is currently working on a Jewish-themed historical novel set in the sixth century BCE. He teaches writing, literature, and other deviant forms of thought at Suffolk Community College on Long Island. Contact him via *Face-bukh* or check out his *veb-zaytl* at http://www.kennethwishnia.com.

Steven Wishnia's books comprise the novel *When the Drumming Stops* (Manic D Press), in which four aging rockers face the impending Great Recession; the short story collection *Exit 25 Utopia*; and *The Cannabis Companion*, which has been translated into six languages. His short stories have appeared in *Long Island Noir* and various magazines, and his memoir/essay "Wie Bist Die Gewesen Vor Punk-Rock?" in *Jews: A People's History of the Lower East Side*. Bassist in the 1980s punk band the False Prophets, he currently plays in Blowdryer Punk Soul, the 13th Floor Klezmer Band,

and the multimedia shows of artist Mac McGill. In his day job as a journalist, he's won two awards for reporting on New York City housing issues; covered urban politics, labor, drugs, and civil-liberties extensively; and written and edited for publications from *High Times* to *Junior Scholastic*. Website: http://www.stevenwishnia.com.

Melissa Yi is an emergency physician who tries to join in Yiddish swearing contests whenever she's invited. Her latest Hope Sze medical mystery, *Terminally Ill*, was hailed as "entertaining and insightful" by *Publishers Weekly* and "utterly likeable" by *Ellery Queen's Mystery Magazine*. Her short stories have been published in *Indian Country Noir* and *Fiction River Special Edition: Crime*, and will appear in *Ellery Queen's Mystery Magazine*. The new Hope Sze novella, *Student Body*, debuted in September 2014. The fourth novel, *Stockholm Syndrome*, is scheduled for 2015. Lights! Cameras! Blog action! at http://www.melissayuaninnes.com.

Dave Zeltserman is the award-winning author of numerous crime and horror novels that have been named best books of the year by the *Washington Post*, NPR, American Library Association, and *Booklist*. His lighthearted Julius Katz detective stories have won the Shamus, Derringer, and *Ellery Queen's* Readers Choice Award (twice). Our last contact with Zeltserman was back in February when we received his manuscript for "Something's Not Right" in an envelope postmarked from the Adirondack town of Clinton. We were able to locate Sheriff Dale Grandy from this same town, but he has so far refused to answer any questions regarding Zeltserman's whereabouts. We are worried.

ABOUT PM PRESS

PM Press was founded at the end of 2007 by a small collection of folks with decades of publishing, media, and organizing experience. PM Press co-conspirators have published and distributed hundreds of books, pamphlets, CDs, and DVDs. Members of PM have founded enduring book fairs, spearheaded victorious tenant organizing campaigns, and worked closely with bookstores, academic conferences, and even rock bands to deliver political and challenging ideas to all walks of life. We're old enough to know what we're doing and young enough to know what's at stake.

We seek to create radical and stimulating fiction and non-fiction books, pamphlets, T-shirts, visual and audio materials to entertain, educate, and inspire you. We aim to distribute these through every available channel with every available technology—whether that means you are seeing anarchist classics at our bookfair stalls; reading our latest vegan cookbook at the café; downloading geeky fiction e-books; or digging new music and timely videos from our website.

PM Press is always on the lookout for talented and skilled volunteers, artists, activists, and writers to work with. If you have a great idea for a project or can contribute in some way, please get in touch.

PM Press
PO Box 23912
Oakland, CA 94623
www.pmpress.org

FRIENDS OF PM PRESS

These are indisputably momentous times—the financial system is melting down globally and the Empire is stumbling. Now more than ever there is a vital need for radical ideas.

In the years since its founding—and on a mere shoestring— PM Press has risen to the formidable challenge of publishing and distributing knowledge and entertainment for the struggles ahead. With over 300 releases to date, we have published an impressive and stimulating array of literature, art, music, politics, and culture. Using every available medium, we've succeeded in connecting those hungry for ideas and information to those putting them into practice.

Friends of PM allows you to directly help impact, amplify, and revitalize the discourse and actions of radical writers, filmmakers, and artists. It provides us with a stable foundation from which we can build upon our early successes and provides a much-needed subsidy for the materials that can't necessarily pay their own way. You can help make that happen—and receive every new title automatically delivered to your door once a month—by joining as a Friend of PM Press. And, we'll throw in a free T-shirt when you sign up.

Here are your options:

- **$30 a month** Get all books and pamphlets plus 50% discount on all webstore purchases

- **$40 a month** Get all PM Press releases (including CDs and DVDs) plus 50% discount on all webstore purchases

- **$100 a month** Superstar—Everything plus PM merchandise, free downloads, and 50% discount on all webstore purchases

For those who can't afford $30 or more a month, we're introducing **Sustainer Rates** at $15, $10 and $5. Sustainers get a free PM Press T-shirt and a 50% discount on all purchases from our website.

Your Visa or Mastercard will be billed once a month, until you tell us to stop. Or until our efforts succeed in bringing the revolution around. Or the financial meltdown of Capital makes plastic redundant. Whichever comes first.

23 Shades of Black

Kenneth Wishnia
with an introduction by
Barbara D'Amato

ISBN: 978-1-60486-587-5
$17.95   300 pages

23 Shades of Black is socially conscious crime fiction. It
takes place in New York City in the early 1980s, i.e., the
Reagan years, and was written partly in response to
the reactionary discourse of the time, when the current
thirty-year assault on the rights of working people
began in earnest, and the divide between rich and poor deepened with the blessing
of the political and corporate elites. But it is not a political tract, it's a kick-ass novel
that was nominated for the Edgar and the Anthony Awards, and made *Booklist*'s
Best First Mysteries of the Year.

The heroine, Filomena Buscarsela, is an immigrant who experienced tremendous
poverty and injustice in her native Ecuador, and who grew up determined to devote
her life to helping others. She tells us that she really should have been a priest,
but since that avenue was closed to her, she chose to become a cop instead. The
problem is that as one of the first *latinas* on the NYPD, she is not just a woman in a
man's world, she is a woman of color in a white man's world. And it's hell. Filomena
is mistreated and betrayed by her fellow officers, which leads her to pursue a case
independently in the hopes of being promoted to detective for the Rape Crisis Unit.

Along the way, she is required to enforce unjust drug laws that she disagrees
with, and to betray her own community (which ostracizes her as a result) in an
undercover operation to round up illegal immigrants. Several scenes are set in the
East Village art and punk rock scene of the time, and the murder case eventually
turns into an investigation of corporate environmental crime from a working class
perspective that is all-too-rare in the genre.

And yet this thing is damn funny, too.

"Packed with enough mayhem and atmosphere for two novels."
—*Booklist*

"From page-turning thriller to mystery story to social investigation, 23 Shades of Black
*works on all levels. It's clear from the start that Wishnia is charting a unique path in
crime fiction. Sign me up for the full ride!"*
—Michael Connelly, author of *Lost Light*

Soft Money

Kenneth Wishnia
with an introduction by
Gary Phillips

ISBN: 978-1-60486-680-3
$16.95   288 pages

Even the best cops burn out. *23 Shades of Black*'s
Filomena Buscarsela returns, having traded in her
uniform for the trials of single motherhood. Once a cop,
always a cop. She may have left the department, but
Filomena's passion for justice burns as hot as ever. And
when the owner of her neighborhood *bodega* is murdered—just another "ethnic"
crime that will probably go unsolved and unavenged—Filomena doesn't need much
prodding from the dead man's grieving sister to step in. Secretly partnered with
a rookie cop, she hits the Washington Heights streets to smoke out the trigger-
happy punks who ended an innocent life as callously as if they were blowing out a
match.

From the labyrinthine subway tunnels of upper Broadway to the upscale enclaves
that house the rich and beautiful, from local barrio hangouts to high-priced seats
of power, Filomena follows a trail of dirty secrets and dirtier politics, with some
unexpected stops in between. In a town big enough to hold every kind of criminal,
crackpot, liar, and thief, from ruthless gangsters to corporate executives drunk on
greed and power, she tracks a killer through the city's danger zones.

*"Great fun… Fil is a hyperbolic character, spewing enough acerbic opinions to fill half a
dozen average mysteries. A spirited sequel."*
—Publishers Weekly

*"Wishnia's world is like a New York subway train—fast, loud, dirty, and dangerous—but
it's well worth the ride with Filomena Buscarsela in the driver's seat. A hard-edged
story gracefully told."*
—Booklist

*"Sharp and sexy… Hilarious and exciting… [Wishnia] has a perfect ear for female
urban angst."*
—Chicago Tribune

*"Nonstop activity, wry humor, mordant characterizations, and a solid dollop of police
procedure make this a hugely appealing follow-up to 23 Shades of Black."*
—Library Journal

The Glass Factory

Kenneth Wishnia
with an introduction by
Reed Farrel Coleman

ISBN: 978-1-60486-762-6
$16.95   256 pages

Ex-NYPD cop Filomena Buscarsela—the irrepressible urban crime fighter of *23 Shades of Black* and *Soft Money*—is back. This time, the tough-talking, street-smart Latina heroine sets her sights on seemingly idyllic suburbia, where an endless sea of green lawns hides a toxic trail of money . . . and murder.

But something is rotten on Long Island. When Filomena discovers that a high-tech Long Island factory is spewing poisons into the water supply, she's sure that the contaminator is none other than her nemesis, a cutthroat industrial polluter with an airtight financial empire. Armed only with an ax to grind, the gutsy Filomena knows she'll have to play dirty to clean up the neighborhood.

Her search for justice introduces her to the unfamiliar scent of privilege—from the state-of-the-art chemistry lab of a local university to the crumbling ruins of a beachfront estate, from a glittering high-society party to an intimidating high-security chemical plant—and immerses her in the all-too-familiar stench of political corruption and personal greed. Once again, Filomena's nose for trouble has drawn her into a case that's more than a little hazardous to her health. As the action heats up, she must juggle the dangers of the investigation with the demands of her adorable three-year-old daughter and the delights of a surprising new romance.

"Wishnia writes with brio, energy, rage, passion, and humor. Brash, sassy, smart, and indomitable, Filomena is purely a force of nature, and The Glass Factory *is another winner."*
—*Booklist*

"Riveting circumstances, a strongly focused plot, and ably described settings make this essential reading."
—*Library Journal*

"Mother and daughter are so appealing, and the case against an unscrupulous businessman is put together so compellingly, the tale keeps one reading to its bittersweet end."
—*Boston Globe*

Red House

Kenneth Wishnia
with an introduction by
Alison Gaylin

ISBN: 978-1-60486-402-1
$16.95   288 pages

First she was a beat cop, then she was unemployed.
Now, Kenneth Wishnia's dynamic Filomena Buscarsela
has apprenticed herself to a New York City P.I. firm
to put in the three years necessary to get her own P.I.
license, which she needs to earn enough money to
support herself and her daughter. Trouble is, she often agrees to take on sticky
neighborhood cases pro bono—like the group of squatters restoring an abandoned
building in the neighborhood—rather than handle the big-bucks clients her bosses
would prefer.

While helping out her more "senior" colleagues with her own superior investigative
techniques bred from years on the beat, Fil agrees to look into the disappearance of
a young illegal immigrant. Then, witnessing the arrest of a neighbor on marijuana-
possession charges that nearly turns into a shoot-out with the police, Fil is roped
into finding out what went wrong. Trying to balance charity cases like these with
bread-and-butter cases, not to mention single motherhood, Fil is quickly in over her
head dodging bullish cops, aggressive businessmen, and corrupt landlords in their
working-class Queens neighborhood.

After years of policing and backstreet bloodhounding, Filomena Buscarsela is
apprenticing to earn her own private investigator's license. She pours on her
Spanish, her clever tricks, and her questionable charms to uncover a labyrinth of
deceit, racial prejudice, and bureaucracy that not only rocks her neighborhood but
also threatens the foundation of the big red house that is this P.I.'s America.

A Washington Post "Rave" Book of the Year

*"Smart dialogue, a realistic and gritty depiction of New York, and the sensitive
exploration of environmental, racial, and economic issues make this another great read
in an energetic series."*
—Booklist

*"An engaging character with a wry sense of humor. The jam-packed plot makes for an
exciting story."*
—Publishers Weekly

Blood Lake

Kenneth Wishnia
with an introduction by
Liz Martínez

ISBN: 978-1-60486-430-4
$17.95   384 pages

"The Ecuadorian Andes is one of the few places on earth where you can get a sunburn and freeze to death at the same time."

When New York City PI Filomena Buscarsela takes her teenaged daughter, Antonia, to see their extended family in Ecuador, it's more than a homecoming. Filomena hasn't been back in years, and the trip brings back memories of her previous life as a revolutionary.

Before she's even had time to adjust to her new surroundings, a priest is murdered, a man who, years ago, saved her life and helped her escape to the United States. She owed him her life; now it's time for the debt to be repaid, and she vows to find his killer. It's an election year, and the dirty hands of politics seem to be everywhere, perhaps even in this senseless death. Filomena's investigation promises to lead her back to the very people she escaped, all those years ago.

As the country is wracked by natural and man-made disasters—landslides, floods, food shortages, protests, crackdowns—Filomena becomes a fugitive from the law, racing across the country toward a climactic confrontation in the Amazon jungle. Wishnia provides a novel rich with the sights, sounds—and dangers—of Ecuador, and a compelling look at the provenance of one of mystery fiction's most dynamic heroines.

"In a stunning portrait of a country just over the line between law and chaos, Blood Lake gives the reader urgent, pulse-pounding prose, an unstoppable, appealing narrator, and a sense that the veneer of civilization may be, in places, very thin indeed.
—S.J. Rozan, author of Ghost Hero

"The first page of Blood Lake is strong, on a dead run; and the rest of the book ain't too dusty, neither."
—Harlan Ellison, winner of the Edgar, Hugo, Nebula, and Emmy Awards

"Wishnia's brand of gritty surrealism jolts the reader with startling images and jarring contrasts. [He] evokes a country and a culture vividly and unforgettably."
—Publishers Weekly

"Successfully serves up exotic atmosphere, complex family relations, social unrest, and dazzling characterization."
—Booklist

Nearly Nowhere

Summer Brenner

ISBN: 978-1-60486-306-2
$15.95   192 pages

Fifteen years ago, Kate Ryan and her daughter Ruby
moved to the secluded village of Zamora in northern
New Mexico to find a quiet life off the grid. But when
Kate invites the wrong drifter home for the night, the
delicate peace of their domain is shattered.

Troy Mason manages to hang onto Kate for a few weeks, though his charm
increasingly fails to offset his lies and delusions of grandeur. It is only a matter of
time before the lies turn abusive, igniting a chain reaction of violence and murder.
Not even a bullet in the leg will keep Troy from seeking revenge as he chases the
missing Ruby over back roads through the Sangre de Cristo Mountains, down
the River of No Return, and to a white supremacy enclave in Idaho's Bitterroot
Wilderness. *Nearly Nowhere* explores the darkest places of the American West,
emerging with only a fragile hope of redemption in the maternal ties that bind.

*"With her beautifully wrought sentences and dialogue that bring characters alive,
Summer Brenner weaves a gripping and dark tale of mysterious crime based in
spiritually and naturally rich northern New Mexico and beyond."*
—Roxanne Dunbar-Ortiz, historian and writer, author of *Roots of Resistance: A
History of Land Tenure in New Mexico*

"Summer Brenner's Nearly Nowhere *has the breathless momentum of the white-water
river her characters must navigate en route from a isolated village in New Mexico to a
neo-Nazi camp in Idaho. A flawed but loving single mother, a troubled teen girl, a good
doctor with a secret, a murderous sociopath—this short novel packs enough into its
pages to fight well above its weight class."*
—Michael Harris, author of *The Chieu Hoi Saloon*

*"To the party, Summer Brenner brings a poet's ear, a woman's awareness, and a soulful
intent, and her attention has enriched every manner of literary endeavor graced by it."*
—Jim Nisbet, author of *A Moment of Doubt*

Vida

Marge Piercy

ISBN: 978-1-60486-487-8
$20.00   416 pages

Originally published in 1979, *Vida* is Marge Piercy's
classic bookend to the Sixties. *Vida* is full of the
pleasures and pains, the experiments, disasters, and
victories of an extraordinary band of people. At the
center of the novel stands Vida Asch. She has lived
underground for almost a decade. Back in the '60s she
was a political star of the exuberant antiwar movement; now, a decade later, Vida
is on the run, her star-quality replaced by stubborn courage. As counterpoint to the
underground '70s, Marge Piercy tells the extraordinary tale of the optimistic '60s,
the thousands of people who were members of SAW (Students Against the War)
and of the handful who formed a fierce group called the Little Red Wagon. Piercy's
characters make vivid and comprehensible the desperation, the courage, and the
blind rage of a time when "action" could appear to some to be a more rational
choice than the vote.

A new introduction by Marge Piercy situates the book, and the author, in the times
from which they emerged.

Dance the Eagle to Sleep

Marge Piercy

ISBN: 978-1-60486-456-4
$17.95   208 pages

Originally published in 1970, Marge Piercy's second
novel follows the lives of four teenagers, in a near future
society, as they rebel against a military draft and "the
system." The occupation of Franklin High School begins,
and with it, the open rebellion of America's youth
against their channeled, unrewarding lives and the self-
serving, plastic society that directs them. From the disillusionment and alienation
of the young at the center of the revolt, to their attempts to build a visionary new
society, the nationwide following they gain and the brutally complete repression
that inevitably follows, this is a future fiction without a drop of fantasy. As driving,
violent, and nuanced today as it was 40 years ago, this anniversary edition includes
a new introduction by the author reflecting unapologetically on the novel and the
times from which it emerged.

Braided Lives

Marge Piercy

ISBN: 978-1-60486-442-7
$20.00   456 pages

Marge Piercy carries her portrait of the American experience back into the Fifties—that closed, repressive time in which forces for the upheavals of the Sixties ticked away underground. Spanning twenty years, and teeming with vivid characters, *Braided Lives* tells the powerful, unsentimental story of two young women coming of age. Jill, fiercely independent, dark, Jewish, an intellectual with Detroit street smarts, is a poet, curious, avid of life—a "professional student" and sometime thief. Donna, Jill's cousin and closest friend, is blond, pretty, and alluring. Together, they grow and change at college in Ann Arbor, where the life of poets and painters contrasts sharply with the working-class neighborhood where Jill's family lives.

Braided Lives is an enduring portrait of the past that has led to our tenuous present. In her new introduction to this edition, Marge Piercy reflects on both the most autobiographical of her novels, and the ongoing battles to ensure the hard-fought victories of the Sixties and Seventies, particularly around sex and reproductive rights.

The Cost of Lunch, Etc.

Marge Piercy

ISBN: 978-1-62963-125-7
$15.95   192 pages   paperback

Marge Piercy's debut collection of short stories, *The Cost of Lunch, Etc.*, brings us glimpses into the lives of everyday women moving through and making sense of their daily internal and external worlds. Keeping to the engaging, accessible language of Piercy's novels, the collection spans decades of her writing along with a range of locations, ages, and emotional states of her protagonists. From the first-person account of hoarding ("Saving Mother from Herself") to a girl's narrative of sexual and spiritual discovery ("Going over Jordan") to a recount of a past love affair ("The Easy Arrangement") each story is a tangible, vivid snapshot in a varied and subtly curated gallery of work. Whether grappling with death, familial relationships, friendship, sex, illness, or religion, Piercy's writing is as passionate, lucid, insightful, and thoughtfully alive as ever.

Send My Love and a Molotov Cocktail: Stories of Crime, Love and Rebellion

Edited by Gary Phillips
and Andrea Gibbons

ISBN: 978-1-60486-096-2
$19.95   368 pages

An incendiary mixture of genres and voices, this collection of short stories compiles a unique set of work that revolves around riots, revolts, and revolution. From the turbulent days of unionism in the streets of New York City during the Great Depression to a group of old women who meet at their local café to plan a radical act that will change the world forever, these original and once out-of-print stories capture the various ways people rise up to challenge the status quo and change up the relationships of power. Ideal for any fan of noir, science fiction, and revolution and mayhem, this collection includes works from Sara Paretsky, Paco Ignacio Taibo II, Cory Doctorow, Kenneth Wishnia, and Summer Brenner.

Full list of contributors:

Summer Brenner
Rick Dakan
Barry Graham
Penny Mickelbury
Gary Phillips
Luis Rodriguez
Benjamin Whitmer
Michael Moorcock
Larry Fondation

Cory Doctorow
Andrea Gibbons
John A. Imani
Sara Paretsky
Kim Stanley Robinson
Paco Ignacio Taibo II
Kenneth Wishnia
Michael Skeet
Tim Wohlforth

The Jook

Gary Phillips

ISBN: 978-1-60486-040-5

$15.95   256 pages

Zelmont Raines has slid a long way since his ability to jook, to outmaneuver his opponents on the field, made him a Super Bowl winning wide receiver, earning him lucrative endorsement deals and more than his share of female attention. But Zee hasn't always been good at saying no, so a series of missteps involving drugs, a paternity suit or two, legal entanglements, shaky investments and recurring injuries have virtually sidelined his career.

That is until Los Angeles gets a new pro franchise, the Barons, and Zelmont has one last chance at the big time he dearly misses. Just as it seems he might be getting back in the flow, he's enraptured by Wilma Wells, the leggy and brainy lawyer for the team—who has a ruthless game plan all her own. And it's Zelmont who might get jooked.

The Underbelly

Gary Phillips

ISBN: 978-1-60486-206-5

$14.00   160 pages

The explosion of wealth and development in downtown L.A. is a thing of wonder. But regardless of how big and shiny our buildings get, we should not forget the ones this wealth and development has overlooked and pushed out. This is the context for Phillips' novella *The Underbelly*, as a semi-homeless Vietnam vet named Magrady searches for a wheelchair-bound friend gone missing from Skid Row—a friend who might be working a dangerous scheme against major players. Magrady's journey is a solo sortie where the flashback-prone protagonist must deal with the impact of gentrification; take-no-prisoners community organizers; an unflinching cop from his past in Vietnam; an elderly sexpot out for his bones; a lusted-after magical skull; chronic-lovin' knuckleheads; and the perils of chili cheese fries at midnight. Combining action, humor and a street level gritty POV, *The Underbelly* is illustrated with photos and drawings.